The Obituary Writer

The
Obituary Writer

Lauren St John

First published in Great Britain in 2013 by Orion Books,
an imprint of The Orion Publishing Group Ltd
Orion House, 5 Upper Saint Martin's Lane
London WC2H 9EA

An Hachette UK Company

3 5 7 9 10 8 6 4 2

A CIP catalogue record for this book
is available from the British Library.

ISBN (Hardback) 978 1 4091 2718 5
ISBN (Export Trade Paperback) 978 1 4091 2709 3
ISBN (ebook) 978 1 4091 2719 2

Typeset at The Spartan Press Ltd,
Lymington, Hants

Printed in Great Britain by Clays Ltd, St Ives plc

The Orion Publishing Group's policy is to use papers
that are natural, renewable and recyclable products and
made from wood grown in sustainable forests. The logging
and manufacturing processes are expected to conform to
the environmental regulations of the country of origin.

www.orionbooks.co.uk

For Tom and Carmel Ramsey,
who taught me the meaning of true love

The Moving Finger writes; and, having writ,
Moves on: nor all your Piety nor Wit
Shall lure it back to cancel half a Line
Nor all your Tears Wash out a Word of it.

Rubáiyát of Omar Khayyám

Prologue

This is it. This is where he kills me.

The thought was gone before it could become fully formed, blasted out of her mind by the wind and swirling white and the church-bell insistence of horseshoes ringing on tarmac, getting faster and faster.

The fog was as effective as a blindfold, a proper pea-souper. Wayward hedgerows made the lane more claustrophobic still. Undaunted, the horse bolted into the invisible unknown. His black mane stung her face as she leaned forward and tried to reason with him. Usually he responded to a few judiciously applied half-halts, but not today. The sports car that had almost hit them had sent him into a frenzy. He was going to run until he reached a place of greater safety or another car stopped him, whichever came sooner.

Rarely did she allow fear to get the better of her around horses, but she was terrified now. The fog had blanked out every other sound and living thing. It was as if they were hurtling towards their doom with no witnesses. She'd told no one she was going riding, let alone bareback, barefoot and without a hat at dawn on a freezing New Year's Day. After the casual cruelties of the previous evening, it had felt like a quiet rebellion against her lover, a way of regaining a modicum of independence and self-respect. It would be most unjust if he were to get the last laugh.

A signpost reared out of the mist: Porthcurno. Seizing her chance, she nudged the horse towards the exit. They clattered through a silent village, across a deserted car park and onto the coastal path. Again, she tried to pull him up but to no avail. Freed from the constrictions of the hard, slick asphalt, he accelerated, gaining speed with every stride. There was no option but to cling on and hope that when they reached the beach, *if* they reached the beach . . .

In mid-thought, something made her glance up. On the edge of the cliff, half in shadow, half in light, stood a man. He was gazing down at her. As the horse swerved down the hill towards the beach, the stranger took a step in their direction. Relief, a great washing balm of it, flooded through her. She was not alone. If the worst were to happen, there was somebody who might help, somebody who might save them.

The beach sand checked the horse's stride. Her heart rate slowed in rhythm with the powdery sigh of hooves. Partly because he was tiring and partly because he'd run as far as the genes of his wild ancestors dictated he should under the circumstances, the horse was now pretending that he'd not been upset at all, not even for a minute, and that he'd needed only to exorcise some ghosts from his racing past, and kick up his heels and be free for a time, just like her, and had never intended to scare anyone. Neck arched and ears pricked, he cantered in neat, carefully described circles, as if he were a dressage horse in training for a competition.

Laughing with relief, she eased him to a halt and slid to the ground. Her feet sank into a silky nest of tiny white and mauve shells. The beach seemed to enjoy its own microclimate. While the cliffs were still swathed in fog, the bay was a Mediterranean turquoise. As the sun rose it scattered the sea with sequins.

On impulse, she gave the horse his freedom, letting go of his reins and walking into the waves. Their lacy edges fizzed around her ankles like champagne. She knew, without knowing how she knew, that the stranger was still watching her and yet, despite the hour and loneliness of the place, she was unafraid.

She knew something else too, knew it for certain. If she were going to die, it wouldn't be today.

One

I

The thing he remembered afterwards was that the clock was changing to thirteen as he rushed onto the platform. The rear lights of the train he should have been on – so easily could have been on – were slipping round the bend with a wiggle and the station was briefly empty, so that he was momentarily alone with a businessman in a creaseless pink shirt, pinstriped suit and shoes that offered a mirror to the sullen sky.

That was another thing that stuck in his mind: the man's improbably perfect attire, perhaps because of the later contrast.

Nick felt disproportionately annoyed at having missed the train. It didn't bother him that he was late, because when it came right down to it the dead were already dead and not about to go anywhere. Nor was he concerned about his deadline, because he'd been scrambling to come up with first-edition copy for nearly half of his thirty-eight years and he'd never failed yet.

Mainly he was irritated because he considered time spent waiting for trains, planes and buses to be time subtracted from life. Minus time. Sure it was possible to make use of it by reading up on the machinations of politicians, or communicating electronically or digitally in an unhealthy number of ways. You could write out your grocery list, ponder quantum physics, or rue the state of your relationship. But you couldn't do anything real. You were just trapped in an urban vacuum, forced to inhale London's rich array of airborne pollutants and watch soot-streaked rats eat garbage off the railway tracks, when you could be in the civilised comfort of your own home making love to a beautiful woman, writing the first chapter of a bestseller, or reading a few pages of Dickens.

The fact that he seldom did the third thing, had never done the second, and did not do the first nearly often enough, and would, had he stayed in his apartment for an extra twenty-one minutes that morning, have frittered it away searching for a lost sock or beating himself up about the novel he'd spent the last eight years intending to write, wasn't the point. The point, Nick told himself, was that it was twenty-one minutes shaved off your lifespan. That was why he resented waiting now.

A lazy flow of passengers refilled the platform at Greenwich station, like the sea spilling in at low tide. There was the usual horde of students, tourists and City-bound commuters, scattered according to the customs of their home nations, their value on personal space. The newer tourists and immigrants were the only ones speaking. Nick watched them sometimes to see how long it was before they nudged each other and lapsed into the voluntary hush observed by everyone else. He was always shocked at how quickly people, who in their own countries filled any public area with their colourful, voluble, sociable chatter, felt compelled, courtesy of a few frozen stares, to join the library quiet of London's transport network.

Naturally, the people who did rebel were the very last ones you wanted to hear from. Most recently, they seemed to be pickpockets taking time off to play the accordion.

At 9.34 the long-delayed next train arrived in an amplified screech of metal. The silent herd surged forward and arranged themselves in a packed arc around each door, blocking the exit of the new arrivals. The selfishness inherent in this action added to Nick's irritation. He and the businessman hung back together, even though Nick had a deadline and the other man appeared to be on his way to a meeting of vital import. His scrubbed, flushed face was focused and set. There was a mutual *tsk tsk* in their body language, a tacit understanding that they alone grasped the futility of standing in front of outgoing passengers in the interests of gaining a split second's advantage in the race for the best seats.

A high-pitched beeping indicated that the train was about to depart. The businessman seized his chance to spring on-board. Conscious of his judgements on others, Nick hesitated in an exaggerated show of politeness. In that instant the doors slammed shut.

'*Hey!*' he yelled at the distant driver, but the businessman had shoved his briefcase into the vanishing gap and was hanging onto the door's rubber edge. Nick wrenched it open a little wider and jumped in.

'Thanks. That was good of you.'

As he spoke, the train jerked forward and the man was forced to snatch at a handrail to keep his balance. He turned away without saying anything.

The last seat on the carriage was situated between a student reeking of dope and an obese, blank-faced woman with an oversized handbag. A static pounding issued from the student's headphones. His left knee jiggled up and down.

Nick did his best to tune the boy out. He'd awoken that morning with a plague of rats chewing at his nerve endings. Repeated checks of his diary had failed to explain why he was gripped by a feeling of foreboding, and it was not until he'd fed himself a breakfast of cornflakes and black coffee and Oliver a can of tuna that he'd given up worrying about it. By then he was already late.

Past Deptford, the world beyond the railway seemed hemmed in by the October sky, leached of colour. It went by in a monochrome strip. The train's passage was an overloud drum solo, drowning out nearly all attempts at conversation or thought. The carriage rolled violently along the steel snarl of tracks. Within minutes they'd be at London Bridge and there'd be another unseemly rush for the door.

Nick pushed past the jiggling student and made his way down the aisle. The businessman was in the final row. He was poring over a sheaf of papers. Among the ordered contents of his open briefcase was an apple. It was, Nick noted as he paused to steady himself, one of those vivid green ones, the kind that were always sour as hell, with chewy skins that got stuck between your teeth. In an ideal universe they'd have been reserved for horses. He was willing to bet that the business-man's wife handed him the fruit as he left for work each morning and that he never ate it and never told her he didn't either, because every apple would have been given and taken with love.

As he passed, the man glanced up and saw him staring. A sheepish smile smoothed his anxious face. Equally sheepish at being caught out, Nick grinned back.

Close to the door the floor bucked beneath his feet and he grabbed at a handrail to steady himself.

That's when the carriage corkscrewed off the tracks.

Time scrambled. The runaway train became a firework display of exploding electrics. The floor swapped places with the ceiling.

Nick felt as if his head had taken up residence in an active thundercloud. The roaring seconds stretched out interminably. His life didn't flash before his eyes, as he'd always imagined it would, but he panicked it might be over before he'd really lived. He wished he'd given more thought to God.

Then pain smashed like an axe into his brain.

Blackness.

A flickering light.

Blackness.

Light.

Nick's senses returned in a rush, letting in a terrible screaming. He had the feeling that a lot of time had passed, but could as easily have accepted it was a fraction of a second. His eyes opened to a war zone.

In the centre of the aisle lay a severed arm, its gold watch still intact. A sack of groceries had spilled and washing powder, pink with blood, was sprinkled throughout the carnage. A teenage girl's mouth was stuck open in a silent cry of anguish. Showers of glass were piled around the broken bodies, like crushed ice surrounding a butcher's display.

Nick hauled himself to his feet and stood reeling, trying to get it together to start helping people. Apart from a ballooning headache and a grazed knee showing through torn trousers, he appeared to be unharmed. It was impossible to take in.

He started towards the petrified girl, but a shivering feverishness overtook him.

Something was wrong. Something was so out of kilter that even amid the chaos the non-rightness of it communicated itself to him. He gripped the back of a seat for support.

What was it that didn't add up?

Then it came to him. The carriage was a bloody battlefield. Every inch of it was filled with people writhing, weeping, crawling, choking or dying.

And he was the only one standing.

2

Two days later, he was back at work.

'Christ, Donaghue, are you planning to write your own obituary?' cried Henry Stillman, his editor. 'Get the hell out of here and go home to bed, or admit yourself to hospital or something. If you hang around here it'll only rebound on me. I'll have the insurance company on my back or acquire a reputation as a heartless slave driver.'

'Not undeservedly, surely,' Nick retorted.

He tossed his messenger bag onto his desk, hung his jacket over the back of the chair and began to sift through his post, throwing anything that came in a brown envelope into the wastepaper basket without looking at it.

The other envelopes came in a variety of friendly or attention-seeking shades. He recognised the handwriting on a couple. One was from the agents of an ageing pop star, a renowned lothario, who kept him updated on all career developments in anticipation of the singer's expiry. Any day now Nick expected to receive a notice regretfully informing him that the singer had passed away in the act of love but that his forthcoming album was being hailed as an artistic triumph.

When Nick had joined *The Times*'s Letters and Obituary section five years earlier, after a decade as a freelance featurewriter, he'd found it macabre in the extreme that certain celebrities, politicians and business high-fliers were so preoccupied with their own legacy, with remaining famous beyond the grave, that they either sent in their own obituaries, to be added to the 5000 the paper kept on file, or routinely supplied new biographical details that might enliven an existing one.

'Such is human vanity that a lot of people would be miffed if they died and their obituary didn't appear in *The Times*,' Phil Baker, the senior obit writer, had told him on his first day. 'Even those who you'd imagine could have reposed secure in the knowledge that a testament to their life's work would be required reading fret about it constantly.'

Phil was Nick's favourite person in journalism. He was old school, cut from the cloth of reporters made heroic by Hollywood movies like *All the President's Men*. He even dressed like them, immaculate to the last detail of his spruce white hair, starched shirts and tailored jackets and waistcoats. He had a droll, pragmatic, humane view of death and the dead, and twenty-seven years in the department had not dulled his passion for his subject. Or his sense of irony.

'An obit isn't meant to be a eulogy,' he'd once remarked. 'The idea is warts and all. At the same time you need to remember that it's about achievement rather than failure. I mean, every naval officer is ego-centric and bossy. That's how they get to where they are. War heroes are ghastly people when you get right down to it.'

Nick dropped the last of the brown envelopes into the bin, switched on his computer and swivelled in his chair to look around the office. In keeping with contemporary newspaper architecture it was open-plan, with lots of steel and glass. It had all the atmosphere of an airport departure lounge, right down to the malnourished potted plants.

It was only then he noticed that Henry was still poised in the door of his cubicle. Amy, the department secretary, had a chocolate bar suspended in mid-bite, and his friend was staring at him as if he'd just tested positive for rabies.

'Someone dial 999,' said Phil, only half joking.

Nick laughed, although it hurt to do so because his body felt as if it had been backed over by an articulated lorry. 'Phil, I'm fine. Really.'

'I'll be the judge of that,' countered Henry, advancing on him through the warren of paper-piled desks.

'Nick, you're obviously concussed, patently delusional, and need to be admitted to the nuthouse without delay,' Phil said matter-of-factly. 'Are you aware that it's not normal to stroll into the office and start going through your post and readying yourself for the day's assignment mere hours after being dragged from the blazing wreckage of a train crash?'

Nick laughed and winced again. 'Seriously, everyone, I'm fine. I'll be coming to work by bicycle from now on, but apart from that I'm a hundred per cent. Well, maybe ninety-nine. No truly, I'm okay. A bit shaken, but okay.'

And he was. He was so fine he was almost worried about how fine he was. With the exception of a couple of category-ten headaches and a palette of bruises representing the full spectrum of the Northern Lights, he was no worse off than he frequently felt after a big night out.

At Becca's insistence, he'd spent the day following the crash in bed. He'd been so weak and nervy that it had been a relief to let someone take over, even if that someone was his pretty blonde ex, now married to his neighbour, Greg.

Becca adored Nick and he was fond of her, but in subtle ways she rarely let him forget that their break-up had nearly destroyed her. It wasn't that he'd cheated on her or in any way treated her cruelly during their year-long university relationship. On the contrary, she freely admitted he'd been the best by a mile of the very bad bunch of men she'd dated prior to meeting Greg. No, it was because at the end of that time, when she was so in love with him she'd have taken a bullet for him, he'd told her that he thought of her as a kid sister, not a lover.

She'd never really got over him until one night, during their annual catch-up, Nick had introduced her to Greg, a muscle-bound black fireman who lived three doors down. They were married six months later. Nick was best man at their wedding.

Any concerns he might have had about having Becca for a neighbour had proved groundless. She was besotted with Greg and the three of them had so much fun together he couldn't remember what he'd done for a social life without them. A couple of times he'd caught himself wondering how things would have turned out if he'd been the one to fall in love with Becca and marry her, but the reality was she'd had a lucky escape. Nick had long since decided that he and relationships were incompatible.

Greg and Becca had raced to his hospital bedside within an hour of him arriving there in an ambulance. They'd sat with him while he was poked, probed and evaluated, and supported him in a brief battle with the admitting doctor when Nick had insisted on going home the same day. Greg had slept on his sofa that night, waking him at intervals to shine a light into his pupils. Becca took over the next morning, skipping work to spend the day puffing up his pillows, bringing him cups of tea and Marmite soldiers. She'd also fielded messages, answered the door to couriers bearing flowers, and kept callers at bay with the brisk efficiency of a drill sergeant.

'I don't understand why everyone's making such a fuss,' said Nick, his gratitude tempered by the lingering guilt he always felt around Becca. 'When I broke my leg skiing and was laid up for months in chronic pain, I couldn't pay anyone to take an interest in me.'

'That's because it was self-inflicted. Weren't there large quantities of Jack Daniels involved? This is different.'

She handed him a tumbler of water and two white pills. 'Here, get these down your gullet and stop complaining or I'll go to the office and leave you to fend for yourself.'

'Is that a threat or a promise?' queried Nick, but he swallowed the tablets.

He was handing the glass back when it slipped from his fingers and smashed. Diamond shards exploded upwards.

His yell came from a long way away. Becca's blonde hair and flushed face faded to black and then he was back in the railway carriage, only this time there was no sound. None related to the crash, at any rate. All he could hear was a squeaking, like that of a straining rope. Conscious of a presence, he looked everywhere to discover its source.

'Who are you?' he yelled. 'Let me see you!'

'Nick! Nick, it's me, Becca.'

Freezing water blasted the train from his brain. Nick came round to find ice cubes sliding down his bare chest. He bolted upright and they clattered to the wooden floor. 'For fuck's sake, Becks, are you trying to kill me? I think you'll find that those kind of nursing practices were outlawed a few centuries ago.'

Behind her rimless glasses, Becca's eyes were wide and staring. 'Nick, this is not a joke. You frightened the life out of me. What just happened?'

'No idea.' Nick felt dizzy and on the verge of a migraine, but he had no intention of sharing that with her. 'Some kind of flashback, I guess. I'm sure it's pretty common with crash victims. Don't make a fuss about nothing. You're not my mother.'

A crimson wave spread down Becca's neck and under her grey cashmere jumper. 'Or your sister,' she said coldly. 'Get dressed. I'm taking you to the hospital.'

Nick grinned. 'You're still beautiful when you're angry. Look, I appreciate your concern. You're a great nurse and I'm the luckiest man alive to have you taking care of me, but I'm back to normal now. Promise.'

'You think it's normal to pass out when a glass breaks? Is that what *normal* people do? And what's worse – what's *really* disturbing – is that for the whole two minutes you were out, your fingers were moving madly, as if you were typing. It was creepy.'

Becca perched on the edge of the bed and smoothed his tousled dark hair. 'Nick, please. Be serious for once. Are you sure you're all right?'

'Positive, but thanks. When I need someone to read me the last rites, you'll be the first person I call.'

'Bastard.'

'Sorry,' Nick responded automatically. As he sank into the pillows and the beginnings of a tablet-induced coma, a wave of depression swept over him. At the first sign of intimacy, he almost always made a joke. He knew he was doing it, knew it hurt people, especially Becca, but he couldn't help himself.

He was reminded of that now, standing in front of his colleagues who, given permission to ask questions about the train crash because he himself had referenced it, were coming up to him in awkward batches while he deflected them with platitudes. This time it wasn't intentional. He simply couldn't describe what he'd been through. Words, his stock in trade, seemed inadequate. He was only able to offer banalities: 'It was over so quickly . . . Life flashed before my eyes . . . A terrible tragedy. The emergency crews were amazing . . . I feel blessed . . . fortunate . . . lucky . . .'

A lapsed Catholic and avowed agnostic, he also repeatedly thanked God, to whom he genuinely did plan to give more thought, just not at this moment when he was only trying to get from one hour to the next and feeling astonishingly cheerful in view of how recently he'd cheated the grave.

At last, when he couldn't cope with any more curiosity or well-wishing, he said politely: 'Do you mind? I really can't talk about this anymore. I have a deadline.'

He returned to his computer after that and began work on an archive piece, the only story Henry would entrust him with, because that way he could pretend not to see the thing he was pretending not to see, now descending on him with the relentless, rapidly accumulating ferocity of an avalanche.

3

On Thursday, three days after the crash, he left the office early for a hospital appointment. His mobile rang as the taxi sped across Westminster Bridge. Nick clicked it through to voicemail without looking at it. It beeped twice as he watched a swan rise from the Thames, wings angel-white in the sunlight.

Guilt, that he had lived to see this day when so many of his fellow passengers hadn't, swelled in his throat. He loosened his tie and checked his phone. He had nineteen missed calls – eight from friends, three from ex-girlfriends and eight from withheld numbers, all doubtless from reporters or editors, many from his own paper.

There was mounting anger at News International over his refusal to provide so much as a line of comment on the train crash, let alone the eyewitness account *The Times* had been banking on. What made it worse was that controversy surrounded the derailment. Even at this early stage, it was clear that somebody or something was to blame. Sabotage and rail company negligence were the accusations being bandied about. Nick was well aware that if he hadn't had Henry shielding him he'd have been hauled before the editor to explain himself and, in the fullness of time, 'let go'. First-person stories by reporters snatched from the jaws of death were among the most prized in journalism. They were held up to a cynical public as proof that reporters were not the sleazy, morally bankrupt liars of myth, but brave and revolutionary truth-tellers, risking their lives in the trenches.

Or, in the case of Nick, ordinary human beings catapulted into extraordinary situations.

A reporter refusing to report was unprecedented. And unpopular.

Nick scanned the list of other calls. He half-expected his parents' number to come up, although of course it never would. For once he was glad. To have their son involved in a national disaster would have been their worst nightmare. It would have devastated his mother. She and his insurance-salesman father had been the kind of people who went 20 mph in a 30 mph zone. Their every waking hour had been spent in the avoidance of risk or anything else foreign or unfamiliar that might threaten their safe, steady march towards retirement – the moment, as they saw it, when life began.

Overprotected as a boy, Nick had in his teens and early twenties rebelled by flirting with death at every opportunity, pushing everything he did – skiing, driving, running, sailing, surfing – to lethal limits. It was a matter of painful regret to him that he'd flaunted his fearlessness in front of his parents. He'd worn his scars like badges of pride. For years his mum and dad had ferried him back and forth to various A&E departments without complaint. They'd rarely criticised him. Mostly they'd studied him with a concerned and kindly bemusement, as if they were certain he'd been substituted at birth but were determined to love him just the same.

He was twenty-four and in his last year at university when the police knocked on the door of his student digs. Earlier that morning, while on their way to church, his parents had been involved in a head-on collision with a truck driver who'd fallen asleep at the wheel. His dad had been due to start his retirement the following day. He'd booked a course of golf lessons. Nick had been asked to identify their bodies.

His parents' neatness in life had come undone in death. Faced with his mother's naked, mutilated body, which he'd been forced to confront in order to verify her identity from a birthmark, Nick had been overwhelmed by the urge to cover her with his jacket. He'd wanted to throw his arms around her and protect her from the gazes of people whom she could never have borne to see her with a missing button, let alone in her birthday suit on a mortuary stretcher, without the dignity that would have been afforded a side of beef; all her years of careful grooming, planning, saving and insuring come to nothing. The injustice of it had been as agonising as the loss.

An ambulance screamed past the cab. Nick almost leapt out of his skin. A forest of red crosses and signs to incomprehensibly named specialists indicated they'd arrived. He paid the fare with shaking hands.

*

Dr Marius Retson was a balding South African with the ruddy good health and thickly ridged forearms of a lifelong sportsman. He exuded a warmth Nick had hitherto found lacking in the medical profession, and an aura of unassailable confidence that came from being prodigiously gifted and rewarded in an area of human anatomy still shrouded in mystery. In among the framed degree certificates on his office walls were photographs of Ferraris and Aston Martins. Nick had not the smallest doubt they were his own.

'You're a most unusual case, Mr Donaghue,' was the neurologist's opening remark. He perched on a corner of his cherrywood desk, arms resting on one thigh.

Nick's heart began to pound. In a single sentence he'd gone from being a slightly banged up outpatient to being – what? Nick had been so preoccupied with trying to convince everyone of his wellbeing that it hadn't occurred to him there could be anything wrong with him. That the CT scan they'd told him was routine on the day of the crash could later have thrown up something sinister.

He wondered how many people had sat in the chair before him and been handed a death sentence.

'I'm sorry to have to inform you . . .'

'. . . an area of concern on your scan . . .'

'An inoperable tumour, probably fatal . . .'

'Call me Nick.' His hands, gripping the chair's leather arms, became clammy.

'Nick,' Dr Retson repeated obediently, his Afrikaans accent enunciating the word precisely. 'How have you been since the crash? Obviously you've been traumatised and it's going to take a while for you to recover emotionally, but how have you been physically? Any headaches? Vomiting? Blurred vision?'

'I'm fine,' Nick burst out, his voice coming out much higher and louder than he'd planned. He tried again. 'I've been very well. I've had a couple of headaches but I feel quite good, considering.' He decided not to mention the incident with the glass. It seemed a trivial thing now.

Dr Retson picked up a silver pencil torch and eased down Nick's lower lids with hot, gentle fingers.

'Why?' Nick blinked in the glare. 'Why am I such an unusual case?'

The neurologist clicked off his torch and returned to his seat on the

16

far side of the desk. 'I didn't mean to alarm you with my turn of phrase,' he said with a smile. 'I have nothing but good news for you. Your MRI was clear.'

'This is what I've been saying to everyone all along – I'm perfectly fine. And now I've had to take half a day off for nothing. I know you're trying to be helpful and I appreciate it, but it's a bit frustrating. I mean, I have a job to do. I'm busy.'

'I asked you to come here,' Dr Retson said patiently, 'so that we could conduct further tests which I consider to be vital. I also wanted to satisfy myself in person that you don't have a brain injury. Three days ago, you lost consciousness. It seems likely that you suffered a blow to the head. Ideally, we'd have kept you in for observation but you insisted on going home. You appear to be well, but if the headaches get worse or if you experience any problems with co-ordination, dizziness, mood or behavioural changes, or light sensitivity, come back and see me immediately. Sometimes in medicine when something seems too good to be true, it is.'

Nick felt a flash of anger. 'Why is it too good to be true? Am I not allowed to be okay? Would you and everyone else find it easier to cope if I had something with a label? A tumour? An aneurism? I was lucky, that's all. It happens. Who knows why some people are spared and others aren't in these disasters. Maybe I helped some old lady cross the road when I was fifteen and I've finally been rewarded for it.'

Dr Retson regarded him intently. 'There's a bit more to it than that. Statistically you've beaten unbelievable odds. I'm not a gambler myself, but they'd have to be millions to one. Do you know what they're calling you around the hospital? The Miracle Man. There were one hundred and twenty-seven passengers on that train. Of those passengers, eleven have died and a hundred and fifteen suffered injuries that we tend to associate with war or terrorist bombings. That leaves you. The only person to have emerged from the crash without a serious, life-threatening or fatal injury. The only person without a scratch. And yet I gather you were in the first carriage, the one that took the brunt of the impact?'

An unwelcome flashback of the moment when he'd gazed around the turmoil of mangled metal and broken people and realised that he was the only one standing seared Nick's memory.

'I have a knee that looks as if it's been attacked by a cheese grater and lots of bruises,' he pointed out in a weak attempt at humour.

The neurologist ignored him. 'You alone, among a hundred and twenty-seven passengers, walk away with barely a mark from a crash they say is the worst in British rail history? That constitutes a miracle in my book.'

'Do me a favour. Don't call me the Miracle Man within earshot of any reporters. They do love a catchphrase.'

'Aren't you a reporter?'

Nick grinned. 'Shhh.'

Out on the rush-hour streets Nick's guilt returned to swamp him. He'd stopped at the hospital reception to enquire about the businessman, whose name he hadn't yet managed to discover. An over-tanned woman encased, like a python, in a glass booth had suggested that the reason Nick was having difficulty locating him could be that he'd passed away.

Nick was aghast. *'Passed away?* Of course he hasn't passed away . . . At least, I hope he hasn't.'

For some reason, he found the mere possibility shattering. If it were really true that the businessman was dead, what right did Nick have to be alive?

Destiny had come like a scythe through a field of wheat and cut down one hundred and twenty-six people and somehow, whether through a fluke of fate or divine intervention, Nick had been let alone. And for what? *Why him?*

'Guilt is a wasted emotion,' Phil had told him over the canteen lunch Nick bought him earlier that day. Phil occupied most-favoured-employee status in the department and Nick wanted him to persuade their editor to reverse his decree that Nick was not to touch an obituary until Henry decided he was fit to do so. Somehow it had turned into a counselling session.

'I was raised a Catholic,' Nick said. 'Guilt is in my DNA. Anyway, I'm not convinced it is a wasted emotion. Surely conscience and accountability are the only things that separate us from the animals.'

'But who benefits?'

'What do you mean, who benefits? Nobody benefits. The whole point is that you're paying a sort of psychological penance for your crime, whether that crime is cheating on your girlfriend, or stealing a loaf of bread, or surviving. The benefits are residual. They're karmic. If you feel guilty about cheating on your girlfriend it might make you be more loving to her, or at the very least she might feel less hurt because she knows you feel awful about it. If you feel guilty about being alive, it's a way of showing the universe that you don't take your survival for granted.'

Phil stirred sugar into his coffee. 'So really it's just about feeling bad for the sake of feeling bad?'

'You've missed the point entirely.'

Now he conceded that maybe it was Phil who had a point. What use was his middle-class angst to anyone? It was not going to make a single person walk again or live again. He'd be better off making the most of the reprieve he'd been given.

He left the crowds behind and took a shortcut down a back alley. He planned to catch a bus home to Greenwich. Ahead of him the under-pass loomed. A train screeched and whined across the top of it. Nick shuddered. God knows how long it would be before he was able to bring himself to use the railways again.

He approached the underpass with caution, pausing before he entered it to squint up through the concrete and steel at the last, heartening slot of sky. A rosy sunset was moving in.

The sooty darkness of the tunnel caught him unawares. He blinked. Overhead, the metallic whiplash of rails gave notice of a coming train. A whirlwind of grit peppered his skin. Nick barely noticed it. He blundered on blindly, his nostrils full of railway smells. He wanted to be through the tunnel and gone before the train was overhead.

A shoulder slammed into him. He had a fleeting glimpse of expensively barbered grey hair and a fat, florid face. There was a whiff of whisky as the man spat: 'Watch where you're going, you fucking moron. Fucking lowlife.'

Pent-up emotion exploded in Nick. Before he could stop himself he'd brought his fists up, ready to smash the man's face in. Only the fear in his abuser's eyes, the way he cowered away like a beaten cur, brought him back from the brink.

'Sorry,' he said, relaxing his hands. The man stumbled away from him just as the train thundered onto the bridge overhead, shaking the ground and setting Nick's teeth rattling.

A wave of dizziness came over him. His vision went black and he heard again that rope-like squeak and, intermittently, a tinkling sound, like ice in a glass.

'Need a hand, mate?'

The clouds rolled back and Nick found himself on the pavement on the far side of the tunnel, with no idea how he'd got there. He focused with difficulty on the freckled hand reaching down to him. The sunset had intensified.

'Thanks,' he said when he was at eye-level with its owner, a twenty-something with a gap-toothed grin and spiky ginger hair.

'No worries. Hardly surprising if you have the odd wobble. You must be pretty fried after what happened. Everyone at the office is talking about how you came back to work two days after the crash when the rest of us lazy bastards would have demanded a three-month sabbatical.'

Nick dusted the grime from his jacket and trousers with unnecessary vigour. His fingers tingled strangely. An electric current pulsed in them. 'I take it you're a reporter. Do I know you?'

'No, but I know you. You're the guy who has every editor at News International spitting nails because you're an eyewitness to one of the worst train crashes in history and you won't return their calls. You won't play their game by being a good news story that sells papers.'

'Do you have a name?'

Again the cheeky grin. 'Damian Dexter from the *Sun*.'

Nick felt his headache return with a vengeance. 'Well, Damian Dexter from the *Sun*, let me make myself crystal clear. It's nice of you to lend me a hand, but I'm not going to discuss the crash. Not now. Not ever.'

'What's the deal with you, Donaghue?' asked Damian, pulling a pad and pen from his pocket as though Nick hadn't spoken. 'You're a hero. I've talked to the ambulance guys and a couple of coppers and they say you were the last passenger to leave the train. That even after the rescuers came, you insisted on waiting until the last survivor had been cut free from the wreckage and stretchered away before you'd even consider getting in an ambulance. They say you single-handedly saved three people. And yet you don't wanna talk about it.'

He bit the top off his pen. 'Anyone would think you had something to hide.'

But Nick had switched off at the first sentence. He was thinking about the man in the tunnel, about the violence of his reaction, his sour breath. His face had struck Nick as familiar.

'Did you get a close look at the man who ran into me? I thought I recognised him from somewhere.'

Damian's nib hovered over the paper. 'What man?'

'The man in the tunnel – who else?' Nick flexed his fingers to ease the pins and needles. He wondered if he was having an allergic reaction to something he'd touched when he blacked out. Poison ivy perhaps. 'You must have seen him. Big guy in his late fifties, early sixties, with a face like a bad banker, overfed and wet-lipped.'

'You're dreaming, mate. I was right behind you. There was no one in that underpass but you, me and a few rats. Hey, if you're feeling shaky and having visions, you might want to visit one of the head doctors at Guy's Hospital. Get things checked out.'

He added slyly: 'Or is that what you've been doing?'

It occurred to Nick that it would be a bad idea to have a newshound like Damian knowing anything about his business, no matter how innocuous. He slung his messenger bag over his shoulder and turned to go. 'Thanks again. See you around.'

'Not so fast,' said Damian, unwilling to give up on a potential scoop. 'What's this about them calling you the Miracle Man?'

4

That night he had the dream for the first time. It came swooping in on dark wings, like a bird of evil portent.

He was accustomed to deadline dreams. Every reporter he knew had them. Those were the ones where his tape recorder batteries went flat during an exclusive interview; or his computer crashed seconds before edition time; or he ran out of petrol on the way to a critical assignment in a foreign town and couldn't find a petrol station because he was continually misdirected by a series of police bullies or hapless pedestrians, none of whom grasped the urgency of the situation.

And all the while the minutes kept ticking away and he knew, just absolutely knew, he was going to miss his deadline and be fired from the paper.

When he woke from those dreams it always took a while for him to convince himself they weren't real, and then it would feel as if he'd been granted some massive favour by the gods. As if, perversely, they had been real.

But this was no deadline dream. It was more like a movie already in progress. Nick had the sensation of being parachuted into it. Of arriving in a scene that was already being played out and would proceed according to script, regardless of his involvement.

He recognised the location immediately. He was in the groping darkness of the underpass and there was someone ahead of him, moving swiftly. From time to time, he glimpsed a swinging black cloak.

'Wait!' he yelled, but his throat constricted and all that came out was a whisper. He started to run, but the cloaked figure effortlessly outpaced him, flying round the bends up ahead. Then it disappeared altogether.

In the dream, he pulled up short and listened. He strained to flee but some unseen force drove him on.

Around the next corner the tunnel ended abruptly, opening not onto the street as it had in real life, but onto a bedroom appointed in velvet drapes and antiques. A chair lay toppled on a Persian rug. Above it, hanging from a rope tied to the brass centrepiece of a glittering chandelier, was the cloaked figure who'd slammed into him in the underpass. A judge's wig sat askew on his head.

The chandelier tinkled in protest at its burden. The rope squeaked softly. The judge rotated to face Nick with a ghastly gurgle.

There was a knock at the door, followed by an urgent hammering. The door handle jiggled. Nick was paralysed with terror, frantic to escape before he was found there, a voyeur culpable if only for doing nothing. A key grated in the lock. Wrenching at his legs in the manner of a man trying to free himself from quicksand, Nick fled in slow motion.

He awoke with a splitting headache, drenched in sweat, the bed sheet strangling him. The window was open but it was a breezeless night, fetid and close, and the Thames air squelched through his lungs. The balcony wasn't much better. Nick peeled off his T-shirt and hung over the railings like a becalmed sailor, wracked with unnamed anxieties.

Most nights he considered the juxtaposition of the Victorian semis that partially obstructed his view and the futuristic neon skyscrapers of Canary Wharf on the opposite bank as the apotheosis of urban beauty. He liked the synthesis of ancient and modern, the brashness of the newcomers versus the stolid middle class. He found solace in the unstoppable flow of the river.

Tonight, though, the water was sluggish. Nick had the macabre thought that its bodies were well buried. He flexed his fingers, which once more pulsed with a prickling current. Wriggling them seemed to relieve it, but the pins and needles soon returned if he quit. He caught sight of himself in the window reflection. There was a blue-black shadow on his jawline. His face, which a candid lover had once observed would be 'boringly handsome if it wasn't so haunted', looked more haunted still. His grey eyes seemed sunken in his skull.

In the fluorescent spill of refrigerator light he drank a coke straight from the can, gulping it down so quickly that it made his teeth hurt, and chasing it with two Nurofen. Its metallic sweetness lingered on his tongue.

He went into his study and switched on his laptop in the darkness. The flare of the welcome screen hurt his retinas. He checked his emails and replied to those requiring no thought. Gradually he became aware that his muscles were locked in a fight-or-flight tenseness, as if he'd just sat through a horror film. In a sense, he supposed he had.

On cue, the nightmare returned to Nick in grisly detail. It had been incredibly vivid, almost as if he'd lived every moment and it had taken place in real time. He felt tainted by its monstrous images.

He began surfing the net for distraction – not porn, definitely not that – just light, frothy things about the misdemeanours of Z-list celebrities or the comeuppances of inept burglars, or anything else he could find that might chase away the squeaking of the rope or that final ghastly gurgle.

But even that went wrong because he clicked on a link that led to a cluster of news stories on the train derailment, and before he knew it he was looking at a photo of the student who'd so irritated him on that day, a barcode of blood on his face, being carried from the wreckage by paramedics.

Already the finger-pointing had begun. The tabloids had managed to unearth a whiff of alcoholism in the train driver's history and his 'friends' were coming forward with lurid stories of his party days. The broadsheets, meanwhile, were focusing on vandalism as the likely cause of the derailment. People living close to the site of the crash had repeatedly complained about a gang of known troublemakers messing about near the tracks, but neither the police nor rail authorities had taken action.

Nick was glad to see that none of the papers mentioned him, but it frustrated him that he had yet to discover the fate of the businessman. He scanned through the names of the dead. There were eight men. One was almost certainly Eastern European and three sounded Asian or African. The most likely candidates were Anthony Cresslick, Steve Hatcher, Patrick Regan and Niles Ashdown. Nick tried to decide if the businessman had been an Anthony, a Niles, a Steve or a Patrick.

He was so absorbed in the reports that he didn't notice a dark shape slip into the room until it had hurled itself at him, hooking claws into his jeans for added traction.

'Listen, you ginger brute,' Nick said softly, 'if I have a heart attack, who's going to keep you in Whiskas? Huh? Think about that.'

He rubbed Oliver's thickly furred cheeks and was rewarded by a deep-throated purr and more painful kneading. He didn't object. The pure, undemanding constancy of the cat's love brought him back to reality, enabling him to separate out from the awfulness of the nightmare.

Already the dream was fraying at the edges. By morning it would be a dim memory. The only thing that stayed clear was the judge's face, seared on Nick's brain.

On impulse and to take his mind off the maddening tingle in his hands, Nick did a Bing search for high-profile judges. Minutes later the man in the dream was before him, identified on screen as Sir Michael Latimer, a Supreme Court judge. In the picture the judge was smiling in front of a Tudor mansion, a topiary bear leering over his right shoulder. He looked well-fed and well-bred, a pillar of the establishment. Yet there was no question that he and the foul-mouthed man Nick had almost punched in the underpass were one and the same.

By chance, Sir Michael had been front-page news that very day, criticising the Home Secretary for grandstanding on the subject of minimum prison terms. That in itself was a comfort to Nick. It explained where the nightmare had come from. His subconscious had seen it, distorted it, and thrown it into the section of his brain still dealing with the fallout from the train crash. The encounter in the underpass had fuelled his imagination further. The result: the most terrifyingly real nightmare Nick had ever had. He almost felt sorry for Sir Michael for having unwittingly participated in it.

It occurred to him that he might cleanse himself of the horrific images by writing an obituary of the judge. That was the thing about obituaries: there was something tidy about them. They were life without the blood, gore or messiness. Life cleaned up. That's not to say there were no villains in them. Mafia bosses were an obituary favourite. But even Godfathers were chronicled without judgement in a way that made them sound like someone you might like to have dinner with, or at least read a book about.

'Who's to say what constitutes a good or bad person?' was Phil's opinion. 'One man's saint is another man's absolute shit.'

Nick did a wider search on Sir Michael and made a few notes. He typed: *Sir Michael Latimer, who has died, aged 62, of . . .*

Of what? The house rule on the obit desk was that the cause of death was not necessary if someone lasted until 80. But Sir Michael hadn't even reached the old house-rule age of 'three score and ten'.

Nick left a space for the cause of death. He continued:

– earned respect and approbation in equal measure for his vociferous campaign for changes to divorce laws.

Although he came from a privileged background and went to Eton, the childhood cruelty and lifelong disapproval of his authoritarian father was to have a lasting effect on him. He once said that it was ironic that his special empathy with the youngsters and single mothers who came before his court was the only gift his father had ever given him . . .

Nick went on in the same vein, describing the judge's starry ascent at Oxford and his controversial early career as a young barrister when a textbook closing argument was said to have led to the freeing of a notorious paedophile. At that, Nick felt sick again. He didn't know why he was doing this – writing the obituary of a living and, judging by his encounter in the underpass, thoroughly unpleasant man. His hands seemed to have a will of their own.

Nick wrapped up the story as quickly as he could, listing two previous marriages and Sir Michael's habit of seeing at least one opera a month. He ended by typing: *He is survived by his wife, Lucia, and—*

The ridiculousness of his self-appointed assignment came home to him. He glanced at the clock. It was after 3 a.m. Abruptly, he switched off the computer and flexed his fingers. The tingling sensation had gone.

5

Nick reached the office two hours later than was usual for him, having overslept and caught two buses to Wapping. If Henry was going to insist that he work on archive stories rather than current events, he wasn't going to break his back getting in. Riding through Greenwich, Deptford and Bermondsey, he caught himself scanning the headlines on passing newsstands on the off-chance that Sir Michael Latimer actually had committed suicide, but the focus that day was on the revelation that the driver of the train had fallen off the AA wagon. No justices of any description had been found hanging from a chandelier.

Nick did his best to laugh at his own imaginings, but the night had been too long and too strange.

'You look rough,' Phil commented when he walked in.

'I've been better.'

Phil folded his arms across his chest. 'And what exactly is stopping you from taking the rest of the month off? Apart, obviously, from sheer martyrdom?'

Because I'm afraid that if I stop for a second I'll be blitzed by an avalanche/whited-out/erased from existence.

Nick crushed down the thought, one strongly reminiscent of those that had plagued him after the deaths of his mum and dad. He hung his jacket over his chair. 'What are you working on?'

Phil's expression registered disgust at Nick's evasiveness. 'The obituary of an unsung hero. A nurse who drove a jeep in France during the Second World War and was caught up in all sorts of mayhem.'

'Those are the best ones.'

A boyish grin spread over Phil's face. 'Aren't they just? People outside the obit department never get that, do they? If a royal or a politician dies, they say: "Big day for you!" They don't understand that the real joy is researching a life that might otherwise have gone un-recognised.'

Nick put his messenger bag on his desk, tucked his post in a drawer where he wouldn't have to look at it, and went to see Henry in his cubicle.

'Ah, Donaghue,' the editor said in a pleased tone when Nick tapped on his door. 'What are you up to today?' He spun round in his chair and undid the top button of his pinstriped blue shirt. 'Christ, you look awful. Is there something wrong with your razor?'

'Henry, I need something I can get my teeth into. If it makes you feel better, you don't have to give me any nuclear physicists or cabinet ministers. I can tackle someone more obscure.'

Henry massaged his right temple. 'Nick, on Monday you were in a train crash that is likely to be headline news for weeks because of the number of fatalities and the mincemeat made of those lucky, or unlucky, enough to have survived. Today is only Friday. While I applaud your enthusiasm and desire to return to normality as soon as possible, there is such a thing as too soon.'

'No, there isn't. According to the neurologist, that's the mistake employers often make. They wrap people in cotton wool and send them home to rest when very often the most healing thing for them is light work.'

'Of course it is. And that's what I've given you: light work. Hunt through the archives and see if there's anyone new we should add. Now go away and let me get on with checking my shares.'

By mid-afternoon Nick could stand the suspense no longer. He had to know. Had to have it confirmed that the nightmare had been no more than the mad ramblings of a shattered psyche. He checked the bylines on the most recent articles on the judge and called Damian at the *Sun*.

'Donaghue!' cried Damian. 'Great to hear from you, mate. How are things in the Dead Centre? Any good stiffs today?'

'Nothing as yet,' Nick said with a grimace. He'd met a lot of reporters like Damian in his featurewriting days and, in the ordinary course of events, avoided them as assiduously as Legionnaire's disease. 'I saw you did an interview recently with Sir Michael Latimer, the Supreme Court judge. Any chance you could give me his phone number?'

'Can't give out his private details,' said Damian, instantly suspicious. 'Wouldn't be right. Anyway, what's in it for me?'

Nick was seized by the urge to put down the phone, walk out of News International and never return. It was at times like these he wondered why it was he'd chosen to work in an industry that routinely brought him into contact with men and women whose moral compass was governed entirely by self-interest. Then he glanced over at Phil, face aglow as he chronicled the adventures of the wartime nurse, and remembered.

'Henry won't allow me to work on a real story because he doesn't believe I'm sufficiently *compos mentis* after the crash, and your excellent piece made Sir Michael sound like an intriguing man for our files.' Nick reasoned that some self-deprecation combined with a small ego massage couldn't do any harm. 'But I quite understand your reservations about giving out his number. I'd be the same. Thanks anyway.'

'No, wait,' said Damian. 'I can't give you his home number, but I can give you the direct line for his PA. I don't know what you'll make of Sir Mike. He's a bit of a weird one. Outwardly he's very posh and polite and he'll talk your ear off about his innumerable campaigns to reform this and reform that. But at the same time it doesn't surprise me he's been married three times.'

'Why's that?'

'See, when I shook his hand, it was ice cold. It was almost as though, beneath the veneer of good will towards all men, he had a refrigerator inside him.'

Nick hung up and dialled the number Damian had given him. It was only when a woman answered that he realised he hadn't worked out what to say. He could hardly tell her his job title. Nick didn't share Phil's conviction that every famous person in Britain lay awake worrying that *The Times* might omit their obituary someday.

'Sir Michael Latimer's office, can I help you?' the woman repeated. She had a home counties accent and sounded like the kind of person who still wore a twin-set and pearls.

Nick cleared his throat. 'Excuse me. I, uh, I'm a journalist for *The Times*. Would it be possible for me to speak to Sir Michael? I'm hoping to set up an interview with him for our Weekend section.'

Was it his imagination or did she hesitate slightly? 'What did you say your name was?'

'Donaghue, ma'am. Nick Donaghue.'

'I'm afraid Sir Michael's indisposed, Mr Donaghue.'

Nick's heart stopped; started up again irregularly.

'What exactly do you mean by indisposed?'

'I mean he's not available right now. He's a very busy man, as I'm sure you can imagine. His diary is full to overflowing. I'm Angela, his PA. Can I take a message?'

'So he's well?'

'Yes, he's quite well. What a peculiar question. Have you heard something to the contrary?'

'No. No, I haven't.'

'I'll leave a message that you called. Good day to you, sir.'

Good day? Did people still say good day?

'Good day,' responded Nick.

He replaced the receiver, not knowing what to think. Until that moment he had been secretly afraid that the nightmare might have some basis in reality. Now it had been confirmed that it hadn't and that the judge was in fact in the best of health and merely busy, he should have been able to put it out of his mind. But he couldn't. He kept replaying the conversation in his head, trying to decide whether Angela had been lying.

Realising that he was becoming obsessive in a not very healthy way, he spent the remainder of the afternoon distracting himself by talking to Amy about her boyfriend troubles, and answering Jason's fact-checking queries on a story he'd done the previous week.

At 5.30 p.m. on the dot, he packed up his things and hurried from the office, unable to bear the strain of being there a minute longer. He was waiting for the lift when Jason came rushing out to tell him that Henry wanted a word.

Nick bit back a curse, summoned an expression of keenness and wellbeing, and returned to the obit department. 'Yes, Henry,' he said, leaning round the door of the editor's cubicle, braced for a quick getaway.

'Donaghue! Thank the Pope that Jason caught you. You'll be happy to hear you've got your wish.'

'My wish?'

'You wanted something you could get your teeth into. Well, they don't come any bigger than this. Breaking news just in: Sir Michael

Latimer dropped dead of a heart attack in his chambers this afternoon. They're going to hold the presses for it but we're going to need to turn it around fast.'

The room receded. Nick fumbled for words, for thought, for air. 'S-Sir Michael Latimer?'

'You know, the Supreme Court judge,' Henry said impatiently. 'You must have heard of him. He is – was – perpetually on the front page. I need twelve hundred words on him ASAP.' He handed Nick a printout from the wires.

Nick recoiled as if he'd been offered a live cobra. 'No! I can't!'

Henry was astonished. 'But only this morning you were pestering me for a story. You gave me a whole speech about the need not to be wrapped up in cotton wool, about wanting a live piece.'

Nick sank into a chair. 'I know I did, but now I realise you've been right all along. I'm not ready. Phil can do it, or Jason. Jason could do with the experience.'

Henry rolled across the cubicle on his ergonomic chair and put his hand on Nick's shoulder. 'This is what I've been telling you all week. You've been harder hit by this crash business than you let on. You're whiter than a snowdrop in winter. But you *can* do this story, I know you can. I need you to do it. Phil is on deadline himself and I don't have anyone else available – not to do a story of this magnitude. You're the best I have. As soon as you sit down to write, it'll come back to you.'

'But I don't like him – the judge,' Nick said desperately. 'There's something sinister about him. Damian Dexter said he had a heart like a refrigerator.'

'What the hell are you talking about?' Henry pushed his chair back and checked his watch. It was 5.46 p.m. 'Since when did that have anything to do with it? If we only wrote about people we liked we'd have very thin newspapers.'

He placed the printout firmly in Nick's lifeless palms.

'Nick, you're a pro. Don't flake out on me now. They're going to hold the paper for it but I need it by six-thirty latest. Get writing. Don't let me down.'

Nick returned to his terminal like a sleepwalker. He switched on his computer and set up a document, but got no further than the judge's name. All he could think was: it's a coincidence. It *has* to be. If Sir

Michael had hung himself there'd be reason for concern, but the judge had dropped dead from a heart attack in his chambers. It was a bit strange that his PA Angela had claimed he was alive and well at three o'clock, but perhaps her office was on a different floor or in a separate building or he'd died a little later than that.

Nick decided the whole thing was a game being played on him by a twisted universe or his own crash-scrambled mind. How could it be otherwise? He wasn't psychic, had never been psychic, and was apparently so lacking in intuition that several girlfriends had cited that as a specific reason to break up with him.

With that strangely comforting thought, Nick went back to work. Or rather, he'd have worked if he could. He seemed to have contracted writer's block. He couldn't marshal a coherent phrase.

Henry kept making excuses to walk past him, so Nick logged onto the internet and gave every impression of earnestly researching his piece.

Phil wasn't fooled. 'Nick! Snap out of it. You look shell-shocked.'

'Only because you're making me nervous. Go back to your desk and leave me in peace. Everything's under control.'

Glancing up at the line of clocks showing times in Sydney, New York, Tokyo, Paris and London, Nick tried, unsuccessfully, not to panic. It was like being trapped in one of his own deadline dreams.

'Nick,' shouted Henry, 'you have five minutes. I hope your fingers are typing at the speed of light.'

Phil rushed over to him. 'Here, I'm finished, let me help you.'

'It's done.'

'How is it done? You have three words on your screen: the guy's name and title. That's it. You have another one thousand, one hundred and ninety-seven words to go. Shift over. We'll do it together.'

Nick put his hand on Phil's sleeve. 'You're the best friend I have. Did I ever tell you that? Thanks but no thanks. It's not how it looks. Just give me a moment.'

Phil returned to his desk, tense with worry.

'Time's up, Donaghue,' called Henry. 'I want the story on my screen in one minute or both of our heads are on the chopping block.'

'No problem,' said Nick. 'Give me thirty seconds.'

Surreptitiously he took a memory stick from his bag, inserted it into his terminal and pulled up the story he'd written in the early hours of that morning. In the space he'd left for cause of death, he inserted: *heart attack.* At the bottom of the piece, he wrote: *He is survived by his wife, Lucia, and their children, Romy and Belinda.*

Then he pressed Send.

A calm feeling came over him.

He was gathering up his belongings for a second time when Henry came over. 'Nick, this is great stuff. Great stuff. I know it was a tough one for you, but you came through and delivered like a pro. Well done.'

Henry wasn't big on praise and Nick knew it was heartfelt. 'Thanks. See you Monday. Any queries, call me on my mobile.'

When Henry was out of earshot, Phil came over. 'How the heck did you pull that off? Every time I glanced up you were frozen.'

Nick smiled thinly. 'Easiest story I ever wrote. It's like it came to me in a dream.'

6

The businessman's name was Matthew Levin. Nick found that out by extensive trawling of online newspapers and blogs. Further investigations by phone brought news that devastated him far more than confirmation of Levin's death would have done. The man's neck had been broken in the crash and he'd suffered extensive spinal cord trauma. He'd been transferred by helicopter to the specialist spinal injuries unit at Stoke Mandeville Hospital in Aylesbury.

On the first Saturday after the crash, Nick took a two-hour, cash-liquidating cab ride from Greenwich to Buckinghamshire, because he couldn't make himself get on a train and didn't trust himself to drive.

'I've heard he's . . . ? Do they think he . . . ? Is he likely to be . . . *paralysed*?'

The nurse was ushering him along a corridor that smelled of antibacterial hand gel and cut-price bacon, not the remembered surgical spirits, marshmallow and gift-shop roses of Nick's youth. Already he was regretting his decision to come. What had possessed him to drag himself out into the middle of nowhere on a Saturday to see a total stranger – a stranger who was unlikely to remember him – purely because of some transitory, no doubt imagined, connection between them?

'There's some paralysis, yes, but it's too early to determine the extent of it. The next few weeks will be critical.'

Nick turned the book he'd brought over and over in his hands. Unable to think of a suitable gift that didn't involve flowers or chocolate, he'd eventually settled on a copy of *The Prophet*, which he hadn't read himself but had heard was inspirational.

The nurse halted before a partially open door. 'He's sleeping at present but I'm sure his wife will be pleased to see you.'

For some reason, it hadn't crossed Nick's mind that the man's family might be visiting. 'Oh, I'll come back another time. I wouldn't want to intrude.'

But it was too late. The woman beside the ghost that had once been Matthew Levin had already spotted him. A month ago her sleek dark bob, yoga-toned figure and elegant dress would have set her apart at the school gates. Today she was a husk. Force of habit brought her to her feet in greeting, but a light breeze would have felled her.

'How is he?' asked Nick after introducing himself. The figure in the bed was immobilised by a neck brace, steel clamps and mummy-type bandages, the flickering monitors and steadily diminishing drip the only indicators of life.

Sarah Levin sat down. 'It's hour by hour right now. Privately they're telling me he'll never walk again. Actually, they're hinting at worse. But if I know Matthew he'll have something to say about that.'

Nick handed her *The Prophet,* which now struck him as a spectacularly inappropriate gift. 'I brought this. I don't know if it's the sort of thing he . . . I mean, I wasn't sure what else he might like.'

'Thanks, that's good of you. Matthew will appreciate it.' She opened the book at random pages and read a few paragraphs in silence. 'How did – how do you know my husband, Nick?'

'I was on the train. We smiled at one another.' Immediately he could have kicked himself. Words, once his friends, had deserted him.

'You were in the crash?' Her eyes ran over him in a slow, appraising way, which under any other circumstances would have been insolent or sexual or both. It made him uncomfortably conscious of his long, muscled legs, flat stomach and swimmer's shoulders, the result of hundreds of hours in the pool and weight room in his former life when those things seemed to matter.

'I'm sorry,' Nick mumbled. As she turned away he thought he saw tears glisten on her lashes at the injustice of fate. But her voice remained steady. She said sincerely and almost forcefully: 'Don't feel guilty about your good health, Nick. Rejoice in it. It will be taken from you soon enough.'

He spent the night at the house of his former university flatmates after drinking too much to make it home. Jim and Jules had not invited him to their annual reunion barbecue. They'd expected him to be on compulsory bed rest, or banned from party-going by a counsellor or doctor.

When Nick had left a message to say that he planned to come as usual, Jim texted: *That's ace, mate, but are you nuts?!!! Shouldn't you still be in intensive care?*

It was Jules who opened the red door of their Fulham house. As always, he felt a twinge of envy at the sight of the homely hallway with its glowing oak and scattered toys. It spoke of family and love. There was none of the hotelish, bachelor feel of his own apartment. When he stepped across the threshold, an old Lyle Lovett tune and the smoky whiff of chargrilled meat drifted in from the garden.

Jules hugged him hard. 'I can't tell you how great it is to see you alive.'

'Yeah, well, it's quite nice to be seen alive, too.'

When he attempted to extricate himself she held onto him. 'Darling, you look—'

'Like shit. I know. Apologies. It's been one of those days.'

'I was going to say you look as if you've seen a ghost.'

An image of Matthew Levin, swaddled in bandages and deathly still, filled Nick's vision. The dark shutters threatened to descend again. He shoved a bottle of wine into Jules's hand and forced a laugh.

'It's the vampire look. Don't you know it's all the rage?'

'Hey, man, you scared the life out of us this week.' Jim strode up the passage and gave him a rough hug. 'We were thinking, "If Nick goes to the big media centre in the sky, who's going to grill the meat at barbecues?".'

'And there I was thinking I'd be missed for my scintillating intellect and lovely personality,' Nick said in mock sorrow. 'Anyway, by the smell of things, I've already been replaced.'

'Like hell you have.' Jim put his arm around Jules and the pair of them regarded him anxiously. They could have been brother and sister. They had the exact same straight, Mediterranean-dark hair, hazel eyes and olive skin. Their lips were pursed in an almost identical way.

They match, thought Nick. They belong together. He himself had never matched anyone, never belonged to or with anyone – not even Becca. If he was honest, he'd never wanted to. He was a lone wolf and happy that way.

Mostly.

Jim said: 'Are you sure you're up to this, old boy? It's not been a

36

week since it happened. Are you certain you want to launch yourself into the whole social thing?'

'Apart from being about three minutes away from full-scale malnutrition, I'm fine. What does a man have to do to get a beer and a plate of chicken around here?'

Nick had come to the barbecue because he wanted to feel normal again. Unfortunately, it had the opposite effect. People he'd known intimately for a decade or more were as remote to him, as they skewered spitting sausages on pulsing orange coals, as actors in a sitcom or dancers on a stage.

Yet he was acutely aware that *they* were the normal ones. They had jobs in IT, PR, HR and recruitment. They had pensions and ISAs, holidayed in Norfolk and Tuscany, and had toddlers in situ or babies on the way. And some were simply carefree singletons.

Then there was him – a freak of nature.

That was how he thought of himself after nearly six days of attempting to recover his old life – his nice, ordinary, pre-crash life – and getting progressively further away from it. He felt like an inexpert windsurfer trying vainly to return to shore, a shore where less than a week ago he too had been able to bask in the sunshine, flirt, sip cocktails and kick a ball about, but which was now lined with people gesturing and staring and a lifesaver or two throwing an ineffectual foam ring.

And he knew with the certainty of his deadline dreams that he was already way beyond the point of rescue.

As the night wore on, he retreated to the shadows and consoled himself with alcohol. At length he was joined by Petra, a forty-seven-year-old friend and work colleague of Jules. She was recently divorced and bitter as quinine about it. When they'd been introduced earlier, she'd greeted him with a lip-curling, all-men-are-bastards disdain. But at some stage in the evening someone had told her about the train crash. Consequently, by the time she joined him in the smoky dark, she was rather better disposed towards him, not least because she was a few Vodka Mules past tipsy. With each fresh drink, she regarded him more and more as if he were a steak she longed to tuck into.

When he could bear it no longer he excused himself under the pretext of getting another beer. The living room was empty, the television left on. Nick paused to watch the Cuban singer Vanessa Diaz performing live on some American chat show. He sank down on the sofa. If he stared at her long enough he might block out the memory of Matthew Levin.

He crept out the next morning before anyone stirred. The only aspect of the party that he could recall with any clarity was being roused by Petra in the small hours. She was nuzzling his chest and mumbling something about him needing someone to take care of him after what he'd been through. Nick, who'd passed out on the sofa in Jim and Jules' lounge, was still trying to shake off the fog of sleep and martial a coherent phrase when he felt her hand slip into his boxers.

Instantly he was overwhelmed by the urge, not to make love to her, but to fuck her as hard as he could until they were both lost in some kind of orgasmic oblivion. He wanted to fuck her until he forgot, and he could read in her hungry face, puffy in the lamplight, that she wanted the same. He pinned her beneath him and kissed her, tasting chewing gum mint and traces of alcohol and stale cigarettes.

'Nick,' she whispered. 'Oh, Nick, I knew this is what you wanted. I knew this is what you needed.'

Five minutes later they were sitting side by side in a state of dishabille – Nick with his shirt unbuttoned but his jeans on and fly done up, and Petra in her black bra and crumpled skirt. Nick was handing her tissues with which to stem the tide of tears, snot and mascara. He hoped her sobs wouldn't wake Jules, who'd come flying down and berate him for seducing – or attempting to seduce – her already heartbroken friend.

'It's because I'm a withered, ugly drunk,' she wept. 'That's what my husband called me when he left me for a twenty-three-year-old wait-ress. Can you imagine how that scars a person? I feel as if I'll never have sex again.'

Ruing the moment he'd ever agreed to attend the wretched barbe-cue, Nick consoled her by telling her that she was immensely attractive, that, yes, she would have sex again, and that the problem lay with him – a combination of delayed shock and too much beer had rendered him unable to perform. At that point, she'd rallied and tried to get him to agree to a date.

His excuses were interpreted as still more rejection. After he said, 'It's not you, it's me,' she flounced from the room.

'Bastard,' she spat as she left.

'If I had a pound . . .' Nick responded wearily.

To kill time and avoid being by himself on a grey, blustery Sunday, he watched two movies back to back in a glittering multiplex in Leicester Square. Afterwards he was unable to say what either of them had been about. On the way home he stopped for a couple of pints and a takeaway. The bus came as he was negotiating a lamb kebab. Attempting to buy a ticket while trying to prevent tahini and chilli sauce from leaking through his fingers onto his already sweat- and barbecue-sauce-stained shirt, he was conscious of watching himself from afar and seeing a walking cliché.

The air in his apartment was stale. Silence lay heavy upon it. If it hadn't been for Oliver, bristling with annoyance at being abandoned for so long yet unable to disguise how overjoyed he was to see a friend, Nick would have shut the door and gone away again. As it was, he threw open every window and the balcony doors and made a big fuss of the wilful ginger mountain that was his cat of five years. Phil liked to tease him that it was his longest relationship. Nick didn't take it personally. More than once he'd thanked whatever lucky star it was that had made him scoop up the bedraggled excuse for a kitten, now an oversized Norwegian Forest cat, which had almost gone under his wheels one rainy night during his first week on the obit desk.

His mobile was on the kitchen bench where he'd forgotten it. There were six missed calls from a withheld number, and a message from Becca. 'Jules called and said you're acting very oddly. We're all extremely worried about you.'

The phone rang again as he was scooping food into Oliver's bowl.

'How could you do that to me?' ranted a disembodied voice.

Nick was startled. 'Damian?'

'Yes, Damian. Remember me? I'm the man whose calls you've been ignoring, the man who on Friday went against his best principles and did you the massive favour of giving you the private number of a Supreme Court judge – the same Supreme Court judge who dropped dead that very afternoon. And yet did you give me the scoop? Did you heck. You just shafted me without blinking.'

Nick dropped the empty Whiskas pouch into the bin. 'Damian, stop. It was a coincidence. I know it's a stretch to ask you to believe that, but it was. When I called the number you'd given me, which, while we're on the subject, is very much in the public domain and not a private number at all, his PA, Angela, assured me he was alive.'

'Why would you ask her that?'

'Ask her what?'

'Why would you ask her if he was alive?'

'Of course I didn't ask her if he was alive.' Nick was unable to believe that an already hideous weekend had taken a turn for the worse. 'Why would I ask her if he was still living when I didn't even know he was dead?'

'That's what I'm wondering.'

'I mentioned that I wanted to interview him and she made the comment that he was well and very busy. Look, Damian, this is ludicrous. I was grateful for your help with the number, but it was pure fluke that he died on the day I started looking into putting his obituary on file. The first I knew of it was when it came through on the wires. Try to accept that. I could hardly have predicted that he was about to have a coronary.'

'I guess I'll have to take your word for it,' Damian said grudgingly. 'Sorry if I attacked you. Personally, I don't believe in coincidences. I mean, why would his PA volunteer the information that he was well? It's not the sort of thing you say, is it? Something doesn't smell right here. I might have to look into it. Okay, mate, I'll see you around. And don't forget, you owe me one.'

Shaken, Nick took a sleeping tablet, something to which he was ordinarily utterly opposed but felt was all but obligatory under the circumstances.

The receding shoreline had just got a little further away.

7

He slept through his alarm and woke at nine with aching limbs and a muzzy head. The first thing he saw was his laptop screensaver swirling on the bedside table.

Nick had an overwhelming feeling of *déjà vu*. Disoriented by a sleeping-tablet hangover, he thought perhaps he'd worked late the previous night and forgotten to put his laptop away. He clicked on a key and the computer came to life. So sure was he that he'd see his archive research on the screen, or his desktop backdrop, a life-affirming photo of snowy mountains against a peacock-blue sky that he'd taken on his last skiing holiday, that it was a full minute before he realised he was looking at something different. That he was, in fact, looking at an obituary.

An obituary with his own byline on it.

Vanessa Diaz, who has died in a plane crash aged 24, was often de-scribed as Cuba's answer to Whitney Houston. Just three years ago, the factory worker's daughter was saved from sharks and hypothermia by US coastguards, who plucked her from a disintegrating raft some 50 kilometres from Miami. Since then, her accomplishments have been almost as miraculous as her rescue. Credited with inspiring a generation . . .

'No!' yelled Nick at no one in particular. He flew out of bed and stood looking at the laptop across a sea of rumpled covers. He tried to get a grip, to get his woozy brain to co-operate. There was a logical explanation for it. There had to be. Obituaries didn't just appear on computers by themselves.

He wondered if he'd had a brainstorm. Was it possible that Vanessa Diaz had died several months back and he'd done her obituary and blanked it out? However, a rudimentary scan of Vanessa's official website revealed that she'd been healthy enough to perform at Madison Square Garden on Saturday night.

Then who? How? *Why?*

Irrationally, his mind jumped to the *Sun* reporter. Damian had done this for revenge. Piqued that Nick had not once but twice denied him a scoop, he'd hacked into Nick's computer and done an obituary of a living person to screw with Nick's head. Either that or he'd broken into the apartment while Nick was comatose.

Watched with alarm by Oliver, who'd come to demand breakfast, Nick rushed from room to room searching for an intruder, even looking in the laundry basket and smaller kitchen cupboards. But the apartment was burglar-free.

He returned to the bedroom and approached his laptop like a ringmaster testing a new tiger. Gingerly he reached out and pressed an arrow key. Scrolling through the story, he discovered that there were 1045 words, complete in every detail. The obituary contained personal and poignant information that could only have been provided by a close family member, friend or colleague. They were details that Nick, who enjoyed Vanessa's music if he happened to hear it but didn't own any of her CDs and knew nothing about her except the bare basics of her rags-to-riches story, could not possibly have summoned up without an hour or two of research.

Nick took ten deep breaths. There were no paper bags in the apartment and he wondered if plastic would do if he started hyperventilating.

There were two remaining possibilities: a) He was losing his mind, or b) He'd had a premonition dream and written the obituary in his sleep. Vanessa Diaz was still alive but was about to die, just like the judge had.

Nick slumped down on the bed. The elephant in his head – the one he'd been ignoring since Friday – was now in full view, trumpeting its presence. What if his nightmare had correctly foretold the judge's death, if not the actual manner of it?

One part of him wanted to cling to the possibility that it was all a giant coincidence. The other part wanted answers.

He threw open the window and gulped in river air. The tide was out and the houses and apartment blocks lining the leaden Thames looked beached on its banks. Soon autumn would give way to winter.

Armed with an espresso, he returned to his laptop and checked the time on the document. It had last been saved at 3.20 a.m., about six hours after he'd gone to sleep. If he'd really researched it in a dream state, there would be evidence.

Seconds later he had it. The internet search history on his computer revealed that someone – Nick was not yet ready to accept that it might be him – had trawled through the websites of EMI, Vanessa's record label; Red Arrow, her management company; various social networking organisations; the *Miami Herald*; and *Rolling Stone* magazine.

Oliver jumped onto his lap. Nick clutched at him like a drowning man, ignoring the cat's squawks of protest. He didn't know what any of this meant. Didn't want to know. He wanted to go down to the muddy shore of the Thames in front of his apartment block, walk into the river and keep walking.

'Donaghue, a word,' Henry said curtly when Nick walked into the office shortly before noon.

'Who's been a naughty boy then?' Phil piped up.

Nick rolled his eyes. He tossed his bag onto his desk, avoided looking at the pile of unread mail and strode across to the editor's pod. 'Morning, Henry. How was your weekend?'

'Donaghue, what the hell's going on with you? Are you back at work or aren't you? I can't have you half here. Don't get me wrong. I'm not putting pressure on you to write if you don't feel up to it. Far from it. I told you from the beginning that you were out of your mind to come back to work so soon. At the very least you should be in counselling. But if you're going to insist on working I need you on call twenty-four seven. I can't have you sauntering in at whatever time suits you. This is a very busy department, as you well know. We're chronically under-staffed. Everyone here has to pull their weight. So what's it going to be? Are you with us, committed and on the ball, or would you like to take an extended leave of absence? Your choice.'

Tirade over, Henry pulled off his red tie, undid the top two buttons of his shirt and flopped into his chair.

'I don't understand what I've done wrong,' Nick said defensively. 'I admit that I was out of sorts last week but I was still recuperating from the crash and I think I made up for it with my piece on Sir Michael

Latimer. I apologise for being late today, but you could have reached me at home if it was something urgent.'

'Believe me, we tried. Your home phone number was engaged and your mobile was switched off.'

'Damn!' Nick took it from his pocket and turned it on. The welcome tone trilled. There were five missed calls on it, all from *The Times*.

'We've been battling to reach you for nearly two hours. That singer, Vanessa Diaz? You know, the stunning Cuban girl with the mega voice who was found half-starved on a matchstick raft off the coast of Miami a few years ago?'

Nick's stomach did a pancake flip.

'The plane carrying her and her band from New York to Canada crashed into the side of a mountain in a storm in the early hours of this morning, London time. Everyone on board was killed instantly.'

But Nick already knew how Vanessa Diaz had died. He saw it as clearly as if he'd been sitting beside her. She was pretending to read *Love in the Time of Cholera* and casting quick, uncertain glances at the rain needling the windows of a small plane. She was terrified, but doing her best not to show it. In the instant before the Learjet exploded, she reached for the hand of the boy sitting beside her and said something that made him laugh.

'Nick? Nick, are you with me? You've gone pale again. I need you to get onto it immediately.'

Nick unclenched his jaw with difficulty. 'You don't have to worry, Henry. I'll do the piece and it'll be on time. That's not the problem. It's just that, well, no matter how long you do this job some deaths hit you harder than others. They seem more of a waste somehow. It sounds trite, but the world will be a darker place without Vanessa Diaz in it.'

'Absolutely it will. Terrible tragedy. How quickly do you think you can turn the story around?' Henry's humour was restored now that Nick was once again firing on some, if not all, cylinders.

Nick held a heated internal debate. If he did this he'd be launching himself into a treacherous unknown. Into the realm of the psychic. Or psychotic. Then again, perhaps he was already there.

'It's on file. I did it a while ago. I'll have to look over it and make a few calls, but you should have it by early afternoon at the latest.'

Henry cupped a hand behind one ear. 'I'm sorry, I think I misheard you. I could have sworn that you said you already have her obituary on file.'

'I did. I do.'

'That's very prescient of you, given that she's only twenty-four.'

'She's a singer. Singers have a habit of dying young from drug overdoses, in crashes of some type, or at their own hands or those of crazed stalkers. Either that or they live long, complicated lives involving multiple marriages to Svengalis or other narcissistic, prescription-medication-addled celebrities.'

'I had no idea you'd given the matter so much thought.'

'Neither had I,' muttered Nick, feeling nauseous and oddly ashamed.

He was halfway out the door when Henry said: 'Hey Donaghue, no hard feelings about my little pep talk, huh? I'm only trying to do what's best for you and the department. I want happy, healthy, productive workers here. I'm not running a slave ship.'

'Right.'

'Oh, I almost forgot.' Henry reached for the *Evening Standard*, lying sports-section up on his desk. 'Keep your phone on in future. You won't believe what a morning we've had.'

He flipped the paper over. The headline read: TOP JUDGE IN HANGING SUICIDE MYSTERY. A photograph showed Sir Michael Latimer, hand in hand with his wife, in front of a mock Tudor mansion in Berkshire. A topiary bear was looking over his right shoulder.

The article wavered before Nick's eyes. He felt himself being sucked back into the vortex of his nightmare, into the sordid bedroom. Once again, he was unable to flee. Once again, he was watching himself from afar – a voyeur in his own horror movie.

'Not our fault but a bit annoying because it's more respectful to the dead, I feel, to get the details right,' Henry was saying. 'It seems our judge didn't have a heart attack in his chambers after all. Apparently his wife issued that statement in a panic on Friday because she didn't want the real story reaching her daughter, who's in New Zealand on a gap-year break, before she'd had a chance to contact her. Said she was worried about her home being invaded by the media. Fat chance now, poor woman. There's talk of kiddie porn being found on his computer and special favours for paedophile defendants and all sorts. It'll be a tabloid scrum.'

'Where did she find him? That is, where was he found?' Nick's voice sounded distorted in his own ears. He felt like a ham actor in a badly tuned radio play.

'She found him. His wife. Lucia, is it? He was in an upstairs bedroom at their country home, dangling from a chandelier in his wig and gown. They'd had a row and she'd followed him home a few minutes later. She arrived too late to stop him.'

8

For reasons Nick could never understand and was reluctant to analyse, those were the clearest dreams, the first two. Increasingly the others took on the fragmented quality of a faulty television, as if the temporary clairvoyance foisted upon him was being taken away again, one spectre at a time.

What was certain was there was no stopping them. They came intermittently – sometimes three in a week, sometimes none for three weeks – but they came inevitably, a macabre parade of the soon-to-be-departed.

At first, he considered the dreams to be random. The coincidence of him colliding with the judge in the underpass and seeing Vanessa Diaz on television mere hours before they both died, he'd persuaded himself was just that.

One morning, he turned on the BBC breakfast news to see a tribute to a veteran Asian bus conductor who'd passed away during rush hour on Oxford Street. Nick was about to change channels when the man's photo flashed up. What shocked him most was that he'd bought a ticket from the conductor on the number 9 bus the previous day. He remembered him because, despite the commuter crush and jostle, there'd been a serenity about the man's white-whiskered features.

Watching him work, Nick had been lost in admiration that anyone still doing such a soul-destroying job in their sixties could summon a smile, let alone the belly laugh that escaped the conductor when a tattooed, shaven-headed youth gripping the studded collar of a Rottweiler told him: 'My dog ate my ticket. You gotta problem, take it up wit' him.'

It was only after a deluge of nightmares featuring the number 9 bus and the image of a leather satchel lying in a gutter that it hit Nick that it was possible, indeed probable, that he'd had some brush with every one of the men and women who stalked his nightmares. He'd walked past them on the street. They'd served him in restaurants, beamed at him from flat screen televisions, or sold him tickets. *He* was the common denominator. People died after encounters with *him*. People were killed when he'd done no more than glance at them.

He'd survived a train wreck only to become an unwitting assassin. A menace to society. A psychic killer.

To ward off what he feared was an increasing tendency towards paranoia, he bought a Native American dream catcher, a pale blue spider's web of woven chamois leather with two feathers suspended from it. A woman in a shop smoky with incense and bedecked with every manner of crystal told him that the Sioux Indians used it to capture the good dreams of life. That evening, the dreams the web caught were more graphic and brutal than ever.

A dream dictionary also proved less than helpful. It suggested that dreaming about a bus driver meant that he was going round in circles and making little progress in life. Dreams about buses in general indicated he was lacking originality and needed to be more independent, and dreams about missed buses were a sure sign that some aspect of his life was out of control.

'No shit,' said Nick as he consigned it to the recycle bin.

Sleep – or rather, no sleep – was the answer. The less he slept the less he'd dream and that could only be a good thing.

He took to pacing the streets of Greenwich at night. It was more effective than caffeine and less excruciating than putting tabasco in his eyes. He'd walk through the silent town in the hours when the foxes, flea-bitten and battle-scarred from a lifetime of urban scrounging, took leisurely strolls among the shops and restaurants, like characters from a Beatrix Potter story. As he became increasingly sleep-deprived and his imagination more feverish, he'd picture rounding a corner and finding them upright in suits, downing pints at the Gipsy Moth.

Looming over the pub was the Cutty Sark ship, restored to full glory after a fire. Wrapped up against the river wind, Nick could waste hours taking in every detail of the tea clipper's majestic rig and imagining life on board in the days of murder, mutiny and plump bales of wool, days when tea was more precious than gold. Lit with purple, the ship seemed to chart a path into the night sky. He wanted to wish himself on it and sail away. Any life, even one involving scurvy, drunken sailors and narrow wooden bunks barely big enough to sleep a child, had to be better than his current one.

His wanderings took him along the river path, past the baroque columns of the Old Royal Naval College, designed by Christopher Wren in the late seventeenth century as a seamen's hospital and now the University of Greenwich. He'd linger beneath the echoing brick edifice of the power station and watch the water crumple and straighten like black foil. When the tide was high, the Thames was often more sea than river. Boat traffic sent waves barrelling up to the embankment and mini tsunamis splattering onto the cobbles.

Most nights Nick paused at the iron gates of a private garden secured with a heavy padlock. He felt drawn to it. Set between the river and the ragged silhouette of apartment complexes under construction, steel cranes watching over them like praying mantises, the garden was like a window onto another era. It was pocket-sized – a tenth of an acre at best – yet it contained all one could ever need in a yard: an apple tree, a luxuriant fig, a sheltering horse chestnut, a shed and greenhouse, a veggie patch, two deckchairs and a barbecue.

Tonight, by chance, the padlock had been left undone. He pushed the gate and went in. Between the lawn and the river, there was no barrier. Nick sat on the bank and dangled his legs over the side. The water, exuding a faint scent of rotting weed and detritus, was barely two metres below. It seemed to exert a pull. He could see its whirlpool eddies. If he slipped . . .

On the opposite bank, the office towers of Canary Wharf laid a path of diamonds across the Thames. To his left were the distant masts of the Cutty Sark and the former palaces of Tudor kings and queens. Adding to the contradictions was the O2 entertainment centre, a futuristic dome set amid the bones of long-dead factories.

Nick lay back on the dew-dampened grass and put his arms behind his head. The garden made him feel like a boy again and he tried using a child's perspective to put a positive spin on his situation. So he was having nightmares. So they seemed prescient. It wasn't good, but logically it would pass. The part of his brain responsible for hallucinogenic visions had been jolted in the crash. All he needed to do was think of it in the same way he might a broken leg. Yes, it was excruciating and at times made life unbearable, but soon it would heal and he'd be able to rejoin the human race. He would, as he kept telling everyone, be fine.

With that absurdly simple thought, he felt a load lift from him. Winter had started, but he was wearing multiple layers and felt more comfortable than he had for weeks in his own bed. Reluctant to leave the enchanted garden, he shut his eyes. He felt safe there. Perhaps he could find out who owned it and pay them to let him spend time in it.

Attempting to analyse why the space made him feel so peaceful, he concluded that it was the absence of a wall between the garden and water. Having submitted himself willingly to the prison that was the city, it gave him a sudden insight into what it was like to be free.

Sleep came like a slamming door. When he was awoken by shuffling sounds and the soft squeak of rubber on cobbles, he thought at first that he was dreaming. Rubbing his eyes, he sat up. What he saw sent a bolt of adrenalin through him. In two silent bounds he was crouching in the shadows. Through the railings, a gang of as many as thirty young men was moving in formation like a militia. There was violence in their silence and Nick, remembering the London riots, knew instinctively that if they were to catch a glimpse of him, alone and vulnerable at 3.15 a.m., the outcome would not be a happy one.

After they'd gone, the garden no longer felt like a piece of paradise. It was more like an elaborate hoax. Nick stayed where he was as the hours ticked by and the sky turned pink and orange and genial local residents retook the streets with their boisterous spaniels and arthritic retrievers, their Saturday-morning papers tucked beneath their arms.

Still he stayed unmoving. By the time he took the river path back to the Cutty Sark his stomach was telling him that breakfast was overdue. After stopping in at Rhodes bakery for a life-saving cappuccino and two croissants, he took a shortcut through the market. The stallholders were setting up for the weekend. It was barely 9.30 but already Eritrean curries were simmering in cast iron pots, salmon was being sliced into sushi and Ruby Tuesday was unpacking inviting rows of chocolate cupcakes topped with plump blackberries.

In among the carved wooden fruit bowls and dragon hand-puppets, Nick found a psychic. She poked a pixie face from the curtain of her booth as he approached.

'Is it too early for a consultation?'

'It's never too soon to see the future. Forewarned is forearmed.'

Her booth was curiously womb-like. He sat on a beanbag and watched her lay out her tarot cards on an occasional table.

'Don't tell me, I'm going to meet someone tall, dark and handsome.'

She picked up the cards and shuffled them again. 'Ah, a sceptic. And yet you're here. I wonder why.'

'I was hoping you could tell me.'

'What would be the point? I'll only confirm your preconceptions. If I say something you believe to be accurate, you'll tell me it was a lucky guess. If I say something you find preposterous, you'll tell me I'm a fake.'

Nick blinked. His eyes were like hot coals in their sockets. 'You're right, I am a sceptic, but my motives in coming to you are sincere. I'm looking for some information and I'm hoping you might be able to provide it.'

'What information – or is that another thing I'm expected to read in the cards?'

'I apologise. I've had a sleepless night. If you don't mind, I have a question. Your gift of second sight or reading cards, is it something you've always had or something you learned?'

Before she could protest he went on hurriedly: 'The reason I'm asking is that I feel as if I've suddenly, overnight, started to see into the future. I'm a pragmatic man and I know that's impossible and yet I have these dreams where . . . Put it this way, there's no other explanation.'

She waited for the punchline. When it didn't come, she seemed thrown. 'I can't speak for your situation. Everyone is different. From what I have seen, people don't suddenly become psychic in their thirties or fifties. They've always been that way. The only thing that's changed is that some life event has caused a shift in their head. They're more open to it. The gift itself has always been there.'

'That's utter rubbish.'

She reached for the deck of cards. 'We can confirm it or not.'

He extricated himself from the beanbag. 'Let's not. Forget what I said. I haven't slept in days and I'm not thinking straight. I don't believe in fortune-telling any more than I believe that you could predict whether or not the sun will shine this afternoon. I'm sorry for wasting your time. How much do I owe you?'

She took his money without a qualm and escorted him from the booth. The jostle and smells of the market were like a slap in the face.

'I can tell you two things for free.'

Nick paused. 'Oh yeah?'

'The sun is not going to shine this afternoon. It's going to rain. I know that because I heard it on the weather report as I was driving to Greenwich.'

'What's the second thing?'

'You'll find what you're searching for, but only when it's too late. My advice? Live in the moment.'

9

'Go away,' Phil had told him back in November, about a month after the crash. 'Go away and don't come back. You've become a rubbish friend and a pretty ropy reporter. If I was Henry, I'd fire your arse.'

'Thanks.' Nick poured gravy onto his canteen-issued chicken-and-mushroom pie. 'With pals like you, who needs enemies?'

'I don't mean for ever. Nick, listen to me. I have a cottage in the countryside . . .'

Nick choked on a crumb. 'I'm sorry, did you just say that *you* have a cottage in the countryside? By countryside, do you mean Hyde Park, or the untamed wilderness beyond the M25, where you're convinced bears, tigers and the odd elephant still roam?'

'I inherited it. Don't ask. At any rate, it's in the back of beyond. Practically in the Atlantic. Mikhail and I visited it last year after Aunt Sadie passed away.' He shuddered. 'That was a weekend to remember.'

'And you're suggesting what exactly?' Nick wiped his mouth and pushed aside his plate. 'That I go into exile until I find nirvana or become a hermit or both? Where is this rural idyll anyway?'

'Cornwall. The cottage is a nature lover's paradise. You'd have the ocean and moors on your doorstep. Okay, so you won't have a super-market at the end of the road and it's lacking in one or two mod-cons, but you'll really feel in touch with the elements.'

'You mean the roof leaks and there's no heating or electricity?'

'Don't look a gift horse in the mouth. Think of the romantic candlelit dinners you'll be able to eat in front of a roaring log fire.'

'Traditionally, romance involves two people. Anyhow, if this place is so great, why are you not spending every spare weekend there?'

'Do I look like a boy scout? Besides, Mikhail has arachnophobia.

Nick, all kidding aside, I'm not sure what's going on with you right now but you don't need me to tell you that you've completely lost the plot. I, for one, am not going to stand by and watch you piss your career down the drain. My cottage might not be the Ritz, but it'll do you the power of good to get away from everything.'

From the vantage point of a grim, grey December, Nick wished he'd taken Phil's advice.

'Talk to me, Nick,' yelled Henry from his cubicle. 'What time can I expect your story?'

Nick didn't respond. Almost six weeks had passed since he'd last written an obituary not handed to him in a dream, and now that he'd been assigned one he was struggling to cope. The well in his head had gone dry.

He consulted his notes again and forced himself to commit a few words to screen. *Theresa Benton was to sailing what David Beckham . . .*

He stopped. It hurt to type. He glanced down at his fingers and was appalled to see that the tips were bleeding. A steady flow of gore dripped onto his keyboard, staining the letters with scarlet. There was a smear of it on his screen, between 'sailing' and 'David'.

'Get you a coffee, honey?' Amy asked, giving his shoulders a squeeze as she passed him. 'You look all done in.'

Nick gave a violent start. The familiar landscape of his desk swung back into place like the seamless transition of a theatre set. There was no blood. No gore. Nothing but a fading concert ticket, the postcard Becca had sent him from St Lucia, the silver-framed photo of his mum and dad and, half hidden, the pile of unopened post. A dark spot of blood showed beneath the plaster on his forefinger, but the one on his index finger was clean. His keyboard and screen were dusty, but otherwise respectable.

'A coffee would be great, thanks, Amy. Black, no sugar.' His voice sounded almost normal.

He borrowed a pen from Jason's vacant desk. His own was at home under lock and key. Two days earlier he'd secured every writing implement, diary and notepad he possessed in his study and given the key to the apartment block concierge. 'Keep this for me until further notice,' he'd told the man. 'Don't give it to me for at least a week, even if I beg.'

So confident had he been that if he had no way of recording his nightmares, they wouldn't exist, ergo nobody would die, he'd risked going to bed early. Had actually looked forward to sleep for the first time since the crash.

When the alarm had shattered the quiet next morning, he'd lain for a long time with his eyes tightly closed. He'd tried to get a sense of the space. The hum of his laptop, the sound that most often greeted him if he'd sleep-written an obituary, was, mercifully, absent. There were only harmless sounds – the drone of an aeroplane sketching a flight pattern; the faraway surf of traffic; the whisper of Oliver's pads on the wooden floor.

Nick opened his eyes a crack. It was still early but the winter sun was trying valiantly to shine. He'd left his laptop at work, and it seemed that his precautions regarding his study had worked. There were no notes on the bedside table.

With a sigh of thanks, he'd swung out of bed and stretched. His toes had touched something cold. His razor was lying on the rug.

'What the . . . ?'

It was then that he noticed a bloody fingerprint on the white sheets. Then another. His hands began to throb. He brought them up slowly. The fore and index fingers of his right hand were lacerated.

Oliver sniffed at them and pulled a face.

Nick clenched his fists, partly to stem a fresh leaking and partly because he knew before it happened what he was going to see next.

On the wall was the name of a football star, written in blood.

Vampire graffiti.

That, to Nick, had been the final straw.

Phil, who had today been assigned the man's obituary, leaned from his chair. 'Nick, what's going on? Why aren't you writing?'

'I'm thinking.'

On an A4 sheet of paper he scrawled: *Theresa Benton's love of sailing came from a most unusual source . . .*

He paused again. His palms were clammy. A vein pulsed unpleasantly in his temple. He gulped down the boiling coffee. A blister swelled on his tongue.

'Ten minutes, Donaghue,' shouted Henry. 'Ten minutes and not a second more.'

Nick screwed up the paper and tossed it into the bin. Purposefully he typed: *Writer's block. The scariest two words in the English language.*

Then he deleted them. Because they weren't. Not by far.

'Nick, you need help,' said Phil, raising his voice to compete with the din in the Captain Kidd pub. 'Stop being so bloody stubborn and proud and admit it. Talk to someone. It doesn't matter whether it's me or a shrink or some tart you pick up in a bar, just as long as you find a way to get out whatever it is that's eating you. Personally, I think you need therapy. Or a lobotomy. One of the two. And while we're on the subject, what's with the plasters on your fingers?'

Nick controlled himself with difficulty. He downed his whisky in a single swallow and signalled to the barman for another. Through the breath-fogged pub windows, the black river seethed. 'Look, I appreciate you giving me a hand with the piece, but I'm telling you for the hundredth time that there's nothing wrong with me.'

'So you keep saying.'

'I had a rough night, that's all. You've had a few of those in your time, haven't you, Phil?'

His friend regarded him with pity. 'Problem is, they're all rough nights for you these days, aren't they, Nick? If you don't watch yourself you're going to be out of a job and on a twelve-step programme at AA. You look like an extra from *Night of the Living Dead*. When did you last get eight hours of sleep? Or three, for that matter? When did you last eat anything that didn't come from a kebab shop? When did you stop caring enough to get your shirt ironed or your jacket dry-cleaned?'

Nick rounded on him. 'What are you, my mother? Oh, I forgot. She's dead. Mind your own business and leave me the fuck alone.'

He slammed his glass down and left the pub without another word. A few doors down, he joined other furtive dependants for a cigarette beneath the smokers' shelter. *Pariahs, more like*, Nick thought resentfully. He'd taken up smoking for the first time in a decade.

Phil emerged from the pub on a wave of yellow light and laughter and walked the other way, the river wind tugging at his umbrella. Nick watched him go. He found a sheltered spot and called Dr Retson's office. When his most loyal friend couldn't give him advice without being savaged, it was time to seek help.

'I see dead people.'

The psychologist regarded Nick impassively across the glass expanse of his desk. Early on in the session he'd counselled him not to interpret this silence as being in any way judgemental. Nor was he to imagine he was being boring or not being listened to with due attention.

Nick had, of course, imagined all of those things. And as was his habit when he was interviewing people, when he often felt like a shrink himself, he had tried to second-guess the psychologist and intuit the diagnosis he must be forming.

'When I say I see dead people, I don't mean I'm like the boy in *The Sixth Sense*. Are you familiar with that film? Bruce Willis starred in it.'

The psychologist, who did not look at all like Nick had guessed he might from his authoritative phone manner and public-school accent, made an almost imperceptible move of his head. It could as easily have been a no as a yes. Equally, he could have been thinking: *This is turning into the longest hour of my life.*

Nick was thinking the same thing. He now bitterly regretted taking Dr Retson's advice. The neurologist had listened with interest to a heavily edited version of his concerns about his mood swings and nightmares, scrutinised an MRI scan at length, and sent him to Harley Street for a psychological evaluation.

'I don't actually see dead people as such. It's worse. I see them before they die. I have nightmares in which I see their last minutes. I predict their deaths in my sleep. I write it all down. When I wake up . . .'

Nick stopped. He'd said too much already.

The digital clock on the glass table showed he'd been talking for fifteen minutes. Having arrived late, he had less than half an hour to go. Doubtless the shrink would read some deep psychological significance into his tardiness when it had to do with nothing more sinister than the diabolical state of London's traffic.

Timing aside, Nick thought he was doing rather well, considering he had always been therapy-averse. So far, he'd talked about the images that haunted him from the crash; about what even he realised was his 'survivor's guilt'; and about what a failure he felt as a friend/lover/human being.

The only thing he'd omitted to mention was the link between his dreams and his job, saying only that he was a freelance feature writer on 'things like sport and music'. He'd decided in advance that the small but important detail about his nightmares becoming reality in the obituary section was best left out. *The Times* obituaries were un-signed so it was unlikely the doctor would ever find out that Nick worked on the obit page, but he wasn't about to take any chances. Who knew what powers were invested in shrinks these days. He didn't want to wind up being committed.

'So that's why I'm here,' he tailed off. He'd expected to experience a rush of relief once it was all off his chest, but his detachment was such that it was only anti-climactic.

The psychologist, a gaunt man in a grey shirt and beige sweater vest, laid down his pen. He had the air of a Victorian detective on the brink of unveiling a murderer. 'What you're describing – feelings of irritation apparently brought on by people suggesting that you take time off work to recover from a physical or emotional condition you don't feel you have, coupled with the nightmares – that's classic PTSD. Post-traumatic stress disorder.'

Nick, who'd been expecting to hear something of the kind, waited for him to continue. He would have killed for a cigarette.

'I'm sure it won't surprise you to learn that I've seen other train crash survivors over the years. But really it's not about whether you were on a train or plane or in a tragic car accident. Essentially, you've experienced a situation in which you've felt helpless or fallen apart. Even if you blacked out while it was happening and weren't afraid except for a millisecond, you've come round and seen the carnage.'

Beneath the X-ray gaze of the psychologist, Nick shifted in his chair. The lid on the sealed box in his head lifted briefly. He relived the instant on the train when his senses rushed back and let in the screaming. He saw the severed arm with its incongruous gold watch.

Like a man wrestling closed a barn door in a tornado, he forced the lid shut again.

The psychologist reached for a sheet of paper. On it, he drew a series of boxes. A consequence of what he called the 'Event' was 'Network Formulation' – the event as memory. 'That's everything you felt, thought or did during the crash.'

From what Nick could understand, the sensory assault of the crash combined with the emotional horror of it tended to result in an 'Ouch Factor'. If his network 'memory' was re-stimulated in some way, the Ouch Factor intruded into his awareness.

'Emotionally, it's very uncomfortable. You'll experience unbidden thoughts, flashbacks and/or dreams.'

Nick sat up straighter. What he wanted most of all was a simple, one-part solution to his problems. 'Go on.'

'Because this intrusion is so painful, most people will do anything possible to avoid any reminder of the disaster, whether it's by refusing to talk about it or steering clear of television programmes with even the most tangential link to the crash, such as a cartoon featuring a smiling train. They're also extremely resistant to counselling. If they do go into therapy, they'll tend to turn up late or get lost in an area they know very well.'

Nick considered himself rapped over the knuckles.

'Empirically, we know that high levels of intrusion are associated with high levels of avoidance. High levels of avoidance are associated with bad psychological outcome. For instance, poor interpersonal relationships and an inability to love people you would normally love.'

He stopped. 'Is any of this sounding familiar? You might also be experiencing impaired concentration, sleep disturbance, a short fuse.'

At this, ironically, Nick's fuse became shorter still. 'At what stage do you ask me if I've ever fantasised about my mother?'

'Would you like me to ask if you've ever fantasised about your mother?'

'Sorry to disappoint you but no, I don't. I'm only using that as an example of the kind of therapy I don't want or need. I'm not interested in having every experience I've ever had unpacked and raked over and viewed through the lens of Freud or Jung or whatever methodology you follow until I recall some repressed childhood trauma and break down in a blubbering heap like Nick Nolte in *The Prince of Tides.* Did you see that?'

'Do you do that a lot? Use cultural references as a diversionary tactic?'

'Not at all. I'm just trying to make a point. But if you haven't seen the film, I highly recommend it. Barbra Streisand's legs alone are worth the price of the rental.'

The psychologist tapped his lower lip with his pen. 'What you're experiencing now is the Ouch Factor. You're avoiding the truth because it's painful to confront it.'

Nick fixed his gaze on the insect trapped inside an amber paperweight. It seemed to him that their situations were not dissimilar.

'Why me?' he asked quietly. 'Why did I survive? One hundred and twenty-seven people on the train and I was the only person with barely a scratch. What did I ever do to deserve that? No, don't bother answering. I can tell you what I've done. Fuck all. I've been a selfish being my whole life.'

'Survivor's guilt is a peculiar thing. You don't feel guilty if you cut your finger and it gets better, and yet if you have the good fortune to be sitting in the one spot in the car, plane or train that doesn't get destroyed in the impact, you do. It makes no sense. That's because it usually has to do with something else. Something that occurred in childhood, perhaps. Guilt is another thing we'll address in future sessions.'

Nick checked the clock. In minutes his time would be up. 'But what about the dead people?' he asked in sudden panic. 'What do my nightmares mean? How can I stop them? *Please,* you have to help me.'

The psychologist examined his spotless fingernails. 'I want to help you, but it's not conducive to your recovery if we run out of time while you're telling me about something that has particular emotional resonance for you. Ideally, I like trauma sessions to be open-ended or around two hours. We need to bear that in mind when we make your next appointment.'

Nick pictured himself lying on the couch week after week with the meter running, while the psychologist dissected the undissectable.

He made a final attempt at a breakthrough. 'All I'm asking for is a tool, a keyword, *anything* that might stop my nightmares. I wasn't psychic before the crash. I still don't believe I am psychic. But there's no escaping the fact that total strangers die horrible deaths in my nightmares and I wake up to find I've chronicled every detail. Have you any idea what that's like? I once sleep-wrote a man's name in blood and the very next day he dropped dead of an aneurism. I felt as if I'd killed him. Rationally, I know it's nothing to do with me . . .'

When he glanced up, the man's demeanour had undergone a disconcerting change, from clinical professional to benevolent uncle. At the same time, there was a new watchfulness about him.

'Why would you feel as if you'd killed him if you hadn't?'

'What kind of question is that? I've just explained to you that I see these people in my dreams and within twenty-four hours they're dead. It makes me feel like a murderer. I'm terrified to so much as look at a woman.'

The psychologist's pen stopped in mid-scribble. 'Why are you terrified? What's the worst that could happen?'

'Surely it's obvious? I'm afraid to meet a girl in case I'm responsible for killing her. Not me, of course, but the voices I hear in my dreams. If I ever had to wake up and find that I'd recorded the death of a person I love, I think I'd . . .'

His chest was so tight he could barely breathe. 'Some nights I envy the passengers who died on the train.'

'Are you saying you're having suicidal thoughts and hearing voices?'

Nick stiffened. He sensed a trap. 'No, no voices. And no, that's not what I'm saying at all. You're deliberately misunderstanding me.'

He wondered if there was a panic button beneath the glass desk, something that, if pushed, brought white-coated orderlies rushing in with a strait jacket and a syringe, ready to whisk him away to a secure facility.

The psychologist continued as if he hadn't spoken. 'You mentioned Freud earlier. You may be aware that he famously described dreams as the "royal road to the unconscious". His belief was that the nucleus of every dream is wish fulfilment. That's often interpreted as a yearning for something pleasurable, but Freudian theory has it that a person can also wish to be punished or to inflict harm. I'm principally a cognitive behavioural therapist, but I believe it is important to be open to other disciplines. For instance, when you think of the images in your dreams, what other things come to mind? This singer, Vanessa. The one whose death you believe you foresaw. I'm afraid I'm not familiar with her music. Were you a big fan of hers? Did you ever previously have any sexual thoughts about her? Or murderous ones, for that matter?'

I'm having murderous thoughts about you, Nick wanted to say. *Does that count?*

It came home to him with brutal clarity that he was on his own with his nightmares. A thousand hours of therapy wouldn't help him.

'See you next week?' the shrink queried as he guided Nick to the door three minutes later, at precisely 4.30 p.m.

Nick smiled. He knew that the psychologist knew that they both knew he had no intention of returning.

'See you next week,' he parroted.

II

Three weeks later, Nick took another cab ride out to Stoke Mandeville. It was Christmas Eve. He could have driven but knew he was likely to want a drink later. A taxi seemed as good a way as any of spending money he would ordinarily be shelling out for presents, turkeys, cards and other Christmas paraphernalia. In the New Year, he planned to sell his apartment and move to somewhere smaller. He craved simplicity.

For the first time in weeks he'd turned on the TV while eating his cornflakes that morning. The staggering range of luxury consumables being marketed to people with credit cards – BMWs they deserved, sofas, watches, sound systems they couldn't live without, and Caribbean cruises that would mean that they, too, could join the ranks of the truly contented – had blown his mind.

The weird thing was that until the crash he'd been one of those people. The part about his last break-up that had upset him most was that the girl, Lucy, had gone off with his favourite Paul Smith shirt. From his current perspective, Nick found the triviality of such a concern belief-beggaring. Increasingly, he found himself staring at his possessions with bemusement. The impulse that had led him to purchase them was lost to him. What he longed for was a stripped-down life, an emptying of everything he'd been and was.

The only exception was his black Mustang, which he'd bought as a wreck seven years earlier with a rather generous payment from an American sports magazine and had spent a small fortune getting lovingly restored. To him, the car wasn't a thing, like a sofa or a fridge. It was family, like Oliver,

'You want ree-seat?' barked the cab driver over a high-pitched volley of Bollywood music.

Outside the car window, ant-like lines of relieved, reprieved, bereaved or just plain devastated visitors moved jerkily in and out of the hospital.

Nick counted out a pile of notes and prepared to join the emotional lottery.

Matthew Levin was propped up in bed watching TV. He was corpse-white and disturbingly thin, but someone, probably Sarah, had seen to it that he was clean-shaven and in a fresh pair of striped pyjamas. He wore a neck brace. His eyes swivelled as Nick entered and he said in a muffled voice: 'You look terrible.'

Nick immediately regretted having come. 'Thanks. You, on the other hand, look a great deal better than you did a couple of months ago.'

'It's the staff here.' Levin had the same piercingly honest gaze as his wife. 'They're incredible. If it weren't for them and for the support of my friends and family, I'd have topped myself by now. You don't realise how selfless people are, and how deep their reserves of love and hope, until something like this happens to you. It really restores your faith in humanity.'

'Oh, it does,' Nick said insincerely. 'It definitely does.'

It was then that it hit him that whatever noble motives he might like to have ascribed to his visit to Stoke Mandeville, uppermost in his mind was the certainty that Matthew Levin was the one person in the world who could be counted on to be feeling worse than he did. To hear instead that the crash that had destroyed Nick's life had restored Levin's faith in the essential goodness of humankind was a blow from which he could not easily recover.

He averted his gaze from the motionless lumps that were Matthew Levin's legs. 'I admire your optimism. It can't be easy.'

Levin scrutinised him. 'Why do I get the feeling that you're here for a reason?'

Nick pulled a chair up beside the bed. 'Of course I'm here for a reason. I wanted to see how you were. To say compliments of the season and all that.'

'That might be your intention, but it's not the real reason you're here. When you entered the room just now a cold front came in with you. I thought to myself: now why is that? You've survived a disaster and you have your health. You should be walking on air, a fit young

64

guy like you. You had a kind of arrogant exuberance about you that day I saw you at the station. You were annoyed about missing your train, but you got over that soon enough. By the time you walked past me on the carriage – which, incidentally, is the last thing I remember – there was a glint in your eye, as if you only had to grin and the whole world would roll over at your feet like a Labrador puppy. I envied you your confidence. Something pretty catastrophic must have happened to change that.'

Levin's directness took Nick off guard.

'To be truthful, something pretty catastrophic has happened . . .'

Then, without warning, without him knowing he was going to do it until he did it, it all came out. He opened up to Levin, the one person who could genuinely empathise with his plight, in a way he could never have done with the shrink.

He told Levin how alienated he felt, how he'd lost his ability to write. He talked about his survivor's guilt and the nightmares that tormented him, although he omitted their link to his day job or the fact that they were prophetic.

Levin heard him out to the end. Above the bulky brace, his face gave nothing away. Throughout Nick's monologue, he stared unseeingly at the characters of a medical drama on the television. At last he said: 'So if I'm to understand you correctly, what you're saying is that because of these dreams, these nightmares if you will, your previously charmed life is in ruins?'

'I guess so,' said Nick, emerging from the rainy dark of his thoughts too late to heed any warning signals.

'You . . . make . . . me . . . sick.'

Levin's voice was so soft that at first Nick wasn't sure he'd heard him correctly. 'You've emerged from a train wreck unscathed, you've had a few unpleasant dreams and your life has gone to the dogs. You poor, pathetic, spoilt baby. You've never had an hour of struggle in your life, have you? Your idea of a bad day is getting to Marks and Spencer and finding that they've sold out of smoked salmon.'

'Now hold on! You have no right . . .' Nick stopped. If anyone had the right it was Matthew.

Levin continued in the same measured tone. 'You want to know what real life is? It's being made redundant by the company you founded, then spending a year being rejected for every job in the

65

universe while the woman you love works twenty-four seven to support you and three children under five. It's being involved in a train wreck on the very day you're due to sign a contract for a new job – and not just any job, a six-figure-salary-plus-multiple-fringe-benefits job – then waking up to discover that not only will that job now not be yours because you'll be spending your time learning how to use a colostomy bag, but that you may never make love to your wife again.

'Shall I go on? It's being forced to accept that your barrister wife has to give up the career she loves to become a full-time carer to her children and paraplegic husband. It's learning that every penny of our savings will be spent on converting our house into something wheel-chair accessible and keeping the bailiffs from the door. That's what real life is, you ignorant, self-pitying prick.'

His voice had risen and the nurse came rushing in. She glowered at Nick. 'I'm sorry, sir, but you'll need to leave now. Mr Levin is very tired and you're upsetting him.'

'*I'm* upsetting him? *He's* upsetting me.'

She squared up to him. 'If you don't go, I'll call security.'

Nick glanced at Levin, but the medical drama still occupied the man. 'I sympathise with your situation, Matthew, but you'll under-stand, I'm sure, if I don't hurry back to visit you.'

He felt the combined heat of their condemnatory gazes as he left. In the car park, it was starting to snow. He paused beneath a bus shelter to light a cigarette in the gloom. He knew very well that he deserved everything Levin could throw at him and worse. He was an ignorant, self-pitying prick. He was a sad, pathetic fool.

It was there that the nurse caught up with him, out of breath and wheezing slightly. She had close-cropped steel-grey hair and a mannish, no-nonsense look about her. Passing car lights gave her face a Martian glow. Not without envy, she watched Nick expel a lungful of smoke.

'For two twos I'd have tossed this into the trash,' she said, handing him his messenger bag.

'So much for the spirit of Christmas,' Nick responded, but without rancour. All the fight had gone from him. 'Why didn't you?'

'Mr Levin insisted I try to catch you.'

'Oh.'

He traded a cigarette for his bag and lit it for her and she smoked for a minute in silence. When she flicked it away with a sigh, orange sparks chased across the tarmac.

'I suppose this is the part where I say Happy Christmas,' said Nick as she turned to go.

'You could. But why bother when you don't really mean it.'

12

Nick groped for his mobile in the darkness, pressing random buttons. ''Lo.'

It rang again and he hit the speakerphone button by mistake. Club music blasted into the room, frightening Oliver off the bed. 'Hello?'

'Hey, mate, it's Damian Dexter. How are you?'

'Damian?' Nick felt for the lamp switch, fighting to free himself from his nightmare. There'd been an overturned car, a platinum plume of flame rising into the sky, and something or someone else. He strained to capture the image but it had dissipated. Smoke from a genie's lamp. 'What time is it? Is something wrong?'

'Wrong? What could be wrong? I just called to say Merry Xmas and all that. I didn't get you up, did I? I mean, it didn't occur to me that you'd be in bed at ten o'clock on Christmas Eve. Oh, crap, you're not alone, are you? Blast, what was I thinking?'

Nick reached for the pot of Nurofen on the bedside table and swallowed two tablets with the remnants of a can of beer. 'To be honest, Damian, now's not the best time for a chat, but I appreciate the call. Happy Christmas. Have a good evening.'

'No worries, mate. No worries. Just one other thing . . .'

Nick covered his eyes with his hand. His fingers were tingling. He wanted the *Sun* reporter off the phone and out of his head so he could try to recall his dream and picture who or what it was he saw in the overturned car.

'Now listen, mate,' Damian was almost shouting above the music. 'I need you to be cool about something. We're both hacks, aren't we? We understand each other. We're in the same business and it's not always a nice business. I don't have to explain to you how it is with newspapers and Christmas. Well, it's another silly season, isn't it? All fluff and no substance. Every second person on holiday leave. My editor, see, he's merciless. He's been banging on and on about me coming up with an exclusive – some holiday-season tearjerker. Naturally I thought of you. Now before you overreact, you wouldn't answer my calls. That's all I'm saying. Remember that. If you'd answered my messages things could have been very different. I think the story's tasteful myself, but with a bit of input from you . . .'

Nick was wide awake now. His fingers felt as if they were being stabbed with needles.

'Damian, what are you saying?' He reached for his laptop and flipped it open. 'Spit it out.'

The screen flickered to life. Nick put the phone on the bedside table. His fingers hovered over the keys.

The reporter's voice, a virtual yell as it warred with the bass line, ricocheted around the room. 'It'll be in the paper on Boxing Day. You'll love it, I'm sure. The only thing you could possibly object to is the headline and pics. You know what it's like. Us journos don't have any control over them. Anyway, forget what I said about you owing me something. We're square.'

But Nick had stopped listening. He was looking at the four words he'd involuntarily typed and trying to make sense of them. The tingling in his fingers was abating, but there were goosebumps on his arms.

He snatched up the phone. 'Damian, never mind all that. Have you been drinking? How are you getting home? Whatever you do, don't drive. Promise me you won't drive.'

Damian laughed. 'I knew you'd be cool about the story. You're one of the good guys, Donaghue, you know that? Re drinking and driving, don't fret. I lost my licence last year doing that very thing, so it's public transport all the way for me now.'

'Great. Then forget I said anything.'

A woman, her voice raised above the din, shouted something in the background. She was giggling.

'What, *now*?' Damian came back on the line. 'Gotta love you and leave you, Nicholas. Think I'm in with a chance. Happy Christmas.'

The music cut off abruptly.

'Damian, wait!' But the phone was dead. Nick jumped out of bed and pulled on his jeans, boots and a thick navy-blue cable-knit sweater. Every second counted. He had to raise Greg and Becca.

En route to the Battersea address where Greg had been dispatched, Becca hurled her Fiat Uno around the icy corners with such abandon that Nick began to believe that it was he and his ex who were going to die in the overturned car he'd seen blazing in his dream. He braced himself and kept silent. Even in the best of circumstances Becca did not respond well to criticism, especially when it came from her ex.

He'd found her in the Trafalgar Tavern in Greenwich, fighting her way through the merry revellers with five white-wine spritzers for her single girlfriends and a cranberry and soda for herself.

Saving the champagne until Greg comes home from his shift, thought Nick, experiencing an unaccustomed pang of jealousy. Taking the tray from her, he negotiated the crush and handed round the drinks, receiving four stony glares and a flirtatious wink for his trouble.

He smiled at the unknown face in the group, the one woman in Britain who didn't appear to hold not marrying Becca against him.

'We won't be long,' Becca apologised, taking his arm in a proprietary way and leading him out onto the cobbled terrace. The night clouds were bloated with snow. They hung low and mean over the river, obscuring the tops of Canary Wharf's skyscrapers.

Becca said: 'Can you believe that Tamara? Did you see the way she looked at you? Honestly, she'd flirt with a lamppost.' She pressed a palm to his jaw. 'It's wonderful to see you, Nicky. I've been worried sick. You haven't returned my calls in weeks.'

Her elation lasted only as long as it took him to explain why he was there, which he did haltingly. After being burned by both Matthew and the shrink, it was hard to choose the right words. 'You're not going to believe this, Becks. I mean, if the positions were reversed I wouldn't believe it either. It's just . . . Well, it's hard to know where to begin.'

'Is this about you getting some girl pregnant?'

'God, no. Becks, I'm serious. Ever since the crash I've been having these premonition dreams. I don't know why it's happening, but it is. Remember when that footballer dropped dead on the pitch a month or so back? I'd dreamed about him. I knew it was going to happen. I know it sounds far-fetched but it's true. When I have these nightmares, they come true within twenty-four hours.'

He tried to tell her about Vanessa Diaz, but she tugged at his arm.

'Nick, you're scaring me. Come back inside. It's perishing and I think you could do with a drink.'

'Becca, I'm here about Greg. I've had a nightmare about a car exploding in a fireball. He's involved in it in some way. I'm afraid that if we don't stop him, he'll die.'

She backed away from him. 'Are you insane?'

'I know how it sounds.'

'That was a rhetorical question by the way. This is what my husband and friends have been telling me for months, Nick. You're not right in the head. Now don't get me wrong. I've loyally defended you every step of the way. Still have that old blind spot where you're concerned, idiot that I am. But this has opened my eyes. You're cuckoo, aren't you, Nick? You've had some sort of mental breakdown. Have you any idea how awful you look?'

Her voice softened. 'Please, Nicky, let me get you some help. I can't bear to see you like this.'

Nick shrugged away from her. They were standing beside a statue of Nelson, close to the river railings. Christmas Eve partygoers were spilling from the pub all around them, sloshing champagne, exchanging beery kisses, fooling about with Santa hats. A year ago, Nick had been one of them. He'd stood in this very spot and felt invincible.

'Becks, please,' he said, catching her hand as she turned to march back inside. 'You have every reason to doubt me. I've been behaving like a lunatic. But I'm begging you to trust me on this. Do you honestly think I would ruin your Christmas Eve and frighten and distress you if I wasn't as sure as I could possibly be? Come on, Becca, this is me talking. These premonitions or whatever you want to call them, they're real.'

It had started to snow again. Flakes were settling like frosting on the admiral's hat and melting into the Thames. The arching green laser of the meridian line was speckled with white.

Uncertainty mingled with fear in Becca's eyes. 'These other dreams you've had, they've come true in less than twenty-four hours? You've had proof? Definitive proof?'

'Incontrovertible. Details I could never have known.'

'So you're saying that if we don't get to Greg in time, he's going to die in a fiery car crash?'

'I'm not saying he will die. I'm saying he might. And it might be in a

71

fire as opposed to a car crash. But I couldn't live with myself if I didn't try to stop him. Could you?'

They'd halted briefly at the fire station, where a young fireman in his first month on the job had almost sent Becca into meltdown by mistakenly informing her that her husband had been due back from a warehouse blaze more than two hours previously but hadn't returned. Fortunately, it transpired that Greg and two colleagues had been diverted to another incident along the way.

Keeping well out of sight of the dispatcher, who'd have had apoplexy at the notion of a fireman's wife and a journalist turning up at a the scene of an inferno, they'd extracted a location from one of Greg's crew members on the solemn promise that they wouldn't do anything 'nutty'.

Nick wondered if running red lights could be classified as nutty.

Becca eased up on the accelerator as their destination drew nearer. 'Nick, are you sure about this? Because if you're wrong, it could be very embarrassing.'

Nick had been trying in vain to extract some concrete detail from the fragments of his nightmare. 'I'm as sure as I can be, Becca, but these things are open to interpretation. I'm not a psychic.'

'What are you then?'

Nick didn't answer. His intestines felt as if they'd been used to secure a yacht in a hurricane. He didn't say that the only basis he had for dragging her out on a midnight chase in a snowstorm were a scrambled dream and four words on his computer screen: Greg Fire Damian Crash.

The sat-nav directed them to a suburban street made quaint by a fresh coating of snow. Christmas-tree lights winked in the windows of its Victorian terraces. Nick's head started to throb again. Nothing looked familiar.

The Fiat Uno slid to a dangerous halt behind the fire truck parked outside number 44. Becca leapt out of the car. Further down the street a dog began to bark.

Nick followed more slowly. There was a strong smell of burning in the air, but no shooting flames. 'Becks, I'm not sure—'

The front door opened and Greg emerged, face black with soot and grease. Becca flew up the path and flung her arms around him. Tears were running down her face. 'Oh, God, baby, I thought you were dead.'

Greg was stunned. So were the firefighters who emerged grinning behind him, one of whom was holding a mince pie. A young couple followed them out.

'Note to self,' the man was saying. 'Check that the deep fat fryer is off before enjoying conjugal relations with wife.'

Greg frowned at Nick over Becca's shoulder. 'What's going on?'

Nick was saved from answering by the intervention of the couple. They were freezing in their dressing gowns and keen to return to bed.

'Thanks, boys,' said the wife. 'I've always wanted to get up close and personal with a fireman, although it would have been nice if it had been in less embarrassing circumstances and when I was single.'

'Steady on,' protested her husband. He gave her a playful shove. 'Inside with you. We're going to have to have words.' He gave a thumbs-up to the firemen. 'A million thanks, guys. You've saved our Christmas.'

As soon as the door closed, Greg said to his colleagues, 'A moment, please, gents.'

When they'd crunched away through the falling snow, he turned on his wife. 'Honey, have you and Nick lost your minds, showing up without even a phone call when I'm in the middle of a job? What on earth made you think I was dead?'

Emotions warred in Becca's face. Her tears had subsided now that Greg was once more before her, rugged and vital in his fireman's uniform, but relief was giving way to humiliation. She cast a sideways glance at Nick. 'I . . . we—'

'It's my fault,' interjected Nick. 'I dreamed that someone was going to die in a fire or a car crash or both. I thought it was you. I had to do something and I persuaded Becca to come along. She was very reluctant but I talked her into it. I'm sorry, Greg. It was an idiotic thing to do.'

Greg clenched a fist and started towards him. 'If I wasn't on duty, I'd be tempted to thump you.'

Becca grabbed his arm. 'No, darling, he's apologised. Leave him alone. He's been through enough.'

'Don't I just know it.' Greg's tone dripped with sarcasm. 'I'm sick to death of hearing about it. It's always Nick this, Nick that, poor Nick.'

He pointed a finger at Nick. 'I've had it with you. You show up here, you embarrass me in front of my crew, you terrify my wife. You're a psycho. Stay away from us. Becca's coming back to the fire station with me. *You* can get a taxi.'

'But what about your shift?' fretted Becca.

Her husband put his arm around her. 'This was my last call. My shift is over. So if I'm going to die, which I'm not, honey, I promise,' he glared at Nick, 'it'll be another day.'

When they'd gone, Becca casting an apologetic look over her shoulder as she accelerated away, Nick walked to the end of the street. A blizzard was raging. He felt numb. There was a whiteout in his brain, as if it had shut up shop for the winter. The person he'd been before his descent into hell was a stranger to him. He could barely recall the man who'd applied wax to his hair, put on a crisp white shirt, blazer and jeans, and set off, brimful of arrogant exuberance, to the job he loved on that blustery morning two months before.

He was stepping into a warm cab when he heard a distant bang. 'What was that?'

'Another accident – bet your life on it,' said the cabbie, pulling out into the traffic. His wipers swished vainly at the whirl of flakes. 'Every maniac in Britain, plus a few imported ones, is on the road tonight. It's like a stock car race out there. Add alcohol and ice to the mix and – kapow!'

There was a loud hiss, then a platinum fireball exploded into the sky. Almost immediately a siren wailed.

'This is going to be ugly,' commented the cabbie. 'It's not like we can avoid it either. It's all one way around here.'

They crawled forward into gridlock, rounding a bend at long last to see the fire truck, some hundred yards distant, a red glow in the snow. Hose in hand, Greg was dousing the skeleton of an overturned car. Becca was nowhere to be seen. He'd either sent her ahead to the fire station or persuaded her to go home.

An ambulance screamed along the pavement, spitting snowflakes. It stopped a short distance ahead. The traffic hiccuped forward. Before Nick knew it, the cab was alongside the ambulance. Its blue light strobed across the passenger seat. Two paramedics bounded out of the vehicle. Bridged by a stretcher, they rushed in the direction of the steaming black carcass.

The traffic had now come to a complete halt, and Nick took the opportunity to have a cigarette on the verge. He stood in the snow sucking in fumes and nicotine, glad of the icy wind that ripped through the holes in his jumper. It distracted him.

The cabbie joined him. 'You all right, mate?'

Nick nodded, not trusting himself to speak. He crushed his cigarette underfoot. The paramedics were returning from the wreck with the stretcher. The businesslike way in which they offloaded the body suggested a corpse rather than a patient.

One of the men wrinkled his nose. 'Not a pretty sight, poor love. Smokies had to cut her out from behind the wheel. The man was thrown clear, but they reckon he was dead before he landed. Like Groundhog Day every fucken Christmas Eve, isn't it? You have to wonder what these people are thinking.'

'That's it, they're not,' retorted his colleague. 'Not with their brains at any rate.'

As he shook out the blanket, a sheet of paper fell from it and became one with the snow.

The cabbie picked it up. 'Hey, you dropped something.' But the paramedic was already hurrying back to the wreck.

Nick and the driver returned to the cab. They crawled forward another few metres before grinding to a halt once again. Sighing, the cabbie turned off the engine and spread the paper out across his steering wheel. It was a page proof from a magazine supplement, dated 26 December, two days ahead.

Beneath the uppercase banner, **SECRET LIFE OF HAUNTED MIRACLE MAN,** was a blurred photograph of Nick emerging earlier that day from the National Spinal Injuries Centre at Stoke Mandeville.

The cab driver caught Nick's eye in the rear-view mirror. Recognition dawned. 'Hey, aren't you——?'

'No, I'm not.'

The paramedics crunched past the window carrying the second victim. Spiky ginger hair, glued into clumps by maroon blood, poked out from beneath the stretcher blanket. Nick stumbled from the cab and was violently sick.

He was rinsing his mouth out with snow when the cabbie lowered his window. 'If you're going to be throwing up, you can find another ride.'

Nick ignored him and climbed back into the cab. 'The man on the stretcher. I know him. Or rather, I knew him.'

All of a sudden he felt more exhausted than he'd ever been in his life. Tired not just to the bone or to the marrow but right down to the DNA. Everything was in pieces and there seemed no way out. No way to fix anything.

'Blimey.' The driver's eyes bulged in the mirror. 'That sucks.'

There was a long silence, during which the queue of cars ahead finally wriggled past the wreck. Greg was at the fire truck, packing away the hose. Nick hunkered down in his seat, not wanting to be proved right in such a horrific way, but his neighbour had his back to the road. The cab's diesel engine gunned. The scene spun away behind them.

After a while the driver ventured, 'Was he a friend of yours?'

Nick saw Damian reaching down to him in the underpass, grinning his cheeky chappy grin. 'Need a hand, mate?'

He shivered. The heat in the cab was causing the snow on his jumper to melt onto his skin.

'Yes,' he said. 'Yes, he was my friend.'

13

On a viciously cold New Year's Day, made unnaturally silent by fog, a low black car travelled erratically along the lanes to Land's End. It sped past a signpost for Porthcurno Beach, only to halt in a squeal of tyres a hundred metres on. Reversing until it was once more level with the turn-off, it headed towards the sea.

A circling gull was the only witness as Nick alighted from the Mustang in an empty car park and set off along a steep path. Later that morning the clouds would roll back to reveal a turquoise bay edged with sand the colour of fresh honeycomb. In the summer months, the beach was a favourite with tourists, enraptured by the geographical anomaly that had somehow transported a piece of the Mediterranean to the southernmost tip of England. But for now it was swathed in white, bleak as an Arctic winter.

Nick didn't notice the view. He hadn't come to Porthcurno for the scenery. Brambles snagged at his jeans and a gorse thorn hooked his hand and drew blood, but he pushed on uncaring, almost running in his haste to reach the top. Close to where the path petered out, a boulder jutted out over the heaving ocean. Nick jumped onto it without thinking. A gust of wind caught him off guard. In the instant before he regained his balance, he saw himself dashed on the rocks far below, battered and broken. Stepping back from the edge, he sat down clumsily. He couldn't do it yet, not without some Dutch courage. After several failed attempts, he lit a cigarette.

The rational part of him knew that it was sheer chance he'd stumbled onto the perfect suicide spot. The other part saw it as inevitable. Saw that he'd been led here. Saw that from the moment he was late for his train on that long-ago morning in October, he was always going to end up in this exact spot, on this exact day, at this exact hour.

He saw too that there was nothing he or anyone else could have done to change things. Not that he didn't wish he'd handled things differently. He wished that most fervently. But he hadn't. That was just the fact of it.

As to why he'd ended up in Cornwall, well, that was down to Phil. With nowhere left to turn, Nick had gone hat in hand to his friend. It was Phil who'd convinced Henry to give him a three-month sabbatical after Nick's obituaries – the ones not handed to him in dreams – had become incoherent to the point of being unreadable. Nobody dared refer to it as writer's block. Phil had also seen to it that Nick had a place to stay, although that, by all accounts, was not necessarily a favour.

Nick got to his feet cautiously. The wind had an animal strength to it. He fingered the cottage key in his pocket. 'I'm sorry, Phil,' he said out loud. 'I'm so, so sorry.'

The previous morning, he'd squeezed Oliver into a basket and loaded up his car with a suitcase and groceries. He'd driven away with Becca, Phil and Mikhail standing on the street looking after him, everyone colluding in the pretence that he was on his way to Phil's cottage for a restorative rest break.

A couple of hours up the motorway, he'd taken a detour via Reading and dropped Oliver off at the local RSPCA with an excuse about how he was moving to Cornwall and had belatedly discovered that his new accommodation did not allow pets. The woman who'd taken Oliver from him had masked her disbelief with a practised politeness. After subtly ensuring that Nick had a guided tour of all the other unwanted cats howling or cowering in their cages, she'd promised to do her best to find Oliver a loving home. At the same time, she'd avoided his question about whether or not his cat would be euthanised if such a home were not forthcoming.

It was his betrayal of Oliver, far more than the fallout from his nightmares, which had tipped Nick over the edge. Humans were so fallible that their judgements could frequently be offset by the know-ledge that they themselves were flawed. But the intentions of animals were pure, and their capacity to forgive almost limitless, so their disappointment was particularly hard to bear. And Oliver had always been the one being in Nick's life who loved him in a way that didn't feel like a burden.

He'd made it as far as Exeter before the urge to get drunk overtook him. After checking into a Holiday Inn Express, he'd done just that, getting through a six-pack of lager, two packets of crisps and several tumblers of whisky in his room. He didn't remember falling asleep but now, as he watched waves crest on a gun-barrel grey sea, he did remember his dream.

He was at a bus stop in a picture-postcard village, head bowed against slanting rain. A cowled figure waited with him. All of a sudden, the person gave a strangled cry and toppled onto the watery street.

In the dream Nick had yelled for someone to call an ambulance, but the village was deserted and no one came. Rain sluicing down his neck, he'd knelt in the street and attempted to roll the person over so he could administer CPR. The effort required had been monumental. First a shoulder lifted from the ground, then a portion of chest. After an eternity, the rest of the body came with it. Nick pulled back the hood.

At that moment a real-life hotel fire alarm had blasted him into wakefulness and he'd bolted upright, drenched with sweat.

The face of the victim had been his own.

Remembrance of the nightmare hardened Nick's resolve. Crushing out his cigarette, he lifted from his messenger bag the dregs of the Jack Daniel's and an unopened pot of painkillers, prescribed for him after he'd broken his leg skiing and never taken on some long-forgotten principle.

There was a constricting tightness in his chest. His 5 a.m. breakfast of nicotine and Red Bull had made him nauseous. He could face neither the pills nor the whisky quite yet. Involuntarily, his eyes wandered to the foaming sea below. If he didn't get it together to do this right, he might wind up drinking soup through a straw.

The trajectory of the cliff bothered him. The physics of falling. Which would be quicker or surer – diving or jumping? Would it make a difference?

When the notion of ending it all had first taken root in his head, he'd contemplated writing his own obituary. He'd decided against it on the grounds that it would suggest his death was premeditated. Better to make it seem like a spur-of-the-moment thing. An accident, even.

Nick raked in a breath. He hadn't, he realised, given any thought to God and it was too late now, although he did consider saying the Lord's Prayer 'just in case'. But in the end, he decided to consign his spirituality, or lack thereof, to history. He'd had the best part of thirty-eight years to make good on his intentions. There was no point in agonising over them now.

He picked up the container of pills. To his frustration, the child-proof lid appeared to be Nick-proof as well, especially since his hands were clumsy with cold. His heart hammered as he wrestled with it. Once, he fancied he heard another heartbeat, drumming in counterpoint, but though he strained his ears for a full minute he could discern nothing but the mournful whine of wind.

A new urgency came over him. Delving in his bag for his penknife, he was surprised to find a book in the side pocket. It was Matthew's copy of *The Prophet*. On the title page was a note written in blue biro:

Nick,

Forgive me. I temporarily forgot my manners. My wife's always telling me I could do with a degree course in sensitivity. At any rate, I think you need this more than I do.

All the best for Christmas and the New Year.

Matthew

P.S. This is the nurse's handwriting, not mine. Mine is a little less flowery.

Enraged, Nick flung the book down. It skidded off the boulder and fell into the gorse. Was this God's – or Matthew's – idea of a joke?

Determinedly, he cut the seal on the pot of tablets and picked up the whisky. He had the pills in his hand when the heartbeat sound came again. This time he recognised it as the distinctive rapid drumming of galloping. He jumped to his feet in time to see a black horse burst from the mist far below him. It came flying down the track that led to the beach. A tangle of forelock blew back between its flattened ears, and its thrusting neck was veined and wet with sweat. Even from a distance, it was obvious it was crazed with terror.

So focused was he on its wild run and the incongruity of its emergence, like a horse out of Revelations, from the dissipating fog, that it was not until it passed directly beneath him that he saw it had a rider. A wraith-like girl with long, tangled hair like that of her mount, only several shades lighter. She was clinging bareback to the colt and trying, without success, to regain control. The pair swerved onto the beach below and whiteness obscured them.

Nick didn't hesitate. He forgot what he was there for. Forgot his despair. Forgot everything except that he had to save this girl the way he'd failed to save the dying on the train, or the innocent in his nightmares. With no regard for the stabbing thorns or the proximity of the cliff edge, he tore down the path, vaulting rocks and ripping his trousers.

It was only as he neared the beach that it occurred to him that, not knowing a thing about horses, he might endanger the girl further if he appeared out of nowhere and tried to grab the beast's bridle. He ducked behind the lifeguard's hut, where he could stay out of sight until he figured out what to do next. There he watched and waited.

At ground level, the mist was burning off in patches. The grey waves had taken an intense blue-green hue. The hazy outline of horse and rider solidified and became three-dimensional. It was immediately clear to Nick that what he now saw was a young woman who was no longer in any need of rescuing – if, indeed, she ever had been. The deep sand had slowed the colt's manic stride. She cantered him in wide circles, guiding him rather than fighting him. And all the while she talked to him in a low, calm voice, one hand stroking his neck.

The emerging sun caught the muscled black hide of the horse and bounced off his neat silver hooves. Close to the surf he slowed to a walk. With a smoke-issuing snort, he finally came to a standstill.

The girl swung off his back, bare feet sinking into the sand. She was wearing fawn breeches and a thin blue sweater. A brown scarf was knotted at her neck. The wind whipped her hair, hiding her features. As Nick watched, she let go of the horse's reins and turned away to roll up the bottoms of her breeches.

The horse tossed his head and did a fast, floating trot across the sand, his arrogant beauty quite startling to behold. The girl paid no attention to him. She walked into the freezing surf. The horse bolted a few strides and braked in a spray of sand. When she continued to ignore him, he walked reluctantly into the surf.

The girl turned and splashed him. Ears pricked, he wheeled away, foam exploding out from under his belly. Round and round they went, churning the surf into a salty bubble bath. The girl's face was flushed with exertion. Both she and the horse were soaked to the skin.

Nick was mesmerised. To witness the joyous abandon of her game with the horse, which threw down the gauntlet to the fog and biting cold and whatever terrifying incident had sent them hurtling down to the beach in the first place, was to experience life lived at a level he'd never even contemplated.

The girl had paused to catch her breath. The horse came up behind her, flanks heaving, and she threw her arms around his neck and kissed his muzzle. Gathering up his reins, she vaulted easily onto his back. They were one as they left the beach. Nick hesitated a fraction too long before retreating behind the hut and worried she might have caught a glimpse of him. But if she had she didn't acknowledge it.

When the clip-clop of hooves on tarmac had been replaced once more by the muted roar of ocean, Nick took the path back to the top of the cliff. He climbed slowly. He climbed knowing that each step carried him further from the person he'd been less than half an hour earlier. Every nerve ending in his body tingled. He felt shaken; exhilarated; shocked awake. A grainy film of the horse and laughing girl played over and over in his mind.

Caught up in the dreamy vision, he was taken aback, then mortified and furious with himself, when he saw the whisky and pills – his suicide props – on the boulder where he'd left them.

The Prophet was lying in the damp grass. As Nick picked it up, it fell open at a dog-eared page. He closed the book without looking at it and tucked it into his bag.

The sweet disgrace of whisky teased his nostrils as he poured it into a crack between the rocks. He disposed of the empty bottle, pills and packet of cigarettes in a car-park bin. After due consideration, he dug out the smokes and put them in his pocket again. There was no point in going overboard.

Chilled after so long in the cutting wind, he dug out the uneaten cheese sandwiches and flask of coffee Becca had prepared for him the previous day. The sandwiches were curling at the edges and the coffee was cold, but he felt a wave of warmth towards his ex. If she'd been here now, he'd have kissed her.

The beach was not sandy, as he'd thought, but a dazzling mix of finely crushed shells of white, mauve and apricot. He breakfasted close to the scribble of tracks, already all but erased by the incoming waves. As the sun climbed, his bones thawed. The bay turned a deep turquoise. The water looked inviting, but not enough to tempt him in.

When he'd finished eating, he returned to the car and drank most of a carton of orange juice in an effort to rehydrate himself for the long drive to Reading and back. He hadn't a clue what his new life was going to consist of but he wanted Oliver to share in it.

Two

I

'You'll be made of sterner stuff than most Londoners – and a good few locals, mind – if you're wanting to move into Seabird Cottage now, what with the place colder than a witch's grave.'

Nick was unsure whether the question was rhetorical, or if he was, as he suspected, being gently teased, but he smiled politely and said: 'Oh, I doubt that very much, but I'll give it my best shot.'

As if to test his resolve, a series of thunderclap bangs recorded the unhappy union of the low undercarriage of his Mustang and the rocks on the unpaved road. He bit back a groan. 'I mean, how bad can it be?' Out of the corner of his eye, he saw Mrs Moreton cough to conceal a laugh.

Flicking on his lights, Nick accelerated up a muddy, tree-lined lane, refusing to allow the caretaker's negativity to dampen his enthusiasm. She could hardly know that a cold cottage, or even a leaking cottage, would be paradise to him if it only meant that he could leave his past behind.

Not that he blamed her for doubting him. He knew what a sight he must be. After eight straight hours of driving, interrupted only by a cheeseburger pit stop and an excruciating trip to Reading to collect Oliver (now glowering through the bars of his carrier box on the back seat, growling periodically), his eyes were bloodshot, and he was in desperate need of both a shower and a shave. In the petrol-station mirror he'd resembled a vagrant.

Prior to turning up at Mrs Moreton's gift shop to collect the keys, he'd donned a clean but extravagantly creased shirt and put on his good boots to smarten up his well-past-their-use-by-date jeans. The overall effect was that of a bankrupt banker. Or an eccentric writer down on his luck, which he supposed he was.

It was barely 4 p.m., but already the winter sun was setting over the fields on his left, lining the horizon with silver. To his right was a barn and farmhouse. The farmer was in conversation with a worker in overalls tinkering with a tractor. A border collie squirmed at his heels. Nick lifted a hand in greeting, but neither man responded.

Mrs Moreton followed his gaze. 'Mr McKenna will sell you all the milk and eggs you can use, and they're the best in Cornwall. But if it's service with a smile you're wanting, go elsewhere. Gordon can be – how shall I put it? Curmudgeonly. It's all a front though, so pay no attention. Beneath the bluster he's about as fierce as a Labrador puppy. Good as gold he's been to my daughter. Well, it's about time someone gave her a break.'

She indicated a branch of even rougher track, arching away from a swathe of desolate farmland. 'Left here.'

Nick gritted his teeth as the underbelly of the Mustang suffered a further assault. 'What does your daughter do?'

'What doesn't she do would be more accurate. Right you are, pull in here. Home sweet home. Mind the mailbox.'

A bracing gust of wind almost plucked Nick off his feet as he climbed out of the car. Fine-mist rain peppered his face. His first impression was that the cottage was one medium-category storm away from being swallowed by the ocean.

He lifted his suitcase from the boot and followed Mrs Moreton up the stone path, inhaling a heady rush of salty, herby air along the way. The cottage was not the ramshackle bothy he'd expected. Framed by the threatening sky and seething mass of ocean, it was oddly imposing. Even empty and unloved, its once-white walls peeling and gutters sagging, it had a proud independence. It had stood four-square to the elements and surging sea for over a hundred years, and neither had defeated it.

'It's magnificent. I thought Phil was having me on.'

Mrs Morton couldn't hide her surprise. She gazed up at the dark windows as if attempting to see the place through his eyes. 'I suppose it does have a certain charm.' She put the key in the lock. 'It's just . . . well, I did warn Phil that it's not suitable for holiday lets, but he said you were very adaptable. "Has a tendency toward martyrdom" was the phrase he used.'

'Did he now?' Nick shrugged. 'Who am I to argue?'

The door scraped open. A weak bulb illuminated a low-ceilinged kitchen, the oak beams of which had been the dining experience of choice for a variety of small creatures over the years. The temperature in the room was scarcely less Arctic than that outside, a situation not improved by the flagstone floor, lack of double-glazing and unlit Aga.

'Had I known when you were coming . . .' Mrs Moreton lifted her hands in a helpless gesture. 'Unfortunately it's been a bit eleventh hour. First, Phil phones on New Year's Eve *of all days* – after six months of no communication, mind, and the place gradually falling to rack and ruin – and informs me that his best friend will be arriving the next day for an indefinite stay at Seabird Cottage. Then last night he woke me from a dead sleep to explain that you may not be coming after all because you aren't answering your phone and have probably gone AWOL. Then at lunchtime today, when I've all but given up, it's yourself on the line informing me that you'll be here in a couple of hours. With a cat.'

She glanced reproachfully in the direction of the car, from which issued Oliver's plaintive meows. 'It's not the way I like to run my business.'

Nick smiled. 'Please. I'm sure everything is perfect.'

She seemed gratified. 'I've done my best. Come, let me give you the guided tour.'

Nick was in bed by nine o'clock, fully clothed in a bid to avoid hypothermia. His attempts to light a fire beneath a chimney that had not seen the services of a sweep for many a moon – something Mrs Moreton had cautioned him against – had smoked out the cottage. Before he'd dropped the caretaker at her own cheerful cottage a mile or so down the road, she'd helped him get the Aga range cooker going. Unfortunately, it took time for its cast iron carcass to heat up. He'd been too exhausted to wait. A cheese sandwich for himself and a can of sardines for Oliver was all he'd had the energy to prepare. He'd climbed into the rickety double bed and fallen asleep in seconds.

At 3.47 a.m. the bed collapsed, tipping Nick unceremoniously onto the floor. For a moment he thought he was back in his old apartment and had stumbled while sleepwalking through a nightmare. He lay without moving, filled with dread. Another instalment of vampire graffiti would, he thought, kill him.

In London most night sounds carried an undercurrent of menace. It was the absence of that aggression that finally reminded him of the long, strange journey that had led him to Seabird Cottage. That and the soft, ceaseless roar of the sea.

The darkness had the impenetrable blackness unique to places far from light pollution. Unable to find the lamp switch, Nick groped for the torch Phil had insisted he bring. His palm touched something warm and squishy.

The torch beam illuminated the tail end of a disembowelled rat, artistically arranged on the rug. Oliver was perched on an armchair in the corner of the room, wearing a beatific expression. In his cat way he was smiling.

Nick slumped against the broken bed. For the first time in months he laughed. 'Okay, I admit it. I'm a monster for taking you to the RSPCA. However, I think you've well and truly registered your disapproval. Are we even now? Can we be friends?'

He disposed of the rodent's remains in the bushes beyond the driveway and brewed himself a coffee on the now radiant Aga. It was a measure of how bad things had been in London that he viewed waking up to a deceased Cornish rat rather than a bloody obituary as a profound relief.

The unkempt, mossy lawn descended in a series of tiers to the ocean. After years of concrete pavements, it felt fluffy and yielding beneath his boots. Six stone steps led down to a bench on a foam-splattered ledge. Nick sat gingerly on its ancient slats. There was nothing in front of him but rocks and ocean – nothing till America.

The fierce heat of the coffee warmed him from within. His breath met the cold air in white speech bubbles. He switched off the torch and let the darkness envelop him. The wind had dropped and left the ocean quietly seething. Using the hood of his jacket as a pillow, he settled back to take in the scene. For the first time in months he allowed his mind to empty. He was conscious of nothing but the fishing boats twinkling on the horizon and the silver-plumed waves swelling against the violet backdrop of sea. Soon he was conscious of nothing.

He came to with the sensation of being watched. A faint stirring of leaves recorded a sinister tread. Instantly, Nick was alert. He cursed himself for his city-boy naivety; for taking it for granted that the countryside was a benign place of gambolling lambs, far from the dark impulses of urban folk. Snatching up a piece of driftwood, he swung to face the threat.

On the top tier of the garden, silhouetted against the cottage lights like a fiery wolf, was an enormous fox. For ten defiant seconds its eyes burned into him. Nick lowered his weapon. When he glanced up again, the fox was gone.

Nick tossed the remnants of his coffee into the sea. It was not yet 5 a.m. and was still pitch dark, but he had no intention of returning to the collapsed bed. He wanted to heat a pot of water, enjoy a leisurely shave and celebrate a nightmare-free first night in Seabird Cottage. With any luck, it would be the first of many.

For the sake of appearances, he'd wait a month or so before calling Phil and offering to exchange his Greenwich apartment for aunt Sadie's falling-down, rat-infested freezer of a cottage. In truth, his mind was already made up.

Come hell or high water, there was no going back.

Ten minutes into his two-mile walk to civilisation, it started to rain. Nick turned his collar up and leaned into it. A week ago he'd regarded inclement weather as a nuisance, something with which to do battle, preferably armed with a steel-tipped umbrella. And only yesterday his response to finding the Mustang out of commission with a slow puncture would have been to call a taxi. Now as he strode defenceless along the edge of a muddy field, naked face stinging, he felt oddly exhilarated.

Mr McKenna passed him in a beat-up Land Rover. Nick waved again but the farmer stared straight ahead, eyes on the road. So much for the famed friendliness of country people, Nick thought, watching him go.

Mrs Moreton's gift shop was on the main street in the pastel-painted fishing village of Lanton. The previous afternoon Nick had not been in any condition to appreciate it, but today he saw that it was a cut above the usual seaside arts and crafts emporium. The delicate watercolours, robust ceramics and cliché-free driftwood sculptures could have graced any gallery in London.

There was no one behind the shop counter. Nick was about to leave a note for Mrs Moreton when he heard a metallic crash at the back of the store, followed by the tinkle of breaking glass. This being Cornwall he thought it doubtful that a burglary was in progress, but there was enough force in the sound to demand investigation. Behind a display of ceramic bowls, a door was ajar. Soundlessly, he approached it.

Through the crack was a partial view of a filing cabinet. There was a dent in the top drawer. In the centre of it, like a bullseye, was a drop of blood. As Nick watched, it began a slowly accelerating descent.

A boyish, cajoling voice said: 'Baby, what's it going ta take for me ta get through ta you?'

Nick pushed open the door. 'You might want to try anger management.'

The man turned on him. 'What the fuck?' He had the looks of a rakish poet – swarthy and sensual, but his dark eyes were murderous. 'Don't you *knock*?'

'In situations of domestic violence, not usually.'

'Domestic violence?' The man threw his head back and gave an abrasive laugh. 'Sasha knows I wouldn't harm one hair on her head, don't you, sweetness?'

With the forefinger of his undamaged hand, he moved to caress the cheekbone of his companion and Nick saw her face for the first time.

The room dipped and swayed.

It was the girl from the beach. She looked the same, only paler.

'That's enough, Cullen,' she snapped, pushing his hand away. She fixed Nick with a spirited gaze. 'I think there's been a misunderstanding. Cullen was a little upset about something, but he's fine now. He was just leaving.'

'That's right,' Cullen agreed. 'I'm fine now and I'm on my way.' His devilish grin suggested that the whole incident had been nothing more than a bit of playfulness between lovers. His dark gaze alighted on Nick. 'Mind how you go. She's a handful.' He winked at the girl. 'Catch you at The Lighthouse later, Sash.'

They heard the shop door tinkle open and click shut.

'Forgive me,' Nick began. 'It was none of my business and I apologise for interfering. It's just that . . .'

He couldn't finish. Couldn't look at her. For reasons he could not have begun to analyse, he wanted to get as far away from her as he could – Antarctica if he could manage it.

'I'm sorry,' he said again and started for the exit.

She reached out a hand as if to stop him, thought better of it, and almost snatched it away. 'It's just that what?'

He hesitated. 'From where I stood, it was hard to tell if he was going to kiss you or kill you.'

'Oh.' Her voice was small.

'I'm sorry,' he said for the third time, and then he was out of the shop and striding down the street in the rain, thankful for the cold, obliterating torrent of it.

Half of him wanted to get into his car and drive back to London. The other part clung to the course that he'd charted for himself in the early hours of that morning, the one where he'd decided to buy Seabird Cottage and make a go of it, as the only way out of the storm.

It was the bus that decided him. According to the timetable, the one bound for Penzance, where he'd been told he'd find a hardware superstore, was due first. None, sadly, were bound for the polar regions.

He stood beneath the shelter staring blindly into the gloom. From the thigh down, his jeans were soaked through. His face and ears were numb with cold. The lights of Lanton were a watercolour blur in the distance. To avoid any unwanted interactions he'd walked up the hill to a bus stop on the outskirts of the village.

The only other person hardy enough – or desperate enough – to wait for a ride in the downpour nodded to him when he walked up. There was no further communication. Since he or she was outfitted from head to toe in an oilskin coat and Wellington boots, Nick had no way of telling if it was a man or a woman. In his current frame of mind, he didn't care.

As he waited, something stirred at the edge of his consciousness. A memory. He refused to let it in. He'd invested too much in the belief that Cornwall was going to be his salvation.

Neither would he think about Sasha. Sasha was off limits and not only because of that lowlife, Cullen. He would think about hardware. He'd concentrate on deciding what tools and supplies he'd need to tackle the DIY disaster zone that was Seabird Cottage.

But as the minutes ticked by and he grew steadily wetter, his enthusiasm waned. He was on the verge of admitting defeat when his companion gave a strangled cry and pitched face-first into the street. For several long seconds, Nick stood petrified. His New Year's Eve nightmare returned to him in technicolor: the picture-postcard village; the driving rain; the hooded figure at the bus stop. He relived the instant when he'd rolled over the body to discover that the face of the corpse was his own.

Only the deathly stillness of the body on the street jolted him out of his stupor. For reasons too horrifying to contemplate, his dream was unfolding in real time, but if he acted quickly he might yet change the outcome. He reached for his phone, cursing when he remembered that he'd left it at the cottage.

'Help!' he yelled. 'Help!'

But the village was out of earshot and all but deserted. Anyone with sense had retreated indoors.

Kneeling in the gutter and using a handful of oilskin as leverage, he attempted to roll the person over so that he could administer CPR. He knew he wasn't dreaming, because the rain sluicing down his neck was comprehensively freezing the few parts of his anatomy still left undrenched.

The lifeless body was heavy, but not the dead weight of his imagination. First a shoulder lifted off the ground, then a portion of chest. Then, after an eternity, the rest of the body came with it. Nick wrenched back the hood.

His relief at finding a stranger beneath it was so great that he felt a corresponding surge of guilt. The woman was in her mid- to late-fifties, amply proportioned without being obese. Beneath the practical cloak, her dress was distinctly bohemian.

There was no time to sprint even the short distance to the village. She'd be dead before he got back. As fast as he could, Nick covered her with his jacket and jumper. Tilting her head back and pinching shut her nose, he began mouth-to-mouth resuscitation. Two breaths, followed by thirty chest compressions – 'between the nipples', as a first-aid instructor had once told him. Two breaths, thirty compressions. Two breaths, thirty compressions.

At intervals, he paused to yell for help and listen for breathing. There was nothing and no one came. A car flashed by but didn't stop. 'Tourist bastard,' he shouted after it. His hands were so cold he could no longer feel them and his upper body, clad in nothing but a T-shirt, was wracked with shivers.

'You have to help me,' he pleaded with his unconscious friend. 'It's *your* life. You're going to have to choose to fight for it. I'm not going to be able to do this on my own.'

Two breaths. Thirty compressions. Two breaths. Thirty compressions. There was no response. Not even a flicker.

A truck flew past, but Nick was too late to signal it.

Then, like a mirage, someone was coming, running up the hill through the deluge, bearing a proper-sized umbrella and, more importantly, a mobile phone. Sasha had the emergency services on the line by the time she reached him and, after an abrupt 'Carry on doing exactly what you're doing', she reeled off all relevant medical details and the patient's location to the operator.

'We're in luck,' she told him. 'They're five miles down the road and already on their way.'

After the ambulance had gone, taking Pattie Griffin with it – alive but just barely – they walked down the hill to the cab office. Sasha offered to drive Nick home, but he insisted, almost to the point of rudeness, on taking a taxi. Equally stubborn, she wouldn't allow him to leave until he'd downed a black coffee loaded with sugar cubes. 'You need it for the shock.'

'I'm not the one who had a heart attack,' protested Nick, but he was grateful for the caffeine hit and the flaring hot sweetness.

Sheltered by a cafe's candy-striped awning, they stood as far apart as civility allowed, waiting for his cab. The rain had slowed to a speckle.

'Shock kills as often as cardiac arrests do, especially when you've spent at least an hour drenched to the skin in temperatures that would freeze a leg of lamb.' She tilted her head. 'I'm not so sure that you shouldn't have gone to A&E as well.'

He made the mistake of looking at her then, something he instantly regretted because her eyes were the turquoise of Porthcurno Bay, flecked with antique gold. He transferred his gaze to the Fair Trade logo of his coffee cup. 'You're a doctor, I take it? Or a nurse?'

'A nurse. Was. A long time ago. Now I help my mum in the gift shop and do the accounts for the cottage rental business.'

'They don't need nurses in Cornwall?'

There was a pause. 'Like I said, it was a long time ago.'

'I didn't mean to pry.'

She smiled. 'You apologise a lot.'

'Sorry.' He grinned then too. Couldn't help it. 'We haven't been properly introduced. 'I'm—'

'Nick Donaghue. Yes, I know. You're the talk of the town. The locals have been taking bets on how long you'll last in Seabird Cottage.'

'Great. And I came here for the anonymity.'

'Anonymity is for cities. In Lanton, if you sneeze in the morning everyone knows you have a cold by lunchtime.'

'I'll remember that.'

He took his time putting his coffee cup into a nearby bin, scanning the horizon for approaching taxis like a castaway watching for a ship. The rain had quit, but the overflowing gutter gurgled like a mountain stream. It struck Nick that bad things always happened to him when he was waiting for public transport.

He turned to find her watching him.

'When you came into the shop earlier, was there something you wanted? I half-expected you to return the cottage keys and go home. Mum thought it unlikely you'd survive longer than one night.'

Home. Nick tried to picture his Greenwich apartment, but it seemed as remote as the moon. He could summon no affection for it. It was like a hotel in which he'd once enjoyed a pleasant stay but had no desire ever to revisit. For now, home was where Oliver was – in Phil's falling-down, one-hurricane-from-the-bottom-of-the-ocean cottage.

It was on the tip of his tongue to say, 'Maybe I am home,' when the taxi swerved up to the kerb. The driver braked with a flourish, adding an extra layer of brackish water to Nick's ruined jeans.

Perversely, he now found himself reluctant to go. 'Uh, I came to ask for advice. Rather humiliatingly, I nearly set fire to myself, my cat and the cottage last night after I ignored your mum's advice and tried to burn a pile of old newspapers under a blocked chimney. In the interests of preserving Phil's dubious inheritance, I was wondering if you or your mum – Mrs Moreton – had the phone number of a sweep? Oh, and the garage roof is leaking, which means the logs in there are either wet or mouldy or both. Any idea where I might be able to buy a cord of dry wood?'

She was laughing at him, he could tell.

'So you're determined to stay. That'll disappoint the people who've laid down a week's wage that you'll be gone by nightfall. No problem. I'll send a sweep over first thing in the morning. For logs, you'll need to speak to Mr McKenna. I expect Mum warned you that he doesn't do service with a smile.'

To Nick's embarrassment, she had the car door open for him before he could get to it. But as he went to climb in, she blocked his escape route.

'What you did for Pattie today . . . she owes her life to you.'

He could hardly avoid looking at her then, so he focused on her mouth and white, slightly imperfect teeth, and that was a worse blunder than before.

'Please, it was nothing. Anyone would have done the same.'

'No,' she said firmly. 'Not everyone would. The simple fact is, not many people could.'

The driver glanced over his shoulder with undisguised impatience. He turned up the radio to convey the extent of his annoyance.

'My amateur first aid would have done no good, *was* doing no good, had you not come running with your phone.'

Her face was as flushed as it had been on New Year's Day, her dark curls wet and tangled. At some stage over the last hour she'd lost her umbrella.

'I only came because I was looking for you.'

A gust of wind wrung a mini rain shower from the awning. Two drops sparkled on her cheek. Nick had an overwhelming urge to kiss them away. He sought refuge in banter. 'Because you intuitively knew that I'd smoked out Seabird Cottage and was on the hunt for a chimney sweep?'

Sasha laughed. 'Precisely.'

The cabbie turned the volume up another notch.

'I'd better go before we get arrested for disturbing the peace.'

She released the door and stood back. Her eyes had clouded over, as if a squall was moving in. When she spoke he had to strain to hear her.

'That thing you said about not being sure whether Cullen was planning to kiss me or kill me? To tell you the truth, I wasn't so sure myself.'

3

Next morning there was a dead dove on the doorstep. It was lying on the mat, looking peaceful, when Nick went to let Oliver out.

'Is it just me or is the country bad for one's health?' he asked the cat, pulling him away. 'Two deaths and a near-death in under three days does seem a little like overkill.'

He was able to view the fallen bird with relative equanimity because, for the first time in months, he'd had a good night's sleep and the worst hadn't happened; he hadn't had another obituary dream. It helped too that in the aftermath of Monday's drama, a warm glow had enveloped him, along with the joyous realisation that he'd saved a life, not been a bystander in the taking of one.

In the cold light of morning, those emotions were tinged with guilt and unease, but he had no intention of untangling them. The only thing that mattered was that he'd had a second, nightmare-free night. There'd been no laptop blinking on the bedside table when he'd opened his eyes. No electronic hum. All he'd heard was the gulls and crashing waves.

It was only on closer inspection that Nick noticed that the dove had not died of natural or even accidental causes. Its neck had been wrung.

A chill went through him then. Foxes, cats and other farmyard predators had equally brutal methods of killing, but only a man could be so cruel.

To tell you the truth, I wasn't so sure myself, Sasha had said.

In the gap between the path and grass, Nick found what he was searching for: a partial bootprint. There was no point in looking for its owner. He picked up the dove and carried it down to the sea. The swirling wind caught it as he threw it and its wings fanned out. When it floated away on a satin sheet of navy blue, it looked as though it were flying.

The way Nick justified it to himself was this. He only saw her again because he went out running, and he only went running because of the unfortunate carpentry incident, and he only took up carpentry because he couldn't write. Could not stand to so much as open his laptop with its sullied memory. And even if he could have stood it, he wouldn't have known where to begin.

Yet the urge was there, indistinguishable some days from other cravings, an itch he couldn't scratch. Following his adventures in Lanton he'd been ill, very ill, partly from spending so long in the freezing rain but also, he knew, because his body understood it could finally relax. The fever had hit him with sledgehammer ferocity right after the chimney sweep left on Tuesday. One minute he was chopping up Sadie's double bed for use as firewood (it transpired that it, too, had been enthusiastically devoured by the same creatures that had laid waste to the kitchen beams). The next, the axe was the weight of a concrete block. Climbing the stairs and crawling onto the mattress in the front bedroom was like scaling the North Face of the Eiger.

For two days Nick drifted in and out of consciousness. He had the sense that his body was purging itself of the past, but it did so with such violence that at the height of his delirium he wondered if Cullen had poisoned Seabird Cottage's air or water in an attempt to kill him. Sweat poured off him until he was swimming in it. He became convinced he was going to die and that no one apart from Oliver would notice. His condition worsened to the point where he didn't care.

Throughout, the cat kept vigil. Whenever Nick woke, Oliver would be perched on the armchair, watching him with a serene expression.

'Are you peaceful because you're confident I'm going to live and continue to open pouches of braised rabbit for you, or are you like that nursing-home cat that was in the news because it sits with residents on the day they're due to pass away?' Nick rasped in a rare moment of lucidity.

Oliver was so pleased at being spoken to after a day and a half of nothing but laboured breathing that he bounded onto the mattress with a meow of delight. He snuggled his furry bulk in the space between the pillow and Nick's shoulder. Nick fell asleep to the sound of the ocean and the cat's ecstatic purrs.

Gradually, the scrambled snapshots of mangled metal, dripping scarlet, and his parents' ghostly bodies laid out in the mortuary gave way to dreams he didn't remember but which left him calm.

On Thursday he was well enough to eat a can of tomato soup and three slices of toast. On Friday, he woke with an erection and a skin-crawling desire to write or be touched or both, which he took as a sign that he was on the mend. To distract himself he had a cool shower, two black coffees and a bowl of cornflakes. Then he lugged the mattress out into the brilliant blue morning and set fire to it. Afterwards, he called John Lewis and ordered a new mattress and a couple of sets of linen and towels. Home delivery was possible for a price.

Inspired, he jumped into his Mustang and rattled over the farm roads to the nearest DIY superstore, where he spent an obscene amount on paint, tools, screws and wooden planks of various lengths. He returned home with a fish and chip takeaway, the car a haze of salt and vinegar. He felt positively euphoric.

It was not until next morning that reality set in.

Two hours after embarking on an ambitious project to transform Seabird Cottage in a weekend, Nick had concluded that the notion that anyone with testicles was somehow genetically wired to put up shelves that then stayed up was one of the cruellest hoaxes ever perpetrated on mankind. It made men, who in their chequered youths had spent every woodwork class smoking in the toilets or engaged in sexual experimentation behind the bike shed, and who had never watched a DIY programme and barely knew a hammer from a saw, feel woefully inadequate.

It was most unfortunate that Mr McKenna should choose that very morning to come roaring unannounced up the driveway at the wheel of his tractor and dump a hillock of logs by the back door.

When Nick went outside, the garden had the nostalgic smell of fresh-cut timber. Mr McKenna was contemplating the logs with a sorrowful expression. A stocky man with a weathered ruddiness, bushy sideburns and a full head of greying brown hair, he was dressed with an almost puritanical neatness in a tweed jacket, white shirt, dark brown tie and corduroys. He made no attempt to conceal his disapproval of Nick, who had been wrestling with the bookshelf since dawn and was unwashed and unshaven, in a ragged grey T-shirt and oil-stained jeans.

'Good morning to you,' said Nick with fake cheeriness. 'You must be Mr McKenna?' He put out his hand. 'Nick Donaghue.'

The farmer scowled at the logs. 'You'd best be getting these inside before the rain ruins 'em. Kiln-dried hardwood, they are. Finest in Cornwall, for all the good it'll do you back in London. S'ppose they'll rot and go mouldy like the last lot. Course, I told her that but she wouldn't listen. Never does. Told her she was wasting her money and my time gifting you a pile of logs as high as Everest, not to mention my good produce.'

He jerked his chin towards the tractor. Beside the wheel was a cardboard box piled with milk, a dozen eggs and winter vegetables – parsnips, potatoes, cabbages and Brussels sprouts. 'Told her you'd be off to London before the end of the week. "No celebrities hiding in bushes," I said. "Nothing to keep him." But she wouldn't have a bar of it. I think she was hoping that if you were warm and fed, you'd be persuaded to stay.'

Nick was unable to suppress a grin. 'That's very thoughtful of Sasha. She told me to contact you about the wood about a week ago, but I hadn't quite got round to it.'

'Sasha? You mean Mrs Moreton's wee lass?' demanded Mr McKenna, as if Sashas were so abundant in Lanton that one might easily get them confused. 'What the heck does she have to do with it? No, Mr Donaghue, it isn't young Sasha who's made you a present of my best logs. It's someone a good deal larger, somewhat less attractive and rather more ancient – if I may say so without causing offence. Nuttier than a fruitcake, too.'

Nick was bemused.

'It's not everyone who'll be thanking you for saving her life, you know. Now don't get me wrong, I have a soft spot for Pattie Griffin myself. But she's a thorn in the side of the hunt lobby, the local council, her neighbours and anyone else who gets in the way of her saving every flea-ridden, bag o' bones stray in the county, and banging on about global warming, population control and you name it. A letter-writing fiend that woman is. No, there's some who'd not have been overly distressed if she had been catapulted into that good night.'

Nick put this monologue down to Mr McKenna's infamous customer service. 'So she's well – Pattie?'

'Well enough to give me grief about how the methane from my cows is decimating the ozone layer.'

'I'm very glad to hear she's recovering. I'll call her and thank her. How much do I owe you for the wood?'

'Paid for in full it is. Pattie wouldn't hear otherwise, much as I tried to dissuade her.'

Nick could hardly wait for the farmer to start up his tractor and go, but the man showed no sign of leaving. The silence stretched on until it became excruciating. Spending another moment in Mr McKenna's company was about as appealing as root canal surgery, but Nick felt obliged to invite him in for a coffee. Too late he remembered the state of the cottage.

Mr McKenna reacted as if he'd been offered bourbon on the rocks before breakfast. 'I'm a tea man myself. PG Tips. None of that queer herbal stuff.'

'I'm afraid I don't have any tea,' Nick began, but Mr McKenna was already marching towards the back door and letting himself in. Sighing, Nick picked up the vegetable box and followed.

Inside, the mess was a thousand times worse when seen through his neighbour's eyes. There was a heap of unwashed coffee mugs and two beer cans in the sink, and a spill of ketchup and the remains of this morning's fried egg and bacon roll on the kitchen table. On the floor was a pile of laundry that hadn't yet made it into the washing machine, including five pairs of Calvin Klein boxer shorts. Stacked beside the fireplace were several choice pieces of Sadie's former bed.

As if that wasn't bad enough, Oliver was sharpening his claws on the arm of the sofa – not something to which Nick usually objected, given that Sadie's furniture was as much of a health hazard as her bed, but which on this occasion served to draw Mr McKenna's attention to the corner of the room occupied by the crooked bookcase. As Nick looked over, a trickle of sawdust joined the chaos of wood chips and scattered tools on the carpet below.

The farmer took his time perusing the scene. 'I'd have thought you'd be off to the bright lights by now. Can't see what's keeping you.'

Nick put the box on the kitchen counter. 'I like it here, Mr McKenna. I've no plans to go anywhere.'

'Never been partial to reporters myself. Morals of alley cats, they have. Always doorstepping the recently bereaved, or championing the rights of drug fiends and looters, or nauseating readers with faithful accounts of knickerless actresses falling out of nightclubs. Not to mention the whole phone-hacking business. It's getting harder and harder to find any news in the newspaper.'

'I don't wish to disappoint you, Mr McKenna, but I'm not that sort of journalist. I'm an obituary writer.'

Mr McKenna was a man rarely lost for words but this floored him. 'That's all you do – write about dead people?'

'Yes, sir. That's all I do. *Did*. That's all I did.'

'Wellll,' said the farmer, exhaling on the word. 'It's not what you'd call man's work, is it?'

'No. No, I don't suppose it is. Out of curiosity, what is it that you consider to be man's work, Mr McKenna? Plumbing? Banking? Farming?'

With impeccable timing, Oliver sprang from the sofa onto the top of the bookshelf. There was a splintering sound, like a boat hull splitting on a rock, and the whole structure collapsed. The weight of each shelf caused the one beneath it to tear from the wall in a domino effect. Oliver fell yowling with them, as did several lumps of plaster.

When the dust had settled Mr McKenna intoned: 'Carpentry. Now there's a man's job. It's a lost art these days, of course. All the young people shop at Ikea. No skill in that, is there? A toddler can assemble a flatpack. But yes, Mr Donaghue, real men understand woodwork.'

Nick showed him the door shortly afterwards.

Undaunted, the farmer pressed: 'So what's an obituary writer doing in the wilds of Lanton then? No dead bodies around here, ha ha.' He clambered onto his tractor, still chuckling at his own joke.

'Not yet, Mr McKenna,' Nick muttered as the tractor roared to life. 'Not yet.'

4

That's how Nick came to be out running at first light on Sunday. Running because the craving had grown so intense he worried that if he didn't do something physical to alleviate it, he might spontaneously combust. Running because if he couldn't write, was missing the carpentry gene, and couldn't take a lover because he couldn't face having sex with a woman whose death he might later foresee in an obituary dream, what was left? What was he going to do with his life? How would he fill up his days?

Nick had never wanted to be anything but a writer. Never considered anything else. Never, to his risk-averse father's distress, been talented at anything else. Jogging into a cold, crisp morning, his tread muffled by the damp earth, he reviewed his options and tried to regulate his breathing. It felt good to be out in the air, working up a sweat, although it alarmed him how out of shape he was. He put it down to the smoking. He'd have to give it up. He'd barely run a mile and his chest was on fire.

Blocking out the pain, he returned to the subject of his career. He could retrain. Journalists he knew had established successful second lives in marketing or PR. He could write press releases waxing lyrical about exciting new developments in cement.

Then again perhaps it was time to get away from writing altogether. He could take a postgraduate degree in business. Later, he could apply for a junior management position with prospects in a local town like Truro or Penzance. He'd marry a woman from HR and acquire two children and a fat golden retriever, and they'd build sandcastles on the beach at the weekends.

But, no, that didn't appeal at all. Maybe the right thing to do was to take Mr McKenna's advice and get a real man's job like plumbing. He could spend his days unblocking U-bends, tiling bathrooms with buxom mermaids and having sex with lonely housewives.

Nick stepped up his pace until his lungs threatened to burst from his chest. It made no difference. The image he was trying to erase from his head, the one that had inserted itself into his consciousness during his fever, refused to co-operate by leaving.

Two raindrops on her cheek, shaken there by the windblown awning.

His legs were killing him, but he set his sights on a blind rise and forced himself to sprint to the top of it. He'd run until the image was gone. Run until *she* was gone. Run until all that remained was him and the elements, and the future stretching ahead, pristine as a spool of new typewriter ribbon.

He and the horse crested the hill at the same moment. Hooves scissored the sky above him, passing so close to his head on the way down that he felt a rush of air. There was a momentary pause, a gathering of oxygen and strength, then the black horse wheeled and bolted with such force and fury that it would have defied all laws of physics had Sasha not gone flying.

In the time it took her to hit the ground Nick saw himself rushing her to A&E with multiple fractures, or watching helplessly as she was dragged across the moors, foot wedged in a stirrup.

He saw it ending before it began.

He did not foresee her landing on her feet with a slight wobble, like a gymnast completing an imperfect routine. She was a little out of breath, but otherwise perfectly relaxed. Easy like a Sunday morning.

'We really must stop meeting like this,' she said.

So she had seen him that day.

'Like what?' he countered, playing for time.

'In dramatic circumstances. You know, life and death on Monday, circus stunts on Sunday.'

To hide his relief he stared after the horse, a tornado barrelling across the russets and greys of the winter landscape. A heron was startled from its path. Hoofbeats aside, no sound interrupted the stillness of the post-dawn world.

'Is this a regular occurrence? The circus stunts, I mean.'

She smiled. 'I could practically set my watch by it. None of the others have managed to unseat me. None, to be fair, have even tried.

But Marillion, bless him, is so blindingly fast that it's pointless resisting the inevitable. I'd only end up with whiplash.'

On the far side of the fallow land the horse came to a stop. He neighed wildly and snatched up a mouthful of grass.

'Should we go after him?'

'He'll be back. At least, I hope he will. That's my measure of whether or not we're making progress, he and I. He has an extreme flight response, but we're working on it.'

Nick wished he'd paid more attention when his pony-mad high-school girlfriends had discussed their mounts. Mostly he'd been thinking about how to relieve them of their clothes.

'Horses are flight animals,' Sasha was saying. 'When they panic, they do what comes naturally: they run for their lives. For the most part that flight distance is fairly short, but a horse that's been traumatised will often gallop until it's out of sight or sound of humans. A year ago, Marillion definitely fell into that category. Still does on bad days.'

She was watching the horse, so Nick stole a glance at her. Her slender, almost boyish frame was clad in the same khaki breeches and light blue sweater she'd been wearing on New Year's Day, with the addition of well-worn long black boots. She did not have on a protective hat. It was none of his business, but it bothered him.

'In case you're wondering how a girl like me gets to own a horse who looks as if he's stepped fully-formed from a Greek myth, it's because there's a story . . . There's always a story, isn't there?'

He looked away before she could catch his eye. 'What's Marillion's?'

'Eighteen months ago, he was one of the top three-year-old racehorses in the country. From everything I've heard, he had it in him to be among the greats. Then a starting gate malfunctioned. The other horses took off; he couldn't. He went berserk. The jockey was in intensive care, Marillion's legs were ripped to shreds. His owner was a foreign zillionaire who didn't want to push up his insurance premiums. He instructed the trainer to do the minimum legally required to patch him up at the track, dose him up with painkillers, and send him to the knackers' yard.

'I was collecting another horse when Marillion came in. He looked as if he'd been flayed alive. He was trembling so much that he could barely stand. Seasoned slaughterhouse workers were in tears.'

Nick had a sudden consciousness of the immensity of the arching sky and sweep of landscape, lent shape by the moors and sea. The far-away horse was a statue in miniature. He took a couple of steps in their direction and paused, tossing his head in defiance.

'How did he get from there to here? I mean, to the untrained eye, he tears around like a Derby winner.'

'I have Lacey Stanton, our local vet, to thank for that. Lacey was so appalled when she saw his injuries that she insisted on operating on him for free. Time, love and Mr McKenna's good hay have done the rest.'

The horse broke into a bucking canter. The swinging stirrups flashed.

'But his flight response still kicks in?' Nick resisted the urge to say: *But he's still a danger?*

'It does, but now at least he bolts for a reason. I mean, I got as much of a fright as he did when you came hurtling over the rise. We're used to having the farm and moors to ourselves at this hour on a Sunday. Most sane people like a lie-in, especially in winter. I'd be having one myself if I didn't have eight horses to take care of.'

'Eight sounds like an awful lot. Do you look after them for other riders or are they all yours?'

'I'm happy to say they're all mine.'

She offered no further explanation and he didn't wish to pry.

The horse slowed as he approached, tossing his extravagantly long mane. He pushed past Nick like a bully at a bar, almost knocking him over. But when he reached Sasha he lowered his head so she could rub his ears. A shuddering sigh escaped him.

He was still for a minute, but no sooner had Sasha untangled the stirrups than he sidled away restlessly. His blood was up from running, his neck wet with sweat. Up close, the latticework of fine scars on his legs was clearly visible.

'He still feels it,' she said, brushing the dew from his muzzle.

'The accident?'

'The need for speed.'

Nick gave a short laugh. 'I can relate. I used to be a bit that way myself.'

She looked at him sharply. 'Used to?'

'Things change.'

He went to stroke the horse's shoulder and it was like touching a live wire. Instantly his fingers started tingling. He jerked his hand away, startling the horse. Sasha was checking the girth and didn't realise that Nick was the cause.

She did, however, notice his pallor. 'Are you all right? You look a bit under the weather. When we didn't see you in Lanton, I worried you might be ill. Mum convinced me that you wanted to be left in peace.'

He forced a smile. 'I'm fine. One hundred per cent.'

Shoving his hands deep into his pockets, he took a step back. His sole preoccupation was getting away from this spellbinding woman and her crazy horse before they ensnared him any further. Or, more pressingly, before they stepped into his nightmares. For all he knew, saving Pattie had been a one-off, never to be repeated.

'Do you always do that?' Sasha asked.

'Do what?'

'Pretend you're okay when you're not.'

'Do you always do that?' he shot back.

'What?'

'Say the first thing that comes into your head.'

She laughed. 'Touché.'

The horse glared at some unseen terror beyond the rise. His ears flattened and he danced on the spot, poised to bolt again.

Sasha gathered his reins. 'I'd better go. He's not good at doing nothing. Mind giving me a leg up?'

Nick took another step back. 'I can't! I don't know the first thing about horses.'

She stared at him in surprise. 'All you have to do is put your hands under my shin and boost me skywards.'

All he had to do.

There was nothing to prevent him from packing up that very afternoon and vanishing without leaving a forwarding address. He and Oliver could start again in continental Europe or somewhere more remote.

New Zealand.

Tristan da Cunha.

The South Pole.

Her boot was butter-soft under his palms. She was lighter than he expected and he practically threw her up in his anxiety not to be near her. Her mouth tightened, but she made no comment. Marillion fidgeted beneath her. She flowed with him, reins loose, until he quieted.

Nick turned to go, wriggling his fingers to ease the pins and needles. His limbs were stiff with cold and aching with the unaccustomed exercise.

She stared down at him, an unreadable expression on her face. 'I could teach you to ride if you were interested.'

Taken off guard, he was more abrupt than he meant to be. 'Thanks, but that's out of the question. I'm fixing up the cottage and working on a book, which means I have my nose to the grindstone pretty much twenty-four seven.'

'Oh, come on, everyone needs companionship. And fun.'

New Zealand.

Tristan da Cunha.

An icebreaker crashing through blue Antarctic bergs.

'I have a cat.'

'I have my horses, but I still need human contact.'

'That's you,' he snapped harshly. 'I don't need or want anyone. Thanks but no thanks.'

He didn't have to worry about escaping then, because she did it first. Before he could blink he was alone with the heron.

Drained, he walked back over the rise. In the centre of the track, still smoking, was a cigarette butt.

Fear lent Nick stamina and he all but sprinted back to Seabird Cottage. Oliver had collapsed by the back door, on the mat where the dead dove had lain. His eyes were glazed and he was gasping. Around his neck was a noose of cobalt blue nylon cord, pulled taut enough to restrict the breath but not to kill. Not immediately, at any rate. A message was crudely etched into the frost-hard dirt of the path.

ACTIONS HAVE CONSEQUENCES.

5

'I have five words for you, Nick. Come back; all is forgiven.'

'So soon?' Nick carried the phone to the armchair in the living room so he could sprawl in Aunt Sadie's decrepit armchair and gaze out to sea as he talked. 'Barely six weeks ago I had the impression that Henry would rather take a barefoot stroll on a bed of hot coals than entrust me with a single assignment.'

'That was before he hired Colin,' reported Phil. 'Now he'd do it naked and throw in a few pirouettes.'

'Do you mind? I've just had breakfast.'

'Seriously, Nick, when are you coming back? The department needs you. *I* need you. If I have to hear about Amy's man troubles, or Colin's eczema, or endure one more of Henry's two-minutes-to-deadline meltdowns, I'll write my own obituary and be glad to do it.'

'Trust me when I tell you, you really don't want to do that.' Nick watched Oliver stalk a seagull across the grass. The wind was giving the cat a ginger Mohican. He'd recovered from his ordeal with no obvious physical effects, but he was noticeably more jumpy. 'As to when I'm coming back, I'm not sure. Maybe in a couple of months, maybe never.'

'Why are you being so evasive?' demanded Phil. 'I know I was hard on you before you left, but you only have yourself to blame. You were acting like a crazy person. But it all seems like a bad dream now. I don't care if it's tomorrow or next week or in a month – I want you back at your old desk and Becca wants you back living down the road from her. Greg's not so keen, but most of us quite like having you around.'

'Is that a fact? Has it slipped your mind that you only talked me into coming to your fridge-freezer, woodworm-infested cottage in the middle of nowhere because you gave me the brochure speech about how it was a nature lover's paradise and I'd be eating romantic candlelit dinners? On my first night here, I narrowly avoided being asphyxiated by a blocked chimney. Then the bed collapsed and almost killed me. Have I mentioned the dead bird on the doorstep? Or the disembowelled rodent? Oh, and yesterday someone almost strangled my cat. You should be prosecuted under the Trade Descriptions Act.'

Phil was immediately contrite. 'Have you had a hideous time?'

Out on the lawn the seagull lunged, screeching at Oliver. Tail like a bottlebrush, the cat fled.

Nick hopped up to let him in the front door. It was a bitterly cold day, but he stood for a moment taking in the wild beauty of the scene. 'It's been an education, put it that way. Everything that could go wrong *has* gone wrong. But as hard as it might be to believe, I'm besotted with the place. It's freezing, uncomfortable, full of vermin and in the middle of nowhere, but you couldn't prise me out of here with a crowbar.'

For a minute, all he could hear was the crackling of the line and the low hum of the obit department – the soundtrack to his former life.

'Wow. I never figured you for the camping type.'

'Nor me. I've always been more of the five-star-hotel type. But there's something about this place that makes me feel alive. I like the rawness of it, the savagery of the elements. Nature is in your face here. There's no hiding from it.'

'I told Mrs Moreton you were a martyr.'

'Yeah, thanks for that.'

He could almost hear Phil's grin.

'What are the rest of the locals like?'

'Variously taciturn, pathological and beautiful.'

'*Beautiful?*' Phil groaned. 'Nick, you've only been there five minutes. Don't tell me you've already fallen under the spell of some ravishing milkmaid?'

'How many times do I have to tell you I don't do love? Or relationships.'

'Take my advice and keep it that way. I started the morning in tears after a row over the marmalade.'

'Besides, she's taken. I think. How can you have a row about marmalade?'

'Crumbs. That's what they don't tell you in the relationship manual.

Or if they do, it's in the small print. Crumbs can lead to divorce. What's wrong with the milkmaid? Can't she see you're worth ten of the local cowherd? Or is he the one that's pathological? What do you mean, you "think"? Either she's taken or she isn't.'

'Phil, has anyone ever told you that you need to get out more? You hold such stereotyped views of countryfolk.'

In the pause that followed, Nick heard Amy offer Henry a coffee.

'Black, two sugars. Co-*lin*, can I see you in my pod, please. Yes, NOW, not next Easter. About this copy . . .'

Phil said in wonder: 'You sound like your old self, Nick. No, that's not true. You sound better.'

Nick turned his back on the ocean view and shut the door with more force than was necessary. The chill seemed to have got to his throat. He said gruffly: 'Thanks, mate, for not bailing on me when any sane person would have – and most did. I owe you more than I can ever repay.'

'Now you're talking bollocks again. If anything, I owe you a Caribbean cruise on a luxury liner for not suing me for the Seabird Cottage experience. Nick, tell me the truth. You're not coming back to London, are you?'

Nick put a match to the kindling in the grate. The flames warmed his cheeks as they flared. 'See you when I see you, my friend.'

Nick could recall almost to the minute when he'd first resolved to become a writer. He'd been eleven years old. The prep school he'd attended was one of those in which no achievement went unpunished. Thuggish dimwits ruled the halls and the teachers were universally doltish, apathetic and cynical. Once, when Nick made the mistake of trying too hard on an essay, his classmates stole it from his bag during gym class, ripped it to pieces and flushed it down the toilet. When he objected, they tried to flush his head down too.

After being sentenced to a week of detention for failing to produce his homework and an extra week for lying about having done it in the first place, Nick had compounded his original error by railing against the injustice of the situation.

'I love writing stories, so it doesn't make sense that I wouldn't do my homework,' he protested. 'Why would I lie about it? And anyway, when I grow up I want to be a famous author or a journalist so it's important that I get lots of practice.'

His teacher, Mr Tracey, had rubbed the red top of his bald pate furiously. It was a tic he resorted to whenever he felt an overwhelming urge to beat the crap out of one of his charges.

'Listen, kiddo, it'll save you a lot of pain and aggravation if you get it through your head now that boys like you – bottom-feeder boys who can barely string two sentences together – don't become journalists, much less authors. You'll be lucky if you end up scraping a living as a tradesman's apprentice. More than likely, you'll be picking your nose in the dole queue along with all the other no-hopers in this place. Your best bet is to focus on doing your sums and maybe when you're older Daddy can help you become an insurance dweeb like him. You're nothing now and that's what you'll amount to – nothing.'

Torn between tears and fury Nick had yelled: 'I will be a famous writer. You'll see, I will. And when I am you'll still be stuck in this shithole, killing kids' dreams.'

Of course, Nick had not only failed to become a famous writer, he'd become an anonymous obituary writer – an unsung chronicler of the dead. Doubtless Mr Tracey, who'd probably perished of heart disease after consuming one too many artery-clogging school dinners, would see some sort of poetic justice in that.

Nevertheless, the perverse streak that had made Nick resolve to prove the teacher wrong at all costs was alive and well in him. That same stubbornness had led him to order a slough of books on carpentry, DIY and furniture-building from the bookstore in Lanton. His Mustang had made so many trips to the hardware superstore for paint and other supplies that, rather than ignoring him, Mr McKenna took to stopping what he was doing entirely when Nick passed, often lighting his pipe and regarding the car's progress as one might regard the descent of a spacecraft from heaven.

Nick paid no attention. What had begun as a mission to prove to the farmer that woodwork was hardly rocket science, and that even feckless city-boy reporters could put up a shelf that stayed up, quickly became a labour of love. Seldom could he recall doing anything more rewarding. It wasn't his cottage and Phil could at any time revoke his right to stay there and put the place on the market. Yet regardless of what became of Seabird Cottage, Nick knew that his efforts would have been worth it. A feeling of home had settled over him on that first morning when he'd glanced up to see the red fox watching him. He'd never been able to, nor wanted to, shake it. He was meant to be there, of that he had no doubt.

Now, gazing around him, he was proud of what he'd achieved. Laptop tucked out of sight in a cupboard, he'd thrown himself into transforming the cottage the way he'd once given life back to the newly departed in his copy. After turning the garage into a workshop, he'd ferreted out damp and waged war on the innumerable spiders, moths and wood-devouring creatures that had taken advantage of Aunt Sadie's hospitality over the years. He'd stripped wallpaper, stuffed holes with Polyfilla and called in an electrician to do enough to make the place legal.

He'd also hired a sander. Beneath the many layers of stomach-turning grime and assorted varnishes that coated the floor, he'd discovered virgin oak. The rush of pride it had given him when it was returned to its former glory was at least equivalent to the feeling he'd got when his first story was printed in the local paper.

Inspired, he carted away the fallen-down shelves and built a proper bookcase. He even tiled the bathroom.

It stopped him from thinking.

His initial attempts at almost everything were atrocious. But with every ruined tile or spilled pot of paint, he learned. Light poured into Seabird Cottage. On sunny days, the waves sent diamonds chasing across the white walls and ceilings. As January shifted into February and March beckoned, daffodils, tulips and bluebells bloomed on the farm and in Nick's messy patch of garden. The fox took to strolling about in broad daylight.

Nick chronicled these small joys, along with his DIY gains and mishaps, in weekly letters to Matthew Levin. He never received a reply and didn't expect one, but since they were not returned to sender he figured that someone, somewhere was reading them. And from a selfish point of view, writing them made him feel calmer.

Most nights he slept the dreamless sleep of a child on his mattress on the floor of the upstairs bedroom, waking refreshed but disoriented. When he came to, his main feeling was one of relief. Every day without an obituary dream was a reprieve.

But the unnameable craving, which he alternately attributed to an addict's withdrawal from writing or a general pining for physical contact, but refused to accept might have anything at all to do with Sasha, still tormented him. His ferocious regime had alleviated it to a degree, but it was always there. The infernal itch.

One morning in March he went out running in a fine, misty rain. On a whim, he took the road signposted No Entry on the far side of Mr McKenna's farm. He'd seen hoofprints on the track leading into a copse a dozen times and always forced himself on. This time his feet carried him there of their own accord. As a precautionary measure, he cut through the dripping trees. The fallen leaves would leave little record of his passing.

He was stealing forward when the soft squeak of leather and muffled rhythm of hooves alerted him to the rapid approach of horses. There was no time to hide. All he could do was dive, like a swimmer, behind the carcass of a fallen tree. Twigs popped like firecrackers when he landed.

Through a crack in the mossy trunk, Nick watched guiltily as Marillion shied hard and spun. Somehow Sasha stayed with him. He galloped a few strides but pulled up quickly, jogging on the spot and blowing steam.

'Easy,' she soothed, stroking his neck. 'Easy there. Good boy. Aren't you an angel? Steady now.'

'What are you like?' scoffed Cullen, riding over to her. His own horse, a showy grey mare, had shied too, but soon submitted to his will. 'You let that animal get away with murder, you do. He'll break your neck one day and it'll be your own fault. Nobody'll feel sorry for you, least of all me. He needs taking in hand, he does. I'll do it for you if you haven't the stomach for it.'

Sasha tensed, but she said in a conciliatory tone: 'Try to be patient, honey. Week on week he's improving, you know he is. What he needs is kindness and love, not a firm hand.'

'The trouble with you, Sash, is you ascribe human emotions to him. Anthropomorphism it's called. Horses respond to discipline and order. All the love on earth is not going to make him think twice if a tractor comes out of nowhere and scares the life out of him. Do you think he'll have loyalty on his mind when that happens?'

They were too far away for Nick to hear Sasha's response, if indeed she made one. He hoped she'd told Cullen to go fuck himself, but doubted that was her style.

A spider crawled over his hand and he leapt up, shaking off rotting leaves. He was filthy. Not for the first time, he questioned his behaviour. Why hadn't he just greeted the pair as they passed and continued on his run? Why did he feel the need to hide? Who was he protecting – himself or Sasha?

At the edge of the copse, the ground shelved steeply. What had once been a quarry or a tin mine was now given over to paddocks, sheltered from the sea winds by a high, grassy bank. Behind them, the ocean roared softly. Directly below Nick were ten stables arranged in a half-moon shape. Cullen was in view. He'd removed the tack from the grey mare and was brushing her down. Marillion was tethered close by. In a nearby school, Sasha was exercising a bay. The pair moved in perfect unison.

From the shadow of the trees, Nick watched Cullen. With his wind-swept dark hair, black polo-neck sweater and navy blue breeches, the man looked more like an elegantly debauched artist than ever. He would not have been out of place on the cover of *GQ*. It was impossible to reconcile the image of the consummate horseman now tending to the mare with the utmost tenderness with the pathological mind that might wring the neck of a dove or half-strangle a cat.

And for what? It wasn't as if Nick constituted any type of threat.

So perhaps Cullen wasn't responsible at all. Perhaps it was Mr McKenna, trying to scare him back to London. Somehow Nick doubted it. The old bastard would have had no hesitation in telling it to him straight.

Who then? A ghost from his past? A dead man walking?

Cullen turned his attention to Marillion. The horse pinned his ears to his head as his tack was removed and he was groomed. He nipped at Cullen when his forelock was brushed, and kicked out when Cullen attempted to clean his rear hooves. Several times Cullen stopped and remonstrated with him. Finally, the horse settled.

Nick had until this minute blocked from his mind the current that had surged through him when he touched Marillion. Now the pins and needles started again. He'd hoped they had been consigned to the past, along with his nightmares, but now they came in waves, causing intense discomfort. What they might signify, he refused to consider.

Cullen was in the process of leading Marillion back to his stable when a plastic bag blew from a bush and startled the horse. The horse shot forward, slamming into Cullen and catching his shoulder with a terrific blow. Sasha glanced over, but Cullen had the horse under control almost immediately so she resumed her work with the bay.

Marillion's stable was furthest away. Cullen emerged and secured the door, keeping a firm grip on the horse's halter. As Nick watched, he reached into the shadows. The horse's eyes went white with terror. It staggered.

Nick craned forward, trying to make out what was happening. Cullen's broad shoulders blocked his view. His impulse was to go tearing down the track and intervene, but it would be his word against Cullen's and what would he say? That from a distance of fifty metres he thought he saw the man do something to cause intense pain to Marillion? Then again, he wasn't sure.

Marillion had vanished from view. Cullen moved away from the stable door. Some instinct made him look in the direction of the copse. Nick threw himself behind a tree and stood motionless, but it was a racing certainty he'd been seen.

For several long seconds Cullen stared upwards. Sasha distracted him by riding over. 'What is it, hon? Everything all right?'

Had Nick not been taking rapid evasive action, he'd have seen Cullen reach for the mare's bridle and help Sasha dismount with a show of gallantry. He flashed a grin.

'Everything's grand, my love. Usual story of Marillion and some of your other favourites trying to get away with murder, which is a little disappointing to be honest with you, but I've come to the conclusion that you're right. It takes patience, but sooner or later everyone learns.'

6

It wasn't until he noticed the broken window in his workshop nearly a week later that Nick realised Oliver was missing. Most nights the cat slept lengthways across the foot of his bed, taking up more than his fair share of space, but that morning his tolerance for Nick's tossing and turning had worn thin in the small hours. He'd stalked from the bedroom, out of sorts. Nick had been too groggy to notice his absence at breakfast and surprised but not concerned when he returned from an afternoon DIY expedition in Penzance to find the bowl of cat food untouched. Shortly afterwards, he chanced upon the shards of glass on his workshop floor and felt the first tinge of alarm,

Even then he didn't worry unduly. If Oliver were on an extended bird patrol, he'd be back when he was hungry or if the weather, which had turned ugly overnight, continued to worsen. The break-in was a different matter. There was nothing in the place worth stealing, but he had a quick look around the cottage just in case. To his relief, the cupboard where he'd locked his laptop was undisturbed and his SLR camera was still sitting on his desk. So was the twenty-pound note he'd forgotten to pick up earlier. Not a break-in then. If there was a culprit, it must be the wind.

Yet something about the air in Seabird Cottage felt different, felt disturbed.

To take his mind off it, Nick lit a fire and turned on Radio Four. He listened to a programme on the history of mathematics while cooking himself a blisteringly hot curry with the help of a jar of paste and a packet of fresh chillies. It was while he was dousing the flames on his tongue with an ice-cold beer that he noticed that the silver-framed photograph of his mum and dad had been moved. Usually, it sat on the right side of his desk, turned outwards as if they were gazing at the view. Now it was face down on the left.

Nick washed his plate, stoked the fire and tried to shrug off the whole thing on the grounds that nothing had been taken and no one had been hurt. Far more alarming was the palpable sense of isolation that had descended on the cottage in Oliver's absence. In the nearly three months he'd lived there he'd never been lonely. Not once. Naturally, he missed sex. A lot. And he missed the easy camaraderie of his old friends – the spontaneous dinners, pub nights and drunken benders. He missed cracking up with laughter about the stupidest things.

At the same time, he accepted that his old life belonged to the past. He was not the man nor the journalist he once was, could never be again. That ship had sailed.

But nothing could have prepared him for the emptiness that bit him with unexpected savagery as he paced the cottage that evening. He couldn't have cared less about the non-burglary. What difference did it make? If he was alone in the world, wasn't everything pointless? Oliver had given life to the space, had given Nick a reason to get up in the morning. Without him . . .

'For crying out loud, he's a cat,' he ranted at himself. 'Get a grip. If he's lost or gotten himself eaten by the fox, it's not the end of the bloody world.'

He stomped into his workshop and grabbed a hammer and a bag of nails from his toolbox. Oliver would be home in time for breakfast. And within half an hour of returning he'd be clawing the sofa, throwing up on important letters from the Inland Revenue, and wanting to go out when he was in and in when he was out and all the other things that frequently made cat ownership a trial.

Nick could hardly wait.

In the corner of his workshop was a bin filled with potentially useful remnants of junkyard furniture. Nick had no trouble finding a board to fit the window. He was about to knock in the first nail when he saw a movement in the darkness. Crouching low, a figure in a grey hoodie crept across the lawn towards the sea, keeping to the shadows.

Nick threw down the hammer and bolted back through the kitchen and out into the night. The intruder was sitting on the bench beside the sea, rummaging in a rucksack. So absorbed was he or she that it was not until Nick was halfway across the lawn that the grey sweatshirt jerked to life. Pausing only to snatch up the rucksack, the figure, a lanky teenage boy, took off around the side of the cottage.

Nick rugby-tackled him as he sprinted for a bicycle propped beneath a tree. They slid through the mud as if they were scoring a try. The boy fought and kicked and even tried biting until Nick put him in an armlock.

'Ow! That fucking hurts. Get off me, you psycho.'

Nick allowed him to sit up, but kept a tight grip on the boy's wrist. With his free hand, he pulled back the sweatshirt hood. A teenager with an angular face and a shock of punk rocker black hair glared back at him. There was a comet-shaped scar on his right cheek. He was inadequately dressed, caked in mud and shivering.

'You've got some nerve,' said Nick. 'You come here, you burgle my cottage, you sneak around my garden in the dead of night and somehow I'm the bad person.'

'Burgle your cottage? What are you on about? I didn't steal anything.'

'Of course you didn't. I suppose you were after some easy drug money. I have to say I'm disappointed. Call me an idealist, but somehow I expected more from teenagers around here. You're surrounded by some of the most incredible landscape on earth and have infinite opportunity for adventure and natural highs, and still you have to resort to artificial ones. It's sad.'

The boy regarded him pityingly. 'Not that you're full of pre-conceptions or anything. I bet you secretly believe that most Cornish teenagers are drugged-up surfie losers on the dole. An idealist, my arse.'

'You've seen right through me. But anyway, we're getting off the subject of why you decided to rob me. I didn't think I owned anything worth stealing. What have you found?'

'I'm telling you for the last time, I didn't burgle your stupid cottage.'

Nick ignored him. He let go of the boy's wrist and seized the rucksack.

'Leave that alone! It's private.'

Nick ignored him. Holding it out of range, he unzipped it. There was nothing inside but an old biscuit tin. In it were eight compartments, organised with military neatness. They contained a couple of cheap floats, three hooks, two weights, some beads and a packet of swivels.

'*Fishing?* That's what this is about?'

The boy took the box, blew on the contents as if Nick had somehow soiled them, and packed it away reverently. 'So what? It isn't a crime.'

'No, it isn't. It's just – not a lot of people surprise me.'

'Yeah, well, you shouldn't be so cynical. You should be enjoying some of those natural highs you were telling me about.'

Nick laughed. 'You're right. I should. But why didn't you simply knock on my door and ask permission? And why here? Aren't there a million other places you could try?'

'I used to come here when the cottage was empty. For shore-fishing, it's hard to beat. After you moved in, people said you were a weirdo recluse so I tried to find another spot. None of them had the same magic. So I thought maybe I could try fishing at night and you'd be none the wiser. Didn't think I'd get assaulted.'

Nick stood and offered him a hand. After a moment's hesitation, the boy gripped it. 'Apologies. My nerves were fried. I came home to find a window broken and my cat missing. I put two and two together and made five. I'm Nick.'

The boy hooked his rucksack over his thin shoulders. His fingers were clumsy with cold. 'Ryan. Good to meet you. Sort of.'

'Ryan, any time you want to fish here, it's fine by me. Only do me a favour. Fish in daylight when there's less chance of you being washed out to sea.'

'Deal.'

'I'm about to make a coffee if you'd like one. If you're into hot food, I've also made a curry that I'm pretty proud of. It's from a jar, but with added personal touches.'

'Aren't you worried that I might case the joint?'

'Like I said, there's not a lot to case.'

Over the next hour Nick learned, not so much by what Ryan said as what he didn't, that he'd never known his father and that he shared a council flat with a mother who was a recovering alcoholic prone to relapses. Despite this, they were close and Ryan, who'd scored some reasonable GCSEs, had ambitions to work at Trelissick or another of Cornwall's tropical public gardens.

As they talked, the wind started to slam around the cottage like a spoiled brat and Ryan reluctantly conceded that fishing wasn't an option. They walked to the end of the garden to retrieve the rod he'd left by the rocks, Nick delaying for as long as possible the moment when he'd be alone once again in the cottage. The waves charged up to the garden bench, flinging out their foaming ends like wind-whipped sheets on a line.

The fishing rod was plasticky and old, its flimsy length mended at least twice with duct tape.

'Catch much with that?'

'Not a lot, but it's not about that. It's about being so close to the ocean that you're almost in it and it's about the game. Free therapy, you see.'

A memory of his time in the shrink's office, the man's wet-fish handshake, returned to Nick. 'Can't argue with that.'

Ryan dismantled the rod and secured it to the back of his rucksack. Nick thought guiltily of the wildly expensive rod and tackle that he'd bought in a moment of madness during one of his DIY trips to Penzance. It was the kind of thing his London self would have done. Afterwards, it had struck him as embarrassingly mid-life crisisish – this notion that he'd go down to the shore like a television survivalist and haul in his own dinner. The rod had never been removed from its wrapper. It was propped in a corner of his workshop, gathering dust. He resolved to give it to the teenager the next time he turned up to fish.

Ryan swung onto his bike. 'Thanks for the curry. You're quite good at the cooking-from-a-jar thing. Now you're sure it's okay for me to come and fish when the weather improves?'

'No problem.'

'You really don't mind? And I can come by any time?'

'I really don't mind and yes, you can come by any time.'

'Cool. Right, see you around.' He flicked on his lights and peddled off down the drive.

'Hey Ryan.'

The brakes squeaked. 'Yep.'

'If on occasion you find yourself with a few haddock to spare, I really wouldn't like it if you dropped by and helped me attempt some home-made fish and chips.'

Ryan grinned. 'I wouldn't like that either.'

He rode away into the darkness, lights bobbing. After a few seconds, the brakes squeaked again.

'Hey Nick.'

'Yeah.'

'I hope your cat comes home.'

7

But Oliver didn't come home. He wasn't there by morning, and an exhaustive search of the surrounding farmland that afternoon proved fruitless. When darkness fell for the second night running with no sign of him, all Nick could do was speculate on possible fates.

Oliver was not, by nature, a wanderer. He was a homebody. Quite apart from anything else, his fuller figure made him err towards the sedentary. He liked his creature comforts. It was highly unlikely that he'd have got so carried away hunting he'd forgotten the way home.

Nick steeled himself to ring the farmhouse. Mercifully, it was Rosa McKenna who answered. She hadn't seen any cats matching Oliver's description, but promised to call if she did. As he hung up, Nick tried to shut out of his mind what he now feared was inevitable – that Cullen had somehow disappeared Oliver. *Actions have consequences.* But what actions and how extreme would be the consequences?

Nick could think of nothing apart from injured pride that would cause Cullen to launch such a vicious vendetta against him. Yet there was no doubt in his mind that that's what was going on. At first, he'd been prepared to let it go. Without proof and with only the flimsiest evidence of anything untoward – a dove that may or may not have died from natural causes; a childish warning scribbled in the mud; a ghost of a chance that Cullen could have let himself into the cottage and nosied around – he could hardly have done otherwise. But if Oliver had been snatched or seriously harmed, things had just got personal. And Nick was not about to take it lying down.

Unable to bear the silent cottage a minute longer, he put on his boots and snatched up his car keys. He had to know. Had to hear what had happened from Cullen's own mouth even if he had to choke it out of him.

The speed at which he drove to Lanton threatened to destroy what was left of the Mustang's undercarriage. Nevertheless, he counselled himself to proceed with caution. In his current frame of mind he was capable of ripping the man's throat out, but the bottom line was he had no proof.

He screeched to a halt outside The Lighthouse Inn, leaving the car in a loading bay. Cullen had made reference to the pub during their first encounter and it seemed as good a place as any to start.

It was a Wednesday night but the place was heaving. The jukebox was so loud that few people turned their heads when Nick burst in, wild-eyed, shaking off an unexpected downpour. Rather more of them noticed as he began pushing his way through the crowd, searching for Cullen. Midway across the room he locked gazes with Sasha, the last person on earth he'd expected to see serving drinks behind the bar. The look she gave him could have frozen vodka.

His enemy stepped in front of him, flashing his devilish grin. He was dressed like an actor on his way to a magazine shoot, in an expensive blue blazer over a crisp white shirt and jeans. His cologne matched his clothes. 'Hey, Sash, it's our reclusive friend,' he cried jovially. 'A big Lighthouse welcome ta you, Nick, me lad.'

Nick hit him. Fortuitously, as it turned out, a drunk fell against his shoulder in the instant before he unleashed the punch, taking the power out of it. There was enough force in the blow to knock Cullen off his feet and draw shocked squeals from several women, but apart from a tiny cut on his chin he was uninjured.

For a split second his eyes met Nick's. Hatred spat from them. He blinked it away before anyone but Nick could register it and laughed as if the whole thing had been staged for comic effect.

The jukebox died and a hush fell over the pub.

Nick hauled Cullen to his feet by his collar and shook him. 'Where is my cat, you bastard? What have you done to him?'

Cullen held up his hands in a gesture of surrender. His expression was one of childlike surprise. 'Ladies and gentleman, boys and girls, are you hearing this or have I lost my mind? I see now what my mum was talkin' about when she advised me not to speak to strangers.'

There was a titter.

'I've met this man only once in me life, for all of five minutes, and now he's accusing me of doing I don't know what with his cat. Not his wife, mind you, or his girlfriend. His cat. What does your pussy look like, Nick?'

More laughter.

Sasha had come out from behind the bar and was staring at the two men, incredulous. Nick knew he was burning every possible bridge, but he yanked Cullen towards him. 'If you've harmed so much as a whisker on Oliver's head, so help me God I will kill you.'

A voice behind him said: 'I might be able to help.'

Mr McKenna's overcoat was dark with rain, his beard beaded with droplets. 'It's a pig of a night out there, Mr Donaghue, and to be honest with you I gave my wife an earful when she ordered me to come out to find you. But I'm thinking now that it was as well she insisted. We've found your big ginger cat. A couple of days ago we had a grain delivery. He must have sneaked into the storeroom and been locked in by mistake. I came upon him about an hour ago when I went to get some chicken feed. Very sorry for himself he was. Rosa soon had him sorted. When I left he was sitting beside the fire, enjoying chopped ham.'

Nick seized the farmer in a bear hug. 'Oh, thank God. That's such a relief. Mr McKenna, I can't thank you enough.'

A cheer went up in the pub.

Mr McKenna went the colour of one of his beetroots. He nearly knocked his neighbour over in his hurry to escape to the bar.

Nick could feel the eyes of every person in the pub boring into him. He extended his hand. 'I'm sorry, Cullen. I don't know what to say. I'm a moron; that's all there is to it. Is there any way I can make it up to you? Can I buy you a drink? Or three or four? A magnum of champagne?'

Cullen gave him a brilliant smile laced with loathing, like a strawberry daiquiri infected with strychnine. He shook Nick's hand vigorously. 'There'll be time enough for champagne later. In the meanwhile, all's well that ends well, that's what I say. No hard feelings. Hey, Sash, let's get our friend a drink. On me. He looks as if he could do with a stiff one. Nothing worse than worrying about a pussy.'

Another cheer.

Trapped by the bonhomie of his enemy, by the crush of the sweaty, boisterous crowd, and by his own calamitous hand, Nick was forced to sit at the bar and drink a pint poured by Sasha and paid for by her lover. It was the proverbial bitter pill.

At the first opportunity he retreated to a dark corner. Mr McKenna joined him.

'Doubtless I've confirmed all your worst suspicions about reporters.'

Mr McKenna took a long swallow of his pint. Stalactites of foam hung from his moustache. 'You're okay, Donaghue. Only . . .'

'Go ahead. Say it.'

'It's none of my business and you'll think I'm a miserable old fart . . .'

'I already do.'

The farmer put down his beer. 'Right then, I'll be off.'

Nick stopped him. 'I'm joking. You've no idea how grateful I am to you and Mrs McKenna for finding Oliver. It probably seems peculiar to you, a grown man getting so worked up over a cat, but I was going out of my mind. It's hard to explain, but we have a history, Oliver and I. Now, you were about to give me some advice.'

'Call me Gordon. My wife's name's Rosa. Now, about Sasha . . .'

'What about her?'

'There's no point in carrying a torch for her, as the old saying goes. You'll not get a look in if you don't have four legs and a tail. Cullen does, but that's only because they were childhood sweethearts. She's as independently minded as that wild horse of hers. She belongs here, to the moors and the sea. She's not for the likes of you, back off to London any day.'

'To borrow another old saying, you're barking up the wrong tree. I barely know her. I appreciate your concern but there's really no need. My focus is on my work. I don't have time for, nor am I interested in, relationships of any description. I especially have no interest in pursuing other men's partners.'

Mr McKenna grunted. 'That's all right then.'

'Yes, it is.'

The pair drank in strangely companionable silence until the waves of drinkers parted to reveal Sasha, framed by the dark oak bar, laughing as she served a customer. The light caught her red dress and tangle of hair and made flames of both. A steel spike of longing stabbed Nick in the groin.

He turned away abruptly. 'I didn't know that Sasha worked at The Lighthouse as well as in the gift shop.'

'I thought you weren't interested.'

'I'm not. But I've seen her exercising horses around the farm and I know she helps her mother with the cottage business. If she waitresses here too, it must keep her pretty busy.'

'No one works harder. Ever since her father passed away she's been like a woman possessed, doing two, three jobs. She has her heart set on this riding centre and it would take a braver man than myself to dissuade her. I know Cullen's tried.'

Nick swirled the dregs around the bottom of his glass. 'She wants to start a riding school?'

'Good Lord, no. Nothing could be further from her mind. Back in London she was a specialist nurse, working with the disabled. When she came back to Lanton to take care of her dad, she rescued a couple of horses from a knackers' yard. That gave her the idea. She has this notion that she can build a place where they can heal each other, the ponies and the people. I'm happy for her to have the land rent-free, but the centre is about a decade off if she's going to pay for it by waitressing.'

The opening bars of 'Lady in Red' boomed across the pub. The cynic in Nick had always considered the song to be the last word in cheesiness – the recourse of teary drunks come over all romantic, or tea-dance DJs in retirement homes. Cullen was near the jukebox. Nick wondered if he had selected the track.

He nodded in Cullen's direction. 'What is it that he does for a living?'

'Not that you're interested.'

'I'm simply making conversation.'

'He's a plumber.'

'Ah, real man's work.'

'Indeed, real man's work.'

Nick wrestled with the twin images of Cullen as he'd imagined him, as a deranged but prodigiously gifted poet/artist, and Cullen spending his days unblocking U-bends, tiling bathrooms with buxom mermaids and having sex with lonely housewives. But no, why would he do such a thing when he had Sasha?

When he looked up the man was waving him over.

He pretended not to notice. 'It's late and I must get back, Mr McKenna. Gordon. Thanks again for rescuing Oliver. I'll be over to fetch him first thing.'

'You're being summoned,' the farmer interrupted.

Nick made his way across the pub as if he were being called to the gallows. The maudlin lyrics cut through the chatter and made his head throb. As he approached, Cullen put one arm around an agitated Sasha. She was saying something to him that he was either laughing off or ignoring. His other arm encircled the shoulders of a beaming woman with an immense bust, tea-stained false teeth and bouncing, poodle-white curls.

'Nick, my old sparring partner, I'm in a dilemma. It's gorgeous Marjorie's seventieth birthday, and she's done me the honour of claiming me for the first dance. I don't want Sasha feeling lonesome, so I wondered . . .'

'*Cullen!*'

'Hold on a minute, baby. Nor do I want her being harassed by The Lighthouse piranhas.' He prodded a portly man festooned in dandruff. 'Yes, Bob, I'm talking about you.'

Bob beamed from ear to ear.

'Cullen!'

'I was wonderin' if you'd do me a favour and dance with my beautiful girlfriend?'

'I don't dance,' Nick said at once.

'And I don't want to dance,' Sasha declared vehemently as Take That began to croon *Back for Good.*

'Oh, go on,' cried Marjorie. 'You're young people. You should be kicking up your heels and having fun – especially you, lady in red.' She grabbed Cullen's hand. 'Come on, handsome, show me a good time.'

He shrugged, grinned amiably and followed her onto a pocket-sized dance floor, where a disco ball had begun to twirl.

Conscious that the crowd would not forgive him for offending their favourite barmaid the way they'd been prepared to move on from his unprovoked assault on Cullen, nor for that matter would he forgive himself, Nick did his best to repair the damage. 'I apologise if I seemed rude. I was taken off guard. It would be my pleasure to dance with you if you're free. I have two left feet, but you're welcome to take your chances.'

Painfully aware that her response was under equal scrutiny, Sasha muttered, 'Let's get this over with,' before heading for the swirling lights.

The floor was full of slow-dancing couples, the noisiest of which were Marjorie and Cullen. Nick and Sasha danced as far apart as they could without creating a spectacle. They touched only when absolutely necessary, avoiding each other's gazes.

'So I'm guessing you think I'm an Arsehole with a capital A,' Nick ventured.

'Correct. Actually, no, that's not quite true. You're an arsehole given to feats of great nobility. That makes you something of an enigma. There aren't too many men who'd go to war on behalf of an animal, especially when they have to humiliate themselves to do it.'

'I suppose not.'

She pulled back and looked at him directly for the first time since he'd stormed into the pub. 'What on earth made you think that Cullen had kidnapped your cat? He's a virtual stranger to you. You have to admit that would make anyone question your sanity.'

'I thought . . . I just . You see, I couldn't think who else . . .'

'But why him?'

'I made a mistake. I'd understand if you never spoke to me again.'

There was a question in her eyes. She said huskily, 'Under any other circumstances, I—'

Cullen inserted himself between them. 'Mind if I cut in?'

The music had stopped but neither of them had noticed. Somebody tapped a glass with a spoon and the pub fell silent, all faces turned towards the dance floor. An air-conditioning vent blew an icy draft down Nick's neck.

Sasha was watching Cullen with a slight frown. He put a hand on her waist and pulled her to him possessively before addressing the assembled crowd.

'Anyone who knows Sasha and I knows we've been inseparable since we were twelve years old. That's when we had our first kiss – May sixth in the stationery cupboard at Lanton Comprehensive, if anyone's interested.'

Lots of laughter.

'Not countin' the years she spent in London giving other men sponge baths –' there were a few chuckles that petered out into coughs and clearings of throats – 'we've been soulmates for half our lives. Now it's time for me to do the right thing, not because she wants me to, expects me to, or is pressurising me to, but because she's my sun, my moon and my stars. She's the reason I get up in the morning. And most of all, because I love her.'

He dropped to one knee and reverently opened a small velvet box. The diamond winked in the mirror ball light. He presented it to Sasha with a smile. It was a smile that had every woman in the room reaching for the Kleenex and the men doing a lot more throat clearing. It was, Nick thought, a smile to make a nun cast off her habit.

He watched from the sidelines, unable to breathe.

'Marry me, darling?' Cullen asked.

Sasha didn't hesitate. 'Yes.'

8

The bed was made of reclaimed oak. Over the months, the chaotic Truro junkyard from which the wood had come, along with the physical labour that followed, had been Nick's salvation.

In London, he'd been interested only in new things. If it didn't come with a five-star rating, if it wasn't so reassuringly expensive that he had heart palpitations when he handed over his credit card, he hadn't wanted it in his apartment. The same had applied to restaurants and clothes. Surrounded by possessions that smelled of the factories from which they came, that had the whiff of luxurious fabric, leather or fresh-from-the-box electronics, he'd felt young, cool and in the know. Cutting edge.

The thrill these toys and treats had given him had been temporary. It was nothing compared to the lasting satisfaction he'd had from stripping the hideous gilt frame off an old mirror and replacing it with one he'd handmade from driftwood washed up on the rocks outside Seabird Cottage. The Ligne Roset sofa he'd so proudly shown off in his Greenwich apartment – a sofa that had almost literally been worth its weight in gold – had not brought him one per cent of the satisfaction he'd felt after refurbishing a dresser rescued from beneath a pile of rotting rugs in the junkyard.

The Aga aside, virtually everything in the cottage had been fixed, painted or changed by him. Ironically, he'd discovered a latent passion for carpentry. There was something about the tactile nature of wood, the way its finely etched grain tied its past irrevocably to its future, which made crafting it into something beautiful a privilege.

Hence the bed. It was a king-size one that smelled faintly but deliciously of newly worked oak of different histories. It had been a challenge to blend the different tones and join the irregular pieces, but it had been worth every hour. The result was a bed that was elegant in its simplicity and, more importantly, a one-off. In the week since he'd completed it, Nick had lain awake for some time each night just enjoying the warm solidity of it. It was his final big project.

The experience of lying in a bed he'd built with his own hands beneath the clean, salty breeze from the skylight windows had given him the courage to call Phil about buying the place. His plan had been to sell his apartment and use the money to purchase Seabird Cottage. He'd been astounded when Phil had suggested a direct swap, with Phil and Mikhail paying the difference. They'd always, his friend confessed, coveted the Greenwich pad. The river view in particular.

Valuations had been done within days. Nick had anticipated there being no more than a few thousand pounds difference. In fact, there was a differential of fifty thousand. To the estate agent's disgust, Nick had immediately reduced the price. Phil refused to accept the discount on the grounds that Nick's restoration work had probably doubled the cottage's value. In the end, Nick had to more or less force him to accept a ten-thousand-pound break.

'You've changed my life,' he told Phil. 'You might even have saved it. You can't put a price on that.'

There was a chain. Phil and Mikhail would have to sell their current apartment before they could buy his, a painstaking process in a rocky property market, but in time it would happen. Seabird Cottage would be Nick's. In the meantime, he had a couple of hundred pounds in rental income left over after he'd paid the mortgage each month – ample when he lived predominantly on the McKennas' eggs, bread and vegetables. Ryan's fish and the occasional expedition to the Lanton chippie supplemented his diet.

It was a simple, almost primal life, but it was the only life Nick wanted. Most days he saw no one except Annie Entwhistle, the gossipy postwoman, who predominantly brought him unwanted furniture catalogues from his old life and talked so much that he felt intimately acquainted with the entire village. Despite his solitude, he felt happier than he had in years because his new life had cured him – that was how he thought of it – of his nightmares. He'd had no obituary dreams since New Year's Eve, five months earlier.

As for Sasha, he refused to admit her to his thoughts. She was banished from his life, his system, and especially his jogging route. She'd marry Cullen and produce a tribe of black-haired, blue-eyed babies and never have to worry about blocked drains. The entire family would forever consider him an arsehole. An enigmatic one, but still an arsehole.

Whenever an image of Sasha as he liked to remember her, her hair and dress aflame in the pub lights, slipped through a chink in his carefully constructed carapace, he congratulated himself. It had been a near thing, but she would shortly be married off. She would never become a victim of one of his nightmares.

One Sunday morning in May, Nick woke up and realised that he'd reached the end of his project list at Seabird Cottage. It was an odd feeling. Pride in what he'd achieved was offset by the awareness that he would no longer get up with a sense of purpose. The old questions returned to haunt him. What would he do with his time? How would he fill up his days?

While clearing out Sadie's cupboards, Nick had come across an antique Remington typewriter of the kind he'd only ever seen in films. He'd not used his laptop since he left London, and had no intention of doing so for the foreseeable future. But the little black typewriter offered the prospect of a clean slate. It sat on the dresser, challenging him. Now as he lay there contemplating it, it occurred to him that he'd run out of excuses not to write.

He was trying not to analyse why this prospect brought him out in a cold sweat when his eyes fell on Aunt Sadie's bedside light. He'd replaced the shade but not the base, which now struck him as characterless and unsightly.

Nick suddenly felt lighter. He'd make a lamp.

Midday found him bent over the lathe in his workshop, engrossed in the delicate business of creating the most perfect lampstand ever made. Until it was complete, he didn't have to write a word. That was his promise to himself.

The garage doors were open, Seasick Steve was growling 'I Started Out With Nothin' and I Still Got Most of It Left' on the CD player, and the sun was streaming in. Nick was in a threadbare pair of jeans and a black polo shirt speckled with sawdust. He hummed to himself as he turned the wood. To date, his whole DIY experience had been relatively injury free, but that was largely because he'd never glanced up and seen Sasha in the doorway, framed by the light.

His hand slipped. There was a split second's delay before a crimson roadmap of blood appeared on his brown forearm. 'Fuck!' he said succinctly.

Before he could move she was beside him. 'Is that a proposition?'

She wore silver pumps and a pale blue sundress printed with tiny violet flowers. Her throat was bare except for a wooden turtle on a leather thong. Sweat sparkled on her upper lip. The urge to put his mouth to it was so overwhelming it made him lightheaded.

'What? No, of course not. Oh, that was a joke, wasn't it? Duh. Sorry, I didn't hear you walk in. Excuse me for a minute; I'll be right back.'

He rushed into the kitchen, unwrapped a snowy expanse of kitchen towel and bunched it around his thumb. The blood soaked straight through.

Sasha watched him from the doorway, making no move to help.

'I could take that personally, you know. The way you said, "No, of course not!" with such vehemence. I could take it that you find me deeply unattractive. Repellent, even.'

Politeness dictated that he lift his gaze, at which time his eyes betrayed him and flickered over the swell of her breasts. He dragged them away. 'Don't say that. You're gorgeous. Insanely so. It's just that . . .'

'What? You're gay? Married? On the run from the law?'

'No to everything.' A pause. 'It's not you. It's me.'

Contempt gleamed in her eyes. 'Oh. That old chestnut.'

She was cool after that. Clinical. Ignoring his protests, she led him upstairs to the bathroom, sat him on the edge of the tub and took the first-aid kit out of the medicine cabinet. Roughly but professionally, she applied pressure to the wound – a deep cut on the fleshy part of his palm. When it had stopped bleeding, she swabbed it with a vicious antiseptic. He winced at the sting of it and saw her smile.

After that, though, she was gentler. She perched on the enamel rim beside him, used Steri-Strips to 'stitch' the wound, and wrapped his hand and thumb in a gauze bandage. The small skylight window above them was open. The ocean roared softly.

Nick was mesmerised by the veins in her hands – her lifelines – exposed each time she passed the bandage over and under. She wasn't, he noticed, wearing a ring.

As if aware of his thoughts, her actions became more self-conscious. Twice she dropped the surgical tape. Her breathing grew shallower until he began to think that she'd stopped altogether.

A forcefield of chemistry surrounded them, binding them.

The pressure built in Nick's jeans. He was relieved she'd put a towel over his groin. He felt as if he was going to explode. As if, at any second, he was going to go off like a teenager. He risked a glance upwards. Desire licked in her blue-gold irises.

He swallowed. What was it she'd said about the flight response of horses? That was how far he wanted to run. He wanted to flee from this town, this cottage and especially from her, and never ever return.

'That's enough,' he said gruffly. 'Thanks for your help.'

She slapped him lightly on the arm. 'Be patient. I'm nearly done. What's your problem with me, anyway? What have I ever done to offend you? It's as if you can't stand to be near me.'

'Nothing!' He almost shouted it. 'You've done nothing.'

He sprang up so suddenly that he knocked her off the bath and had to grab her to keep her from falling. Self-preservation forced her to snatch at his shirt with one hand and his bicep with the other. Caught off balance, he fell forward himself and for an instant they were arched together like dancers.

With effort, he recovered and thrust her from him forcibly.

Tears shimmered in her eyes. She straightened her dress and half turned away from him.

'I'm sorry,' he said inadequately.

'There's something wrong with you,' she burst out. 'You have some sort of phobia about human contact. Or maybe it's just me. You have a phobia about me.'

Don't touch her, he thought.

Don't touch her.

Don't touch her.

Don't touch her.

Don't touch her.

He touched her.

Afterwards, Nick could never remember how they'd got from the bathroom to the bedroom. He only knew that he went from hell to heaven in the time it took to say her name. A trail of clothes marked their frantic passage. Then the wet, velvety heat of her was enclosing his hardness, and her mouth, soft as rose petals, was locked on his. They came within seconds of one another, her first, both crying out with animal sounds that Mr McKenna probably heard half a kilometre away.

'There's a lot to be said for delayed gratification,' murmured Nick as they lay moulded together in the aftermath.

'No, there isn't,' Sasha said indignantly. 'It's been torture.'

In the afternoon, they went for a picnic on the cliffs above Friday Beach, taking the champagne Jim and Jules had given Nick before he left London and drinking it out of coffee mugs. Sasha sat between his thighs, leaning against his chest, feeding him strawberries. Seagulls wheeled above the panorama of rocks and sea.

As to why she'd shown up unannounced at Seabird Cottage, startling Nick so much that he'd almost ended up in casualty, she'd said simply: 'I wanted to see you.'

Nick watched a guillemot perform a kamikaze dive. 'Dare I ask how Cullen is?'

'I don't have the faintest idea. Last time I saw him he was in the hospital, being fitted for a set of dentures.'

'You're kidding!'

She turned to face him. 'No, I'm not. He screwed one too many married women and a husband came home early one afternoon and registered his disapproval. With a seven-iron. Knocked out all his front teeth.'

Actions have consequences.

Nick laughed before he could stop himself. 'Sorry, but it couldn't have happened to a nicer guy.'

Her brow furrowed. 'You detested him, didn't you? It's understandable given the circumstances of your first meeting, but I never did figure out why you thought he might have stolen Oliver.'

With Cullen out of the picture, Nick was not about to go into his suspicions about what had or hadn't transpired with the dove, Oliver and Marillion. 'The way I see it, most character traits are common to everyone, to a greater or lesser degree. We're all capable of honesty or dishonesty, kindness or temper, good judgement or lack of it, laziness or industry. But cruelty is a choice. It's premeditated. You make a decision to inflict physical or emotional pain on a person or animal and then you act on it. Sometimes repeatedly. I find that incomprehensible.'

She was silent for a long time. 'He always found it difficult to forgive and forget. Little things would upset him – a client who tried to short-change him, or someone who spoke to him as if he were the hired help. He could harbour a grudge for years. When you walked into the shop and calmly but very confidently accused him of domestic violence, you belittled him. He was never going to let that go. Plus you're very hand-some – in a haunted, bachelor writer sort of way . . .'

'Thanks. I think.'

'Like a lot of cheats, he was insanely jealous. The reason he was in such a rage that day is because he'd got it into his head that I'd flirted with a customer.' She gave a short laugh. 'He was even jealous of Marillion. He couldn't stand how much I loved him. He saw all of life as a competition for my attention.'

She dipped a strawberry into her champagne and fed it to Nick.

'And yet you loved him enough to agree to marry him?'

'I guess it had become a habit. At school and in my early twenties, I worshipped him. He was a free spirit. We had so much fun. Plus he was as horse-mad as I was.'

'What changed?'

She took a sip of champagne and they kissed for a long time. He was so aroused he could have taken her there and then, but more than that he wanted to listen to her. For ever, if that was an option.

'Life. It disappointed him. As a teenager, I was a straight-A student. I'd decided very early on that I wanted to do a nursing degree and I worked for it. When I left school I was fortunate enough to be accepted into the university I chose and end up in a job I loved. Before I gave it up to take care of Dad, I was having a ball.

'Cullen, on the other hand, was obsessed with becoming a racehorse trainer. He spent five years and every penny he possessed trying to break into the scene. With zero success. For whatever reason, it didn't work out for him. There were a couple of bad accidents – not his fault, but he acquired a reputation and it stuck. He's a gifted horseman, but the experience soured him. He could never think of horses in quite the same way. There were times when I wondered whether on some level he actively hated them. Eventually, he had to admit defeat. He qualified as a plumber – a good job and one in which he makes a lot of money, but not exactly what he'd pictured for himself.'

'And the lonely housewives – when did that start?'

'When I was in London we had an open relationship. Or rather, he had one. It wasn't going to work any other way. I came back to Lanton when my father got Alzheimer's. Cullen and I got back together and he promised to be faithful. It didn't take me long to figure out that the name of his business, In and Out Plumbing, was literal. Back then I excused it because Dad occupied so much of my time. It's ironic, but I was the one who felt guilty. I blamed myself for being permanently exhausted and never in the mood for making love. I figured that the screwing around would stop once we were married and he felt secure about me.'

The breeze had chilled and Sasha had goosebumps. Nick wrapped his arms around her. 'I'd put both hands in a furnace before I cheated on you. No, I take that back. I'll never cheat on you. Period.'

As soon as the words were out of his mouth, he regretted them. 'Sorry, that sounded presumptuous. I'm not assuming that . . . I mean, I'd like . . . but, you know, I'm aware that you've only just . . .'

Sasha laughed. 'I'm not assuming anything either, but on the subject of cheating I can promise you one thing. You'll never have a reason to.'

She unzipped his jeans. 'Now, if you're done talking, there's something I'd like to try.'

Later, they lay in the oak bed and listened to the waves storm up to the rocks at the bottom of the garden. Oliver was snuggled into the crook of Sasha's right arm.

'Will we ever be this happy again?' she asked.

'Yes, a million times.'

He fell asleep with her heart against his and her breath on his cheek, smelling of champagne and strawberries.

When he woke up she was gone.

9

In contrast to every other obituary dream, it was late afternoon before he remembered it.

At the time, he was checking his phone for messages. Until a couple of hours earlier he'd been too preoccupied by the note Sasha had left on her empty pillow to be concerned about why she hadn't called: *Be seeing you x.*

Was there ever a more ambivalent sentence? What did it mean? Was she saying that it would be great to bump into him if their paths happened to cross in the supermarket? Or would she actively be seeking him out? If so, when? Today? Next month? In three years' time?

Nick felt profoundly annoyed by his own insecurity. Usually when he slept with women he couldn't wait to see the back of them. He'd have been overjoyed if the vast majority of them had crept out before he woke up and was forced to recall their names and any drunken promises he might have made, or had to face them over the breakfast table when their hair was sticking up on end and they were looking round his apartment and, after one shag, sizing him up as a marriage prospect.

Be seeing you x, with its open-ended meaning and non-committal kiss on the end, was the kind of line he'd have written himself once upon a time. But it was the last thing he wanted to receive from Sasha. His only thought before sleep had claimed him had been: I can't wait to see her lovely face in the morning.

But when he'd awoken, her lovely face was gone, as was her lovely lithe body, and he hadn't a clue when he'd be seeing either again.

At 12.45 he rang the gift shop, hoping to catch her on her lunch break if she had one. Unfortunately, Mrs Moreton answered. He hung up without speaking. By mid-afternoon he was checking his phone at regular intervals. By four, he was wondering whether it was broken and if he should race into Lanton and replace it.

To distract himself, he brewed a coffee he didn't want to drink and prepared a sandwich he couldn't face eating.

'An impossible dream,' he said to Oliver, who was draped across the back of the sofa, basking in a square of sunlight. 'That's what this is.' The cat stretched and went back to sleep.

That was all it took. One word.

Nick had the Turkish coffee pot in his left hand and was checking for messages with his right when a remembered nightmare came roaring into his brain like an express train. The silver pot hit the kitchen tiles with a crash, splattering his jeans with boiling liquid. Fragments of his mobile joined the stew.

Billowing colours: red, yellow, white, blue, green.

Mr McKenna crossing the horizon on his tractor.

The post van pulling out of the drive.

Sasha turning to smile at him over her shoulder.

Marillion rearing.

Nick slid to the floor, arms wrapped tightly around himself. He reviewed the images without being able to make head or tail of them. It was impossible to see how they were related. For all he knew they were random.

When the dark clouds receded, he found himself sitting in a puddle of cooling coffee. From a dry perch on the kitchen counter, Oliver watched him anxiously.

'You poor bugger,' said Nick. 'It can't be easy living with a nutcase.'

It took him the best part of twenty minutes to clean the kitchen. The Turkish coffee pot was intact, but droplets of coffee had found their way into every conceivable nook and cranny. His mobile phone was beyond help. Now if Sasha did call, he'd never know. She'd decide that he was as bad as that bastard Cullen, and never contact him again. At the present moment Nick found that a relief.

In the upstairs shower, barely a metre from where he'd kissed her for the first time, Nick scrubbed himself raw. He had already made up his mind to have no further contact with Sasha. It would be agony, but he could see no other choice. It was the honourable thing to do. The right thing to do. It might also be the only way that he could save her life.

He closed his eyes and leaned against the shower wall. A tidal wave of self-loathing swept over him. If he hadn't frittered away those fateful few minutes back in October and been late for the train, his life would not have been derailed. Would not, in effect, have been cursed. He would not now be in a position where he had to walk away from the most incredible woman he had ever known and never see her again.

It was not until he was sitting on the bench staring disconsolately out to sea that evening that he realised how illogical this was.

All but one of the people in his obituary dreams had been strangers. He'd only had the briefest of contact with each of them. In the case of Vanessa Diaz, he'd done no more than watch her on television. And yet in not one instance had he been able to save them. The only person with whom he'd had any prolonged contact was Pattie Griffin, whom he had been able to help. Pattie's recovery had, in actuality, been so dramatic that she'd been back in her studio within ten days, restoring sofas. The magnificent couch in the living room, which Oliver was under pain of death not to scratch, was one of Pattie's. In between saving whales and firing off missives to the *Telegraph,* she salvaged them from tips or street corners and worked her magic on them. Nick's intervention at the bus stop had enabled that magic to continue.

Viewed in that light, Nick could be Sasha's guardian angel. If the pictures in his dream did turn out to be a prediction of some kind, he might be able to spot the threat in advance. He could protect her. She *needed* him.

More to the point, he needed her.

'What are you thinking about?' she asked.

He started guiltily. She was perched on the final tier of the garden, a little way above him. He had no idea how long she'd been there. 'You.'

'What about me?' She walked down the steps and sat beside him on the bench. They were separated by an expanse of salt-scarred wood, not touching. The tide was coming in. Seagulls dipped and cried over the ocean.

He reached for her hand, but she pulled it away.

'I should leave. I'm not sure why I came. I should have driven away when I knocked at the back door and got no response. Instead, I felt compelled to find you. God knows why.'

'Sasha, what's going on?'

'It's too soon. For this. For us. And maybe there'll never be a right

143

time. I've only been out of a long-term relationship for a month and, as you so succinctly told me, you don't want or need anyone. You have your work.'

New Zealand

Tristan da Cunha

An icebreaker cutting through the blue bergs of Antarctica.

There was still time for him to walk away from his life with nothing but the clothes on his back and Oliver. But if he were gone, who would protect her? More importantly, who would love her?

Nick stood up and walked over to the rocks that were all that stopped Seabird Cottage from being swallowed by the ocean. 'You're right. I've never wanted or needed anyone. I've made damn sure of it.'

Without knowing he was going to do it, he told her something he'd never told another living soul. Not even Becca. About how he'd planned to catch a train to Oxfordshire to see his parents one Saturday when he was twenty-four years old. It was their thirtieth wedding anniversary and his mother was cooking a special dinner. He'd promised her he'd be there; had given her his word. He'd told her how much he was looking forward to it.

On the way to the station he'd stopped for a quick pint at his favourite pub. One had become two, three, five and eight, because his mates had turned up and kept buying rounds. Somewhere in between he'd struck up a conversation with a dense but sexy beautician. Later, she'd blown him in the toilets. The last thing he remembered before he collapsed in a drunken stupor in the room of his university digs was starting to dial his parents' number. In the end he was too ashamed to call.

Behind him Sasha made no response. For all he knew she could have left. Still, he forced himself on.

He told her how he'd never forgiven himself for not being there to snatch his mum and dad from the path of the sleeping juggernaut driver as they drove to church the following morning. How he'd been haunted by the pain he'd caused his mother on her last night on earth, and the knowledge that his parents' final thoughts about him would have been ones of hurt and disappointment. How even in death he felt he'd failed them, because there was nothing he could do to shield them from the prying eyes of the police or the coroner. How something inside of him had shut down that day. How he'd turned away from the lie that was God. How he'd never again allowed anyone in.

'In case they went out the door and never came back?'

'I expect that's what a shrink would say.'

'In case you made them a promise that you couldn't keep?'

He didn't answer. There was more to it than that, but there was no point going into it. If he told her about his obituary dreams she'd run a country mile.

He thought she might anyway and was startled when he felt her breath on his neck as she said his name. Turning, he found himself pressed up against her. She'd come up behind him like a wraith.

'Thank you for telling me,' she said softly. 'It helps me understand who you are and who you've been. There's just one more thing . . .'

The contours of her body were warm against his. He had a flashback to the previous afternoon when he'd made love to her on the picnic blanket on the cliffs, the sea pounding far below. The corresponding rush of blood made him dizzy.

'You said there was one more thing?'

She pulled away in order to read his expression. 'Why are you here? In Lanton, I mean. For what it's worth, Cullen is convinced that you're either a certified lunatic or a criminal with a past, as is half the village; Pattie Griffin thinks you're the closest thing to a knight in shining armour the twenty-first century has to offer; and our local mis-anthropist, Gordon McKenna, seems to have a grudging regard for you – a world first when it comes to outsiders, let me tell you. Mum's theory has always been that you came here to recover from a broken heart.'

'What's your opinion?'

'To begin with, I went along with a relationship breakdown as the most likely explanation. Why else would you be so reclusive, moody and driven? Then I heard you were a writer and thought it possible that you had writer's block.'

'And now? What do you think now?'

'After yesterday I don't know. Sunday was one of the most blissful days of my life, but it doesn't alter the fact that your past is full of secrets. Frankly, that terrifies me.'

The tide was roaring in and peppering them with icy drops. Nick took her hand and led her inside. He poured her a glass of Cloudy Bay and built a fire with pinecones, newspaper and Mr McKenna's best logs.

She regarded him warily from the sofa.

'Can I persuade you to stay for dinner? I'm not sure what I have in the cupboard, but if you don't mind pot luck . . .'

'You were telling me how you came to be in Lanton.'

Smothering a sigh, Nick tossed down the poker. 'The short version is, I came here because I had nowhere else to go. Initially, my plan was to stay a week or two, long enough to get my bearings until I figured out what to do next. I'd been involved in a crash and it had triggered a mid-life crisis. I'd burnt a lot of bridges. My whole identity was tied up with what I did. When I lost my ability to do it, I no longer knew who I was. That changed when I came to Cornwall. Within hours of arriving in Sadie's igloo of a cottage I saw a fox and that started me on the path to remembering. By then I was already in love with the place.'

She sipped her wine and watched him over the top of her glass. 'What is it that you do? For a living, I mean.'

'I'm an obituary writer. *Was* an obituary writer.'

Out of the corner of his eye, he watched for her reaction. Women tended to take his career choice badly. A reporter for *The Times* was generally well received. A journalist who wrote about dead people was creepy.

'You're such a talented writer, Nick, why can't you write about something beautiful?' one ex-girlfriend had demanded. 'Writing obituaries seems morbid. Depressing. It can't be healthy, day after day, a constant parade of death.'

'What would you have me write about, Camille?' he'd demanded. 'What constitutes a nice subject, in your opinion? Stella McCartney dresses? Luxury holidays to the Bahamas? Hollywood stars?'

Which wasn't what he'd meant at all. What he'd really wanted to say was that, to him, writing obituaries was beautiful. Not always, obviously. Not in the case of assassinated mafia dons or movie stars who'd over-self-medicated. But more often than not, an obituary bookended a life of quiet heroism or sublime achievement. At other times, it put a full stop on a simple life lived well. A lot of obituaries were testimonials to the triumph of the human spirit. They were good news.

'You're an obituary writer!' Sasha was incredulous.

'Is that funny?'

She sobered. 'No, of course not. It's just that the obit page is my favourite bit of any paper, although I particularly enjoy the one in *The Times*. It's the first thing I turn to. Cullen used to find it macabre. I'd try to explain that, to me, obituaries are a celebration of life.'

She came to a decision. 'All right. I'll stay for dinner . . . But then I'm going,' she added, in case he got any ideas. 'Anyway, you need someone to repair your dressing. You've done a horrible job with the bandage.'

'Sasha . . .'

'Mmm?'

'Shut up and let me kiss you.'

For dinner they ate the food she'd brought and almost taken away again, a rich, garlicky arrabbiata sauce served with fresh fettuccine and salad. They wiped their bowls with crusty white bread.

In the grate, Mr McKenna's best logs hissed, crackled and popped. After clearing away their plates, Nick hauled the sofa nearer to it. He and Sasha sat entwined, eating homemade vanilla ice cream drizzled with melted chocolate and kissing at intervals.

'Did you bring your toothbrush?'

Sasha slipped a hand beneath his denim shirt. 'Nick, in case it's skipped your mind, we only got together yesterday.'

He licked chocolate off the corner of her mouth. 'You think we're taking it too slowly?'

She giggled. 'Has anyone ever told you that you're incorrigible? If we took it any faster I'd go into orbit. I feel as if I'm in the eye of a hurricane, travelling at twice the speed of sound. Seriously, Nick . . .'

'Seriously, Sasha,' he mimicked. 'Look, we could waste a lot of time playing the usual *Men Are From Mars, Woman Are From Venus* games, or we could agree that I've spent thirty-eight years without you and you've spent – how old are you?'

'I was twenty-nine on December twenty-sixth.'

'A Christmas baby? Don't worry, I'll buy you two presents . . . So you've spent twenty-nine years without me. Speaking for myself, I do not, if I have any choice in the matter, want to spend another minute of my life without you.'

'I don't want to spend another minute without you either, but . . .'

'So don't. Tomorrow morning we can book a moving van and

everything you possess can be relocated from . . . Where are you living at the moment? At the place you shared with Cullen?'

'At my mum's. I packed my bags and walked out on Cullen within hours of him being admitted to hospital with no teeth and several broken ribs. Call me unsupportive, but enough's enough.'

'Okay, so we'll get a moving van to collect everything you own from your mum's and brought to Seabird Cottage. If you want to be here, that is. If not, I can move in with you. Not at Mrs Moreton's house, obviously, but anywhere you choose in Cornwall. Or we can go somewhere else entirely.'

She got up to stoke the fire. Sparks flew. 'What you've done with Seabird Cottage . . . it's transformed. Anyone would want to live here. But Nick, do you know what you're saying?'

'I'm saying that I want your cosmetics cluttering up my bathroom and your breeches thrown over the back of the armchair in my – *our* – bedroom. I'm saying that I want your face to be the last thing I see before I go to sleep every night and the first thing I see every morning.'

Sasha snuggled up to him again. 'I thought this was the kind of thing only lesbians do – meet on Sunday, move in Monday.'

Nick raised his eyebrows. 'Is that what they do? Do you know, I've long thought that gay women are some of the most sensible people on the planet.'

Later, he watched over her as she dreamed in the oak bed. Her face, bathed in the silver light of a full moon, was wholly peaceful and ethereal. The intensity of his feelings for her made his heart feel too big for his chest. He prayed to the God he wasn't sure existed that he was equipped for the challenges ahead. Some instinct told him that those challenges would be formidable, and that they would be many.

'I love you,' he whispered, startling himself. His mum and dad aside, they were three words he'd never uttered to anyone.

He was sliding into oblivion when he heard her say, 'I love you, too.'

At dawn, something compelled him to get out of bed. He left Sasha sleeping and went downstairs with Oliver to make coffee and open the back door.

The black typewriter was sitting on his desk in front of the living-room window that overlooked the sea. Setting down his mug, he rolled in a clean white sheet of paper. Experimentally, he typed: CHAPTER ONE. The clacking of keys sounded thunderclap-loud to him. He hoped it wouldn't wake Sasha.

He scrolled down the page. The story he wanted to tell was very close to him and he wondered if that indicated a wholesale lack of imagination. But in the end, wasn't everything autobiographical?

Oliver jumped onto the desk and made himself comfortable on Nick's sweater. The orange sun crept slowly above the shifting line of sea. Nick inhaled a shot of industrial-strength black coffee.

He typed: *The thing he remembered afterwards was that the clock was changing to thirteen as he rushed onto the platform. The rear lights of the train he should have been on – so easily could have been on . . .*

10

The shipping forecast was predicting a 'north-westerly four or five, occasionally six' and a 'moderate or rough' sea state when Sasha threw open the patio doors, breathed in the mineral-laden wind and said: 'Let's sail around the coast to Botallack and go exploring.'

Nick followed her out. 'Let's not. It looks like rain.'

She took the cup of coffee he handed her. 'Darling, there's hardly a cloud in the sky.' When he didn't respond she said: 'Well, I fancy going. You're welcome to stay here and write.'

Nick hesitated. Sailing had its risks, but if it would keep Sasha away from the horse that stalked his nightmares, it had to be done. He forced a smile. 'What? And miss the chance to be out on the ocean with you? You must be kidding. What's a small storm between lovers anyway? We're not going to melt.'

Sasha pressed her mouth to his. 'Besides, there's this little secluded cove I know . . .'

It was never going to be easy. That much he'd known. What he hadn't anticipated was that it would be like walking through a shelled-out town, watching for a sniper.

In London, his nightmares had always yielded up some clue as to cause of death. His current, recurring one could mean anything or nothing. Had it not been preceded by the familiar sensation of walking along a dripping, dark tunnel, his legs like concrete but moving forward against his will, he'd have questioned whether it was an obituary dream at all.

He found it impossible to interpret the five signs, if that's what they were.

Billowing colours: scarlet, marigold yellow, forest green, white and ultramarine blue.

Mr McKenna crossing the horizon on his tractor.
The post van pulling out of the drive.
Sasha smiling over her shoulder.
Marillion rearing.

Mr McKenna was forever roaring about on his tractor, the post van visited the farm three or four times a week, Sasha smiled all the time and Marillion reared at the drop of a hat. As for the rippling colours, millions of things had some or all of those hues, but Nick could think of nothing that had them in that particular sequence or shape.

He could not even be sure who, if anyone, was in danger. For all he knew, the horse could be the potential victim after bolting his required flight distance. Not a person. Not Sasha. After all, it was Marillion, not her, that had caused his fingers to tingle.

'Penny for them?'

Sasha was standing in the doorway in jeans and a pale blue vest, her red bikini beneath. She had towels and waterproofs slung over one arm.

'I was thinking about how much you love Marillion. Would you ever consider selling him? What I mean is, if it turned out that he wasn't suitable for your riding centre or something?'

There was a note of warning in Sasha's tone. 'Just so you know, nothing on earth would induce me to part with Marillion. We belong to each other, he and I. The trouble with Cullen was he never understood that.'

On the contrary, he understands it only too well. Nick found it difficult to think of her ex in the past tense. It seemed too good to be true. Only yesterday Annie Entwhistle had mentioned 'in passing' that Cullen had left town with no forwarding address, but Nick found it hard to believe they'd seen the last of him

He put his lips to the satin skin on the nape of her neck. 'As someone who started a bar-room brawl over a missing cat, I feel I've proven where my loyalties lie when it comes to animals.'

She laughed and the moment passed. 'So you have. Now if you're not ready in five minutes, I'm setting sail without you.'

She handled the thirty-two-foot yacht with the same natural-born ease with which she rode horses and made love, and Nick thrilled to the snap of sails and the Prussian blue ocean rolling sensuously beneath them.

'Has it occurred to you that this could put p-p-paid to our sex life?' he'd asked her during the course of the previous day's riding lesson, as he bumped painfully around the school on Caprice.

'Men have been riding bucking broncos and galloping bareback across plains for centuries with no obvious ill effects. Concentrate and try to rise on the diagonal. When her right foreleg is going forward, you should be going up. Relax and you'll find yourself doing it naturally. Horse riding is a lot like making love. All you have to do is find your rhythm and go with the flow.'

Nick had gritted his teeth and willed the time to pass quickly. He'd had three riding lessons in three days and everything hurt. So far, he'd struggled to see the appeal of equestrianism, although he had no trouble understanding the allure of horses in general. They fascinated him. Partly because he saw in them a means of understanding Sasha, but also because he appreciated the wonder of them. Their athleticism, sensitivity and intelligent, dark eyes. They were barometers of kindness.

Prior to coming to Lanton, his only experience of horses had been a three-hour trek with Becca during a university camping weekend on Dartmoor. Had a bomb exploded in the ear of the piebald cob he'd been assigned, it would not have moved one step faster. If Nick had been informed that the beast had passed away several years before, been stuffed by a taxidermist and returned to service with a failing battery, he'd not have been surprised in the least.

But Sasha's horses – with their radar ears, velvet muzzles and traumatic pasts – were bewitching. It was a privilege to earn their trust. Every morning and evening for two weeks now, he'd groomed seven of them – all except Marillion – while Sasha lunged or did lateral work with the black horse and any other requiring special attention. A girl from the village came during the day and exercised the rest. His London friends would never have believed it, but Nick enjoyed the routine of mucking out stables and buffing dull coats to a shine. He'd volunteered for the job, overriding Sasha's protests. Without Cullen, she'd been doing almost everything on her own.

Sasha preferred to brush and feed Marillion herself, explaining somewhat unnecessarily that he could be a trifle unpredictable. She never let anyone else ride him. Nick was relieved. It saved him the trouble of thinking up an excuse for staying away from the beast.

Taking care of the horses forced him out of bed early. It cleared his head before his writing day.

That in itself was a miracle, that he had a writing day. The slim sheaf of manuscript beside the old typewriter was growing at a glacial pace but it was growing all the same. That was all that mattered.

Why the block had unblocked, he was reluctant to question. He was only conscious that everything felt new and precious: Sasha; the horses; writing; *life*.

He leaned forward as the yacht, an old Contessa 32, bequeathed to Sasha by her father, rode another blue-green swell. When a wave curled over the bow and threatened to swamp them, he laughed out loud at the adventure of it.

The old tin mines of Botallack were dotted along three and a half miles of the Land's End peninsula, clinging to the black granite cliffs like castle ruins. For centuries St Just miners had risked life and limb to work the submarine shafts for copper and tin. Father and son had toiled side by side in cramped, lethal conditions hundreds of fathoms beneath the sea. They'd hand-drilled shot holes and blasted them with gunpowder.

Touching the stone walls of the engine rooms, which perched on the extreme edge of a grassy cliff edge, put Nick's worries of the morning into perspective. The dangers faced by the men and boys who'd descended daily into the deepest shaft, some 500 metres below sea level and stretching almost as far out into the ocean, had been real rather than imagined. No amount of money could have convinced him to do the same. It was hard to think of an environment more nightmarish than those dank, claustrophobic tunnels with the sea pressing down on them. The bone-lacerating cold in winter. The killing fumes. Surely the bravery of any man capable of enduring such a career was at least equal to that of any soldier.

Sasha took his hand and led him up the steep path. 'My father used to bring me here all the time when he was teaching me to sail. He believed it was important as a way of honouring the men who worked so hard here, and those who lost their lives. There were a series of awful tragedies at Botallack in the late 1800s that eventually led to the shutting of the mine. In the worst accident, nineteen men and a boy were drowned.'

It explained the eerie feel of the place. Human endeavour had been thwarted by greed and nature. Still, it was hard not to be won over by the magnificence of the landscape. Birds, butterflies and bees flitted among clifftop heather and hedgerows alive with colour. Thyme, thrift, sea campion and centaury. Each breath was an aromatic rush. Two wide-eyed seals rose and fell on the waves far below.

They picked their way between the spiky gorse and starry succulents, squinting in the sun's golden glare. Interspersed with fuchsia-pink heather was moss so thick and springy that Sasha kept pausing to bounce on it like a delighted child.

'If there are ghosts here, they must be nice ones,' Nick said.

She gave him an appreciative glance. 'I think that's true. As a child, I used to have nightmares about skeletons crawling from the disused shafts. Botallack always held a mixture of fear and fascination for me. But gradually, I came to see it through Dad's eyes, as an almost spiritual place – a place to honour. That's why I wanted to share it with you.'

And her fingers, threaded through his, squeezed tighter.

The lone occupant of the secluded cove was a cormorant. The tidal pool was several degrees warmer than the sea but still gasp-cold. They stripped off and paddled like seals, pausing to kiss and fool around. Nick thought he'd never desired a woman more. He felt dizzy with it.

They dried off on the warm black granite, gulls wheeling overhead. Nick lay on his front watching Sasha. Arms behind her head, she gazed up at the sky. Her pale, fit body was a study in sculpted perfection, her nipples hard beneath the thread of polka-dotted red bikini. Water-dark tendrils of her hair were splayed across the rock.

'Your riding-centre dream,' he said. 'When did it start?'

She was silent for so long that he wondered if she'd heard him. Her gaze never left the slowly knitting wisps of cloud. 'It came in increments. It was never a conscious decision. The thing they don't teach you in nursing school is that fate is no respecter of circumstance or age. Nobody explains that there'll be days when children as wise as old men will wipe away your tears because nothing has equipped you to deal with the pain you will necessarily cause them. No medical journal admits that those same kids will be brought to their knees, not as you'd imagine by the betrayals of their own body, but by a system designed to dehumanise them. Nobody tells you that you'll be forced to stand by and watch proud, vital men like my father become trapped by their minds or bodies until they're no better than birds in cages.'

Nick thought of Matthew lashing out at him through the bars of his loathsome new cage. *Your idea of a bad day is getting to Marks and Spencer and finding they've sold out of smoked salmon.*

'Was it rescuing Marillion that inspired you to start a place where horses and people could heal each other?'

'Marillion was the start of everything, but each new horse has taken me one step further. They all have something to teach and something to learn. And it's not just about healing. Riding is a great equaliser. It removes gender, age and disability from the equation. A strong horse can make a man with no limbs feel whole. That same man's compassion can change the destiny of a traumatised horse. It's an exchange.'

Nick traced the outline of her hips with gentle fingers. 'An exchange that costs money. Even with Mr McKenna's rent-free land, it's not exactly going to be a cheap proposition.'

'Believe me, everyone from my mother to my bank manager thinks I'm crazy. Not that it'll stop me.'

'I don't think you're crazy.'

'You don't?'

'All achievements, even the tiny ones, are only dreams made real. Most start with a picture or a feeling or an embarrassed kernel of hope.' He thought of his novel, just such a kernel, and wished he were better at taking his own advice.

'I'll bear that in mind,' murmured Sasha, and she reached for him again.

They were blasted awake by the storm's fat drops. It stung their exposed limbs and smacked down on the rocks. The sea was a grey-green cauldron.

'It might be best to try to get out of here by road,' said Nick as they tugged on wet clothes. 'We could flag down a passing car. We'll return for the boat when the weather improves.'

But Sasha was already moving towards the wall of rocks that separated them from the cove where the sailboat was moored. 'The tide will have cut off the cliff path. Our only way out of here is by sea. Don't worry, there's a radio on board if we get into trouble.'

Nick felt a stab of misgiving, but he refused to acknowledge it. He grabbed the rucksack and ran to catch up with her. 'Careful, Sasha,' he cautioned as she slipped and almost fell on the first rock she stepped on.

All he got was her back, moving upwards and away from him. If anything, she climbed even faster. He rushed to close the gap between them, skidding once and bashing his ankle on a rock. The pain was so excruciating that for a moment he thought it was broken. Unfortunately, there was no time to stop and examine it. The incoming surf was foaming at his heels.

He was below and slightly to the left of Sasha when she reached the top of the bluff. The wind slammed into her, catching her off balance. From Nick's angle, she seemed to pitch into space, out over the ocean. How he caught her he would never know. In the lashing rain, on ice-rink rocks, he moved with the speed and strength of gods and monsters.

Yet even as she clung to him, a blinding rage came over him. Furiously, he held her from him. 'Dammit, Sasha, how am I supposed to protect you when you're forever taking risks and putting yourself in harm's way?'

The shutters came down in her eyes. She dropped her hands and twisted away from him. Her tone was more chilling than the wind and rain. 'Don't smother me, Nick. I'm not made of glass. That's not who I am.'

They were almost at the boat when Nick spotted something he'd not noticed previously. The *Cassandra* was painted white with a thin stripe of ultramarine blue. The spinnaker was red, marigold yellow and green. Together they made up the colours in his recurring nightmare.

Dread trickled like acid through his veins. The game, if that's what it was, was on. His dream was unfolding. Disastrously, he was unprepared to do anything about it. His university single-handed dinghy-sailing skills had been based more on fitness, willpower and daring than technique. He'd never tackled anything other than mildly choppy seas.

They got off to a bad start. Clambering over the stern rail, Nick tripped over the VHF radio antenna, snapping it. They wouldn't be radioing anyone. That might have been less of a disaster had Sasha not left her mobile lying exposed by the tiller. It was now swimming in brine.

'It's unlikely we'd have been able to get a signal even if it was working,' said Nick, trying to make amends for his outburst. 'Don't worry about it; we'll be fine. Tell me what you need me to do and I'll do it.'

If Sasha heard him over the storm's roar, she didn't acknowledge it. She was reefing the mainsail and tying it to the boom with practised efficiency. Her face was set, but not afraid. She gave the impression that she'd have managed with or without him.

Once at the mercy of the elements, however, they had no choice but to work as a team. Nick paid out long ropes at the back of the boat, looped two wavelengths back to slow it down. Sasha worked to helm the yacht safely through the swells that came at them from every angle. The water thwacked the hull like concrete.

It became a test of nerve and endurance, made harder by the ocean's numbing bite. Nick felt oddly calm. His limbs were leaden, his reactions dulled by cold, but his mind was razor-sharp. He felt as if he were watching himself from a distance. Whatever happened next was going to happen and there was very little they could do about it.

Twice the mast tipped so low it almost touched the water. The third time, a wave hit them broadside before they could right the boat, coming over the beam in an avalanche of white. Instinctively Nick gulped in a breath. It was his last before he was swept into the ocean, slamming hard against the boat edge as he went.

Death by a thousand cuts. That's what the freezing surf felt like. Down he went, pummelled by the current, his hands unable to locate his safety line. Which way was up? There was nothing but blackness and bubbles. Every promise of air, of release, came to naught.

Sasha. Where was Sasha?

Time expanded the way it had during the train crash. Only a few months ago this was exactly what he'd wanted. An easy exit from the torment of his nightmares. The beckoning embrace of the grave. But not now. Now he wanted life. Life and Sasha. Life *with* Sasha, for better or worse.

His lungs screamed for air. Fuelled by a burst of adrenalin, he kicked out with all his might. His fingers found the safety line. Again and again he pulled for the surface. Again and again it receded. Then, quite suddenly, the night air was fresh on his face and he was sucking in oxygen so fast it hurt. The boat was before him, somehow upright.

The panic he felt when he heaved himself aboard and saw no sign of Sasha made everything he'd been through since the crash seem as nothing. Her safety line was broken. Frantically, he scoured the grey ocean. The rain was abating, making it easier to see, but she had vanished. His cries were guttural. If he'd believed in prayer, he'd have begged God for help, but he didn't. There was nothing and no one out there. He and Sasha were alone. He wanted to fling himself back into the ocean, dive deep and search for her, but he knew that would mean certain death for both of them.

If I'd seen the colours sooner, if I'd made the link, this wouldn't have happened. I'd have made some excuse. I'd have done everything in my power to stop her from going sailing today.

She burst to the surface, coughing up sea water. With each fresh wave threatening to wash her further away, Nick snatched a spare halyard from the mast, attached it to the safety line and threw it to her. On his fourth attempt, she caught it. The cockpit winch did the rest.

When he reached out and pulled her on-board, she collapsed on the deck, as white as the sail. All he could offer her was his thin wind-cheater. With what remained of his strength, he got the yacht moving again. It was a good ten minutes before Sasha sat up. Nick put an arm around her and pointed. They were in sight of home.

At Lanton Harbour, Sasha made no protest when Nick anchored the yacht. Nor did she resist when he held out his hand for the car keys. The fury that had blazed through him on the bluff was long gone. He was glad that the rain on his face and the looming darkness masked the extent of his emotion.

When they walked through the door of Seabird Cottage, Nick switched on the kitchen light. Sasha tried half-heartedly to stop him. Her eyes were the colour of the sea they'd left behind. There was a pleading in them.

'Warm me up, Nick,' was all she said.

He lifted her into his arms and carried her upstairs to the shower, where he stripped her of her wet things and shampooed the salt from her hair. Afterwards, she did the same for him. The ankle he'd bashed on the rock was purple. Neither of them spoke. They stood beneath the scalding water until they'd stopped shivering. Steam rose from their mottled skin.

After he'd dried Sasha and put her to bed, Nick swaddled them both in a duvet and blankets and kissed her swollen lips. The heat of her when he thrust into her was almost shocking.

12

'I know what you're thinking and I don't want to hear it,' Nick told Mr McKenna when he stopped by the farmhouse for eggs and vegetables the following Sunday.

'Still warm from the nest,' the farmer said, tapping the carton. 'Don't get that in Tesco. And don't let me find you've wasted a single one of my good vine tomatoes. Have a sniff of them. Sunshine in a salad they are. No need for dressing. Not like the ones you find in the Lanton grocer. You'd get more flavour if you put ketchup on a sponge.'

The fruit's rich, iron smell started Nick's stomach rumbling. Mr McKenna's tomatoes were one of the many reasons he'd fallen in love with Cornwall.

'It's no use pretending that you couldn't care less. I *know* you. Your disapproval is obvious. But Sasha and I are consenting adults. We know what we're doing. We don't need your opinion or your advice.'

'Wouldn't waste my breath,' Mr McKenna responded mildly. 'You'll not be the sort to take a well-meaning word. Only don't say I didn't warn you.'

'Wouldn't dream of it.' Nick hoisted the box onto his shoulder. 'Look, I'd have been the first to agree with you that she's not for the likes of me. But she seems to feel differently.'

The farmer made a great show of lighting his pipe. He took several leisurely puffs, blowing clouds into the sky. 'If you say so.'

'I do.'

'So you'll not be minding that young Cullen's back in town? And with the Hollywood smile. Not courtesy of the NHS, I'll be betting.'

'Don't care. Nothing to do with me. Live and let live, that's my motto.'

'Just as well,' said Mr McKenna, 'because he's down at the stables with Sasha.'

At Seabird Cottage, Nick filled a wastepaper basket with pages of meaningless phrases. He couldn't focus on his novel. He kept picturing Cullen and Sasha as he'd first seen them, locked in some intense, emotional battle, their beautiful faces close together.

Possessiveness was not his style. Never had been. He'd never acted the jealous boyfriend. He couldn't stand that in men – the implication that women were objects to be owned, collected or controlled. That they were status symbols like BMWs or Rolex watches. What he loved best about Sasha was that she was exactly as Mr McKenna had described, as 'independently minded as that wild horse of hers'.

To say that he didn't like the thought of Sasha shooting the breeze with her ex was an understatement, but under ordinary circumstances he'd have coped. He'd have stewed quietly about it, probably been a little nervous about it, but he'd have rationalised it and soon moved on.

But he didn't trust Cullen. Not one inch. He'd been too quiet. In some ways, that was hardly surprising. The most arrogant man alive would have been humbled by a seven-iron bashing and the simultaneous loss of his front teeth, his fiancée and, one assumed, his mistress. As conceited as Cullen was, he was far from being that. However, he did consider revenge a dish best served cold.

What were they doing? What were they saying? He trusted Sasha, but . . .

There was no but. He trusted her. Full stop.

There was a pounding at the door. Nick's chair went flying as he rushed to get it, tripping over Oliver, who was chasing a ball of mangled prose.

'Nice out today, fresh and clear, makes you feel alive, a day for the beach and not for the van, sign here,' said Annie Entwhistle in her usual stream of consciousness way. 'Sasha not in?'

On an ordinary occasion, Nick found it difficult to decide which part of the postwoman's rapid-fire delivery to respond to. Today he mumbled: 'Absolutely. Thanks, Annie, on the phone, gotta run.'

He seized the box from her – fly repellent for the horses, ordered by Sasha – and purposefully shut the door with his shoulder. As it slammed closed, he saw Mr McKenna on his tractor, crossing the horizon. He wrenched it open again. The post van was pulling out of the drive. Two images from his nightmare.

A thrill of horror went through him. Cullen was alone with Sasha.

He snatched his car keys from the hook near the kitchen door. The delivery gave him the excuse he'd been wishing for. Now he would not be the jealous boyfriend, tearing up to the stables as if he were afraid of what he might find. He'd be the caring partner, so concerned for the wellbeing of Sasha's horses that he wasted not a moment in delivering their fly treatment. 'Why Cullen, fancy meeting you here,' he could say in a relaxed, friendly tone. 'How's life treating you these days? Played any golf recently?'

He was so determined to appear casual and on the right side of sane, especially to Mr McKenna, bumping across a field in his tractor, that he drove at half his normal speed in the direction of the stables. He'd been wrong before and could be again. On the other hand, the BBC had recently reported that domestic violence was at an all-time high. One in five women were victims. Statistically, most women were killed by someone they knew.

Sasha knows that I would never harm one hair on her head, don't you, sweetness?

The memory made Nick accelerate.

He was approaching the edge of the copse when Cullen's truck shot from the track signposted No Entry. It seemed to Nick that he emerged in a guilty rush, though there was no trace of anxiety in his demeanour when he pulled up alongside the Mustang.

Nick climbed out of the car and leaned against the door, arms folded. Cullen didn't follow suit.

'Good day ta you, Nick, me old mate,' he said, leaning from his window in an open-necked black shirt and flashing teeth that would have been considered naturally white only in Los Angeles. 'Where are you off ta in such a hurry? Not worried that Sasha might have some lingering feelings for her old flame, are you? Not worried that we might have been doing the nasty on the stable floor? Erotic things, stables, you know. Tried them out yet?'

A month ago, Nick would have hit him. Now he felt something close to pity for the man. He'd never grow up. At sixty, he'd still be playing the same tired hand. Still, he was glad he'd punched him when he had the chance.

'What are you doing here, Cullen?'

Another dazzling grin. 'I've come to say goodbye to Sasha. And Marillion. Couldn't leave without payin' my respects to Marillion.'

'Goodbye?'

'I'm off to my homeland, to glorious Galway Bay. Plenty of openings there, in a manner of speaking, for In and Out Plumbing. Loads of fillies in the paddock. So you're welcome ta Sasha, Nick. Personally, I never was too keen on other men's leavings.'

'That's not what I've heard.'

Again, that fleeting gleam of hatred. 'Yeah, well, you can't win 'em all. Long as you come out on top when the bets are in, that's what I always say.'

He revved the engine. 'It's been a blast but I must be on my way. Seriously now, take care of her. She's a good girl, our Sash. She's . . . what's the word? Impetuous. You'll have your hands full keeping her out of trouble, but she's special. One of a kind. It pains me to admit it, but you're the better man for her. We got off on the wrong foot you and I, but I guess I always knew that. Truth be told, you're what she needs.'

He reached out a hand and smiled warmly. 'Good luck ta you, Nick.'

Nick had a momentary insight into the boyish charm, almost a sweetness, which had attracted Sasha. He immediately felt the lesser man for having villainised Cullen for so long, without a shred of evidence. The man might be a cheat, but that didn't make him a bunny boiler. Nick could well have been mistaken about the dove on the doorstep. It could, after all, have died of natural causes. The incident with Marillion might have had nothing to do with Cullen. The horse had probably freaked out for other reasons entirely. No question about it, he was psychologically scarred.

As for the noose around Oliver's neck, it could easily have been placed there by any of the bird-loving hikers who used the public footpath that passed near Seabird Cottage. Or even Ryan, the teenager who fished in Nick's front yard. Nick had heard from Annie Entwhistle that Ryan had been excluded from school for violent behaviour. He appeared to like Oliver, but who could tell? Perhaps he had latent feelings of anger that manifested themselves in random acts of aggression.

Nick felt an unexpected wave of goodwill towards his former rival. He gripped the other man's hand. 'And to you, Cullen. Apologies again for what happened at The Lighthouse. Hope it works out for you in Galway Bay – the openings.'

He was about to step back when he saw the coil of nylon cord on the passenger seat of Cullen's car. It was cobalt blue.

Cullen put the truck into gear. 'Great. Then I'll be off.'

His foot was on the accelerator when something made him glance up. He followed Nick's gaze to the passenger seat.

He laughed. 'Almost got away with that, didn't I? Ah well. Like I said, win some, lose some. Got quite a bite on him, your cat. Should have finished him off when I had the chance. Mind how you go now.'

His wheels span in the dust.

Couldn't leave without payin' my respects to Marillion.

Nick abandoned the car and ran.

13

Sasha was leading the black horse from the stableyard when Nick came tearing down the slope, sending shale shooting in all directions. Marillion reared.

The third image.

In rapid succession, Nick registered that Sasha's T-shirt was navy blue and white, that Marillion's saddle blanket was red and that the feedbag propped against the fence was green with yellow lettering. The colours from his dream. His fingers had started to tingle.

Sasha laid a soothing hand on Marillion's neck as he pranced and snorted. 'Nick, darling, unless it's a matter of life and death, don't ever run like that around horses. Guaranteed, someone's going to get hurt. What's wrong? Is there an emergency?'

'Yes, there's an emergency. Well, sort of. Sasha, there's no way you can ride Marillion today. That monster's done something horrific to the horse.'

She sighed. 'This is about Cullen, isn't it? Honey, he turned up out of the blue, I swear it. Almost gave me a heart attack too, looming out of the tack room in his black shirt like the Grim Reaper. Anyway, it's good news. He's leaving the country. Apparently the women of Galway Bay can't wait to make use of his services.'

She reached up and kissed his cheek. 'If it helps, I find him repellent these days. Vain, shallow and tainted. I can't believe I ever found him attractive. I feel as if I was hypnotised by a snake.'

'Sasha, listen to me carefully. Did Cullen touch Marillion? Did he go anywhere near him?'

She frowned. 'He offered to saddle him for me, because I was putting a poultice on Rebel's abscess. He was actually very helpful for once. Nick, what's this about? Did you and Cullen have words? What on earth happened?'

Nick was fixated on the horse. He lifted the saddleflap nearest to him. His fingers tingled maddeningly. 'Sasha, I haven't wanted to say anything before, but Cullen's dangerously unhinged. Pathological. He's been waging a silent war against me since the day we met. He broke the neck of a dove and left it on my doorstep – that's how deranged he is. He as good as admitted that he tried to strangle Oliver. Now he wants revenge against Marillion and possibly you. He loathes the horse; you said so yourself. He's done something potentially lethal, I know he has. He's cut the girth or tampered with the bridle or maybe poisoned him . . . Oh, I don't know. Help me out. What would someone do if they wanted to cause a riding accident?'

Sasha was wide-eyed with disbelief, staring at him as if he'd suddenly morphed into an axe murderer. She placed herself between him and Marillion. The horse's ears flickered uncertainly. 'The girth is fine. The bridle's fine. Everything's fine except you, Nick. Why don't you calm down, if that's possible, and tell me what's going on?'

Nick drew an uneven breath. There seemed no way to get enough oxygen into his lungs. 'I didn't tell you before because he was gone from your life and there didn't seem any point. I thought he'd inflicted enough pain. But he did something to Marillion once – some kind of acupressure torture thing. I saw him. I was watching from the copse.'

'You were spying on us from the trees?'

'Not spying, looking. I couldn't make out what was going on, but Marillion was plainly terrified.'

'You observed this and said nothing?'

'Well, I couldn't be sure. I was a fair distance away and it was hard to be positive that anything untoward was happening. It's more of a theory. It fits his profile. But what's beyond doubt is that he tried to kill Oliver.'

Sasha groaned. 'Not the cat again. Nick, let it go. Mrs McKenna locked Oliver in her grain store by mistake. Surely you're not suggesting that she and Cullen were in on it together?'

Nick felt as helpless as he had when the train was derailed. He could hear in his own ears how ridiculous he sounded, yet he ploughed on regardless, crashing and burning. 'Soon after I met you, he overheard me talking to you. He scrawled "Actions have consequences" on my garden path and put a noose around Oliver's neck. I saw the blue cord in his car.'

Sasha shook her head. 'I think I've had about as much of this as I can stand. I'd strongly suggest that you go home to Seabird Cottage and have a long think. Calling a therapist would be a good idea. You'll find me at my mum's house when you've regained your senses. Right now I'm going for a ride.'

Nick seized her wrist. 'I'm not going to let you ride him. I won't. You'll be hurt or killed or something terrible will happen to Marillion. I'm not going to stand by and let that happen.'

'You have precisely three seconds to let me go or this relationship is over.'

Nick tightened his grip. Marillion snorted, pawing the ground in agitation.

The love that had shone in Sasha's eyes when Nick ran down to the stables only minutes earlier had vanished as if it had never been. She was cold but eerily calm. 'I've had it with jealous, controlling, paranoid men who smother me. One of the many reasons I fell in love with you was because you seemed the polar opposite of Cullen. Now I realise that you're identical. Evidently, that's my pattern.

'Oh, you'd never cheat on me, of that much I'm certain, but I'm not going to live my life with you breathing over my shoulder, obsessively concerned that I'm going to slip, drown, fall off my horse or trip over the bathmat. I admit I was reckless on the day we sailed to Botallack, and that my recklessness could have got us killed. But it didn't. Your courage and quick thinking saved the day, and the God I trust to protect me, protected me. Protected *us*. But on an ordinary day, I'll take my chances. I want to be free to live and love with joy and freedom and abandon. With you, that wouldn't be possible. So I'm going to do it without you.'

Nick said nothing. There was nothing to say.

Sasha continued in the same detached tone. 'Over the next few days, I'll send for my things. Don't try to contact me – not today, not tomorrow, not ever. Stay away from me and from my horses. I never want to lay eyes on you again. All I want now is to forget I ever knew you.'

Nick's hand dropped to his side.

Sasha swung into the saddle. She didn't look at him and he couldn't look at her. He listened to the hoofbeats until they faded and then he walked into a future devoid of hope, faith or love.

It was exactly thirteen days later that Sasha found the thorn. It was a long blue-green spike, with an odd vanilla smell. She would not have seen it but it pricked her finger, drawing blood, as she was squeezing Marillion's red saddle blanket into the washing machine. It was threaded through the underside of cloth. By some miracle it had remained flat. Had it pierced the noculus barrameter nerve, or indeed any point in Marillion's back when they were at a flat-out gallop . . .

Bile rose in Sasha's throat. It didn't bear thinking about.

She began a feverish search of the flora around the stables, although she already knew that she'd not find the bush from which it had come. She and Rosa McKenna, a keen botanist, had gone over the place with a fine-tooth comb before a single horse had moved in. An astonishing number of plants were poisonous to the animals.

At the farmhouse Rosa identified the thorn in a matter of minutes. It was from a Crucifix Tree. 'South American. Very rare. Would never have known it, but I saw it myself in Trenance Gardens not a month ago. It was lost for decades and rediscovered a couple of years back. It's the smell of custard that's the giveaway. Where did you find it?'

Sasha got blindly to her feet. She felt faint. Mr McKenna sat her gently back down, but she stood up again as soon as she was able.

'If it helps,' Rosa said, 'he's a wreck too.'

'Oh, Rosa, I've been an absolute idiot. I've said things, unforgiveable things, things I can never take back. And now it's too late.'

'The best of us are idiots from time to time. But it's never too late to put it right.'

'This is about Donaghue, I take it?' Mr McKenna butted in. 'I'll be honest, I always thought it was a terrible idea, you and him—'

'Gordon, don't interfere,' chastised Rosa. 'You're not helping.'

'Over the years I've learned that you can tell a lot about a man from his woodwork. When he first arrived here, he could barely use a hammer, never mind put up a shelf. Couldn't hit a cow's arse with a banjo.'

'Gordon!'

'What I'm trying to say is that I was wrong. He's a good man. A bit eccentric and prone to strong emotion and flights of fancy, in the way of these artistic types, but I'll wager there's not a bad bone in his body.'

Sasha said nothing. All her preconceptions and resolutions came crashing down like glass. Her heart felt as if it was being excavated from her body with a teaspoon.

'It's never too late,' Rosa said again.

But Sasha was already halfway out the door, bolting across the fields like Marillion. The thorn didn't explain everything but it explained a lot, and she was willing to listen to the rest – not least because at a subconscious level she'd known it all along. That there was something not right about Cullen. Something potentially lethal. Her refusal to face it might have cost her the love of the best man she'd ever known. Even at her most devastated, there'd been times over the last couple of weeks when she'd have happily listened to Nick recite the phone book if only she could hear his voice again. If only he would hold her again, make love to her again.

A stitch bit into her side, but she didn't slow. The fear that he'd be gone with no forwarding address, as untraceable as the wind, drove her on. When she saw his car in the drive her heart flipped over in her chest.

She was crossing the lawn at Seabird Cottage when she heard voices. Unprepared to face anyone but Nick, she slipped behind the hedge.

The kitchen door opened and out came a woman with a flushed, pretty face, a shining cap of blonde hair and a body that could have been made to model tight jeans. Nick followed. He was unshaven and pale, but he was laughing. They walked arm in arm to her car with the ease of people utterly familiar with one another.

He opened the door for the woman and she put her arms around him and clung to him for a long time. His head was on her shoulder and his eyes appeared to be closed.

'I've missed you so much, Nicky,' she said. 'Promise me you'll take care of yourself.'

'It's you who needs taking care of, not me. I'll be thinking of you, honey.'

'Same here. See you, gorgeous.'

'See you soon.'

14

The worst mornings were when he woke up thinking she was there. The breeze from the skylight, cooler with the approach of autumn, would caress his skin, and in the daze of departing sleep he'd fancy it was her touch. A smile would tug at his mouth. The agony of finding her gone would take his breath away.

Had it not been for his novel and Becca's impromptu visit, he would, he knew, have fallen apart. Once he might have packed his suitcase and departed with Oliver for the far-flung destinations that until recently had seemed so attractive. Now he was aware that he'd run as far as he could go. There were no more hiding places. He had to turn and face his demons.

Writing helped. He'd been afraid that without Sasha his block would return, but words poured out of him. A couple of times he wrote three or four thousand in a day. The only thing he was unclear on was how the novel would end. Should it be happy or sad? In his current frame of mind he inclined towards the tragic.

'Has anyone ever told you that you have a tendency to be morose?' Becca had remarked, coming across him staring bleakly out of the kitchen window. He'd been making coffee and had glanced up to see Sasha trotting towards the moors on the bay mare, Caprice. That was the trouble. She could choose not to see him. He seldom had the same luxury.

'*You* have,' he answered. 'Many times.'

'I don't suppose there's any point in reminding you that there are plenty of fish in the sea?'

Had he been given a choice in the matter, Nick would never have sanctioned a visit from Becca when he was at his lowest ebb since he'd stood on the cliff edge on New Year's Day. Yet there was no denying it had helped. She'd turned up unannounced twelve days after Sasha had walked out of his life, unchanged and unapologetic.

'Before you remind me that you don't like surprises, let me just say that you make life impossible for yourself by having no email address, no Facebook page and refusing to answer your phone. What was I supposed to do? Use a carrier seagull? Anyway, Phil was fretting that you'd been murdered by the local cowherd in a *crime passionnel* and buried under the floorboards.'

'Phil has watched one too many episodes of *Emmerdale*. Cowherds don't do that kind of thing around here. Plumbers, on the other hand . . .'

But that wasn't the reason she'd come. Nick guessed it when he offered her a glass of wine with dinner and she turned it down.

'I had to tell you face to face. Even if you were a normal person who answered their phone or used the internet, it wouldn't have felt right. When Jane called and suggested a girlie weekend in Cornwall, I jumped at it. She and Lizzie – not to mention Greg – were a bit pissed off when I announced that I needed to spend one night with you, but after I explained how much it meant to me they understood. Even Greg, dear man. As you can imagine, he's beside himself with joy at the prospect of being a father.'

She lifted her hands. 'So here I am. A size eight, but not for much longer.'

Nick was taken aback by the effect the news had on him. It was like being seared with a red-hot poker. He'd never wanted kids and had made no secret of it. Some of his worst rows with women had been caused by him likening child-rearing to a life sentence.

'If I wanted to sacrifice fifteen or twenty years of freedom, I'd buy a ball and chain,' he'd told one broody girlfriend. 'At least I wouldn't have to change its nappies.'

Yet when Becca announced that she was pregnant, he was devastated. It wasn't that he was jealous. He couldn't have been more thrilled for her and Greg. What hit him with unexpected savagery was the realisation there was nothing he would have liked more than to have a child with Sasha. The knowledge that that would now never happen hurt almost as much as their breakup – a breakup caused by him. He'd destroyed Sasha's trust, no one else.

The worrying part was that as a consequence of his actions he could no longer protect her from the coming threat – if that threat should be made manifest.

Over and over, he replayed the events of that fateful day in his mind. If he'd paused to reflect before haring down to the stables to confront Cullen and warn Sasha, this would never have happened. There were hundreds of ways in which he could have persuaded her not to ride Marillion that day. He could have seduced her in the stables, as Cullen had suggested. He could have sweet-talked her into allowing him to whisk her to St Ives for a romantic afternoon of beach walks and art galleries, followed by dinner at the Porthminster Beach Cafe. They could have fallen asleep to the sound of the ocean in the upstairs bedroom at Seabird Cottage. Bodies entwined. Happy.

At the first possible opportunity, he could have checked the stables and tack for any trace of Cullen's lunatic hand. He could have dealt with whatever had been done discreetly. Sasha would never have had to know.

Then he'd have to remind himself that nothing *had* happened. Cullen's threat had been an empty one. Had to have been. Every other day, Sasha and Marillion galloped past his window as free as birds. Unharmed. Whatever the cause of his symbol dreams, they'd so far proven to be meaningless – nothing more than a series of familiar images on a loop.

Unfortunately, rationalising his nightmares wasn't the same as stopping them. And recently two of the pictures had been especially vivid: Sasha smiling at him over her shoulder as she turned to go, and Marillion rearing, his eyes wide with terror.

The postcard featured a bucolic scene of New Forest ponies grazing in a poppy-strewn meadow. It got straight to the point.

Don't be an idiot. Do whatever you have to do to get her back.
Matthew

It was the first reply Nick had ever received from the man, but that wasn't what made him have to pretend for a moment that he had something in his eye. What got to him was the brevity of the card and the tone. It was a note written by a true friend, one who'd read his letters, sized him up and got the measure of him.

'He's right,' declared Annie Entwhistle. 'You're an idiot if you don't do whatever you need to do to get her back. The sooner you do it, the better if you ask me.'

'I didn't ask you,' said Nick. 'That's because it's none of your business. Didn't they teach you in postwomen school that it's rude to look at other people's mail?'

'It's a postcard, not a letter – that means the sender has declined to use an envelope to protect the privacy of its contents. By definition, that's an invitation to read it.'

Nick's response was to shut the door firmly in her face, but Annie's boot blocked its passage.

'They're all in a tizz up at the farmhouse today; don't think I ever seen Rosa in such a state. As for Gordon, he's pacing about in a right temper, slamming doors and sending the chickens scooting.'

Nick did a mental eye roll. Politeness dictated that he now had to enquire why the McKennas were so stressed or distressed when all he wanted was to be left alone.

'Well, it's Sasha, isn't it?'

'What about her?'

'Off to London to resume the nursing lark.'

Nick stared at her, uncomprehending. 'She can't. She wouldn't. I mean, what about the horses?'

'Going today, the lot of them – all except the mad black one. Sold, given away, who knows. Riding centre down the drain. Gordon and Rosa did their best to talk her out of it, but she wouldn't have a bar of it, mind made up. Always headstrong and passionate was our Sash. Could give a mule lessons in stubbornness, but then you'll know more about that than me. Gotta love ya and leave ya – letters to deliver, postcards to read. There's the lorry now, lost, I daresay. Fate that it's headed your way. If you're going to take your friend's advice, you'd better get a move on.'

Nick was reeling. The post van rattled away into the dull grey day. No sooner had it exited the drive than the lorry – a dark green horse transporter – rumbled in. The brakes hissed and the engine petered out. A man, sporting clown-like tufts of hair on either side of his head and a grubby shirt stretched over several low-slung bellies, hoisted himself from the cab.

'Nick?'

'Yes, but I think you've taken a wrong—'

'I 'ope you're more 'elpful than that sod of a farmer,' the driver interrupted, waggling a sheaf of sweat-moistened paper at Nick. 'Right misery guts 'e is. Threatened to have me arrested for trespassing. When I showed 'im the job sheet confirming that I'm 'ired to collect seven 'orses from this farm, I thought 'e was going to blow a gasket. Bent me ear for about ten minutes about 'ow I was taking advantage of a vulnerable woman. Flat out refused to direct me to the stables. Just as I was thinking that they don't pay me enough to put up with this crap, 'e suddenly relented and directed me 'ere. Said you're the partner of this . . .' he glanced at his papers – 'Sasha Moreton, and you'd be glad to point me in the right direction.'

There was a tragic comedy to the situation and Nick gave an involuntary laugh. The old bastard never missed a trick.

The driver's eyebrows scrunched together like mating caterpillars. 'Not you as well. I feel as if I've taken a wrong turn to the funny farm.'

'I'm sorry. You see, there's been a mistake. There'll be no horses leaving here today. I apologise if you've had a wasted journey and also that you had to deal with Mr McKenna. Take it from someone who knows; he can be . . .' What was Mrs Moreton's word? 'Curmudgeonly.'

'Now 'old on a minute. If you think I'm leaving 'ere without being paid, you've got another think—'

'I will pay you in full,' Nick interrupted, 'plus I'll throw in an extra hundred in cash to compensate you for the inconvenience. Will that do? Now if you'll excuse me for a minute, I'll get my chequebook.'

The driver brightened. 'What about this Sasha – your wife, is it? Girlfriend? Should I 'ave a word? After all, it was 'er who booked the job and she seemed pretty certain.'

'That's a kind thought, but if you don't mind I'll talk to her myself. To tell you the truth, this is all my fault.'

15

The horses were standing in their stables, forelocks neatly combed, like children ready for a school outing. Slung over the paddock rail were seven gleaming sets of tack. Sasha emerged from the storeroom with a bucket. Her face was drawn, her dark hair tangled and unkempt. When she saw Nick, she halted in confusion before pushing straight past him.

'Nick, this is not a good time. Whatever it is, can it wait for another day? I'm expecting someone.'

'He's not coming.'

'Oh God.' She wiped her forehead with the back of her hand. 'Nick, I really can't do this now. What do you want me to say? That you were right about Cullen and I was wrong. That he *was* all of the things and probably *did* all the things that you accused him of. Okay, I admit it. Now will you go?'

Nick stayed where he was. 'Sasha, what's going on here?'

She picked up a cloth and began rubbing at an imaginary mark on an already burnished saddle. Behind the trees, the ocean kept up a muted roar. A sad wind added to the atmosphere of melancholy. 'What does it look like?'

'Like you've given up.'

'Not you as well. Gordon's put you up to this, hasn't he? First I can't move for people telling me that only an insane woman would contemplate single-handedly opening a riding centre for the disabled with eight traumatised horses and no money, and now the very same people – people like the McKennas, who blew a gasket when I first suggested it – are telling me only an insane woman would give it up. Well, I am giving it up and that's final.'

'I always believed in you and your riding centre,' Nick reminded her. 'That's never changed.'

Sasha stopped what she was doing and stared at him as if she'd only just taken in his existence. Her eyes were empty, their sparkle gone. 'That's true, you did. Not that it matters anymore. I've found a job in London and I'll be leaving as soon as I've managed to persuade someone to take Marillion. The others are all going to good homes. Any minute now a lorry will be arriving to fetch them.'

She glanced at her watch and frowned. 'The driver should have been here half an hour ago. You need to go. I still have a ton of stuff to do.'

Nick risked a step nearer. 'I've sent him away.'

'Sent who away?'

'The driver. I told him you wouldn't be needing his services after all. Not today, nor at any time in the future. I paid him for his trouble.'

'You did *what*? How dare you? What gave you the right? You're not even *with* me – in fact, you're with someone else, and you still want to control me. It's unbelievable.'

'Someone else? What the . . . ?' He groaned. 'Oh. Oh no. You saw Becca, didn't you? Either that, or the infamous Lanton gossip mill has been at work. She was here for one night, Sasha. She's pregnant. She wanted me to know.'

'If you're trying to make a bad day worse, you're going about it the right way. Pregnant? Well, that didn't take long.'

Nick raked his fingers through his hair. 'It's not my baby – it's her husband, Greg's. How could you even think that? Sasha, I've explained about Becca. She's like a kid sister to me. Always was. That's the reason we broke up fifteen or sixteen years ago and it'll never change. As for me wanting to control you, this riding centre is not about me, or us. It's not even about you. It's about the horses you've rescued and the people you're going to heal.'

Sasha raised her chin. Her eyes were red-rimmed but now there was fire in them. 'Don't guilt trip me, Nick. I've done enough of that to myself. I felt like Judas this morning, feeding the horses their last supper. They trust me to take care of them, Marillion especially. They've no idea their world is about to be turned upside down.'

'So don't do it.'

'You don't understand. I can't do this alone. I thought I could once . . . before . . . but now I'm certain I can't. Anyway, what business is it of yours? You and I, we're nothing to do with one another. It's over. Now if you'll excuse me, I'm going to call the lorry driver. By the time I return, I expect you to be gone. Get out of my head, my heart and my life. You're poison.'

Nick was almost at the gate before an impulse he couldn't control sent him striding back across the yard. Sasha was in the tack room, tapping numbers into her mobile phone. Tears were streaming down her cheeks.

He took the phone from her unresisting fingers and set it on the bench. 'It is my business because I love you. It is my business because nothing is more important to me than your happiness. If you want me to leave and go to the ends of the earth so that you'll never have to lay eyes on me again, I'll do it gladly. But I'm not going anywhere until I'm sure that you're okay. Nor am I going to stand silently on the sidelines while you throw away your dream. If you're seriously telling me you want to abandon the horses you've put your heart and soul into rescuing, that you're fine with betraying Marillion, then so be it. There's not a lot I can do about it. But don't lie to me, Sasha. More importantly, don't lie to yourself.'

He ached to hold her but he took a step back. Like a sapling in a gale she swayed towards him, and somehow she was in his arms and his mouth was on hers and they were kissing as if the world was going to end in five minutes.

She tore her lips from his and pushed him away.

'What's *wrong* with me? Whenever you're around, I lose my mind. You don't love me, Nick. You're not capable of it. Your heart is in lockdown. There are prisons with less fortification. Oh, on paper, you're the best man I've ever met. Brave. Decent. Honourable almost to a fault. You were right when you said that you're the opposite of Cullen. If we got back together, I don't doubt that you'd be faithful to me, take care of me. But what difference would it make when you'd never let me in? Whatever happened in your past – and you know as well as I do that I'm not talking about the death of your parents – is sealed in a vault in your head. You have nothing to offer anyone. Nothing. So don't lecture me about lying to myself. *You've* turned it into an art form.'

Nick's hands dropped to his sides. He moved to the doorway, breathing in the mingled smells of sea air, leather and saddle soap. The horses' heads were turned in his direction.

'You're right. Everything you say is true. I am poison. I love you with all my heart and there's nothing I want more than to be with you, but I can't. I can't be with anyone. I'm sorry for what I've done today – coming here, making a mess of what must have already been an impossibly hard day for you. Hurting you. If it's any consolation, I feel an absolute shit. Give me twenty-four hours and I'll be gone from Seabird Cottage and you'll never see me again. But first . . .'

He steeled himself to step into the abyss. 'First, I owe you an explanation.'

She folded her arms across her chest.

'Last October I was in a crash . . .'

'I'm well aware of that. You told me about it, remember? It triggered a mid-life crisis was how you put it. That's how you ended up here. Was it your fault? Were you driving? Is that it?'

He shook his head. 'It was a train crash.'

Her eyes went dark with shock. 'Not *the* train crash? Not the derailment at London Bridge? Nobody has ever been held accountable for it.'

'That crash, yes. Only I wasn't injured. At least, I thought I wasn't. I barely had a scratch. But then—'

There were goosebumps on her arms. 'Then the nightmares started?'

When he didn't answer, she said wryly: 'I did share a bed with you, Nick. Many times. It's not exactly something you can control – what you do when you're unconscious. I have to admit, it frightened me a bit. A lot. Some nights you looked as if you were in pain. Your fingers would type madly as if you were trying to meet a deadline.'

Nick said defensively: 'Most people . . .' He cleared his throat. 'Most people who've been through some kind of trauma have nightmares. Post-traumatic stress disorder and all that. It's not the end of the world.'

'But it has been the end of *your* world, hasn't it, Nick? What is it about your dreams that's different? What do you see?'

Sweat trickled down Nick's chest. His vision went wavy around the edges. His secret had eaten him alive for the best part of ten months, but he could still prevent it coming out. He only needed a minute to clear his head. He started across the stableyard, but it was all he could do to stumble to the paddock rail. The ground felt about as steady as the yacht had in the storm. He reached for his cigarettes with a shaking hand before remembering that he no longer smoked.

When Sasha touched his arm, he flinched as if he'd been burnt.

'Tell me what you're hiding. Tell me what makes you the way you are.'

'I kill people,' he yelled. 'Is that what you want to hear? I can never be with you or anyone else because I kill people.'

She gave a nervous laugh. 'Oh, so now I don't just have one pathological ex, I have two. What do you do? Strangle hitchhikers and bury them under the patio?'

'No, but after the crash something shifted in my head. I'm not psychic, but in my dreams I see things.'

'Next you'll be saying they come true.'

'What if they do?'

'I'm assuming you're joking. Nick . . . ? Nick, you're starting to frighten me. Tell me that this is just you being melodramatic. That you are who you've always been and you're only saying this in some misguided attempt to stop me giving away the horses and—'

'I'm the common denominator. The people in my dreams, they die after encounters with me. That's why I moved into Seabird Cottage – to be isolated. To hide from everything and everyone. For a while it worked. Well, apart from the premonition about Pattie Griffin, but then I saw that before I even reached Cornwall. The difference between Pattie and all the rest is that she was the only one that I - we – you, really – managed to save. After that, the nightmares stopped altogether. I thought they had, at any rate.'

Sasha's gaze was fixed on Marillion, restless after a morning cooped up. 'Let me guess. They started again when you and I got together?'

Nick didn't respond. Telling her felt like a purging, but it also felt like a suicide mission. He'd come here to stop her from leaving. He'd finished up giving her a hundred reasons to do exactly that.

'You've seen something, haven't you?' she persisted. 'Something to do with me?'

It was on the tip of his tongue to deny it, but the lying had to stop. It was the avoidance of truth that had got him into this mess in the first place.

'I'm not sure. When the dreams first started I saw every detail. Complete strangers – I'd know their most intimate thoughts, see every frame of their deaths. I'd wake up with this uncontrollable urge to write about it. Obituaries. If I tried to suppress it, it got worse.'

'And now?'

'Now I see random things. Symbols, pictures, colours. Everyday scenes like the post van pulling into the drive. I don't know what they mean.'

'But you've seen me?'

'Yes, but only—'

'That's why you were always trying so hard to save me? Why you wanted to protect me? That's why you fought so hard to keep from getting involved with me?'

His throat felt as though a golf ball were lodged in it. Every word threatened to choke him. 'I couldn't face the thought that I might one day see the face of a woman I loved in a dream.'

'And then you did?'

'And then I did.'

Sasha's face was white, but her expression was resolved. 'I think,' she said, 'you'd better start at the beginning.'

16

They were married on Saturday, October fifteenth, a year and five days after the crash and on his thirty-ninth birthday. Since Nick was a lapsed Catholic and didn't think they'd miss him, and Sasha preferred what she called a 'more personal relationship with God', they chose the Anglican chapel, which had a famously liberal vicar. It stood on a promontory west of Lanton, high above the pounding seas. Its stained-glass windows reflected its environment, with angels rescuing sailors in distress and Jonah being gobbled by the whale.

Throughout the ceremony the wind tugged so hard at the stone church that Nick could have sworn he felt it sway. The proximity of the elements lent additional resonance to the already charged words, 'Till death do us part'. Yet when Nick lifted Sasha's veil to kiss her, her face radiated a quiet joy.

Phil was Nick's best man. 'If I'm the best man, how come she didn't marry me?' he quipped at the reception hosted by the McKennas at the farmhouse. In Sasha's honour, the meal was vegetarian (cue much grumbling from the farmer), although Oliver – wearing a white lace neckerchief despite Nick's protests that it was undignified – was given special dispensation to have a plate of poached salmon.

The wedding cake was black forest gateau, Nick's favourite, baked by Sasha's mum. She cornered him in the kitchen as he searched for clean glasses.

'Nick, my dear, I couldn't be happier for you both, but please promise me that you'll take extra special care of her. After what she's been through with her dad and Cullen, she deserves . . . she needs . . . I mean, she's not as tough as she thinks she is. I guess what I'm trying to say is that Sasha's always had this wild streak. She's always flown too close to the flame. I see her with Marillion and I'm not ashamed to admit that it terrifies me. I'm hoping that you'll be a steadying influence on her. I want you to give me your word that you'll keep her safe from harm.'

Nick took her hands in his. They were his lover's hands, thirty years on. 'Peg,' he said gently, 'that's not a promise I can make. I've learned the hard way that no human being can guarantee the safety of another. I'm Sasha's husband, not her keeper. Her amazing spirit is the best part of her. I couldn't stifle that even if I wanted to, and I don't. What I can promise you is that she's the love of my life. If it's within my power to make her happy and to cherish and protect her, I'll move heaven and earth to do that.'

His gaze fell on the single rare orchid that had been the wedding gift of Sarah and Matthew Levin. Attached was a card written in Sarah's artistic hand:

Love one another but make not a bond of love:
Let it rather be a moving sea between the shores of your souls.
The Prophet

Much joy to you both.
Love Matthew & Sarah

On a day of high emotion, few things moved Nick as much.

When he'd asked Sasha to marry him, Matthew had been the first person he'd told, or at least written to. They were now exchanging letters as often as three times a week. Nick's missives were a sort of country diary of farm life and the odd priceless quote from Mr McKenna. Matthew sent clippings from the *New Scientist* or ranted about government cock-ups or hapless junior doctors.

Sasha teased Nick about their correspondence, calling it an 'old-fashioned courtship'. 'Are you sure it's me you want to marry? Oh, that's right. Matthew's already taken.'

Phil and Mikhail had been driven down to Cornwall by Greg and Becca, who was now sporting a cushion-sized bump. Nick wasn't sure whether to be relieved or concerned that his ex and Sasha had hit it off the instant they'd met. Whenever he looked over, they seemed to be in fits of giggles. He hoped they weren't comparing notes.

'Bound to be,' Phil remarked unhelpfully, 'but there's no need to be insecure. You've got the girl, remember?'

Across the room, Sasha, in conversation with Rosa, Becca and the vet, Lacey Stanton, glanced up and gave him a heart-stopping smile. It was hard to take in but true. Against all odds, he'd got the girl.

Greg was so over the moon at the prospect of being a father that all past wrongs were forgiven. Still, Nick apologised profusely for his behaviour in London. 'I don't know what to say. I wasn't in my right mind.'

The fireman stopped him in mid-flow. 'It's forgotten, mate. Say no more about it. Besides, I've been doing some thinking and I've come to the conclusion that regardless of what went down last year, I owe you big time. I mean, if you hadn't been dumb enough to pass up on Becks, I wouldn't have landed the most beautiful woman in the world. Not that you've done too badly yourself. She's a great girl, your Sash, and sweet with it. You take good care of her. You're one lucky son of a bitch.'

'Don't I know it,' said Nick with feeling, thinking it ironic that now that he'd made peace with the fact that he couldn't control the destiny of so much as a hair on Sasha's head, everyone was exhorting him to protect her.

'Death and taxes,' was how Sasha had said they were to think about his dreams. 'How *you* have to think about them. Death is inevitable. Plenty of people manage to defraud the taxman, but not one of us can cheat the grave. The best we can hope for is that it's a long way off. If we obsess over every nightmare you have and what it may or may not mean, it'll destroy us. Besides, I'm not sure what you have in mind but I plan on growing old with you. You're stuck with me whether you like it or not.'

'Oh, I like it,' he'd responded with a grin, taking her into his arms. 'I like it very much.'

Since he and Sasha were not leaving for their honeymoon in Paris until Monday, when they'd fly from Bristol to Charles de Gaulle, and since Greg and Becca fancied a romantic weekend of their own at a hotel in St Ives, Phil and Mikhail stayed at Seabird Cottage. In the dead of Saturday night, Mikhail let out a blood-curdling screech. Nick suspected that it had very little to do with Phil's prowess in the sack and quite a lot to do with the massive, hairy spider Nick had chased under the wardrobe a few days earlier and been unable to reach. It looked like an import. He'd forgotten that Mikhail had arachnophobia.

In the lead-up to their visit, he'd worried that his friend would take one look at the cottage and decide that he did want it after all. Since they had yet to exchange contracts on their properties (the sale had been held up by Phil's struggle to sell his apartment in New Cross), there was nothing to stop him changing his mind. Nick had pictured the boys relaxing by the fire or gazing out at the ocean at Seabird Cottage – which had been transformed by Sasha into a homely but stylish space of wood, white and muted shades of blue – then coming to the conclusion that a rural retreat might not be a bad idea after all.

In fact, the reverse was true. Over cake and mugs of hot chocolate, the only dinner anyone could manage after the excesses of the wedding feast, it emerged that Phil and Mikhail were equally fearful that he might renege on his offer to swap his Greenwich apartment for Seabird Cottage. They'd taken it for granted that now Nick and Sasha were married, their first order of business would be to return to London.

'Why on earth would we do that?'

'Theoretically you still have a job, Nick,' Phil reminded him. 'I know Henry agreed to an extension on your sabbatical, but that year will be up in a few months and he's as keen as mustard to have you back.'

'Top of my to-do list when I return from my honeymoon is to write to Henry and tender my resignation for the third time,' Nick said drily. 'He never was any good at taking no for an answer.'

'So that's it then? There's no hope of you coming back to save me from the dross of Colin's copy or Henry's tirades?'

Nick drew Sasha close. She had exchanged her wedding dress for a grey sweatshirt and jeans and looked, if anything, more delicately beautiful than before. 'Zero.'

Phil sighed. 'Can't say I blame you.'

'Hey, why are you suddenly so keen on getting us to London?' demanded Sasha. 'Do you have designs on our – sorry, *your* – cottage?'

'Darling, if it weren't for the alarming proximity of nature in general and spiders in particular, we very well might, but under the circumstances we'll leave you in peace. Anything less would be immoral. Besides, we've already moved into the Greenwich apartment in our heads. We've practically decorated it. That said, if we weren't wildlife phobes you'd have good reason to worry. Nick, what you've done to

Seabird Cottage is unbelievable. You've turned a ruin into a virtual work of art.'

'That's Sasha's doing, not mine. All I did was put up the odd shelf.'

'Ignore him. He's talking nonsense as usual.'

'That's nice. We've been married all of . . .' he glanced at his watch, 'eight hours and seventeen minutes and you're already—'

'The point my Phil is making,' Mikhail interrupted in his impeccably accented Russian-English, 'is that even if we were the world's most hard-hearted people, which we are not, we would never take away your home. Your roots. And this is your home now, I think?'

Nick and Sasha simply nodded and gazed at one another adoringly.

'Don't mind us,' said Phil. 'We'll take Oliver and retreat to the spare room.'

Upstairs in the oak bed, Sasha lay against Nick's bare chest and opened the card given to them by Gordon and Rosa McKenna, which the farmer's wife had appealed to them not to look at 'until dinner time at the earliest'. Unusually for a wedding card, it was in a large, board-backed brown envelope. As Sasha tipped it up, a certificate fell out.

She clapped both hands over her mouth. 'Oh my God.'

Nick read the card.

Dearest Nick & Sasha,

We hope you like your wedding gift, although we have to confess to a couple of ulterior motives. We figured that if we actually gave you the land on which your riding centre will stand (ten acres), it would a) incentivise you to stay in Lanton and on our farm for ever, and b) (this one is a purely selfish one from Rosa!!) stop Gordon moaning about how your horses are eating his 'good grazing'.

Only kidding!!

All our love to you both.

Rosa & Gordon

'Is it possible to die from too much happiness?' asked Sasha. 'Because right now I feel that if I got any happier or was any more in love with you than I am, I'd explode.'

Nick kissed her eyelids. 'I don't think there've been any recorded cases, but I'll hold you tightly just in case.'

Sasha yawned, then sat up guiltily. 'It's our wedding night. We should make love.'

'We should,' Nick agreed, 'but to tell you the truth I think I've eaten too much cake.'

Sasha patted her stomach. 'I've definitely eaten too much cake. Plus I'm . . .' She yawned again. 'Exhausted.'

Nick put a hand on her forehead. Beads of perspiration dotted it. 'Are you feeling all right, Sash? You're burning up. Do you think you might be coming down with something?'

'Nah, I'm just a hot chick.'

He laughed. 'What percentage of people make love on their wedding night, do you suppose?'

She considered. 'Haven't a clue. Seventy per cent maybe.'

'I was thinking more like fifty. And of those fifty maybe ten per cent have great sex. The rest are too drunk, too full, too pissed off with their new in-laws, too riddled with post-stag night guilt, too—'

'Are you saying that we shouldn't risk jeopardising our record?'

'Of mind-blowing sex, you mean?'

'Of mind-blowing sex. Exactly.'

'Mmm, maybe not.'

She traced the outline of his lips. 'Do I still get a kiss and a cuddle?'

'You can have all the kisses and cuddles you can bear.'

When Nick came bounding down the stairs early next morning, he startled Phil, who was seated at the desk in the living room.

It took Nick a moment to process that the sheaf of paper Phil was holding was his own manuscript.

Phil put the chapter he was reading face down on the desk, aligning the pages neatly as if that would somehow right the wrong. 'Nick, I'm sorry. Forgive the intrusion. My spider-phobic boyfriend had a midnight meltdown that almost ended in him calling a taxi and demanding to be taken to a hotel. Afterwards, I couldn't sleep. I only picked this up because I was curious to see what you were working on. I thought it might be local freelance stuff – you know, who won the prize for the best heifer. I didn't know it would be . . . Nick, this is wild. If it's true it explains everything.'

'It's fiction,' Nick said furiously. 'It explains fuck all.'

'If you say so.'

Phil pushed the chair back and stood up. He was barefoot and wearing a white vest and blue pyjama bottoms. Out of his customary starched shirt, tie and waistcoat, he looked oddly vulnerable. 'What are you planning to do with it?'

Nick's anger dissipated like mist. Part of him recognised that he'd left the manuscript on the desk for a reason, though what that reason was he could not have said. 'I'm not sure. Maybe nothing. I hadn't thought that far ahead. It's a sort of exorcism.'

'I have a friend, a literary agent.'

'I don't know. It's too soon. I'd need to think about it.'

Phil's gaze went to the stairs. 'Does Sasha know the whole story?'

'Yes. No! What is this – twenty questions? I've told you, it's a novel. Fiction as opposed to non-fiction. But in case you're worried, she knows everything and loves me anyway. For better or worse.'

'Far be it from me to suggest that there are similarities between you and your novel's protagonist, but reading between the lines I'd say you love her almost too much.'

'There's no such thing as too much. I love her the way she loves me, for better or worse. Of course, with her there are really only good bits.'

'Then you'll be fine. That's all there is to it.'

17

It was Nick who found the lump.

Four days after returning from Paris, he was idly caressing his new wife while drifting off to sleep when he became conscious of a nodule under her left arm, close to her breast. He sat up and turned on the light.

'It's nothing,' Sasha assured him. Woken from a sweet dream, she was dopey and smiley, as loose-limbed as a newborn foal. 'It's a fibro-cystic, uh, cyst. I saw a doctor about it a year ago. They come and go with hormones or times of the month. It went away for a bit and now I guess it's back.'

'Okay, babe. Sorry for disturbing you,' murmured Nick. What he really wanted to do was rush her out of the door to A&E and have a specialist triple-check that she was fine, especially since she seemed feverish again, her skin moist to the touch. But a bedrock principle of their marriage was that they respect one another's independence.

He switched off the light and moved close to her, but not so close he would make her even hotter.

Sasha squeezed him in the darkness. 'Don't worry, honey. To be on the safe side, I'll make an appointment first thing. Now go to sleep and keep your hands to yourself.'

The oncologist's lips were moving but no sound was coming out. All Nick was able to take in was that beneath his grey suit trousers the man wore green and red Cat in the Hat socks. It was only when the pain in his arm became excruciating that he realised that Sasha's nails had bitten so deeply into his flesh they'd drawn blood.

Extracting his arm with difficulty, he tried to take her hand in his. She affected not to see it and gripped the side of the chair instead.

'That's impossible,' she was saying. 'I'm only twenty-nine. I'm fitter than most sixteen-year-olds. I don't smoke. I've never done drugs or lived on junk food. I drink but only in moderation. Well, mostly. I mean, at university . . .' Her voice tailed off.

The oncologist's face was a kind one, but there were furrows of weariness beneath his eyes. He was close to retirement and looking forward to it.

'Anaplastic large-cell lymphoma is a rare disease, but unfortunately it preys on the young. And before you ask, no, you've done nothing to bring it on. Cancer doesn't discriminate. In some instances, factors like diet can have a bearing, especially if there are no aggravating environmental issues – exposure to radiation and such like – but it's just one piece of the jigsaw. Olympic athletes get it. Genetics can be key. Anecdotally, we know that life also plays its part. The many stresses of modern existence. Too much expectation. Too much pressure. We're bombarded by multi-media of one kind or another twenty-four seven, and, of course, we bombard others.'

'But I'm not under stress. I've just got married. I'm in love. Thanks to my husband, I've stopped working three jobs and now spend hours of every day with horses. That, too, makes me ridiculously happy. Yes, I work hard, but then so do millions of other people. I send the odd email and watch the odd film but I'm hardly an addict. Test me again. There must be some mistake.'

Nick found his voice. 'It's impossible. Test her again.'

He said it to be supportive and in the vain hope that simply speaking the words out loud might make them true, but he knew very well that there was no error. That much had been obvious the minute Sasha's GP had examined her breast area and all but shoved her out of the door to the hospital for a biopsy and a whistlestop series of tests.

He knew, too, that the inconsequential minutiae of this day would be ingrained on his mind – the Cat in the Hat socks, the rip on the black faux-leather seat of his chair, the rudely healthy faces of the three grandchildren grinning from the photo on the desk.

The oncologist crossed and uncrossed his red and green ankles. 'I'm afraid there's no mistake.' He added almost accusingly: 'Sasha, you're a nurse.'

Sasha's fingers groped for Nick's. 'I haven't been a nurse for nearly three years. I don't see how that's relevant.' Her grip tightened. 'What I need to know . . . I need you to tell me . . . What are my chances of recovery?'

'I'll be honest with you: ALCL is a highly aggressive non-Hodgkin lymphoma. The good news is that the prognosis for a cure is optimistic in the majority of cases. But first we have to do a battery of tests – a CT scan, blood tests, a bone-marrow biopsy, a lumbar puncture – to determine how far it's spread. Try not to be alarmed. Even when it's in the spleen, bone marrow or liver, we still get good recovery rates. That's not where the real danger lies.'

Nick could have throttled the man. He wondered if years of delivering death sentences had inured him to the horror of his words. 'What can be worse?' he demanded. 'If an aggressive cancer is not real danger, what the hell is?'

The oncologist inclined his grey head. Over the decades he'd heard every conceivable reaction to the bad tidings he brought. He understood that it wasn't personal. At the same time, extreme emotion could lead to some sticky situations.

He turned a stern but sympathetic gaze on Nick. 'What you should understand is that this is a cancer of the lymphatic system, which is an integral part of the immune system. When we blitz it with chemotherapy – and by blitz I mean it'll be twice as strong as the level we'd use for Hodgkin's lymphoma – we'll basically be waging war against Sasha's body's defences. Inevitably, there are consequences.'

He looked at Sasha. 'To be clear, this is not palliative care. We advocate the CHOP regimen. It's named after the drugs we use: cyclophosphamide, doxorubicin – the chemical name of which is hydroxydaunomycin – Oncovin and prednisolone. I'll direct you to a website that'll explain everything in layman's terms. We treat with the intent to cure, but we're dealing with a paradox. In order to kill the cancer cells, we have to kill the healthy ones, effectively destroying your immune system.'

'And in the process you could kill her?' said Nick.

'I wouldn't put it like that.'

'How would you put it?'

'There is a risk that Sasha's ability to fight infection could become so compromised that she is unable—'

'Believe it or not, I am still capable of participating in the conversation,' Sasha broke in. 'I haven't yet been reduced to mute invalid status. Now tell me about this CHOP. How soon do I start?'

'If I don't make it through this, I need you to promise me that you'll take care of Marillion.'

The red orb of the traffic light blurred before Nick's eyes. Another scene engraved on his brain. In the colourless dome of sky above the windscreen a kestrel twisted like origami.

'Nothing is going to happen to you, Sasha,' he said, accelerating so hard onto the motorway that the tyres squealed. 'I won't allow it to. We're going to fight this thing.'

'I don't think it works that way, darling, and I refuse to approach this as if it's a fairytale. We're going to get real and face facts. But if you make me this one promise, at least I'll have some peace of mind. If the worst happens, I want to know that you'll always look after Marillion. The other horses are so sweet and well trained now that you'd have no difficulty finding homes for them. But not many people would take on Marillion.'

Nick's hands tightened on the steering wheel. 'How can you even ask me that? You should know me well enough to know that *if. . .*'

He couldn't bring himself to say it. 'In the unlikely event that anything were to happen to you, I'd look after him as if he were my own son.'

He was going too fast and almost missed the farm turnoff. The driver behind leaned on his hooter as Nick veered left without indicating.

Given an option, he wouldn't have driven at all. He felt drunk with shock. Nauseous with it. At the back of his mind lurked the conviction that this was somehow his fault. His premonition dreams had cursed her.

Sasha said: 'And while we're on the subject, we need to talk about us.'

'*Us?* What about us? We'll get through it. No matter how tough it gets, we'll manage. It's going to be okay; we have to believe that.'

'It's not going to be okay. That's one thing it's not going to be.'

They sped past the farmhouse. Rosa waved from the chicken coop. Sasha lifted a hand in response. 'I want the marriage annulled.'

Nick swerved, smacking into the makeshift wooden sign that

pointed down the track to Seabird Cottage. It exploded into matchwood, pinging off the Mustang's bonnet.

Sasha clung to the dashboard in silence as he righted the car, drove the last three hundred metres with tortoise slowness and braked outside Seabird Cottage. She was out of the door before he'd even turned off the engine. Nick punched the steering wheel, but it was no use. The hurt on the outside was never going to match what he felt on the inside.

Sasha was in the living room, staring out to sea. She looked as fragile as a new bird, as if the mere diagnosis had sucked the marrow from her bones. The first thing she'd done on leaving the oncologist's office was buy a bag of cheap chocolate snowballs and cram at least six into her mouth. Her eyes had been glazed, crazed. Already, she seemed to have gone to a place where Nick couldn't follow and that terrified him far more than any disease could have done.

He put his arms around her stiff frame. 'I'm sorry, Sash. I know that was the very last thing you needed after the morning you've had. But for future reference, it's best to wait until your husband is not behind the wheel before you threaten him with divorce after just thirteen days of marriage.'

Sasha twisted to face him. 'I said annulment, not divorce. There's a difference. Don't you see that I'm giving you a chance to get out now, while you can? This is not exactly what you signed up for, is it? A dying wife.'

He caught her cold, resisting hands. 'I meant my vows. "In sickness and in health."'

'Of course you did. You're a decent, honourable man. I'd expect nothing less. That's one of the many reasons I adore you. It's because I love you so much that I don't want this for you. You're young enough to start again with someone else, have children. If you go now, nobody will be any the wiser. I'll start treatment but I won't tell anyone I'm ill for as long as I'm able to maintain a reasonably healthy façade. We'll simply say that we realised within days of getting married that we'd made a monumental mistake and that it's purely coincidental—'

'Stop!' The black fury inside Nick had erupted into a volcano of sadness. 'Just stop it. Nobody is leaving anybody and there will be no annulment or divorce or any other kind of parting. The oncologist told us that for most people with Ana . . . Ana . . .'

'Anaplastic large-cell lymphoma.'

'Right, for most people with ALCL, the prognosis is good. That's the outlook I'm going to focus on. Secondly, even if it was bad, how could you not know that I'd rather spend one week with you than five lifetimes with another woman?'

Her eyes were as big and blue as the ocean and rimmed with tears. 'Really?'

'Yes, really. Idiot.'

He had to grab her then because she collapsed into his arms.

Neither of them could face lunch and in the early afternoon Sasha announced that she was going upstairs for a nap. It was the first time she'd ever done such a thing and Nick had to hide his astonishment. But all he said was, 'Great idea. I think I'll go check on the horses.'

He put on his running shoes and went out to face the world. Jogging didn't work because his chest felt as though an elephant were standing on it. The October wind sparred with him like a heavyweight boxer. In the end he simply walked as fast as he could cross-country, choosing the rocky path over the road.

The horses had been turned out in the field by Tam, the village girl, who was feeding and exercising them until further notice. When Nick let himself in the gate, Marillion's head shot up. The others were too busy guzzling grass.

Nick crossed the field to the black horse. He never knew what to expect with Marillion. He had the sense that the animal liked him – or that he didn't actively dislike him the way he had Cullen – but he'd never penetrated Marillion's reserve. There was a fortress around him with an armour-plated gate to which only Sasha seemed to have the key.

But as he approached the horse now, Marillion gave a low whicker of pleasure. His ears pricked and he walked forward.

Nick was taken aback by the effect this response had on him. It was as if a candle had been lit in the icy darkness of his heart. He ran a hand down Marillion's sleek, warm neck, taking care not to flinch and startle the horse when the inevitable tingling started in his fingers. They stood together quietly. Nick breathed in the smell of horse and salty air; Marillion gazed off into the distance, his big body shielding Nick from the wind, his delicate nostrils fluttering as he exhaled. Beyond the cliffs, the waves hissed and crashed.

Across the far fields, Mr McKenna's tractor traced an ant-like trail. He'd be taking food to the sheep. The image familiar from countless nightmares jolted Nick from his trance. It was then he realised that the fear which had fuelled his nightmares since the day he met Sasha now had a face. The monster was no longer unknown – a thing that could come from anywhere, in any form. It was before him. The Big C.

He couldn't decide whether to feel relieved or guilty. How could he be glad that Sasha was ill? But it wasn't that at all. Nothing could be further from the truth. It was simply that now that his opponent had a physical form, he could tackle it head on. He could pick up his sword and do battle with it.

He'd been motionless for so long that Marillion gave him an impatient shove. Nick smiled for the first time in days. He gave the horse's forelock an affectionate tug.

'Hey you, there'll be none of that. We're going to need each other, you and I.'

18

When Nick woke the following morning, tense and unrested, Sasha was propped on one elbow, watching him with a smile. She leaned over and pressed her mouth to his in a slow, deep kiss that gave him an instant hard-on. Then she bounced out of bed.

'Wait! Come back here. Don't start something you have no intention of finishing.'

'You finish it,' she said heartlessly. 'I need to hop in the shower. I have my operation at midday, remember?'

She paused at the bathroom door. 'You'll be pleased to hear that I'm going to roll up my sleeves and get on with it. No more tears. The quicker I stand up to this and get practical, the quicker I'm going to recover. I refuse to be a victim.'

It all came roaring back then. The news that had smashed their world.

Nick slumped back into the pillows, grief-stricken, as if the worst had already happened. Elsewhere, life went on as usual. The seagulls cried, the waves rolled interminably and the cock crowed, as it did every day, with increasing hysteria and arrogance. On the bedside table, the second hand of Nick's watch ticked inexorably onward. His heart clenched painfully as he was reminded of Auden's 'Stop all the clocks'.

Oliver jumped up, meowing for breakfast. Nick gave himself a mental slap. What the hell was wrong with him, wallowing in self-pity? Only yesterday he was thinking about taking up swords and slaying dragons. Today and every day, that was the only way forward. If Sasha could roll up her sleeves and face down her would-be killer with a smile, he could bloody well do the same.

*

The nightmares that had driven him to Cornwall returned as he dozed off in the armchair beside Sasha's hospital bed after a delayed operation to remove a cluster of lymph nodes from her armpit. These were not his symbol dreams – a now-familiar parade of images. These were violent and ghoulish movies of the dying or soon to be departed in the wards and wings around him. A teenager who'd overdosed. A business-man with arteries too fatty and far-gone to survive a triple bypass. A toddler with meningitis, diagnosed too late.

Once, inexplicably, he dreamed about Ryan. He saw the boy dying on an operating table. A surgeon, who looked first like the hanged judge, then like an actor playing Falstaff and finally like one of the judges from The Muppets, was staring at his scalpel with almost comic puzzlement. A nurse screamed silently at him.

Nick was on the phone to the teenager before breakfast, using the excuse that he'd wanted to tell him about Sasha and asking him if he'd mind cat-sitting Oliver for a couple of days. Ryan was still half asleep and distraught to hear about Sasha, but otherwise appeared to be perfectly well. As a precaution, Nick then texted Rosa and asked if she'd do him a favour and check on Ryan because, he lied, the teenager seemed under the weather.

That afternoon she'd replied that while Ryan was very well, her pantry was not. She'd invited him for lunch and he'd eaten his way through half a chicken, four slices of bread, a hunk of cheese, four tomatoes, most of an apple pie and half a pint of custard.

'If this is him under the weather, I'd be fascinated to see what he gets through when he's well.'

'You're dreaming again,' Sasha observed a few days later, by which time they were home again. She was pale and sore, but in good spirits, all things considered. 'You were thrashing around in your sleep.'

Nick shovelled cheesy scrambled eggs onto a slice of toast, added a sprinkling of chives and brought it over to the sofa on a tray for her. 'Was I? Don't remember.'

'Don't believe you.'

He fetched his own plate and the Worcestershire sauce and sat down between her and Oliver. The cat had taken to following Sasha around like a dog. He picked up the TV remote. 'Want to watch something?'

'Don't change the subject, Nick. This is important. I'm going to be in and out of hospital having chemo for months. I couldn't bear to think that on top of everything else you'll be dealing with, my situation might cause you horrific nightmares.'

'Of course it won't. Don't be silly.'

She continued to look at him.

'Don't fret about it, Sasha. It's not going to happen.'

'Judging by the way you were writhing and moaning last night, it already has. Darling, it's enough for me that you're here for me and love me. It's more than enough that you'll be doing the lion's share of the horse care for the next goodness knows how long. You don't also have to be my taxi to the hospital. Rosa and Mum have offered to take it in turns.'

'But I'd like to take you. Please, I want to.'

He didn't tell her that while she was still sleeping off the anaesthetic, he'd had to run down to the hospital gift shop and buy a notebook in an attempt to alleviate the pins and needles in his fingers. The voices in his head had been so loud that he'd gouged holes in the paper trying to tell their stories and make sense of their ends. Later, he'd secretly transferred those tales to his manuscript, changing all names and altering many details. In an echo of his former life, he'd pounded at the typewriter keys until the prickling in his hands finally abated.

The thought of enduring months of these nightmares was beyond awful. Not so long ago, they'd pushed him to the brink of suicide. Now he knew that they were nothing compared to what Sasha was going through. For her, he'd deal with ten times more.

He caught sight of the Mousehole postcard he'd bought to send to Matthew. It was lying on his desk, ready to be written. But what to say? The only reason he'd told Phil about Sasha's diagnosis was because his friend had called with the contact details of a literary agent and caught him off guard. On hearing the news, Phil had broken down. Holding the receiver from his ear as great gasping sobs echoed down the line, Nick immediately resolved not to tell anyone else.

'Nick, you know that Mikhail and I are here for you any time, day or night,' Phil managed when he'd regained control. 'One word from you and I promise we'll be on the first train out of Paddington, spiders or no spiders.'

Nick knew it was a promise he could take to the bank, but they both knew he'd never call it in. And Matthew, the one person he would have given anything to see, and in whom he did want to confide, was out of reach. Nick could hardly leave Cornwall to go to visit him and it felt wrong to convey the news in a letter. He'd have to limit his correspondence to light-hearted chitchat about the farm and horses.

Sasha nudged him. 'Your dinner's getting cold. Where have you gone to in your head?'

'Nowhere. I was thinking about Matthew. I must write to him.'

'Tell him everything. Rant and rave to him if you need to. Say "How can this be happening to me when I've barely been married a fortnight?" Say anything you like; just keep communicating. It's important.'

It was easier said than done. On Sunday, a week after her operation, Sasha left Nick to labour over his letter and went to visit Rosa at the farmhouse. She was gone for so long that he grew worried and went in search of her.

Mr McKenna was in the yard, taking advantage of a spell of weak sunshine to bag winter vegetables for his customers. He nodded towards the kitchen door. 'I'm not sure what's going on in there, but judging by the giggles we'll not be liking it, either of us.'

He sucked on his pipe. 'How are you holding up, son?'

Nick kept moving, the collie dog squirming and wagging its tail around his legs. 'Fine. Pretty good, you know. Right, thanks, Gordon. I must get Sasha.'

'When you're not fine, we're here,' the farmer called after him.

Nick knocked at the farmhouse door. The laughter and a buzzing noise ceased.

'Come in,' called Rosa.

Ordinarily, Nick considered the McKennas' kitchen everything the heart of a farmhouse should be and more. It was cosy and smelled of delicious roast lunches, rhubarb crumbles and Victoria sponges. The flagstone floor was dominated by a magnificent, scarred oak table. Gordon had made it for his wife on their first anniversary, nearly forty years before. Copper pots and pans hung from hooks on the back wall. Every other surface was crowded with fat jars of preserves, colourful teapots, bowls of eggs and happy plants.

But Nick noticed none of these things. He was transfixed by his wife. She was sitting on a kitchen chair, wearing skinny brown corduroys and a chunky pink sweater with a bear on the front, neither of which he'd ever seen before. Rosa was standing behind her with a pair of clippers. But that wasn't what caused his blood pressure to surge.

'Oh, dear,' Sasha said. 'I told you he wouldn't like it.'

Rosa laughed. 'Well, I think you look hot. It'll grow on him. Shaven-headed women have a long tradition of sexiness. Think of Demi Moore in *GI Jane* or Sinead O'Connor.'

Neither of which I'd have touched with a bargepole, Nick thought cruelly, but he couldn't help himself. The shock of seeing his gorgeous wife, whose tangled dark locks he adored, looking like a football-hooligan skinhead, was too much for him.

She was still beautiful. If anything, baldness enhanced her delicate features. But without hair, her youth, vulnerability and the violet shadows beneath her eyes were magnified. To Nick, it was a look that screamed of illness.

'What's going on?'

Sasha gave him an over-bright smile. 'I thought I'd pre-empt things. Take control. When I start chemo tomorrow, any hair I do have is likely to be dropping out in chunks. Rather than getting depressed about it, I thought I'd go for a funky new look. I kind of like it. It's empowering.'

But walking back to Seabird Cottage in the twilight, towards the platinum line of sea, her confidence evaporated. 'You really hate it, don't you?'

Nick took her hand. 'Darling, no. Look, it's a bit of a surprise, but as Rosa said it'll grow on me. I wish you had said something, that's all.' He nodded towards the sports holdall she'd insisted on carrying. 'What's with the new clothes?'

'They're not new. Well, the underwear is. We nipped into Lanton to get it. But everything else is from Rosa's attic, clothes worn by her daughters or granddaughter. It was Rosa's idea. A friend of hers who had breast cancer did it. You become someone else, take on a different character, for the time that you're being treated. It stops you from being engulfed by the disease. Prevents it defining who you are.'

She gave an embarrassed laugh. 'That's why I'm wearing the kind of things I'd never normally be caught dead in.'

Intellectually and on a compassionate level, it made perfect sense. Yet every time Nick looked at the bald stranger beside him, the blood simmered in his veins. The cutting of her hair had been a symbolic act that separated them. He felt emasculated by it. A chasm had opened up between them. If they weren't careful it would quickly become a raging river, impossible to cross.

There was still distance between them when they climbed into the oak bed that night. Sasha had just returned from a late evening visit to see the horses.

'Any week I'm having chemo, I don't want to be around them. They're so sensitive that they'll smell it oozing from my pores for days afterwards. I want them always to associate me with good things. I don't want them to think of me as some toxic unknown quantity.'

But you are, Nick thought. *You've as good as admitted that you intend to become someone else for the duration of your illness.*

To make amends for his reaction to her shaved head, he held her tenderly. But even that backfired because she was wearing Rosa's floral perfume and didn't smell of Aveda shampoo and hemp soap the way she usually did. Leaving aside the baldness, she didn't look the way she normally did either. As long as he'd known her, her underwear of choice had been cute white cotton panties beneath her breeches, or silky thongs in colours like red or cream in bed. The thick black knickers she had on tonight put him in mind of a Catholic girls' boarding school, and not in a good way.

Even when she slipped the offending panties off and said, 'Make love to me one last time, Nick,' he didn't get aroused because her body was not the same. Always lean, she'd lost a disturbing amount of weight in less than two weeks.

'It isn't going to *be* the last time,' he snapped, glad of an excuse to get angry.

'Nick,' she said patiently, 'we have to face reality. From tomorrow, everything will be different. When I was nursing in London I saw the effects of cancer treatment firsthand. It robs you of desire, of dignity, of strength, of your femininity. Who knows when I'll be able to face having sex again. I'm trying hard to be positive, but the word chemotherapy alone makes me feel as if I'm being sent to the electric chair.'

Nick stuffed down his rage, ill with shame. He hated himself for his shallowness.

'I love you,' he said. 'You're not going to go through this alone. I'm here for you.'

Closing his eyes, he gave her a lingering kiss. He conjured up a picture of Sasha as she had been on the first day they made love. Crazed with passion, he'd torn off her sundress and white knickers and she had helped. Her silky brown thighs had parted and her beautiful body had arched against him as he entered her in a rush.

'Look at me, Nick.'

He opened his eyes. The image vanished.

Her face was sad. 'I asked you to make love to me, not to resort to fantasies.'

'I wasn't . . .'

She pulled away from him.

He kissed her shoulder. 'Sweetheart, please. I'm sorry. I want to do this.'

They tried again, but despite her best ministrations his traitorous body wouldn't co-operate. His cock lay flaccid against his thigh.

She got up, put on her robe and went out. A chill breeze came in after her. He could hear her settling down in the spare room. Less than a month had elapsed since they'd made a pact never to go to sleep on an argument or sleep in separate beds.

But that wasn't the worst part. The worst part was, he let her.

19

Nick added an extra pinch of sea salt, a grating of parmesan and a few basil leaves to the minestrone and tasted it for the umpteenth time.

'For goodness' sake, stop fussing over that soup like an ancient grandmother and bring it over here before I collapse of starvation,' said Sasha. 'There'll be none left if you carry on testing it. You're not Gordon Ramsay, you know.'

'And that's a bad thing why exactly?'

Nick put an extra grinding of pepper into the pot, gave it a quick stir and ladled the minestrone into a bowl. Sasha had lost her sense of taste and he may as well have given her cut-price cup-a-soup, especially since in the twenty-four hours following chemo she had trouble keeping anything down, but over the past two months Nick had challenged himself every day to find the perfect set of ingredients to stimulate her appetite. The right combination of nutrients would, he was convinced, restore not only her health but her taste buds. It was just a question of finding them. Most times he had to settle for a smile, but that in itself often felt like a victory.

He carried the tray over to the sofa, where Sasha lay wrapped in a duvet. Oliver's whiskers and pink nose poked out from beneath it. There was a pile of headscarves beside her.

'What's your opinion, kind sir?' she said, holding them up for his consideration. 'What takes your fancy? Shall I go for the pirate look, or would you prefer me as an urchin, vagabond or gypsy queen?'

'Personally, I've always rather fancied the idea of a gypsy queen. I could cross your palm with silver and you could tell me my fortune.'

'And what will you give me in return?'

She handed him the scarf and he tied it around her bald head, taking care not to pinch the gossamer skin at the back of her neck.

'Now that's a leading question. I suppose I could tell you yours.'

She smiled. 'Go ahead.'

'I predict that you'll love the minestrone and secretly think your husband is such a fine chef that it's a crime he doesn't have his own television show. I can also say with confidence that, very shortly, a tall, dark handsome man will want access to your duvet.'

'That's a bit conceited, don't you think – describing yourself as handsome?'

He draped the remaining scarves over the rather sparsely decorated Christmas tree. 'Admittedly there was a bit of poetic licence involved. What should I have said? How did you put it when we first got together? There was some remark about how I was "good-looking in a haunted, bachelor writer sort of way".'

'Did I really say that? I can't believe how brazen I was in those early days. Well, you're still a bit haunted and wounded, but I wouldn't describe you as good-looking.'

He flopped down beside her and tore a chunk from a crusty roll on her tray. 'I'm not sure my ego can take much more of this. How would you describe me?'

'Hmm, let me think. As the most devastatingly attractive man I've ever met.'

'You old charmer, you. You're only saying that to butter me up.'

She kissed him on the cheek with chapped, swollen lips. Mucositis had invaded her mouth, stripping the lining and leaving it ulcerated and raw. It was one of chemo's more vicious side effects. 'So what if I am? Now do you want to hear my predictions for you?'

'Will I require therapy afterwards?'

'Don't think so.'

He took her hand and pressed his mouth to her palm. 'That's in lieu of silver.'

'I predict that wherever I am, whether it's on earth or if I'm a star in the sky, I'll love you across space and time for all eternity. Across universes if I have to.'

He braced himself against a wave of emotion. 'Good try, but that's not even close to how much I'll love you. However, my affection's conditional. In the next half hour, you have to eat at least two spoonfuls of soup.'

She managed five, albeit with difficulty, and followed it with half a pot of strawberry yogurt. By recent standards, it was a triumph. The meal might even have stayed down had she not had a coughing fit while they were watching a movie. By the time she'd finished, her skin was a ghastly grey. Blood oozed from her gums and a sore near the corner of her mouth. Nick wiped it away with a tissue. As these things go, it was normal.

Out of habit he put a hand on her forehead to check her temperature. It was hot enough to fry an egg. He tried to decide whether that, too, was normal. In the morning, she'd begin a five-day course of prednisolone tablets and start exhibiting flu-like symptoms. She'd be weak with a tiredness that would grow more debilitating by the day. Strong smells such as the 'sour' stench of coffee or bad breath of strangers would be abhorrent to her. The previous month, even the scent of horses that lingered on Nick's jeans after he'd worked with them had repelled her.

She'd also been wracked with abdominal cramps and constipation so severe she'd been in tears. The take-no-prisoners CHOP regimen was corroding her stomach lining.

By comparison, the last week of the twenty-one-day cycle had been a breeze. She'd been able to taste and enjoy tea or the simple treats Nick made her, and spend time with Marillion and the other horses.

Sasha put a hand to her mouth. 'Nick, the bucket!'

He grabbed the bowl from the downstairs toilet and raced back to hold her head as she began to retch. 'Ready? Steady? Aim.'

Black humour was the only way to deal with it. They'd discovered that through trial and much error. It was either that or fall head first off an emotional cliff. They'd been there, done that, didn't want the T-shirt.

In a way, it was the stripping away of everything superficial, sex most of all, which had enabled them to get through it. Not that Nick had coped at first. He cringed to remember how he'd behaved. If he lived to be a hundred, he'd never forgive himself for his monumental selfishness in those early days. Perhaps that's why he worked so hard to make up for it.

For the first three weeks of her treatment they'd slept in separate beds. The raging river Nick feared had quickly become a flood. Ironically, the situation had been exacerbated because Sasha had sailed through the initial round of chemo with zero side effects. Nick wasn't surprised in the least. It would be typical of Sasha if she romped through this as she did everything in life, thumbing her nose at death and danger.

He'd tried to be supportive and there for her if she needed him, but he'd felt alienated by her new persona – part gap-year student, part ashram dweller – and by the constant stream of well-wishers through Seabird Cottage. Every five minutes someone was banging on the door. It was like rush hour at Charing Cross station. The living room was a perpetual hen party.

Relegated to the kitchen to make yet another round of teas and coffees, Nick would hear Sasha telling her friends: 'There's no sense in romanticising it. You have to roll up your sleeves and get practical, get healing fast.' She'd say: 'I don't want any of this to be for nothing. I'm trying to turn every situation into an opportunity to learn.'

It was like listening to the audio version of the self-help books she had piled up on her bedside table.

Internally – and that almost made it worse, because he wasn't honest about it – he'd railed like a spoilt teenager at the simultaneous withdrawal of her affections and focus on him. For a time, he'd lost his compass. His reflection of himself through Sasha had taken a battering. The part of him that wholeheartedly believed he loved all of her had been shattered to discover the degree to which he valued her beauty and the chemistry between them. It had terrified him that the cancer would take those things away.

Then came the second round of chemo at the end of November. On the first day, Sasha once more emerged from the hospital with a bounce in her step. At home, she decided against taking her anti-nausea tablets because she refused to have any more chemicals in her body than was absolutely necessary. 'I'll chew on a piece of ginger if I feel queasy.'

He'd been awoken hours later by the sound of violent hurling. It went on and on. A ghastly silence followed. He'd burst into the bathroom to find Sasha collapsed on the floor in a puddle of sick.

For a second he'd been convinced she was dead. That's when everything changed for him.

When her eyes fluttered open, he'd been so thankful he almost wept. He'd sponged her down, wrapped her in a blanket and cradled her while she vomited until there was nothing to throw up but blood. By 6 a.m., she'd deteriorated to the point where he almost called an ambulance. As it was, she was barely conscious by the time he got her to A&E.

Once there, she'd been sucked away into the system by a surfer-dude junior doctor and a couple of hatchet-faced nurses. It had been hours until he could get any information out of anyone. When the teenage doctor finally emerged and said that Sasha was going to be fine, Nick had locked himself in a toilet and sobbed for the first time since he was eleven.

On the day that she'd come home to Seabird Cottage, he'd carried her upstairs to the oak bed. She was as spindly as a fawn in his arms.

He sat on the mattress beside her and took her hand. 'I'm sorry. I've been a terrible husband – everything I swore I wasn't going to be. I haven't known how to handle things.'

A smile tweaked the corners of her mouth. Her vocal chords had been stripped raw and she was barely audible. She put a finger to his lips. 'No apologies, but no more separation either. Kills me. I've missed you.'

'Missed you too.'

The raging river was no more.

Nick put the remains of the minestrone in the fridge and turned off the Christmas-tree lights. Oliver was dead to the world in his igloo near the Aga, so Nick put the presents under the tree. There were four – two from him to Sasha, one from her to him, bought by Rosa, and an exceedingly large and heavy one from Phil and Mikhail: a dinner service, if the rattling was anything to go by. Matthew and Sarah had sent a card and a bottle of champagne.

If only they knew that we have nothing to celebrate except the surviving of each new day, thought Nick. For him, that was the greatest celebration of all.

As he climbed the stairs he could hear Sasha coughing. It worried him. She was twenty-four hours into the third cycle of CHOP and her immunity was non-existent. The previous week she'd insisted on letting a local charity bring twenty underprivileged kids to see the horses. The children were mostly well-behaved and a couple were precociously adorable, but every other kid had had a lurgy of some kind. They were like mobile petri dishes of flourishing bacteria.

Within forty-eight hours Sasha had developed a hacking cough and now there was a distinct rattle in her chest as she breathed. In bed, she was propped up against the pillows looking unnaturally flushed.

'It's the heating,' she explained. 'We need to turn it down. It's like an oven up here.'

'Clearly it's not the reading material.'

She didn't answer. She was absorbed in a passage in her Bible. When he'd met her she'd opened it once in a blue moon. Now she read it . . . well, religiously.

Not that religion had anything to do with it. As far as Sasha was concerned, religion had been hijacked centuries ago by men who liked to twist it for their own wicked ends. Faith was what mattered. Faith healed. It was about unconditional love. Faith moved mountains.

Nick had a quick shower. When he climbed into bed, she was still engrossed.

He lay watching her, little sparks of anger spitting in him. 'Do you ever ask yourself why the God who supposedly loves you would give you a lymphoma that could be fatal at the very moment you were happiest?'

She looked up, surprised. 'No, I don't. Why not me? Should I wish it on someone else? And I don't believe that God inflicts anything on anyone. We do these things to ourselves with the world we've created. We rape the land and poison the water. We manipulate food and spew chemicals and carcinogens into the air. Then we wonder why we get ill. It doesn't make sense.'

He picked up his book, a thriller. After a couple of pages he put it down again. 'The trouble with Christians is that most of them are like Gordon McKenna – pious on Sunday and miserable old sods for the rest of the week.'

She smiled. 'Really? Is that a true reflection of how you see him? Sure, he presents a grumpy face to the world, but as you know better than anyone that's mostly tongue-in-cheek. Consider what he does, not what he says. I mean, it's a source of constant amazement to me that the farm stays afloat. Gordon gives most of it away. Half the elderly in Lanton are kept alive by his free eggs and vegetables, and last year there was a rumour that he delivered his best ram and a couple of ewes to a struggling farmer – just dropped them off in the middle of the night. He never did admit it. Told the man he must have a screw loose. He flatly denied ever seeing the animals before.

'When I approached him the year before last about keeping a menagerie of rescued horses on his farm, with a view to ultimately opening a riding centre for disabled people, he moaned like a stuck pig. Said he'd never heard anything so half-baked in his life. At the same time, he couldn't do enough to help me. He built the stables almost single-handedly. I'd arrive at the site to find a fortune's worth of timber or bags of cement that he claimed to have found lying forgotten at the back of some barn. No matter how much I pleaded with him, he wouldn't take a penny. I tried tackling Rosa about it, but she was almost as bad. Told me I was doing them a favour by taking the stuff off their hands.'

She snuggled up to him. 'And now they've given us ten free acres, which means that one day my riding centre could become a reality. I don't know about you, but I'm not sure I've met many people kinder than that miserable old sod. Anyone can string together a bunch of pretty words, Nick. Love is an action.'

Before he could reply, she succumbed to a coughing fit that tore at her thin frame and left her with streaming eyes. Afterwards, the rattle in her chest was significantly worse.

Nick threw on jeans and a crumpled shirt and went downstairs to make her a hot lemon and honey drink. He would not go to sleep until he was sure she was okay. If in doubt, he would not go to sleep at all.

Love is an action.

While the kettle was boiling, he paged through recipe books. With what could he entice her on Christmas Day? Something tasty but soft like aubergine parmegiana? Or was it better to go for a relatively bland soup, like leek and potato? For dessert, it would have to be something soothing for her mouth. Rhubarb compote, perhaps, with a teaspoon or two of vanilla ice-cream.

He caught sight of the clock and realised he'd been gone for twenty minutes. Re-boiling the kettle, he poured it over the juice of one lemon and a tablespoon of manuka honey and hurried upstairs. Sasha was asleep. Crestfallen, he put the mug on her bedside table. He was reaching for the lamp switch when he saw beads of sweat on her forehead. The high points of colour on her cheeks had intensified. She was running a fever.

For the next few hours he kept vigil. Sasha's breathing grew increasingly laboured. When a coughing bout woke her, he took her temperature. It was 100 degrees and climbing. Ignoring her protests, he dialled 999. He didn't want to risk driving her to hospital only to have her spend six hours freezing in A&E on Christmas Eve.

The ambulance took an hour and a half to arrive. By then Sasha had a temperature of 103 and was hallucinating, and Nick was on the verge of a nervous breakdown.

'Apologies,' said one of the paramedics as he charged up the stairs. 'Pileup on the A30. Cutting people out of burning cars, they were. Christmas madness. Sex, drugs and tourists. Recipe for disaster.'

Nick had a flashback to Christmas Eve the previous year. Damian on the stretcher, his red hair maroon with dark blood. An hour earlier he'd been laughing, talking to Nick on the phone. He hadn't known he wouldn't live to see morning.

In the bedroom, Sasha was shiny with sweat and tugging weakly at the sheets. 'Right as rain by tomorrow,' she rambled, twisting away from the paramedic. Her eyes were glazed and unseeing. 'Right as rain . . .'

Into Nick's mind came a picture of Sasha on a mortuary slab, like Damian and his mum. He seized the arm of the paramedic.

'Please, she's the most precious thing on earth to me. You are going to be able to help her, aren't you?'

The man's face was a professional mask. 'All we can do is get her to the hospital as fast as we can. Put it this way, it's a good thing you called us when you did.'

As he picked up the stretcher, his eyes fell on the Bible. He glanced from it to Nick. He didn't say anything but the implication was clear.

Pray.

20

'A double whammy,' said Dr Reena Mehta, recently arrived from Gujarat, India. 'That is what we're up against. Your wife has a type of fever associated with the destruction of white blood cells during chemotherapy. Unfortunately, she has also developed pneumonia. I'm sure you don't need me to tell you that the consequences could be very serious indeed. She is in the Critical Care Unit and we are doing all we can, but you need to prepare yourself.'

She didn't elaborate on what he should be preparing himself for. 'Believe me, Mr Donaghue, the last thing I feel like doing on Christmas Day is delivering this kind of news, but it's not going to do either of us any favours if I lie to you. Now, do you have anyone you can call? A friend?'

Nick was aware of the doctor talking for a few minutes longer, but she was like a television with the sound turned down. He could have been looking at her round, bespectacled face on the news. Eventually, her footsteps receded.

The world whirled away. Nick was conscious only of an aggravating buzz in the overhead strip light and a spider web of cracks in the grey floor. An hour ticked by, then another and another. White plimsolls shuffled past, followed by trolley wheels, a vacuum cleaner and two gossiping nurses, one of whom made the mistake of trying to move him on. Distant sirens popped. An elderly lady, bent almost double, squeezed his shoulder.

At lunchtime, somebody brought him a coffee and a mince pie, which he left untouched. The doctor returned with an update. Nick was allowed in to see Sasha. She was so drugged up she barely recognised him, and the sight of her lying beneath the flickering monitors, her thin arms chock-full of tubes, was more disturbing even than his imaginings.

He returned to his spot in the corridor near the CCU. As the gloomy day darkened into evening, he was dimly aware of the chair beside him scraping under the weight of its new occupant.

'Might have known you'd be sitting here like the ghost of Christmas past, as if forgoing dinner is going to be of any use to Sasha whatsoever. Here, get this down you or Rosa will have my guts for garters. She's off giving the nurses a grilling. Wants to know every detail of Sasha's care. Believe me, if they had any ideas of giving Sash anything less than star treatment, they'll be thinking again.'

Nick managed a glimmer of a smile. 'Thanks, Gordon. I appreciate you both coming. Unfortunately, I don't think I can eat anything.'

The farmer thrust an open lunchbox into his hand and put two cups of steaming tea on the table. 'It's Rosa's best turkey and cranberry sandwich. Everything's homemade, including the bread. If you dare to insult her by not eating it, I'll tell everyone about that time I came to Seabird Cottage and that appalling carpentry effort of yours – an abomination of a bookshelf, I believe – came crashing down.'

'No doubt they've heard it all a million times,' Nick said wryly. He took a bite out of the sandwich. It was delicious and reminded him that he'd not eaten in nearly twenty-four hours. McKenna was right. If he didn't keep his strength up, he'd be useless to Sasha.

They sat in silence until Nick had finished the last crumb. There was a slice of Christmas cake too, but he couldn't face it.

'Thanks for the sandwich. World class. You were right, I needed it.'

'Don't be daft. By the way, Peg Moreton is on the hunt for you. Ran into her in the waiting room.'

'I've been avoiding her. What must she think of me? I promised to keep her daughter safe from harm and I've failed.'

'If it's the rot you'll be talking, I'll be off,' Mr McKenna chastised. He put a hand on Nick's shoulder. 'Son, if it was Rosa in there, I'd be raging like a bull. I'd be breaking things. You know me. I do that on a normal day. I can't tell you why we have to face these terrible trials, but I do believe they happen for a reason. What that reason is may not be obvious for weeks or months or even decades. But one day it'll become crystal clear.'

Nick stared him straight in the eye. 'When I was twenty-four, my mum and dad were killed in a head-on collision with a lorry driver who fell asleep at the wheel. Some evil bastard fuckwit, greedy for a few extra quid, stole my parents' lives. I had to identify their bodies. I saw my mother laid out in the morgue. What purpose did that serve?'

'Apart from turning you into a man who uses foul language, you mean? It's made you a good man, a compassionate man, a man strong enough to deal with this situation and deal with it well. It also made you a man who could empathise with the deaths of strangers and write beautifully about it . . . Surprised you, haven't I? Yes, I've read your *Times* obituaries. Looked them up online. Knew which ones were yours because the you that's underneath comes through in every line. There's never been a writer born who could hide his true nature on the page.'

Nick raked his fingers through his hair. 'I feel so useless, Gordon. There's nothing I can do to save her.'

'Ask for help. That's all it requires.'

'You're talking about prayer, I suppose. I'm afraid I don't believe in that.'

'Not asking you to, although personally I've always found it helpful. When everything else is going tits up, to borrow an expression you yourself might use, it's good to have something you can depend on. A rock.'

'What rock? It's like depending on sea mist. If it's okay with you, I'll put my faith in science. Doctors. Cutting-edge medical research. Things that are visible and have been proven to work and exist.'

'Great,' Mr McKenna said easily. 'Keep me posted on how that works out for you.'

He stood and Nick stood with him. 'Seriously, Nick, Rosa and I, we're here for you and Sasha, night or day. Anything you need, be it a turkey sandwich or a punch bag, pick up the phone and we'll be there.'

'I know that, Gordon. Thank you.'

The farmer packed away the sandwich wrappings and picked up the empty cups.

'Gordon?'

'Yes.'

'I think Sasha would like you to pray for her. If you don't mind.'

'Can't guarantee that the good Lord will pay attention to an old reprobate like me, but no, I don't mind at all.'

*

Sasha's condition continued to worsen. Nick was allowed torturously brief glimpses of her, each more frightening than the last. On Boxing Day, which, agonisingly, was also Sasha's thirtieth birthday, he checked into a soulless hotel a block away from the hospital. Later, he drove home to pack a bag with clothes and his typewriter. Light-headed with tiredness, he nearly had two accidents en route.

He felt none of the usual pleasure on entering Seabird Cottage. It was freezing, for starters, and the McKennas were taking care of Oliver, so there was no friendly face to greet him. His boots rang loudly on the stripped wood floor.

The bed had been made – probably by Rosa – but there were tell-tale signs of Christmas Eve's flight. Scattered toiletries, a couple of which had spilled. The mug of lemon and honey, never drunk, tucked behind the curtain. A cream negligee trapped in the chest of drawers. In his panic, he'd found it impossible to decide what Sasha would need where she was going.

He leaned against the wardrobe door and shut his eyes. Where was she going? Would she be back? He realised that a piece of him was already in mourning.

A hammering at the kitchen door almost gave him a heart attack. Ryan was on the doorstep, hopping from foot to foot like an anxious crow. His black spikes quivered in the cutting wind. The scar on his cheek, a fishing-hook injury, was bright pink. As usual, he was inadequately dressed for the weather, in a leather jacket, grey hoodie and pipe-cleaner jeans.

'Nick. Umm, I didn't know if you'd be here. Just wanted to say how sorry I am about Sash. Hope she's better soon. She's the best.'

'Thanks, Ryan. That's nice of you. It's sort of day by day at the moment.'

Out of the corner of his eye, Nick saw the recipe books on the counter. A lifetime ago, he'd planned to cook Christmas dinner for Sasha. Their presents lay unopened beneath the tree.

He wished Ryan would go, but the boy lingered in the doorway. It was obvious he had something to say. Not that he was in any hurry to admit it.

'Are you sure there's nothing I can help with? My cleaning skills are not brilliant, but I could definitely vacuum the cottage or catch you a fish . . . Anything you need, consider it done. I don't mind hanging out with you for a while either. Shitty time of the year to be alone.'

'Thanks, Ryan, but I wouldn't inflict myself on anyone at the moment. I'm moving to a hotel room near the hospital. I want to be as close to Sasha as possible.'

'Right. Course. Well, you have my number if you need me. I'll be out of action for the next couple of days but you can get a message to me and I'll come as soon as I can. If I can't, I'll send a mate.'

'Ryan, what's up? Is there something on your mind?'

The boy squirmed. He resumed his hopping. 'No. It's nothing. Feel guilty even mentioning it when Sasha's at death's door.' The scar on his cheek glowed scarlet. 'I didn't mean—'

'I know. Spit it out.'

'Weird coincidence. Going to hospital myself tomorrow. Same one as Sasha. Appendix is coming out. Doctor insisted 'cos it keeps flaring up.'

'You nervous?'

'Shit scared.'

'It'll be cool. Nothing to it. All that happens is they put a needle in your arm, you count to three, then they're waking you up and telling you it's all over. Easy peasy.'

'Really?'

'Really.'

They gripped hands. Thought about hugging. Didn't.

Ryan was swinging onto his bike when the dream of a couple of months earlier came back to Nick. It was too faded to be trustworthy, and he had trouble recalling anything beyond the fact that a red-nosed surgeon had been bent over a dying Ryan, but he knew he had to say something.

He had to sprint to catch up with the teenager and nearly didn't make it. Ryan was on the farm road and picking up speed. Nick yelled to make himself heard above the iPod and the swirling wind.

Ryan swerved to a halt, plucking out his headphones.

'Ryan, I don't know how to tell you this . . . You'll think I'm nuts, but . . .'

'No change there then.'

'At the hospital there's a surgeon who looks like one of the judges from The Muppets. Younger, but you get the picture. Broken nose.

Whatever you do, don't let him operate on you. No matter what pressure they put on you, say no. Promise me.'

Ryan gripped Nick's hand again, causing the pins and needles to intensify. 'Give you my word. No Muppet surgeon's getting within ten metres of me.'

Nick listened to his bike crunch away down the farm road and thought how crazy it was that men were seen as being somehow stronger than women simply because they could lift heavier loads. Right now, he felt as much of a scared boy as Ryan. The thing in him that was keeping going, putting one foot in front of the other, came from Sasha.

Even when she was asleep (he couldn't bear to think of her as unconscious), he had the sense of an invisible current flowing from her to him, fuelling him, giving him the power to stand upright. It was that strength he drew on now as he trudged back to the cold, empty cottage to pack his suitcase and prepare once more to go to war.

21

Carole Jackson stood on the hospital fire escape smoking a cigarette under cover of darkness. It was against the law, but of course they all did it – the nurses, surgeons and ambulance drivers. How else did the bean-counting ignoramuses who mismanaged the National Health Service expect them to deal with the stress? If it had been up to her, nicotine would have been prescribed free to all medical staff, along with chocolate and alcohol.

Carole checked her watch and had a last nip of brandy (a winter warmer was how she thought of it) before returning to the Critical Care Unit for her shift. Not too much, because she didn't want to end up like that old soak Dr Davey Roper, frog-marched from the building that morning for being drunk on the job. Among the nurses, she alone had sympathy for him. When Bea from radiology had demanded to know why she cared, Carole had retorted: 'Because there but for the grace of God go us all.'

Not that Carole believed in God; she most certainly did not. It was simply an expression. It would have been more accurate to say, 'Because a lot of us sail a bit too close to the wind,' but that might have aroused Bea's suspicions.

At any rate, Carole had been sad to see Dr Roper go. He could very well lose his medical licence, and all because some punk-haired adolescent with an attitude had refused to let him take his appendix out. The resulting row had brought a senior surgeon running. It had been she who clocked that Roper, long rumoured to be alcoholic, was so drunk he could barely hold a scalpel, let alone perform an operation.

Despite this cautionary tale, Carole took another swig of brandy. She'd need it if she was to have any hope of getting through the remainder of her twelve-hour shift, during which she would be expected to nurse her ex-lover's ex-lover back to health. A laugh that was part sob escaped her. Of all the sodding luck. The woman who'd been the architect of her ruin was now under her care. Carole couldn't decide if that was a disaster, or a gift of an opportunity too perfect to pass up.

Only that week, she'd learned that she'd be getting nothing in the divorce. As if that wasn't bad enough, the combination of her reduced circumstances (she was back living in a shared flat with two ditzy student nurses) and the weight she was piling on meant that her chances of snaring another wealthy husband were shrinking by the day. What was it that Germaine Greer had said all those years ago? Something about a woman over forty having more chance of being killed by a terrorist than getting married. Those odds had worsened, not improved. These days you couldn't even fly to Ibiza without worrying that some nutter with a bomb in his Hush Puppies might be about to blow you to smithereens.

If only she'd done things differently with Cullen. Been more discreet. She could have had her cake and eaten it. Jeremy, her soon-to-be ex-husband, was a nice man. His looks and personality would never have set the world on fire, but he'd been besotted with her. Carole only had to snap her fingers and he'd fallen over himself to buy her jewellery, clothes and pretty things for the house.

As befitting the wife of a man who owned an electronics chain, Carole had also been the proud owner of a flatscreen television that took up half the living room and all the gadgets her heart desired. She and Jeremy had been to the Caribbean three times. However, all that had paled beside the gift he'd bought her for her last birthday: a midnight-blue, custom-fitted MG that had been the envy of the entire hospital.

Seizing Carole's sports car had been the most agonising of the many blows the scorned Jeremy had chosen to inflict on her.

Perhaps she should have killed him while she had the chance. She and Cullen had often joked about it – doing away with their partners and starting a new life in a tropical paradise like Belize with Jeremy's millions. Cullen had a cruel streak. Frustratingly, he'd always been less focused on getting rid of Sasha than he had on tormenting the man he'd decided she fancied – the reporter who'd moved into Seabird Cottage.

For reasons that remained unclear, Cullen had detested the guy on sight. From time to time, he'd regaled Carole with the latest episode in his mission to drive the man back to London. Once, he'd even got it into his head to strangle the man's cat because he'd overheard Sasha's mother saying how much he doted on it. Another time, he'd broken into the cottage to search for evidence that Sasha had been there. Finding nothing, he'd kidnapped the reporter's cat and carted it across the fields to the farmhouse in the hope that the McKennas' border collie would find it and kill it.

That kind of behaviour had given Carole pause. She'd demanded to know how Cullen could claim to be in love with her when he continued to effectively stalk Sasha. But Cullen maintained that he'd done these things on principle, not because he was jealous. As long as Sasha belonged to him, he was not going to put up with her screwing around on him – especially not with some prick of a Londoner who'd had the temerity to insult him.

When Carole had pointed out the obvious, Cullen snapped: 'Double standards are better than no standards at all, pet.'

He'd said something similar when he got engaged to Sasha mere hours after spending the afternoon in bed with Carole. Carole had gone ballistic when she found out. Cullen's excuse was that he'd felt under pressure to 'do the right thing'.

'I don't understand why you're giving me a hard time when *you're* married yourself,' he'd ranted at his lover. 'You're a hypocrite, you are.'

Carole needn't have worried. Afterwards, their affair became steamier than ever.

Ducking away from an onslaught of midges, she took a final swig of brandy and headed back to the CCU via the bathroom. In the neon glare, she brushed her teeth and shook the smoke out of her lank blonde hair. The face staring back at her in the mirror was a study in despair. Not so long ago, she'd been beating off admirers. Now the bags under her eyes were tea-coloured, her roots were showing and there were unsightly grooves in her décolletage from years of sun exposure.

With hindsight, it was her own fault that events had taken the dramatic twist they had and poor Cullen had been beaten half to death by a scarlet-faced Jeremy wielding a golf club. In the weeks leading up to that attack, Cullen had been pushing her to leave 'Mr Tubby'. But Carole had been playing an age-old game. She'd wanted to keep her lover while continuing to enjoy the trappings her husband's money afforded her. She adored Cullen, but she didn't trust him. As soon as she belonged to him, he'd do to her what he was doing to Sasha.

The rules of the game changed after Jeremy threw her out. Desperate, Carole had turned her attention to salvaging her relationship with Cullen. She'd nursed him and listened to his woes. The money she'd spent years squirrelling away, in case she ever decided to leave Jeremy, she'd used instead to send Cullen to a cosmetic dentist. His new teeth, although alarmingly white, had made him look more dashing than ever. He'd declared his undying love for her. Her hopes for the future were further raised when he returned from a trip to Ireland full of talk about how they were going to move to Galway Bay and start again. Galway was not as hot or exotic as Belize, but it had its attractions, not least that it was far from Sasha.

Unfortunately, Cullen's continuing obsession with his former fiancée soon took its toll on their fledgling relationship. He'd been enraged to learn that Sasha had moved in with his nemesis – the reporter. That piece of news alone had caused him to fume and moan for days.

'I'll teach her a lesson she'll never forget,' he'd raged. 'It's not over till it's over.'

Carole had been unable to repress a thrill at the thought of her lover taking out his wrath on the woman she hated, however unjust that attack might be. She had a suspicion that Cullen's way of hurting Sasha would be to destroy the black horse she worshipped, a creature he detested. Sadly, nothing happened. Despite spending the best part of a week acting as if he were plotting something truly sinister, it all came to zip.

One afternoon, he'd returned to their rented holiday apartment and announced that he was leaving for Ireland within hours – alone. He vowed that as soon as his business was up and running in Galway Bay, he'd send for her. Two weeks later she'd received a text: *Sorry, pet. It's over.*

Now she was expected to play Florence Nightingale to the woman who, as Carole saw it, had taken everything from her.

Back in the CCU, she leaned over the unconscious patient, her face mask-like in the greeny light of the hospital room. In her heart of hearts, Carole was well aware that Sasha had not destroyed her life and that the reverse was in fact true. If anyone had been wronged it was Sasha. But she loathed her just the same.

Her health aside, Sasha had everything. A cottage by the sea and a good man who'd not only married her but was, by all accounts, devoted to her. The departing day nurse, Violet, had practically been in tears as she'd related how he'd sat in the corridor for hours on end, like a little boy lost. She'd tried to comfort him, but he'd wanted to be on his own.

'Ever so nice he is. Gorgeous, too, in a sleep-deprived, wounded-soldier sort of way. But I got the impression that if something happened to his wife, he wouldn't care less if he lived or died.'

Her curiosity piqued, Carole had been unable to resist getting a close look at the man who'd driven Cullen to distraction. She'd taken him a cup of tea and a couple of biscuits. It was the kind of thing that would have incensed Cullen and in the midst of her misery it made her feel good to get back at her ex, even in a small way.

Nick had been pale, unshaven and polite. He'd mumbled a thank you and said something about how kind everyone had been, but he hadn't really looked at her. That annoyed Carole. Until recently most men had registered her in a favourable way, whether they were nineteen or ninety.

'I'm Sasha's night nurse,' she told him. 'I'll be taking the best possible care of her. Go home and get some sleep, Mr Donaghue. Try not to worry.'

He'd run an anxious hand through his hair. 'Are you sure? What if she wakes up and needs me?'

For a split second his emotions had been naked on his face and she could see how close he was to the edge. Unexpectedly, her heart had gone out to him. She'd put a hand on his shoulder, intending to tell him again that Sasha was in safe hands, but he'd jerked away as if he'd been electrocuted. A spasm of revulsion had rippled across his face.

Before she could work out what she'd done to cause such an extreme reaction, he'd escaped down the corridor, leaving more polite thank-yous and you're-too-kinds in his wake. The tea and biscuits had been left untouched.

A shadow fell across Sasha's hospital bed. 'Everything all right, Carole?'

'Dr Mehta! Yes! One hundred per cent!' Fright gave Carole a life-and-soul-of-the-party voice. Hastily, she toned it down. 'I mean, she's stable at the moment. It's great to see.'

The new doctor had a piercing intellect and genuine compassion for her patients. She also had a directness of gaze that had a tendency to make Carole feel guilty, even though she had not, as yet, done anything wrong. She was thankful when Dr Mehta transferred her attention to the monitors.

'Yes, it is, but she remains critical. I'll admit to you, Carole, I am deeply concerned. Keep a close watch on her over the next few hours. Any change for the worse, no matter how minuscule, call me at once. I'm going to A&E for an emergency consult.'

After she'd gone, Carole scowled down at her patient with renewed bitterness. As gratifying as it was that Sasha had lost her looks and resembled a prisoner of war as she lay lifeless in the sterile hospital bed, it was not enough. If she recovered, she'd return to her perfect life by the sea with the man who loved her, while Carole spent a thousand lonely Friday nights eating tubs of cookie dough ice cream in front of dire romantic comedies packed with propaganda about true love. And all because Cullen had been too cut up over Sasha to stay in Lanton.

In reality, Carole knew that Cullen would have forgotten about both her and Sasha within twenty-four hours of arriving in Galway Bay and was at this moment doubtless tucked up with some ravishing Irish girl. But he wasn't here. Sasha was.

A chilly smile flitted across Carole's lips as she surveyed the machines keeping Sasha alive. Violet had once told her a story about a bed in a South African hospital that had gained notoriety because every Friday someone died in it. Around the hospital, it became known as a cursed bed. After an investigation was launched to see if anything untoward was going on, it was discovered that the hospital cleaner had been unplugging the life-support machine in order to power her vacuum cleaner.

Carole had laughed till she cried when Violet reached the punchline of the tale. It had appealed to her sick sense of humour. Few nurses survived without one. But she wasn't laughing now. She was recalling the grim hospice she'd worked at after graduating, where the easing of elderly patients into the next world was actively encouraged in order to free up beds.

During her night shifts, Carole had dispatched quite a few of these old biddies and gents without so much as a twinge of conscience. She had, she felt, done them a favour. Getting rid of Sasha would be no different. It would have an equally positive outcome – not for Sasha and the bereaved reporter, perhaps, but for Carole. There could be no more effective way of cutting Cullen to the core. Once he returned to Lanton for the funeral, as she was sure he would, she'd win him over with her own special blend of comfort.

Her nails bit into her palm. Could she do this or not?

Nobody at the hospital knew about Cullen. Carole had confided in several friends about her affair, but she'd never disclosed the identity of her lover. Even after her marriage broke up and she and Cullen moved in together, they'd kept their relationship under wraps in the hope that Carole would get the biggest settlement possible in the divorce. Fat chance now. But it did mean that there'd be no reason for anyone to connect her with Sasha. According to the lawyer, Jeremy was out of the country on an extended leave of absence. If she knew him at all, he would not have told a soul that he'd caught her in bed with a plumber. His fragile ego could not have stood it.

Dr Mehta was a couple of floors down. All Carole had to do was turn off the life-support machine and waste a critical couple of minutes before turning it on again and sounding the alarm. A crash team would be there in moments, but with luck it would be too late. Sasha would have been erased from existence. If anyone got the blame, it would be the new doctor – leaving the bedside of a critically ill patient to go elsewhere.

Carole experienced a rush that beat the high of any drug she'd ever taken. For the first time in months, *she* was the one in control. *She* held the power.

Moving quickly to the doorway, she peered out. The triage nurse, Nina, was at the far end of the corridor, arguing with a visitor. They had their backs to her. The woman yielded and the pair disappeared round the corner. Carole checked her watch. It was 2.08. Snores echoed from the room across the way and she could hear the faint murmur of a faraway phone conversation, but otherwise all was quiet.

Carole returned to Sasha's bedside. She smiled as her hand hovered over the switch.

22

For the first time since the crash, Nick prayed for a nightmare. Before he'd ever met Sasha, his greatest fear had been seeing a lover's death in a dream. Now he was terrified that his wife might die alone surrounded by strangers, or because of simple human error or another easily preventable complication, all because his clairvoyance had failed him on the one occasion he needed it to work. If he could see the worst, as he had been able to do with Ryan and Pattie Griffin, he might be able to prevent it.

Infuriatingly, Sasha appeared to be his one blind spot. The only time she ever featured in his dreams was as part of a random collection of images, and a snapshot of her smiling over her shoulder could in no way be shown to hint at cancer. Nor, for that matter, could Gordon McKenna crossing the horizon on his tractor or Marillion rearing.

He'd never figured out what the billowing colours meant. An exhaustive search of the flags of the world in an encyclopaedia in Lanton bookshop had not produced a match. As prescient dreams go, the symbol ones had been about as useful as a watering can in a wild-fire.

He picked up his mobile. He needed a friend. If he didn't speak to someone, he felt he'd go mad. Scrolling down his list of contacts, he paused first at Becca's number, then Phil's, then the McKennas'.

The person he most wanted to talk to was Matthew, but how could he ring the man in the middle of the night and say, 'Sasha's in intensive care – I'm petrified I'm going to lose her,' when he hadn't even told him she was ill?

The nurse; perhaps he could ring the nurse.

The outline of her, as she stood bewildered in the corridor while he stammered and stuttered in his haste to get away, swam into his mind. Not even Marillion had caused such a reaction in him. It was like being struck by a bolt of lightning. But whereas the horse had caused his hands to tingle as if an electric current was pulsing through them, the nurse's touch had triggered something akin to revulsion. As he'd backed away down the passage, he'd had the sensation of having been brushed by something unclean.

Thinking about it now, he was embarrassed. His own wife had been a nurse. Technically, she still was a nurse. He was well aware that nurses were not only paid atrociously, they were frequently under-valued and abused by meddling administrators, arrogant doctors and an ungrateful public. Sasha's night nurse had taken the trouble to visit him and attempt to reassure him that she would be taking the best possible care of the woman he loved, and his response had been to treat her like a leper. He couldn't even remember whether or not he'd thanked her for the tea and biscuits. It was shameful. If he saw her again, he'd have to make a grovelling apology.

No, he couldn't call the nurse. She definitely wouldn't want to hear from him. It could potentially make matters worse.

He began to pace the room. It was then that he remembered *The Prophet*. He'd found it while looking for a book that might distract him and had shoved it into his bag on his way out of Seabird Cottage.

Nearly a year had gone by since Matthew had returned it, yet Nick was no wiser as to its contents. He opened it to the dog-eared page. Even from a distance of twelve months, he could recall the power of the wind that had come close to sucking him off the cliff edge that New Year's Day. The fury that had risen in him when he saw the words in Matthew's card came back to him with cinematic clarity. Now, for the first time, he looked at the page beneath.

Your pain is the breaking of the shell that encloses your under-standing . . .

Over and over he read the lines below. They had a truth that was especially devastating because it spoke directly to him in the way of a song lyric heard at a moment of heartbreak. He felt listened to and understood.

But when he reached the last sentence, he cast the book aside. 'I can't, Matthew. Why the fuck should I accept any of this, let alone in silence and tranquillity?'

The same compulsion that drove him time and time again to reach for his typewriter and tell his character's story drove him now to take the much-edited script from his bag. He couldn't control what was happening in real life, but he could change the outcome in his novel.

Picking up the hotel phone, he ordered a room-service toasted sandwich with chips and a pot of strong coffee. He expected the worst, and it went some way to restoring his spirits when it came and was really quite tasty. A steaming shower revived him further. He climbed into bed in his boxers and fanned through the sheaf of pages. By his calculations, he'd written around 85,000 words. All the book really needed was an ending.

Using the complimentary hotel pen, he began to write with the same urgency that had possessed him since he'd been compelled to type the first line. In spite, or perhaps because of his nightmares, he spent his days trying to distance himself from anything that even vaguely smacked of the supernatural. That was at least part of his problem with God. But what was undeniable was that from start to finish his novel had felt channelled. It was as if the story was being told to him; as if, in a parallel universe, it already existed. In essence, he was merely a conduit.

He was unaccustomed to writing in longhand and his handwriting was terrible, but his pen flew across the paper almost of its own accord. And once committed to the page, the words became more real than reality. He wrote on into the night, fuelled by caffeine and Rosa McKenna's Christmas cake, until at last he came to the final sentence. It should have felt momentous, but he was so exhausted that it was all he could do to finish it and scrawl: *The End*. Still, he felt lighter. In prose, if not in life, he'd done what he could to fix things.

Drained, he lay down. It was 2.08 on the bedside clock. He refused to sleep. He would not sleep until he knew she was safe.

He slept.

An hour earlier, Rosa McKenna had put another log on the fire in the farmhouse living room and settled into an armchair with a mug of tea in one hand and a PD James novel in the other. Oliver was on her lap, glowering at Skip the border collie. It was after 1 a.m. but sleep was the furthest thing from her mind. A feeling she was unable to identify gnawed away at her. Initially, she'd put it down to the extra portion of cauliflower cheese she'd served herself at dinner. It was famously rich and often gave her heartburn. But when a Rennie failed to shift it, she'd left Gordon snoring and come downstairs.

Of course, with Sasha in the CCU it was nigh-on impossible to drift off. Gordon was only sleeping because he'd spent the last three nights tossing and turning. It had finally caught up with him. At dinner, he'd almost nodded off into his trifle.

It frightened her sometimes how much Sasha had come to mean to them. She was the daughter they'd never had. 'Not for want of trying,' Gordon had told people in his inimitable Gordon way when he and Rosa were still young enough for their childless state to be of exhaustive interest even to strangers. She'd been glad when the first grey hairs appeared and she no longer had to explain that she was barren. That was the word she'd always used. It was an old-fashioned term and offensive to some, but it was the truth.

In the early days of her marriage, she'd begged Gordon to leave her while he was still young enough to start again and have the family he so desperately wanted.

'Don't be daft,' was his standard response. 'Where would I find another woman who'd put up with me?'

He had a point. Not because nobody else would put up with him, but because Rosa was certain that no other woman would appreciate as much as she did the funny, thoughtful and impossibly generous man who hid behind Gordon's dour, grizzly-bear exterior.

Not that he was perfect. He could be a royal pain in the arse. In the years when she was still sensitive about such things, it used to infuriate her when he said of their childless state that it had happened for a reason. He was confident that that reason would one day be revealed to them.

To Rosa, who in her thirties and early forties had on numerous occasions locked herself in the bathroom and sobbed into a towel after excruciating visits to friends blessed with abundant, bouncing kids – children they frequently seemed not to appreciate – there could be no good reason for a womb that wasn't fit for the purpose. There'd been times when it had severely tested her faith. And yet the day Sasha had knocked on the farmhouse door asking if there was any chance they might lease her a plot of land for a couple of rescued horses, because she had a pipe dream that she might eventually be able to start a riding centre for disabled children, the parched, cold place inside Rosa began to thaw.

Over the past two years, it had been a joy to have Sasha near them and to share in her vision. Within months of meeting her Gordon had wanted to change their joint will, leaving Sasha the farm, but Rosa had refused to go along with it until Sasha married Nick. She'd never trusted Cullen. For one thing, Skip cringed away from him. For another, he was too smooth. At one stage Rosa had become convinced Sasha was being abused by him. She didn't seem the type to put up with it, but in Rosa's experience there was no type.

As a child she'd witnessed her own mother, a brilliant mathematician and gregarious, outspoken beauty, become a creeping, agoraphobic shadow without her father so much as raising a hand to her. It had taught her that, to some people, love and hate were not opposites but on a continuum, and that while fists and guns could maim or kill, nothing inflicted pain like a cruel whisper. She'd vowed to marry a man who was the polar opposite of her father and she had. There were plenty of men with more social graces than Gordon, but there was no one kinder.

When Nick moved into Sadie's ruin of a cottage, Rosa had for a long time kept her distance, imagining he was either a tourist who'd been deceived by the brochure pictures or a starving artist friend of Sadie's nephew, Phil. She was afraid that if she visited him, she'd be compelled to invite him to move into the warm farmhouse and that if he was the latter he'd never leave.

For several months, she and Gordon's usual roles had been reversed. Ordinarily, it was Rosa who welcomed newcomers to the area with open arms. Like a mother hen, she almost always tried to set them at their ease and ply them with food and drink.

Gordon had made no attempt to do that with Nick. He wasn't that sort of person. Even on his best days, he simply wasn't capable of it. But he did do something surprising. He gave Nick the benefit of the doubt. Their abortive first encounter – a version of which had been hilariously recounted at so many dinner parties that it had passed into legend – had demolished his preconceptions of the young journalist.

Privately, Gordon had confided to her that although there was something quite pitiful about Nick's terrible DIY and hopeless attempts to keep body and soul together, his determination to make his new life work in the face of whatever unseen horror was hanging over him showed courage 'the like of which I've not seen in a long time'.

But what had really won him over were Nick's good manners. Under extreme provocation – 'I ribbed him a little – had to be done' – Nick had remained civil and even respectful, as well as demonstrating a talent for self-deprecation. At the same time, he'd not been cowed. Far from it.

Thus in a single meeting the seeds of an unlikely friendship had been born. The fact that Nick had saved Pattie's life hadn't hurt either.

Rosa had taken longer to warm to Nick, not because he wasn't inherently likeable (it was hard not to admire a man who'd go out in a rainstorm and start a pub brawl because he was so desperate to find his missing cat), but because from early on it had been clear that Sasha was falling for him. Rosa had been convinced it would end in tears.

Yet at every turn Nick confounded her. While Cullen revealed himself to be a philandering shit of the first order, Nick, in a hundred unexpected ways, had been Sasha's rock. Not that he was without flaws. There'd been a shaky period after Sasha was diagnosed with lymphoma. The day he'd walked into the farmhouse kitchen and seen his wife's shaved head, he'd looked on the verge of a volcanic eruption.

By then, however, Rosa had come to love him like a son. She understood that he was reeling. There was so much chemistry between Nick and Sasha that the air practically crackled when one was around them, and to have that taken away within days of the honeymoon, to have your partner look like someone else, *be* someone else, be potentially dying, was something very few people could take. She'd feared it might be the breaking of him.

Instead it was the making of him, and with every passing day she was more thankful that it was Nick who'd been at Sasha's side, not Cullen, when the storm struck.

At the thought of Sasha's ex, Rosa's sense of unease deepened. She tried once again to figure out what was niggling at her. Like Gordon, she was beside herself with worry about Sasha, but it wasn't that. It was something she'd seen or heard. A snippet of conversation. A fractured image. A face she knew without knowing she knew it.

Out of the blue it came to her. Shortly after Cullen and Sasha had got engaged, Rosa met a friend for lunch in St Ives. While tucking into tapas at the Porthmeor Beach Cafe, she'd glanced out of the window and been sickened to see Cullen strolling along the beach rather amorously nuzzling the neck of a woman who wasn't his fiancée. It had taken her a long time to forget the woman, who was pretty in an expensively tarted-up way, or the anguish that seeing the pair had caused her.

That night, she hadn't slept a wink. She'd spent hours agonising over whether to break the news to Sasha, or to stay silent but confront Cullen. An apoplectic Gordon had suggested a dozen unchristian things such as putting sugar in Cullen's petrol tank, or a prawn in the back of his laptop, or just giving him a 'bloody good hiding'.

As it turned out, the decision was taken out of their hands. Less than forty-eight hours later, Cullen self-destructed. The seven-iron wielded by the anonymous woman's husband, some kind of electronics millionaire from Truro if Lanton gossip was to be believed, had been a much more effective deterrent against future cheating than a lowly prawn.

Sasha had taken the news better than expected, but the whole experience had been so harrowing and had soured Rosa against Cullen to such a degree that she'd made a conscious effort to bury the St Ives memory. Until now. Now that it was critical she recall his mistress's face, her features were fuzzy. She hovered just out of view. What she did remember was that the woman was said to be a nurse.

Rosa wished she still had the faculties of a twenty-year-old. At the hospital earlier that evening, she'd been too preoccupied with grilling the day nurses and checking on Nick to take much notice of her surroundings. She'd barely noticed the nurse who arrived to take the night shift as they were leaving. Yet that fleeting impression had been sufficient to sow a toxic seed that had infected her whole system.

Rosa tried to marry the two images: the cunning sensuality of the woman on the beach and the shadowy nurse. Were they the same? Yes, they were. Out of nowhere, the woman's face came burning into her brain.

Rosa leapt from her chair, startling Skip into a volley of barking. Oliver shot under the sofa. A note. She must leave a note for Gordon. A hasty scrawl and then she was rushing out into the dark garden, her hands shaking so much that it took her several attempts to get the key in the ignition. The engine purred to life, illuminating the dashboard.

Rosa exited the driveway so fast that she almost took out the gatepost. It was 1.33 a.m.

The Hotel Atlantic was not the most salubrious establishment in Cornwall, but it did have double-glazing that muted all but the most cacophonous of the traffic noises on the streets below. As a result, Nick was still sound asleep when rush hour, such as it was, began on Monday morning.

As he started to resurface, drifting up through the layers from stage-four sleep to the REM sleep responsible for dreaming, the landscape of his nightmares swung into place. A dripping tunnel, claustrophobic and dank. Rats in the gutters, claws skittering. Nick tried to turn back but already it was too late. A force outside of him and apart from him propelled him onwards.

He stopped fighting and allowed himself to be carried along, waiting with an awareness that was almost conscious for the horror to unfold. But as he neared the next turn, the tunnel suddenly became lighter. The walls shimmered like mica. He tensed for the bleakness that always awaited him. The tragedy of lives half-lived and slipping away.

It didn't come. Around the corner was a lagoon flanked by a white beach. A rainbow arched over it. The sun emerged and stole into his bones, warming him by degrees. The weight on his chest lifted. He felt lighter than he had in years.

Nick opened his eyes and lay unmoving, trying to hold onto the unfamiliar feeling of serenity. Then he caught sight of the clock. It was after eight. Cursing, he shot up in bed and pulled on his jeans and a jumper. Pausing only to splash his face and rinse out his mouth with toothpaste, he grabbed his jacket and flew out into the hard, bright morning. It was December 28th and it felt like it. The streets crawled with people on a post-Christmas comedown, lethargic and queasy.

He had to get to Sasha; that's all he could think. Something was wrong and he had to get to Sasha.

As the lift doors opened on the CCU corridor, Nick saw the backs of two black-uniformed police officers. They moved swiftly to intercept him.

'This area is off limits at the moment, I'm afraid, sir. You'll need to go back down—'

'I'm not going anywhere. Dr Mehta promised I could come first thing. I need to see my wife.'

'I'm sorry, sir, but that's not possible. This area is a crime scene. We've cordoned off a section of private rooms. If you go back down to reception, they'll explain—'

'A crime scene? My God, what's happening? I have to see my wife.' Evading the officers' grasp, Nick ran down the passage, but they were lighter on their feet than their bulk implied and before he'd got halfway their heavy hands were clamping down on him.

'Try that again, sir, and we'll have you in cuffs,' said the taller one. He took out a notebook. 'Name and address, please?'

Nick straightened his jacket and tried to contain his fury. 'Have you no compassion? My wife is on a life-support machine and you're treating me like a criminal.'

The other officer's face changed. 'Let him go. It's the husband.'

It's the husband.

Dr Reena Mehta materialised at the end of the green corridor. Her homely face was as welcome as a lighthouse in a tempest.

'Mr Donaghue, thank goodness you have come. Despite specific instructions to ring your hotel, the person I asked to call you kept trying your mobile and home number, both of which kept going to voicemail. Then Rosa McKenna, your neighbour, told us we should let you get some sleep.'

'Rosa? I don't understand. What does she have to do with anything? And what is this about a crime? Has a patient been hurt? Please tell me what's going on with Sasha.'

She took his arm. 'To be honest with you, Mr Donaghue, we've had quite a time of it. Sasha flatlined overnight. There was this nurse, this mentally disturbed nurse, who tampered with the ventilator. I had a bad feeling about her, but of course you can't dismiss people because you have an instinct about them. If Rosa hadn't come when she did . . . But don't worry, the police have taken her away.'

Nick was suddenly so weak he could barely stand. 'They've taken Rosa?'

'Not Rosa, the nurse.'

'Just give it to me straight. What's happened to Sasha?'

'Nick, do not distress yourself further. Not only did we manage to revive her but she's made what I can only describe as a miraculous recovery. She's sitting up in bed and she's asking for you.'

'Sasha's conscious and she's asking for me? Dr Mehta, you're a genius. The greatest doctor in the world. I can't thank you enough.'

She laughed. 'You're most welcome. It's a good feeling for us too.'

Take that, Gordon McKenna. The triumph of science and medical knowledge. Tangible, provable. Not God gobbledygook.

'Unfortunately, I can't take any credit in this instance. It's all down to Rosa. In the middle of the night she remembered that the nurse was once the lover of Sasha's ex-fiancé. She had a gut feeling that such a person might not be the best nurse to be in charge of a vulnerable patient and she risked life and limb to reach our Critical Care Unit. I can only say that had she not left her farm when she did, had she hesitated for even a few minutes, it would have been too late.'

So Cullen had had his revenge after all, if only by proxy.

A memory came to Nick. Sasha talking about the day the yacht went over in the storm. *The God I trust to protect me, protected me.*

'No,' Nick said vehemently.

'No?'

'No. Obviously I don't know the details and if Rosa has done what you're saying, I'll be indebted to her for the rest of my days. But we both know that it was your skill and medicine that saved my wife. It was science.'

Behind her thick glasses, Dr Mehta's brow knitted in puzzlement at his persistence, but her smile was both relieved and unexpectedly happy as she steered him towards Sasha's room. 'I know what you're asking, Mr Donaghue, but I'm not the right person for the question.'

'Meaning?'

'Meaning that I did my medical degree in India, spent a couple of years working for a charity in Rwanda and now I live in rural Cornwall. I've seen some things. In my experience and for what it's worth, love trumps science every time.'

23

Nick sat on the top rail of the paddock fence and watched Sasha canter Marillion around a field strewn with tulips and poppies. It had been anybody's guess how the horse would behave after a long, idle winter and only limited exercise (the village girl, Tam, had found him impossible), but in the fortnight since Sasha had started riding him again he'd been a true gentleman. As she trotted him over to the gate, he arched his neck regally and shook his great mane. The pining he'd done during Sasha's long absences had melted some of the flesh from his bones, but he still looked as she'd once described him, as if he'd 'stepped fully formed from a Greek myth'.

'That,' she said breathlessly as she swung out of the saddle, 'was pure heaven.'

The way she staggered and grabbed Nick's arm on landing betrayed the weakness of her limbs, but she was getting stronger every day. Her recovery continued to amaze her doctors.

Nick took her riding hat. She'd finished the final cycle of the dreaded CHOP regimen in late February and five weeks on, her hair was growing back beautifully. 'Glad you enjoyed it, gorgeous.' He ruffled her auburn spikes and gave her a cheeky grin. 'Or should I call you Tintin?'

'Not if you expect to see me naked ever again.'

His mobile rang before he could think of a suitable retort. He tucked the phone between his ear and shoulder and answered it while undoing Marillion's girth and lifting off the saddle.

'Nick?'

The voice was familiar but he couldn't place it. 'Speaking.'

'It's Sarah Levin, Matthew's wife. I'm not sure if you remember me.'

'Of course I do, Sarah. How could I not?'

He handed the saddle to Sasha, mouthing, *'Matthew's wife.'*

Cupping the phone to shield it from the sea breeze, he said: 'It's really good to hear from you. I think of you and Matthew often. As strange as it may sound, he's one of my closest friends.'

'He thinks the same way. At least he did.'

'Did?'

'He says that in recent months your letters have become more distant, as if you were losing interest in corresponding with him. Nick, I'm not sure why I'm calling you except that I'm at my wit's end. Short of the Samaritans, I've nowhere else to turn. Matthew won't stop going on about assisted suicide. He's begging me to take him to a clinic in Switzerland and have him "put down like a dog". That's the phrase he keeps using. He feels that as long as he's around I won't be free to move on and meet someone new. He doesn't believe me when I say that I don't care if I never have sex again. I only want to be with him.

'Nick, he wants to die. That's what he tells me. He says, "If you really loved me, you'd let me go." Is that love – having someone euthanised? Or is it murder?'

Nick was stunned. 'Sarah, I'm so sorry. I don't know what to say.'

'What?' Sasha whispered. 'What's going on?'

'I shouldn't have bothered you, Nick. I probably did the wrong thing, calling. I suppose I thought that if you could talk to Matthew, if you were face to face . . .'

Sasha was leaning close to the phone, trying to hear.

'I wish I could,' Nick said. 'Unfortunately, I don't think . . . You see, it's not a great—'

Sasha took the mobile from him. 'Hi Sarah. This is Sasha, Nick's more coherent other half. How soon can you get here?'

'We came without the children,' explained Sarah as she climbed out of a clapped-out Renault the following Saturday, kissed Nick on both cheeks and began unfolding her husband's wheelchair.

'Well, most of them,' said Matthew. 'When she agreed to have three babies, my wife had no idea she'd end up with a fourth.'

Sarah looked as if she'd like to crawl under the nearest bush. She turned her back on her husband and took in the scenery. 'Wow! Double wow! What a view! You get to wake up to that every single morning?'

Nick let his gaze rest on the ocean, iridescent in the spring sunshine. From this angle, the charging waves always looked to him as if they might swallow the white cottage whole. 'Pretty much.'

'I can see why you've never been back to London. You haven't, have you? Not since you left. What is it now? A year and three or four months?'

'That's right. Not been to the Big Smoke once. Never felt the need.'

Matthew's wheelchair bumped painfully and deliberately over Nick's foot. 'Why would he need to escape when he has a hot woman to keep him warm? The view is just a bonus.'

Nick didn't react. He was too busy trying to conceal his astonishment at how much they'd both aged. Ten years would be conservative. When he'd first seen him at Greenwich station, Matthew had been handsome in a businessman-in-a-suit sort of way. Beneath a cap of neat hazelnut hair, his decent face had been boyish and vulnerable. Even in the hospital he'd looked better than he did now, greying, hangdog and poorly shaven.

And Sarah, once traffic-stoppingly attractive, looked close to broken. Misery permeated every line of her body.

Nick mustered the phoney enthusiasm of a third-rate hotelier. 'It's fantastic to see you both after all this time. Sasha apologises that she isn't here to greet you. Annoyingly, the feed delivery for the horses came late. She'll be here shortly. Meanwhile, let me show you to your room and get you a drink. You must be worn out after your long journey.'

'A little,' confessed Sarah. She looked close to tears.

'Can I help you with your luggage?'

'You'll have to,' Matthew said. 'Fat lot of use I am. You see, darling, if you got yourself a real husband, he'd be able to do things like that for you.'

Nick led the way into the cottage, a suitcase in one hand and holdall in the other. He was wondering how long to leave it before he suggested that they'd find it infinitely more comfortable in a Lanton bed and breakfast. If it weren't for Sasha, he'd have done so the previous week, but she'd been so excited about meeting them that he'd allowed himself to be carried along on her enthusiasm.

Under her instruction, he'd used his newfound DIY talents to transform his workshop into a pretty bedroom with disabled access.

The biggest headache had been bathroom facilities. Fortunately, there was a downstairs loo and Gordon had come to the rescue at the eleventh hour with a power-shower solution. And first thing that morning, Sasha had picked violet and yellow crocuses for the vase beside the bed. Yet when Nick showed him the transformed space, Matthew's only response was a grunt.

We have to put up with these people, these *strangers*, for five entire days, thought Nick. He scowled as he brewed Matthew a coffee. If he made it through the next hour without clubbing the man, it would be a miracle.

Sarah was in the bedroom freshening up. Or crying, more likely.

Matthew had wheeled himself to Nick's desk. He was holding a white-framed photo of Sasha before she got ill. She was laughing at the camera, her long dark hair blowing in the wind. In her red polka-dot bikini top and cut-off denim shorts, she looked tanned and beautiful. Matthew leered at the picture until Nick wanted to snatch it away from him.

'I'll put this over here, shall I?' he said, banging the mug down on the coffee table. To add to his irritation, Matthew's clumsy attempt to pick it up caused it to slop all over the latest issue of *National Geographic*. He had the idea that his visitor took pleasure in watching him mop up the mess and throw away the ruined magazine.

'It's usually best to keep me separated from boiling liquids,' Matthew said with bitter cheerfulness. 'Hasn't been that long since I stopped drinking soup through a straw.'

He tapped the glass photo frame with his forefinger. 'You didn't tell me how foxy Sasha is, and it wasn't apparent from that rather formal wedding photo you sent. She's drop-dead gorgeous. What a bod. Hot to trot. I suppose you're at it all the time like rabbits. In every position. Practising the *Kama Sutra*. Can't say I blame you. Time was, I'd have done her like a shot. Don't worry. Couldn't do a blow-up doll now. Dead from the waist down.'

A floorboard squeaked. The blood drained from Matthew's face.

Sasha was standing by the kitchen bench. Backlit by the sunshine that streamed through the open door, her spikes glowed red, accentuating the ghostly pallor of her skin. Her mauve polo shirt and chocolate-brown breeches hung loosely from her thin frame.

She gave no sign that she'd heard, although it was obvious to both men she had.

'You must be Matthew,' she said, coming forward with her hand outstretched, her smile warm and genuine. 'A pleasure to finally meet you. I've heard so much about you and Sarah from Nick – all good – that I can't wait to spend time with you. Now I'm sure you must be starving. How about we have some lunch? I bet my husband hasn't mentioned that he's a fabulous cook.'

'I'd completely understand if you punched my lights out,' Matthew said as Nick helped him out of the car and into his wheelchair at the stables. Sasha and Sarah had walked on ahead to meet the horses, deep in conversation. 'In fact, you'd be doing me a favour if you kept pushing till we reached those cliffs over there. One rotation of the wheel and I'd be out of everyone's hair. A burden no more.'

Nick removed a stone from the path of the chair and threw it hard against the water trough in exasperation. 'Can we stop with the pity party? Besides, there's probably a law against assaulting paraplegics.'

Matthew covered his eyes with his hands. 'Nick, I'm so sorry. I'm such a cretin. But why the devil didn't you say something? You wrote to me practically every week during the period Sasha must have been having chemo, and not a dicky bird. I should have known something was up when your letters stopped making me laugh. For months, they were like epistles from *Cold Comfort Farm*. Then overnight it was *Pollyanna*. It didn't ring true. I put it down to you losing interest in writing to a man who does nothing more entertaining than change a colostomy bag.'

'I wanted to tell you, but it isn't something you can put in a letter, is it? "My wife has an aggressive lymphoma that could kill her and I'm terrified twenty-four seven." And as wonderful as it is that she's survived the chemotherapy, I'm still afraid because it's not over yet. She gets chronically tired and has excruciating bouts of abdominal pain, which we try not to read anything into. In a month's time, on April twenty-first, she has a test which will determine whether she's going to be around for the next fifty or sixty years or if the cancer has come roaring back. So I admit it: I'm petrified.'

'Nick, people who've been through what you and I have together shouldn't have secrets from one another. Not those kind of secrets, at any rate.'

'That's a bit hypocritical when you've not exactly been straight with me. Why didn't you tell me you were feeling so low?'

'And what if I had? What could you have done about it? My sister almost died from breast cancer so I can empathise with what *you've* been through. You, on the other hand, how could you possibly know what it's like to be betrayed by your own body? To be reduced to the point where you can't even take a dump by yourself? Oh, at first I was the world's greatest optimist. At Stoke Mandeville, they said they'd never met such a fighter. Why do you think I felt qualified to rant at you? Then I got home and reality bit. This paralysis business sucks, Nick. Big time. Believe me, there are some worse things than dying.'

Nick glared down at him. 'Yes, there are. But there is nothing better than living.'

'Any chance you guys will be finished gossiping before dark?' called Sasha. 'There are horses here waiting to be saddled.'

Gordon McKenna roared up to the stables in his Land Rover just as Sasha was introducing Matthew to the horses. Nick, who was in the tack room fetching the specially adapted saddle Sasha used in training, emerged too late to intercept him.

'What have we here?' demanded the farmer with unaccustomed joviality. 'Has the riding centre opened without my knowledge?'

'As if we'd want anyone other than you to be the cheery public face of our new centre,' said Sasha, tongue firmly in cheek. 'When we finally get it off the ground, you'll be the first person we call. Matthew and Sarah, can I introduce you to our neighbour, Gordon McKenna? Part agricultural maestro, part grumpy angel, he's responsible for giving me the land on which you now stand. Gordon, these are Nick's lovely friends from London. Matthew rode a bit as a boy and has kindly volunteered to be our first client. Or should that be guinea pig? All he has to do is select the horse he'd like to ride.'

Matthew manoeuvred his chair along the line of seven horses tethered to the hitching post. Then he glanced over at Marillion, who was tearing up and down the paddock fence a little distance away, frantic to be with his pals.

'I'll take the black one.'

'I'm afraid that's not possible.'

'Why not? He looks strong enough to carry ten paraplegics.'

'He is. But he isn't safe. He's an ex-racehorse with a traumatic past. He's very fast, very unpredictable and famously difficult to control. Come and meet Caprice. She's a sweetheart.'

'If I can't ride the black horse, I don't want to ride at all,' Matthew said petulantly. 'I'm sick and tired of being mollycoddled.'

The smile left his wife's face. 'Be reasonable, darling. You don't know what you're saying.'

'He may be a cripple, but he's still a man,' Gordon interrupted. 'I'm sure he knows his own mind. Let him ride Marillion.'

There was a shocked silence, broken when Matthew burst out laughing. He held out his hand. 'I like you, sir. In a year and a half of being legless, as it were, you're the first person to call a spade a spade.'

Sasha looked helplessly from Sarah to Nick. Sarah turned away. Nick simply nodded.

'Marillion it is,' Sasha said.

24

'The closest thing possible to flying without wings,' was Matthew's verdict as he sat beside Sasha on the sofa that evening, wrapped in a matching rug. She'd teased him that they were a couple of old crocks. 'Hands down, one of the best experiences of my life. Course, I'll probably spend the next five years in therapy, but that's beside the point.'

He grinned at Sasha. 'Joking! No, seriously, a million thanks. I gathered from Nick during the ticking off he gave me afterwards that Marillion is your special horse and you're the only one who ever rides him. Apologies again, but if it makes a difference, it was a life-changing encounter. For twenty perfect minutes I experienced a freedom I thought was lost to me for ever. Can I do it again tomorrow?'

'No, you cannot, you stubborn bastard,' said Nick, getting up from the fireside where he and Sarah had been toasting coconut marsh-mallows. He handed Matthew a plate. 'If we have to endure a repeat performance of you haring off over the horizon on Marillion, perhaps never to be seen again, *we'll* be the ones seeing a shrink.'

'In your case, that should be a statutory requirement anyway, but no, I wasn't referring to the black horse. As exhilarating as it was to be strapped to a bolt of lightning, once was ample. Can't you tell I'm shattered? If I'm allowed to ride again, I'll leave the choosing up to the experts. I'm thinking something rather more sedate.'

'Sedate would be good,' Sasha agreed. 'I'd advise nothing more strenuous than a rocking chair.'

Watching his wife from the kitchen as he brewed a pot of Turkish coffee, Nick worried that she'd overdone it. Her eyelids were at half-mast and every now and then, when she thought no one was looking, they shut altogether. He had to resist the urge to pick her up and carry her off to bed. Her recovery was going well, but she was by no means out of the woods.

At the same time, he wouldn't have changed a thing about the day. There was something about Matthew's wild ride that had bonded the four of them in a way that would never have happened had they not been forced out from behind their respective walls of preconception and pain. By the time they sat down to a candlelit garden dinner of garlic prawns, coconut rice and Nick's latest speciality, a spinach and lentil dish, it was as if they'd known each other their whole lives.

'While I was cantering across the moors today . . .' Matthew began. He laughed incredulously. 'Gosh, it feels good to be able to say that. While I was cantering across the moors – well, it was a bit quicker than a canter – I spotted this strip of honey-coloured sand below the cliffs. It looked quite magical. However, I'm guessing that it's neither vehicle nor wheelchair accessible.'

'No, but it's horse accessible,' Sasha told him. 'That's Friday Beach. If you're game and the weather is decent, we could have a picnic the day before you leave.'

Matthew's face lit up as if someone had just handed him a winning lottery ticket. 'I'm game if Sarah is up for it.'

Sarah was already glowing from the heat of the fire but she glowed a bit more. 'I haven't been on a horse since our courting days, when I took riding lessons in an attempt to impress Matthew. But it sounds good to me. Wouldn't miss it for the world.'

'Great. Now what do you fancy doing tomorrow? Would you like to take a boat trip to see the dolphins?'

As so often happened when the British winter had extended its grim, grey tentacles further into March than the spirits could endure, compensation came in the form of a dazzling spring. On Friday Beach, the air was like champagne.

'I like them,' said Sasha, watching Matthew and Sarah trot through the waves with the abandon of a couple of teenagers. 'What you see is what you get. They're genuine to their core. Smart, too. I would have loved to see Sarah in action during her barrister days. On the one hand, she seems too nice to be a lawyer, but I can imagine her niceness being a highly effective weapon in the courtroom. I bet most of the people she was up against didn't realise that they'd been lulled into a false sense of security until their cases had been sliced to ribbons. Now she's a legal clerk in some gloomy office. Seems a waste.'

Nick shook out the picnic rug and unpacked some local cheeses, olives, salad and baguettes. For dessert, there were strawberries and clotted cream. Popping the cork on a bottle of fizz, he chased bubbles through four glasses. When he looked up, their guests were coming towards them. Sasha helped Sarah unsaddle the horses, while Nick lifted Matthew onto a fold-out camping chair.

'Any closer and we'd have to get married,' Matthew quipped as he released his grip on Nick's neck. 'Nice aftershave, mate.'

'Don't get any ideas,' Sasha said. 'He's taken.'

Sarah collapsed onto the rug with a groan. 'That was bliss, but already I'm aching in parts I didn't know existed. By tomorrow, I'll be begging to use Matthew's wheelchair.'

'No pain, no gain,' her husband told her.

Sarah swiped an olive from the dish and lay back with her hands laced behind her head. 'What colour is the sky, would you say? Duck-egg blue? I feel as if I could dive right into it and swim away to paradise.'

She sat up again. 'Wouldn't the kids love it here, Matthew? The freedom. We wouldn't have to be afraid for them the whole time. They could be out in nature, living life.'

Matthew took a sip of champagne. 'It isn't only the children who'd benefit, honey. You and I could do with a dose of nature and living life ourselves. It's been years since I felt so free. Thinking about it now, I was crippled long before the crash, just in different ways. Crippled by stress, by money worries, by the constant need to be seen to be climbing up the ladder and "doing better". It took me a while to realise that, for most of us, it's not a ladder at all. It's a wheel. Most people are simply hamsters, running to stand still.'

'So stop,' Nick said. 'Turn your back on the rodent existence. Move to Cornwall. Be free.'

Sarah giggled. 'Don't tempt us.'

Matthew looked over at Sasha. 'Don't suppose you need a good business manager for your riding centre, Sash? I used to be one once. Before people decided that losing my legs somehow equated to a lobotomy.'

'I'll definitely need a good business manager when it's eventually up and running. My accountancy talents, or lack thereof, are so appalling that I was once fired as a bookkeeper by my own mother. But the reality is that the riding centre is still a figment of my imagination. I have the horses and the land, but I'd need equipment, insurance, at least one off-road vehicle, an office and a zillion other things, all of which cost a king's ransom. Nick's busy writing a bestseller that he insists is going to pay for all of it, but until then . . .'

'It will. I sent the first draft to an agent a couple of months back. He said it showed promise. Haven't heard anything since but I'm trying not to read anything bad into that.'

'What if the riding centre became something more than a distant dream?'

Sarah wore a focused, determined expression that Nick suspected she'd frequently worn when putting forward her clients' cases in court. 'What if Matthew and I relocated to Lanton and the four of us formed a partnership where we worked towards making your vision happen?'

There was a spark in Sasha's eyes that matched the glittering ocean. 'Are you serious?'

'Very. What do we have to lose? At present, Matthew, the kids and I are squashed into a house we can't afford in London, where the world from our windows looks uniformly grey. We scrimp, save and squabble. That's the sum total of our existence. I work part-time as a legal clerk and loathe every minute, and Matthew feels worthless.'

'I do. I feel as if I'm wheeling myself into an early grave. All I want is to be useful again. Needed. If we moved to Lanton, we could probably afford a house with a bit more space and I could throw my energies into figuring out how to get your riding centre funded. And when it is, I could show you how to manage it as a viable business that turns lives around. I would get the biggest kick out of helping disabled children get a taste of the joy and sense of liberty I've experienced this weekend. Actually, what I'd like most is to feel as if I'm helping for a change, rather than being helped.'

Sarah said excitedly: 'And I could carry on working part-time, hopefully in a nicer law firm than I am now, while helping Sasha decorate the centre, or build a client list, or exercise horses or . . .'

She stopped. 'What am I saying? Sasha, Nick, forgive me. You've known me for all of five minutes and here I am assigning myself a job at your unbuilt riding centre and practically putting the seal on the contract.'

'Sorry,' Matthew said sheepishly. 'We got a little ahead of ourselves. It's the sea air. Blasted stuff's gone to my head like cheap wine. Pay no attention to us.'

'We don't want to ignore you,' Sasha told him, refilling his glass. 'We kind of like you. And if you meant any of it, I like what you're saying.'

'So do I,' said Nick. 'Especially the part, Sarah, where you were going to help take care of the horses. Does that include mucking out? I love them to bits but they do eat a lot, these creatures, and what goes in comes out.'

'Nick!' scolded the women in unison.

He grinned. 'As a recovering wheel-treading rodent, all I'm trying to say is that I think you should do it. Move to Lanton and help us make Sasha's riding centre happen. Ride horses, sail boats, live life.'

'We can't,' said Sarah. She reached for her husband's hand. '*Can we?*'

'I don't see why not. It's not as if we can do anything hasty. We can go back to London, put our house on the market and have a cooling-off period where we're sensible and think it over. If at the end of it these two still want to be associated with us, we'll move to the sun and sea.'

His wife looked as if someone had lifted a concrete block from her shoulders. Too emotional to speak, she simply smiled and nodded.

'Let's drink to that,' said Sasha with feeling. 'To health and happiness.'

Four glasses clinked.

'To health and happiness,' agreed Matthew.

'Your nightmares?' Matthew said, as he handed Nick his holdall to put in the toy-cluttered boot of the Renault. 'Do you still have them?'

'Sometimes. The bad ones went away for a while, but plagued me again when Sasha was in the hospital. More commonly, I have a symbol dream that I can't interpret and seems pointless. I thought it had stopped when Sasha got ill, but I had it again last night. It's a series of random images.'

'Such as?'

'I see colours. Rippling colours. They're attached but separated, if that makes sense, like triangles on the tail of a kite. There's writing on each piece. A foreign language. I thought it might be Arabic, but it's difficult to tell because it's blurred. Who knows? I've come to the conclusion that it doesn't mean a thing. The crash probably jolted something in my head. Some picture I've seen on television is stuck on repeat.'

'I doubt it. Jung believed that recurring dreams demand attention. As far as I understand it, his view was that they were essentially messages to the dreamer, presenting him or her with revelations that could uncover and help resolve emotional or religious problems or fears.'

Nick smiled. 'In that case, I'd better get used to them.'

'Well, I'm always on the end of a phone line if you need me. Perhaps one day I'll even be living down the road. Meantime, I'll be thinking of you both, especially when Sasha goes for her final check-up. It'll be fine, I know it. I like to believe that good things happen to good people.'

'They don't always. They didn't for you.'

'No,' said Matthew. 'But being here has made me understand that what's happened might ultimately make me a better man and give us all a better future. Made me understand something else too. That whatever life throws at you, the important thing is to get through it with grace. For a long time, I forgot that. Lost my centre. Close friends withdrew from me, kicked me in the teeth. Unlikely people, you chief among them, stood by me, even when I behaved monstrously.'

He lowered his voice so as not to be overheard by his wife, who was helping Sasha bag up some of the McKennas' fruit and vegetables to take back to London.

'I have a beautiful family who love me, but at a certain point I convinced myself that they'd be better off without me, Sarah in particular. I'm ashamed to admit it but I've put her through hell. I got myself all knotted up about sex. Stupid, really. The doctor says that it's all in my head. Plenty of things we can do and try. But I've had a mental block about it. Hence my childish outburst the other day. Talk about wanting the ground to open up and swallow you.'

Nick grinned. 'It's easy to get knotted up about sex. Most people are paranoid that everyone else is having more and doing it better than they are. I know I am. But when you boil it right down, it's not about that, is it? Just love her. That's all she really needs.'

The women started towards them, laden with produce. Nick closed the boot. 'By the way, the stunt you pulled with that book – *The Prophet* – putting it in my bag when I came to see you, while it didn't exactly go down well at the time, it helped.'

'Did it? I'm glad. All I can remember from that period is lecturing you rather harshly. Do you remember me telling you that your idea of a bad day was getting to Marks and Spencer and finding they'd sold out of smoked salmon?'

Nick grinned. 'It's seared on my brain.'

'Boy, did those words come back to haunt me.'

'Water under the bridge.'

'Yes, it is, but I—'

'Is this what it's going to be like when we move here, Matthew?' interrupted his wife as she deposited the baskets on the back seat. 'You and Nick gabbling non-stop like a couple of old biddies at a market?'

'Oh, I doubt it. Nick will be too busy shovelling horse manure to enjoy idle conversation, and I'll be hiding in my office with the accounts. Anyway, even if we were, you and Sasha wouldn't have time to notice. Aren't you planning world domination?'

He shook Nick's hand, suddenly awkward. 'Thanks for everything. It's been . . .'

'Unforgettable,' Sarah finished for him as she started the car. 'It's been unforgettable.'

Matthew watched in the wing mirror as the white cottage, tropical patch of garden and inky wash of sea faded into the haze behind them. The lump in his throat was more painful than anything he'd endured in the crash.

They were halfway to London before he opened the package Nick had given him. As he did so, the desolation he'd felt as they drove away from the farm evaporated. His mouth tugged up at the corners. On the inside flap of *The Prophet* was a single line:

You make me glad I was late for my train that day. N.

25

'What would you do if you had one day left to live?'

They were sitting on the garden bench with the Sunday papers spread out around them, eating warm croissants and drinking coffee strong enough to stand a spoon in. The ocean fizzed and sparkled at their feet.

Nick was horrified. 'Don't say that. Don't even think that. You're going to go to the hospital tomorrow morning and be given the all-clear.'

Sasha kissed a crumb from his cheek. 'Darling, I'm not being morbid. I'm talking hypothetically. I only mean that it's an interesting question. It throws everything into sharp relief. If you had one day left to live, what would you do with it?'

'Seriously?'

'Seriously.'

'And this is not about tomorrow?'

'It's not about tomorrow. Promise.'

'I'd ride Marillion. With your permission, of course.'

'You'd *ride* Marillion? In the entire time we've been together you've never even hinted at wanting to ride him. I know that deep down you secretly adore him as much as I do, but it never occurred to me that you might be hankering to take him out for a gallop. Caprice would be miles better. Besides, she's your favourite.'

'No, it would have to be Marillion.'

'But what if he does one of his things?'

'What things?'

'One of his quirky fight or flight things that only make me love him more, but could cause him to inadvertently hurt you?'

He reached for another croissant. 'What's the worst that could happen? And anyway, what would it matter? If I broke my arm with only a day to live, it would hardly be the end of the world.'

'It would matter to me,' she said indignantly. 'We'd squander at least six of your precious twenty-four hours in A&E. What kind of last day is that?'

He grinned. 'We're playing a game, remember? You asked me what I'd do if I only had twenty-four hours to live. In those circumstances you're allowed to do anything you want, however eccentric. It's like a prisoner's last meal before an execution. If they ask for a curried burrito with a meringue on top, it has to be granted.'

'They've changed the rules on that in Texas, but let's not get pedantic. Okay, carry on. And yes, of course you could ride Marillion.'

She topped up their mugs with coffee and debated whether or not to have a second pain au chocolat. They were very moreish.

Reading her mind, he handed it to her. 'All right, here goes. With your permission, we'd start the day with that sleepy, slow-burning sex that begins when we're barely awake and kind of fumbling around like teenagers, but gets more intense by the minute.'

She giggled. 'You mean the kind we had this morning?'

'The kind we had this morning. Now I've lost my train of thought.'

'You were describing your perfect day; or at least what you would do if you only had one more day to live, which is not necessarily the same thing.'

'Good point. I always did think that perfection was overrated. Far better to accept that you're hopelessly flawed and concentrate on the really important things in life, like eating high-calorie breakfasts and watching the ocean. Next on the agenda would be a trip to Kittiwake Cove. We could swim naked. Be at one with nature. I've never done that, you know. Skinny-dipped. Too repressed.'

She rolled her eyes. 'Oh, yes, you're terribly repressed. Shy and retiring are the first words that come to mind when I think of you.'

'If these really were my final hours, I would hope you'd be less of a tease.'

She hitched up the skirt of her sundress and straddled him. 'What's it worth?'

'Will you stop! I'm trying to concentrate.'

She zipped her mouth. 'I'm all ears.'

He put his palms on the warm skin of her thighs. 'After we'd dried off, you'd make me one of your cheese toasties and then we'd gallop full pelt across the moors. I'd cook dinner. Something simple like mushroom risotto with loads of garlic. Afterwards, we'd lie on the sofa and listen to Bach and cheesy pop music. Naturally, I'd end the day by making love to you again. We'd fall asleep with the ocean crashing outside and you'd smell of strawberries and champagne.'

Recalling with a jolt why they were having the conversation in the first place – because of Sasha's real-life appointment – he was annoyed that he'd allowed himself to become so caught up in the fantasy.

He lifted her off him and stood up with a grimace, brushing crumbs from his jeans. 'I don't think we should be doing this. Tempting fate.'

She laughed. 'Darling, don't look so serious. I'm going to get the all-clear tomorrow, remember? Not to state the obvious, but even if I didn't, I'd still be around for quite some time. Years, possibly, if I could keep fighting it off. However, if this really was my last day, yours sounds pretty perfect to me. Would you mind very much if I shared in it?'

The water was heart-attack cold. Nick immediately regretted his decision to leave his Speedos in the Mustang. Sasha screamed when she jumped in.

'This might be your idea of a good time, but I'm erasing this section from my own final day,' she gasped. 'If I caught hypothermia in the first hour I wouldn't be able to enjoy the rest of it.'

He splashed her. 'Fine, but you'd be missing out on an opportunity to experience the perfect union of your physical being with the elements.'

'I'd be missing out on catching my death, which would seem to me to be a good thing. Might I remind you that my body was intimately acquainted with the elements on the night we capsized in the storm and it's not a union I'm keen to repeat.'

A scoopful of icy water hit her in the midriff.

She glared at him. 'Nick, if you splash me again, I won't be answerable for the consequences.'

He couldn't resist. When he made matters worse by laughing at her when she tripped on an unseen rock while trying to escape, she was spitting mad. He offered her a hand, but she refused to take it.

Water streamed from her as she struggled to her feet. 'That's it. I know this was my stupid idea, but I've had enough. I want to go home.'

He grinned. 'It's not stupid in the least. As a matter of fact, I think it's a marvellous idea.' She tried to wriggle free, but he began kissing her from head to thigh. She shoved him away crossly, but ruined it by bursting into helpless giggles. 'Nick, I think we should stop. What if someone sees us? A tourist with a video camera or a mobile phone?'

'Nobody ever comes to this cove. That's why I suggested it. It's totally deserted. And so what if they do? If I only had twenty-four hours to live, the last thing I'd be worried about would be whether or not I was going to wind up naked on YouTube.'

'Yes, but given that you're likely to be around for another forty or fifty years, you might want to reconsider.'

Warmer now, they began to swim, only stopping when they were so far from the shore that the beach was almost obscured by the waves. It was risky because riptides were not uncommon in the area, but they did it anyway and felt as liberated as dolphins.

When Sasha first suggested that they live out the day as if it were their last, it had been on the tip of Nick's tongue to refuse. Now he was thankful he'd agreed. One glance at her shining face told him all he needed to know about whether or not she could cope.

Exhilarated, they returned to the car. They were walking hand in hand in their birthday suits when a tall woman with a weathered elegance and two springer spaniels rounded a bend in the path.

She arched an eyebrow. 'Adam and Eve, I presume?'

Nick, who'd stepped in front of Sasha to preserve her modesty, belatedly realised his error and rushed to cover himself. 'Excuse us, ma'am. Apologies. We thought the beach was deserted. We didn't mean to offend anyone.'

The woman took a fraction longer than was decent to size him up. The spaniels were tugging at their leashes. 'No excuses necessary, young man. I can't recall when I last enjoyed the local wildlife quite so much.' She winked. 'A very good morning to you and your lady friend.'

'Good morning,' they replied in unison.

As soon as she was out of earshot, Sasha mimicked: 'I can't recall when I last enjoyed the local wildlife quite so much.' She fell about laughing.

'What's so funny?'

'I thought she was going to ask you for a guided tour. "Young man, is that a squirrel beneath your navel or are you just pleased to see me?" '

'I wouldn't have minded but my lower extremities are so frozen that they've shrunk to the size of peanuts.'

'And that's different from their usual proportions how?'

'You're lucky that I love you so much,' Nick said crossly and stalked off to the car. He retrieved his boxer shorts from the back seat and towelled himself down.

'Or what?' Sasha wanted to know, catching him up. 'What would happen if you didn't love me so much?'

He pulled on his jeans. 'Ooh, I don't know. I might tickle you to death.'

'At least I'd go laughing.'

She was doing up the buttons on her sundress when he put his arms around her. 'I do, you know. Love you, I mean. More than anything on earth.'

She stood on tiptoe to kiss him. 'Ditto.'

It was then that he spotted the distant headland where he'd stood a year and five months ago, on that dank, foggy New Year's Day. A shadow crossed his face. Had he jumped, none of this would have happened. Not one thing. He'd have died before he ever really lived. Or loved.

'What is it?' She turned to see what had caught his attention. 'Oh.' 'Oh?'

Their eyes met. Something about the gold-flecked blue of her pupils had always made him feel as if, on a clear day, he could see for ever. Now he felt exposed. More naked than he'd been without clothes.

'It was you, wasn't it, that day on the beach? When I came tearing along on Marillion. It was you on the edge of the cliff.'

It was less of a question than a statement. His happiness evaporated. The roar of the surf filled his ears. 'How long have you known?'

She pulled away from him, not meeting his eyes. 'I'm not sure. It dawned on me gradually. It was no one thing. Or rather, it was several small things. The way you stand. An impression of you, like an artist's sketch. One day it all clicked into place.'

Hot and cold waves of shame swamped him. 'I wanted to tell you a thousand times, but I couldn't find the words. I thought you'd think less of me. Think I was weak. I mean, what was I supposed to say? That I was standing there because I wanted to end it all? That I was so desperate to be free from my nightmares that jumping to my death seemed an attractive option? Do you want me to say that when you and Marillion came flying out of the fog like phantoms, it stopped me from going over the edge?'

'You can say anything,' she said softly, 'if it's true.'

'I never believed in love at first sight. Not until that day. But in the space of ten minutes you not only saved my life, you changed it out of all recognition.'

'You saved your own life. All I did was provide a diversion. The funny part is you were watching over me even then.'

He snorted. 'Hardly. I was a self-obsessed wreck. Oh, I had all sorts of noble intentions, but when I reached the beach it was obvious that you weren't in any need of rescuing. Just as well. Back then, I was barely capable of tying my own shoelaces.'

'That's not true. By the following afternoon you were giving CPR to Pattie Griffin.'

'What had happened? What had caused Marillion to bolt?'

'A speed merchant in a Maserati. Probably still drunk from New Year's Eve. It was the one time – the *only* time – when I felt that Marillion's flight response had the potential to kill us. He was tearing along totally out of control through fog so thick it was like a blindfold. Without a saddle, I couldn't get enough purchase to stop him. If a car had come along from either direction, it would have been the end of us.'

She was leaning against the car. He moved a little nearer. When she didn't move away, he leaned gently against her, lowering his head so she couldn't read his eyes. The sun beat down pleasantly but the wind had a real bite to it.

He rubbed her arms to warm them. 'Then you saw the signpost to Porthcurno and the rest is history?'

She lifted his chin and forced him to look at her. 'Yes . . . but it's important that you know something. When I caught sight of you as we raced towards the beach, I felt profoundly relieved that I wasn't alone. I was suddenly filled with the certainty that if something were to happen to me and Marillion, you, a complete stranger, would help us. I felt that very strongly. The sand and space gave me the opportunity to slow him and turn him, but you being there – even though you were mostly invisible – calmed me. All I had to do then was win back Marillion's trust . . . I thought of speaking to you, you know. As I left the beach.'

'Why didn't you?'

'I didn't want to break the spell.'

Her hand was on his heart, warm against his chest. 'Strange to think that if the Maserati driver hadn't come along at that exact minute, and if Marillion hadn't bolted, you and I would never have been brought together. Two planets colliding. But they did and we did. What do you call that?'

'I call it fate.'

'How about divine intervention?'

'Aren't they the same thing?'

26

It was not until he was saddling Marillion that the prickling in Nick's fingers confirmed what he already knew. He should not be riding the horse.

'You don't have to do this, you know,' Sasha said, coming over with Tia Maria, a big-boned, mild-mannered silver mare. 'It's not compulsory. Or is this some kind of macho challenge you've set yourself? Matthew did it so you have to? Riding is supposed to be fun. *We're* supposed to be having fun. You look like a dead man walking. Is that what Marillion is to you? The equine equivalent of the gallows?'

In a flash of self-awareness, Nick realised that's exactly how he viewed the horse. Not on an ordinary day, when he almost regarded him as a supernatural being, but right now. Despite his conviction that his obituary dreams had ended with Sasha's recovery, he could not quash his superstitions about Marillion. How else to explain the tingling in his hands?

Get a grip, Donaghue. Horses pick up on fear.

What frustrated him most was that he'd never previously been afraid of the horse, only of what he signified. He was proud of the bond that he and Marillion had formed during Sasha's illness. They'd got through the worst of times together. So why was he so jittery? In the nearly three years that Sasha had owned the horse, no one had ever been injured by him. Not unless you counted Sasha's many bruises and Tam's sprained wrist.

Cullen didn't count. He'd deserved a good kicking.

Nick tightened Marillion's girth. 'Hardly. I was just picturing your expression after I've raced you across the moors and you realise that you've been beaten by a rank amateur.'

'Is this you throwing down the gauntlet?'

'Why? Afraid you might not be up for the challenge?'

'When have you ever known me to walk away from a challenge?'

Nick grinned. 'In that case, you can consider the gauntlet tossed down.'

As he swung astride Marillion, Nick had a sense of his dreams being made manifest. He did his best to quash the feeling. More than anything, he was desperate to believe that they'd faced all they would ever have to face and that Sasha was safe in perpetuity. At the same time, the part of him that had endured all he could possibly take wanted to throw down the gauntlet, not to his wife but to the unseen forces that continued to stalk his nightmares. He wanted to shout: 'If you want me, come and get me.'

Nothing in his limited riding experience had prepared him for the sheer power of Marillion. Intensive training sessions with three of the other horses had limited Sasha's time with the colt over the past ten days and he was the definition of a coiled spring. He jogged, yanked at the bit and fidgeted. He spooked at a bird in a hedge. A field of cows he'd passed a hundred times before caused him to dance like a Lipizzaner, goggle-eyed.

'If you want to swap horses, it's fine with me,' suggested Sasha. 'On days like this Marillion can be a real challenge. I wouldn't wish him on my worst enemy. It's a pity because he's been an angel recently.'

'Stop fretting and concentrate on your own horse,' Nick responded through gritted teeth. 'I'm having a great time.'

'Yes, and it shows,' she said drily. 'Honey, if you relax, he will too. Try softening your hands. Flow with him.'

They'd barely been riding for twenty minutes and already Nick's arms ached with the effort of keeping a check on the thunderbolt beneath him. It didn't help that the pins and needles in his fingers made holding the reins both difficult and painful. He'd have given anything to take back his rash words of the morning. He'd already decided that if he ever did discover he only had twenty-four hours remaining, he would not be including riding volatile ex-racehorses on his bucket list.

Ahead of them, the open moors beckoned. Nick had zero confidence that he'd be able to hold onto the horse once they reached them. His only hope was Sasha's advice. He loosened his hands. Marillion snatched at the reins. Nick's instinct was to wrest them back, but he forced himself to resist.

He stole a glance at Sasha. It was hard to tell who was more chilled out – her or Tia. To Sasha, riding was meditation. Equine Zen. The more a horse played up, the more deeply she breathed and calm she became.

Nick tried taking a leaf out of her book. He focused on relaxing one muscle group at a time. If Matthew could cope with the horse, so could he. On the other hand, it was not exactly a level playing field. Matthew, it had transpired, was something of an expert. He'd not simply 'ridden a bit' as a boy, he'd misspent most of his adolescence and early twenties riding athletic, excitable warmbloods over ever more challenging fences at eventing championships up and down the country.

Marillion stopped fighting for his head but lost none of his bounce. His neck was soapy with sweat.

Up ahead, the moors were a shadowed sea of chestnut, maroon and yellow. The sun had been obscured by a band of sullen clouds. They bumped like great sheep over the hills on the horizon, chased by a strengthening wind.

Sasha nudged Tia alongside Nick. 'The weather's on the turn. We can head back if you like. With Marillion in the mood he's in, that might be best, to be honest.'

'What mood? All he needs is to feel the wind in his face and the grass under his heels. Race you to the boundary line.'

She laughed nervously. 'Nick, I don't think that's a good idea.'

'Why not?'

'Babe, I don't have a good feeling about it. Call it gut instinct. We can have a race some other time. You're probably right. We shouldn't tempt fate.'

'Afraid you might lose?'

The old fire glinted in her eyes. 'Lose? Me?'

He gathered his reins. 'See you there.'

Once, when he was eleven, Nick had begged a ride on the motorbike of a mate's older brother, a chain-smoking, rather nerdy-looking rebel without a cause. Nick had worn a helmet but not a visor and the subsequent face-peeling, heart-palpitating thrill of that blast down the motorway had triggered his love of speed.

Motorbikes, however, could be managed. You could put on the brakes, change down a gear or turn off the ignition. Horses had minds of their own. Not only could they be wilful, nervy and unpredictable, they had spindly legs that could step into rabbit holes. Their imaginations could transform a lone dandelion into a rampaging dragon. They also weighed a ton. That made them potentially lethal.

All of these thoughts went through Nick's head as Marillion surged forward. Over the past year he'd ridden a fair amount and come to thoroughly enjoy it, mainly because it was an excuse to spend time with Sasha and because he liked the personalities of the horses. They were real characters. For that reason, he had no trouble understanding her obsession with the animals. It was the riding part he had difficulty with. While fun, the hacking and basic schooling he'd done so far did not have the adrenalin rush of skiing or kite surfing, or the physicality of rugby. It was not psychological warfare, like rock climbing.

But that, he saw now, was because he'd never ridden a horse like Marillion. The acceleration alone tested every muscle in his body. The G-force crushed the air from his lungs. He had to grab a handful of mane in order to stay with the horse. The grey and the black were neck and neck, then neck and belly as Tia slipped behind. Nick had a last glimpse of Sasha and then he and Marillion were alone, sweeping across the moors at a speed that went way beyond galloping.

For the first time Nick got it. Why it held Sasha in thrall. The freedom of it, and how at a certain point you and the horse became merged, almost as if you shared the same nervous system. He was no longer afraid. A peace that was tangible took possession of him. He didn't fight the horse, didn't panic, didn't for a moment believe that Marillion would put a foot wrong or that he'd be raced over the horizon and never heard from again. All he felt was a rightness that went to his core.

When Marillion slowed it was almost by tacit agreement. Afterwards, Nick had no memory of touching the reins. The horse came to a gradual, blowing walk and finally an easy halt close to the stone wall that formed the farm boundary. The sea was a silver shroud.

Marillion's veins made squiggles on his sweat-soaked shoulders. He shook his long mane and stretched down to swipe a few mouthfuls of grass. Nick stroked the horse's wet neck while he waited for Sasha to catch up.

'Talk about the tortoise and the hare,' he teased as she and Tia came trotting sedately through the heather.

'The race was cancelled at short notice. Poor Tia got a stone in her shoe. It's a miracle she isn't lame.'

'Oh, please. Is that the best excuse you could come up with?'

She laughed, reaching out of the saddle to rub Marillion behind the ears. 'As a matter of fact, it was. I think the skinny dip this morning froze all creative impulses in my brain. Well, what did you think?'

'I'd say that Matthew is right. Riding Marillion is the closest thing on earth to flying without wings.'

'So now you know.'

'Now I know.'

She gave a contented sigh. 'It's getting dark. We should probably get home. I know a shortcut.'

They heard the motorbikes before they saw them. One moment they were riding up a narrow, wooded lane with no sound but birdsong and the musical clop of hooves, and the next a chainsaw roar was reverberating through the trees.

There was nowhere to run. No time to hide.

Minutes before Nick had been thinking about the tingling in his fingers and wondering why it still plagued him. Consciously or unconsciously, he'd pushed the black horse to do his worst – to be the architect of his doom if that's what he intended – and the opposite had happened. At the very moment when Nick should have felt most at risk, most fearful, most threatened, he'd felt cradled. It was hard to think of a time when he'd felt safer.

Now Marillion was spinning in circles, ears flat against his head, wild-eyed.

'There's nothing we can do except keep the horses as close to the edge of the road as possible,' said Sasha. 'We'll never outrun the bikes and we could kill ourselves trying. Keep your hands soft and relax your body. Do anything you can think of to communicate to Marillion that you're in charge and are going to look after him.'

Three joyriders burst out of the dusk. They were skinny youths in T-shirts and full-face helmets riding abreast. Playing chicken. Any hope that they might slow when they saw the horses was in vain. One braked only so that he could rev his engine and gloat as the horses plunged in terror. Another leaned on his hooter.

Marillion reared. Nick saw the barbed wire fence wink in the headlights, saw the asphalt and gravel, saw Tia spin and prepare to bolt.

The scene in the railway carriage came back to Nick. The shattered, bleeding bodies. The moment when he realised that he was the only one standing.

Destiny, long delayed, was playing out.

Marillion exploded into a crazed gallop. Pursued by the machine-gun clatter of the biggest boy's bike, he blasted up the road at breakneck speed. Nick had no thought for his own safety. His only aim was to outmanoeuvre his attacker and get back to help Sasha.

Ironically, it was the swinging headlights that provided him with an escape route. Where the barbed wire fence ended there was a wide ditch. Marillion saw it at the same time. Swerving out of the path of the bike, he leapt. Nick held on as the horse soared over the gaping hollow, landed and began to gallop.

There was a crunch of metal behind them and he guessed that the rider had come to grief. There was no time to look back. Marillion was hurtling into the shadowed forest and it took everything Nick had to stay with him as he spooked and swerved. Yet his earlier fear of the horse had gone. Laying a reassuring hand on Marillion's neck, he gentled him, slowed him and persuaded him to return at a rapid trot to the road.

An unnatural quiet had descended on the scene. A motorbike smoked silently in the ditch. There was no trace of Sasha. The blood thudded in Nick's ears. *Kaboom, kaboom, kaboom.* He looked up and down the road. What had happened? Had they taken her? Which way had she gone?

Marillion threw his head up and whinnied violently. Tia came trotting from the trees on the other side of the road, her reins broken and trailing. A thousand terrible thoughts went through Nick's head, but he did what Sasha would have wanted him to do, dismounted and coaxed the grey mare towards him. He loosened her girth so she could breathe.

When he looked up, Sasha was crossing the road towards him.

'You're a natural,' she said with a smile. 'No one would guess you hadn't been doing this your whole life.'

Nick rushed over to her and hugged her tightly. 'When Tia came back without you, I was afraid—'

'With good reason. They were thugs, those boys. Fortunately, they were neither brave nor bright. When their leader fell into the ditch it scared him so much that he jumped on one of his pals' bikes and scarpered. Tia's usually bombproof, but the whole thing was too much for her. I made the beginner's error of getting off in an attempt to control her from the ground and she broke her reins and bolted.'

She took the mare's reins from him. 'You and Marillion, on the other hand, put on a riding masterclass. You were like brothers in arms.'

He grinned. 'Brothers in arms. Yes, I suppose we were.'

They walked back to the farm hand in hand, with the horses stretching out alongside them. Having faced down a roaring monster and lived to tell the tale, Marillion amused them by being almost cockily confident and pleased with himself. He strode eagerly towards the distant stables, worn out from all the exertion, his velvet muzzle brushing Nick's arm.

As they walked, Nick found to his surprise that he was thinking less about the wanton aggression of the joyriders, and much more about the freedom he'd felt as Marillion swept across the moors. It was a feeling he could not have described. Much more than ecstasy, it was a kind of releasing. An acceptance that whatever would be would be.

Up ahead, the last gasp of sunset trailed threads of saffron against the steely sky. The storm had changed course and moved away. Nick put an arm around Sasha's waist and pulled her to him. 'Are you happy? Or is that an odd question after what we've just been through?'

'It's not an odd question in the least. And yes, I am happy. Blissfully so. I'm with you, aren't I?'

In a little while, when they got home to Seabird Cottage, she'd cook spaghetti and they'd listen to cheesy pop music followed by Glenn Gould playing Bach. They'd lie on the sofa eating clotted cream ice cream and sharing a bit with Oliver. Later, they'd make love in the sweet, lazy way of the utterly exhausted.

They'd fall asleep knowing that it had been the best of all possible days: perfectly imperfect.

27

She went to the hospital alone.

Under normal circumstances, Nick would have insisted on going with her, but he had a blinding headache. It had come on during the night and had so far proved immune to paracetamol. The last thing he felt like was breakfast, but he was determined to maintain an optimistic front. When Sasha emerged from the shower, he was clumsily making pancakes, unhelpfully aided by Oliver, who'd been allowed to sit on the kitchen counter and drink a bowl of cream as a special treat.

Sasha burst out laughing when she saw the pair of them covered from head to paw in flour. 'A snowman and a snow leopard! Just what I always wanted.'

She put her bare arms around Nick's waist. 'Everything's going to be all right. You do know that, don't you, darling?'

He flipped a pancake and kissed her. 'Don't have the slightest doubt about it.' And all at once he didn't.

But when it came time to eat neither of them could manage more than a few bites. Sasha left shortly afterwards. Nick stood at the kitchen door and watched her stride loose-limbed and cheerful into the overcast morning, as if she were heading off to nothing more challenging than a day spa.

'Sasha . . .'

She paused in the midst of ducking into the car, looking round with a smile.

'Nothing, I . . . Drive safely.'

She blew him a kiss and was gone.

When the sound of her car engine had been replaced by the ocean's soft percussion, he sat at his desk and tried to conjure up work. At the bottom of the garden, Ryan cut a lanky silhouette. Having acquired both a girlfriend and a placement with a local hotel garden, he rarely had time to fish at Seabird Cottage these days, but his presence now was a welcome distraction. There was Zen in the boy's graceful casting. Over and over, the silver thread of line shimmied towards the waves.

A mobile phone burst into discordant song. Ryan spoke into it, flung down his rod and disappeared.

Nick fed a sheet of paper into the Remington and typed a chapter heading. Ellen Glass, the literary agent recommended by Phil, had written to say that his manuscript was doing the rounds of various publishers. For the time being, it was past the point of change, but to kill time Nick made a meal out of editing several pages and retyping them with obsessive neatness. On the spur of the moment, he also changed the ending. Was it happy or sad? He supposed that was open to debate.

Ellen found it incomprehensible that any twenty-first-century author would voluntarily struggle with a typewriter belonging in a museum. According to her, writing novels in longhand was still viewed as eccentric and rather charming, but using a manual typewriter was 'just plain weird'.

That was her blunt opinion when she agreed to take Nick on as a client. 'Suffice to say that my lovely assistant had no choice but to scan every page – all three hundred and twenty-seven of them – before we could even consider sending your typescript out. If it ever does get published – I'll be doing my best, but understand that the book world is in tumultuous times – you may have to overcome your objections to the internet. Reclusiveness is a luxury of the past. JD Salinger wouldn't have lasted a day in modern publishing. Not if he refused to use Facebook.'

Scooping up Oliver, who was flopped, as usual, across the very pages he needed to read, Nick carried him out into the yard. The cat's purrs vibrated through his chest. The tension in the cottage had made him clingy.

They sat side by side on the bench and stared out to sea. Already, the cloud was breaking up, chased by a brisk wind. A splinter of sun pierced its woolly underbelly and tore a hole in it, unveiling a better shade of blue.

The sea air filled Nick's lungs and alleviated his headache. The timeless beauty of the scene put things into perspective. He was filled with an intense joy. An absolute certainty that Sasha would be found to be cancer-free took hold of him.

Even so, he found himself saying a prayer just in case. *If it's a negative result, take me instead.* It was the wrong thing to do, he knew. God didn't make deals. But the fragment of him that was petrified for Sasha sought comfort in the only prayer he felt capable of praying. A life for a life. It seemed a fair trade.

If it's a negative result, take me instead.

The sound of a car engine penetrated his thoughts. He took the garden steps in one bound. Sprinting across the lawn he tripped over the fishing rod he'd given Ryan, which was hidden in the overlong grass. As he pitched forward his temple made contact with the corner of a flowerpot. It was no more than a glancing blow. He sat up, rubbing the sore spot.

'Hello, the house! Anyone HO-O-ME!'

It was Annie Entwhistle.

Sick with disappointment, Nick scrambled to his feet as the post-woman, stumpy and straining at the seams of her blue uniform, rounded the house. Ryan followed close behind.

She shook the mail at him. 'Going deaf, you are. I've been knocking and yelling. Would have driven away, but the lad here swore you were in. Sign here, please.'

Nick was confused. Wasn't it only a moment ago that he'd heard the post van engine and mistaken it for Sasha's car?

Ryan dropped to the grass. 'Fuck's sake. My rod! The line's all tangled up. Has that blasted cat been using it as a toy?'

A thought came to Nick, a fragment of a dream, but he couldn't quite grasp it. 'Sorry, mate, it's my fault. Didn't see it lying there. Here, let me help you.'

Annie's hand was on her hip. 'Am I invisible? Do I look like someone who has all day?'

'No, of course not, but—'

'S'alright,' Ryan said. 'I can manage. My own fault for leaving it there. Gotta pack it in, anyway. Boss is on my case. Thought I could sneak away for a few hours, but no such luck. Always some fucken crisis.' He picked up his fishing box with a grimace. 'Be seeing you.'

He took a few strides before halting, face thoughtful. 'Never thanked you, Nick.'

'No need.'

'Every need. This is me saying it now.'

'What for?' Annie wanted to know. 'What's Nick done apart from giving you a place to play truant?'

Ryan grinned. He spread his arms wide and turned three hundred and sixty degrees, taking in the ocean, moors and cottage. 'Oh, nothing much. Only everything.'

Nick's headache had returned with a vengeance. It wasn't a migraine. More like a brainstorm with accompanying lightning bolts. His neurons appeared to be short-circuiting. It was the tension. If only Sasha would come home. Whatever her test results, they'd cope. It was the not knowing that made waiting so unbearable.

'Apologies, Annie. I'm not very with it today. Sasha has gone to the hospital and that's all I can think about. Now, what do you need me to sign?'

When the post van had gone, bumping away up the drive, Nick sat at his desk and examined his mail. Top of the heap was the registered letter he'd had to sign for – sent by Dr Marius Retson of Guy's Hospital. It had been to several addresses. He opened the one from Ellen Glass. Better to get the rejections over with first.

A cheque fluttered out. Nick picked it up and gasped. It was for £10,000 and had his name on it. He pored over the agent's words, trying with difficulty to hang on to each separate phrase.

Dear Nick,

I really must implore you to embrace the concept of email or at the very least pick up your voicemails. If you hadn't authorised me to act on your behalf, I'd be tearing my hair out by now . . . Astonishing news . . . You'll be wondering about the cheque. It's a bit unorthodox, to say the least, but I've promised to forward it to you. It's a 'no obligation' signing bonus. Out and out bribery, I call it, but what can you do?!!

After nineteen rejections, I have to admit I was close to giving up hope. Then three publishers came along all at once. They've been scrapping like roosters over your script, all of which I could have kept you abreast of had you answered your mobile phone occasionally. I've detailed the numbers (the important part!) below. There'll be sleepless nights

265

all round till you decide. Your earliest communication would be appreciated.

As ever,

Ellen

P.S. Congratulations!!

Nick whooped. He grabbed Oliver and squeezed him so hard that the cat gave a squawk of protest. 'We did it,' he said, laughing out loud. 'Oh, mate, against all odds we did it. I'm going to be a published author. An *author!* Who'd have believed it?'

He felt a rush of indescribable happiness, but quickly sobered. It didn't seem right to feel celebratory when Sasha was going through what she was going through. But then it occurred to him that, regardless of the outcome at the hospital, it was within his power to put a smile on her face.

Sitting at his desk, he wrote two notes. The first was to Ellen, thanking her profusely for her efforts and instructing her which of the three publishers to choose. To him, it was a no-brainer. The 'bribe' wasn't the only factor in Nick's decision, but it helped.

Next he endorsed the £10,000 cheque to Matthew Levin and put it in an envelope along with a pink Post-it note: *Relocation expenses and your first month's salary. See you in Cornwall. N*

Lastly, he telephoned his bank. A woman in Mumbai helped him transfer the balance of the money he'd received from the sale of his apartment to Sasha's account. It wasn't a fortune but it would be enough to make a proper start on the building of the riding centre.

After that, who knew? His novel could sell three copies, be a bestseller, or something in between. Over the years, he'd met many journalists who moonlighted as authors or had given up reporting in order to follow creative muses, and their fortunes had been decidedly mixed. The only thing certain was that the book trade was a lottery. But that was all right because he knew the score from the outset. He hadn't written the novel for the money. He'd written it because it had become a compulsion that would not be denied.

The post box at the end of the drive was for outgoing mail as well as incoming. After depositing the cards for Matthew and Ellen Glass, Nick scanned the horizon for the faintest puff of dust that might indicate the return of Sasha. The only thing he saw was Gordon's tractor, bumping slowly along the fenceline towards the sheep.

Back in the kitchen, he brewed himself a super-strength vat of coffee and took another two headache tablets. Sasha had been gone for three and a half hours. His ears were on hyper-alert for her car engine. After putting his mobile on the kitchen step where the signal was strongest, he went in and out like a yo-yo, checking for vital calls or texts. He was furious with himself for not insisting he go with her.

Returning to his desk with a second mug of coffee, he picked up the envelope from Dr Marius Retson. Something about it made his stomach feel as if it was falling down a lift shaft. The fact that it had gone to several addresses. The fact that the neurologist was writing to him at all.

A car rolled into the drive, spraying gravel. Shoving the letter, still sealed, beneath his typewriter, Nick flew to open the door.

28

Sasha's smile had left her face the moment she was out of sight of Seabird Cottage. It had been a relief to pull out of the drive and drop the pretence that she was feeling on top of the world when, in fact, she'd rarely felt worse.

In the midst of her shower that morning, she'd been overwhelmed with nausea. It had come on so fast that she'd had to leave the water running and bolt for the toilet. It had been some time before the accompanying abdominal pains subsided and she could compose herself sufficiently to go downstairs. When she did, Nick was making pancakes. In her fragile state, pancakes were the very last thing she felt capable of enduring, but the sight of her boys – that was how she thought of Nick and Oliver – covered in flour brought on a tidal wave of love that almost swamped her. A year and a half on from their first meeting, the power of her feelings for Nick still caught her by surprise.

Most mornings Nick woke before her, but on those occasions that she beat him to it she had to restrain herself from nudging him awake just so he'd open his grey eyes and look at her. Nightmares tended to leave them shuttered and sad, but at other times they flamed with desire or crinkled at the corners with love.

It had been Nick who'd saved her sanity and, quite possibly, her life over the past six months. Not that he'd been perfect. There'd been times during the initial course of chemotherapy when she'd cheerfully have strangled him. But the terror that had come over her when he saw her with her newly shaved head and she'd realised that his feelings for her might be based largely on attraction, and that those feelings would go away if the disease made her hideous, had entirely dissipated.

It was true that her illness had tested their relationship to its limits. For different reasons they'd both had to fight the urge to run, to shut down emotionally, to hole themselves up in steel vaults that locked the other out. Teaching themselves to pull towards one another, not flee every time there was a crisis, had been a steep learning curve.

The end result was nothing short of amazing. They were soul mates in the real sense, so close that she sometimes found it hard to tell where Nick ended and she began. Theirs was a love she'd believed only existed in films. Forever love.

All of which made the current state of affairs especially agonising. It also compounded the guilt.

Sasha turned into the hospital car park, switched off the engine and pressed her forehead to the steering wheel. She shut her eyes.

For there was one thing about which she hadn't been honest. How could she be? How could she look into the eyes of the man whose happiness meant more to her than anything on earth and say, 'You know how I felt like a million dollars for six weeks or so and effectively convinced us both I was cured? Well, I don't feel that way any longer. Truthfully, I feel like shit.'

That was why she'd talked Nick into living the previous day as if it was their last. Despite her denials, she'd had a sense of foreboding about the results of her test. Suddenly it had seemed incredibly important that when she sat across from the oncologist she had those precious few hours to hold onto. She'd wanted the physicality of the day fresh in her mind – the salty cold of the ocean, the exhilaration of galloping, the heat of Nick's skin. The looming appointment had turned life into a ticking time bomb. Leading up to it, she'd wanted to cherish every second.

Earlier, when Nick had called out to her as she walked to her car and then pretended he'd forgotten what he was going to say, it had occurred to her that he might know the outcome already. He'd looked as ill as she felt at breakfast. That was the trouble with having a husband who had prescient nightmares. It was a double-edged sword. His dreams could show him that she'd live or tell him that she'd die. Perhaps it was just as well that he claimed to be unable to decode them.

Somebody rapped on her window. She glanced up to see a nurse squinting in.

'You okay in there, hon?'

Sasha forced a smile and opened the window a crack. 'I'm fine. Thank you for asking. Just a little tired.'

The nurse didn't move. 'You have an appointment, dear, or you just had one? What is it? Blood test making you feel faint? You don't wanna drive like that, hon.'

Sighing, Sasha grabbed her bag and climbed out of the car. The nurse looked to be in her early fifties and of Caribbean extraction, her smile framed by crescent-shaped dimples.

Sasha smiled back. 'It's sweet of you to check on me, but there's nothing at all to worry about. I'm a little nervous about an appointment I have shortly with an oncologist – my last ever with any luck – but otherwise I'm well.'

The nurse fell into stride beside her. 'If you say so. All the same, I'm goin' to just walk with you, dear. You're deathly pale.'

Now that she was upright and walking, Sasha felt as bad as she had at any time during chemo. She had the sensation that her head was about to float away from her body. As they passed through the hospital doors, she spotted a bathroom. She barely had time for an 'Excuse me' and she was on her knees in the ladies', throwing up again.

When she emerged rather shakily some while later, the imperturbable nurse was reading an article about Kate and William and waiting for her with a cup of sweet tea. 'Nora,' she said, holding out a cool hand.

Sasha sank weakly into a chair. 'Nora, you're a godsend. I can't thank you enough. I'm Sasha and I can't tell you how pleased I am to meet you . . .'

The nurse closed the page on the Royals. 'Nerves?'

'I guess so. I hope so. I don't know.'

'Mmm, that's a whole lotta uncertainty. Any symptoms?'

'Where to begin? The nausea you already know about. General fatigue, abdominal cramps, strange taste in my mouth, frequent peeing, a bit of pink spotting.'

Nora clapped her hands together and let out a hoot of laughter. 'It ain't an oncologist you're wanting to see, honey, it's an obstetrician.'

Sasha was incredulous. 'You think I'm pregnant? That's impossible.'

'Impossible or you don't want it to be true?'

'Impossible. We never had sex while I was having chemo and then when we did . . . What I mean is, mostly we use protection.'

'Mostly?' Nora handed her the magazine. 'Wait here. I'll get you something to set your mind at rest.'

Sasha was attempting for the umpteenth time to read the first paragraph of an article about a shoplifting, alcoholic actress when the nurse returned with a pregnancy test kit. 'My shift is starting, hon, so I'm gonna love you and leave you. How you feeling? You want me to send another nurse to watch over you?'

The sweet tea had gone a long way to reviving Sasha. She was reeling, but she was not about to pass out. 'I feel a lot better. Thank you for taking care of me. You've no idea how much I needed someone to be kind to me just then.'

'You're most welcome. Good luck with all of it. I'd say God bless, but the hospital management forbid that nowadays, case we offend someone.'

Sasha smiled. 'You can say it to me. I'll take all the blessings I can get.'

As her new friend walked away, she thought about the other nurse – the one they said had tried to kill her. The police had asked her if she'd testify if the case went to court but she'd wanted no part of it. The woman had been sacked in disgrace and would be struck off by the General Medical Nursing and Midwifery Council. She'd also lost her home, her husband and been royally screwed by Cullen. As far as Sasha was concerned, she'd been punished enough.

Back in the bathroom, Sasha sat on the toilet lid and watched with disbelief as the line on the applicator stick changed from clear to blue. Shock mingled with euphoria and a crippling fear. She took her mobile from her bag and dialled Seabird Cottage, but clicked off before it could ring. As much as she wanted to share the news with Nick, she didn't want anything to detract from the specialness of sharing it with him in person. She couldn't wait to see his face.

In the days leading up to their marriage, he'd stunned her by confiding that one of the reasons he'd been so gutted by their break-up was because he'd realised that he would never have a child with her. Having always been almost virulently anti-kids, he had, he admitted, been taken aback to find how desperately he wanted a son or daughter to be a joining and an extension of him and the woman he loved.

Sasha had been almost speechless with astonishment. At the time of the conversation, she'd not yet turned thirty and had barely given children a thought. It went without saying that she wanted them eventually, but it had always been a long-term plan, something that would happen in her late thirties or early forties after her riding centre was established. Nick's confession had made her think seriously about babies for the first time. His babies. She'd revised her schedule down by a few years. Perhaps she'd have a child when she was thirty-six or thirty-seven.

Then, of course, she'd fallen ill and children, and the fact she might now never have them, had become the elephant in every room.

On her darkest days, she'd hated herself for the time she'd wasted by not leaving Cullen the hour she fell in love with Nick. She could pinpoint it exactly. They were standing under the Good Brew coffee shop awning after putting Pattie Griffin in an ambulance and she was trying to will him to look at her while he did his best to look everywhere but.

He was a wreck. There were purple bruises of exhaustion under his eyes and he was so wet and cold that his coffee cup shook in his hand and his mud-splattered shirt and jeans clung to him, and yet there was something about his sad, strong face that had caused her sleepless nights afterwards. She hadn't been able to identify it then but she knew what it was now: an intrinsic goodness that overrode everything else – even, and perhaps especially, his nightmares.

And as he stood there, framed by silver threads of rain, some chance remark she made finally forced him to meet her eyes. That was it. Call it love at second sight. She knew then, only she was too cowed by Cullen, too brainwashed by his promises and his hurting brand of obsession, to do anything about it. So she had seen Nick into the taxi and closed the door when all she wanted to do was walk into his arms and stay there for all eternity.

But it was okay. They'd got there eventually. And now a little piece of him was growing inside her.

The door of the cubicle rattled. 'Any chance you'll be out this millennium?'

'Every chance.'

Sasha popped the applicator with its tell-tale blue stripe into her bag, flushed the toilet for appearance's sake and walked out with her head held high as the women in the queue glared at her. When she was done at the hospital, she'd take home a nice bottle of Sauvignon Blanc – her last for a while in all probability – and tell Nick over a candlelit dinner.

But as she stood at the basin, rinsing soap off her hands, a feeling of pure, unadulterated terror went through her. If the cancer had returned, she wouldn't have any of it – not Nick, not the baby. In her excitement, she'd jumped the gun. She'd forgotten that there was still the small matter of her appointment with the oncologist. What if that went badly? What if it was, in effect, a death sentence? What then?

She glanced at her watch. It was time.

29

When Nick opened the door, Sasha was flushed, impossibly pretty and carrying a large cardboard box, which she set down on the kitchen counter. Nick lifted her off her feet and whirled her round. It increased his headache tenfold, but it was worth it.

She was bubbling over with good news, fizzing with it. 'I'm still trying to take it in. No more chemo. No more probing and poking and men in white coats. No more poisons running through my veins. Like the oncologist told us, the amazing thing about this particular lymphoma is that once you're cured, you're cured for ever. It's never coming back. So I'm free! Can you believe that? I'm truly free.'

She kissed him again. 'Sorry if I was longer than I meant to be, darling. You weren't too worried, were you?'

'Barely gave it a thought.'

He drummed his fingers on the box. 'Been shopping?'

She lifted it again, hugging it to her. 'I bought us something to mark the occasion. A celebration present. No, let's not open it here. It's such a heavenly day. Come on, let's go out into the sunshine.'

Out in the yard the wind, sharp as a sushi chef's knife, had shaved away the last threads of cumulus, leaving behind a glorious day. Blue, clean and clear with a hint of sea salt and cut grass.

Sasha took an age to untie the knots after unwisely involving the cat, but each time Nick tried to help she blocked his hand with a smile and an, 'Oy, you, be patient'. Oliver sat on the garden table and swiped at the string with his claws. He rolled on his back and wrestled with it, a plump, ungainly tiger.

At last, Sasha managed to prise the lid free. Nick let out an involuntary gasp as the box opened. Rippling colours unfurled from it – triangles of fire-engine red, marigold yellow, snowdrop white, forest green and ultramarine blue. Bound together like the tail of a kite, they were the precise hues and shapes he'd seen in his dreams. As Sasha shook them out and tied them to an assembled flagstick, he saw that each was crisscrossed with Sanskrit.

'A Tibetan prayer flag. Of course.' He was short of breath, as if he'd climbed the Himalayas to witness some ancient ritual.

'A prayer flag, yes. Isn't it glorious? I couldn't resist it. A Nepalese man was selling them on a market stall outside the hospital. It seemed appropriate somehow. Symbolic.'

It all made sense to him then. Everything. He might have laughed out loud had the storm in his head not relocated to his heart.

'Don't you like it?' she asked, suddenly unsure.

'It's beautiful. Really exquisite – like you.'

He pulled her close, holding her so tightly she winced. Moulded to the slender warmth of her, he marvelled that after everything they'd been through they still fit together.

She tried to move, but his arms were locked around her. Part of him wanted to imprint the essence of her on his soul; part of him just needed her help to stay upright.

He pressed his lips to the velvet place behind her ear. 'Sasha, you've been my best friend and the sweetest love I could ever have imagined.'

'Hey, what's with the past tense? I'm yours for always, remember?' Keen to resume her task, she kissed him and stepped away.

'Sasha, there's something I need to tell you,' he began, but as he spoke thoughts drained from his mind like the sea in retreat.

What was it? What was it that he wanted to tell her?

She stopped what she was doing, half listening, half thinking about something that caused a secretive smile to flit across her face. 'There's something I want to tell you too, babe, but you go first.'

'There's a letter on my desk from Ellen, my agent. It exthp . . . *explains* everything . . . Sasha, you musht . . .' What was it that she had to do? He couldn't remember. It was vital that he communicated something to her, but he couldn't recall what it was.

Now he had her full attention. Tenderly, she brushed a strand of hair from his forehead. 'Darling, you're slurring your words. I think the strain of everything has been too much for you. Have you got a migraine? You're extremely pale. Would you like to go inside? We can do this later. What were you saying about Ellen? Has she heard from any publishers yet?'

'Sasha, listen to me, I'm incredibly happy for you . . . for uth. Us,' he said, shaping his words with difficulty. A thought hovered close enough to grab. 'You have your whole life ahead of you now. You must do your riding centre. Don't let anything stop you.'

'Of course I'll do it. *We'll* do it. The money will happen. Somehow it'll happen. Your book will be published and become a bestseller, I'm certain of it.'

She smiled and picked up the flagstick. 'I have some news for you, too, but first I want you to put this in the ground. It's said to give the planter long life.'

The pain exploded in him then. He only just managed to stop himself from groaning. It was as if someone had launched a grenade in his skull. The scene before him blurred. He sucked in a breath. 'No, Sasha, I want *you* to plant it.'

But as she raised the flagstick, Nick caught her wrist. Her pulse beat steadily beneath his fingertips. He opened his mouth but speech was beyond him. Words, like untethered balloons, floated away. He reeled them in at last. 'To a fresh start.'

'To a fresh start,' she echoed, and plunged the pole into the ground.

The wind caught the flag and it reared up, a rainbow horse. Sasha turned to Nick, triumphant.

Next thing he knew, he was on the grass and Sasha and Oliver were looking down at him and he wasn't sure how they'd got there, into their respective positions.

There was panic in her voice. 'Nick, stop fooling around.'

He tried to answer but he couldn't. He was spinning into the blue heavens, into infinity.

'Nick! Oh my God, Nick, you're bleeding. Are you hurt? Where's it coming from? Have you hit your head? What on earth happened? It's dark blood, like treacle. That means . . . Oh, please, no. Nick, my phone's inside. I'm running to call an ambulance. Lie very still and I'll be right back.'

'No!' Fear revived him. 'Don't leave me. I need you near me.'

'Don't do this, Nick. Please don't do this.' Her tears rained down on his cheeks, melting into his skin like glycerine.

She fell to her knees. 'It was you all along, wasn't it, Nick? You were dreaming about yourself. All those times when you tried to save me, you really needed saving yourself. I should have been watching over you. *I* should have been watching over you.'

Somehow Nick found her hands and covered them with his. 'Hush, sweetheart. Don't cry. You're going to be well. That's the only thing that ever mattered.'

'Nick, I need to tell you something. Nick, I'm pregnant. I'm having our baby.'

His tears mingled with hers then. 'Oh Sasha . . . Sasha, that's the most wonderful news I've ever heard.'

But he no longer knew if he was saying it out loud or only thinking it. Her face, the best face in the entire world, began to fade.

She bent closer, straining to hear him.

'Thank God for you,' he whispered. 'For this place. For Matthew, Oliver and Gordon . . . For everything.'

Thank God.

It went through the fog in his head that, for an ending, it felt a lot like a beginning.

Blackness.

A flickering light.

Blackness.

Light.

Acknowledgements

I wrote *The Obituary Writer* over the course of four years and it wouldn't have happened without the advice and support of a series of wonderful people. First and foremost, thanks to Catherine Clarke, the best, loveliest agent in the world, whose enthusiasm for the book remained undiminished throughout and who uncomplainingly read sections and gave me feedback, even when she was insanely busy. My other sounding boards were Jules and Lisa. A thousand thanks. Words can't convey how much the unflinching confidence of both of you kept me going when I was assailed with the usual novelist doubts.

Special thanks, too, to Susan Lamb for having faith that I could make the leap to adult fiction, and to my editors, Genevieve Pegg and Eli Dryden: Gen, for believing in the novel when it was mostly still in my head and for doing such a visionary first edit, and Eli for seeing it through with such passion and commitment.

I feel immensely fortunate to be published by Orion, which seems to be staffed by boundlessly enthusiastic, quite extraordinarily nice people. Thanks especially to my children's book editor, Fiona Kennedy, for being so supportive and flexible on deadlines! Huge appreciation also to Lisa Milton, Malcolm Edwards, Gaby Young, Laura Gerrard, Graeme Williams, Mark Stay and especially to Jo Carpenter, who routinely moves mountains. Jo, you've already made my year, but feel free to make it again!

Lastly, I am indebted to the experts who patiently answered my questions and entered the strange world that is the imagination of a writer with a yet-to-be-written book. Thanks to Claude Zitz, Samra Turajlic and the real-life obituary writer on *The Times* who helped me four years ago when the novel was little more than an idea. I am more than grateful to you all. Any technical mistakes in the novel are mine and mine alone.